Praise for

UNLAWFUL CONTACT

"Powerful, sexy, and unforgettable, *Unlawful Contact* is the kind of story I love to read. Pamela Clare is a dazzling talent."
—Lori Foster

"A spellbinding, gut-wrenching page-turner with a gripping plot. This story is unique and creative with an imperfect hero you can't help getting sweaty palms over . . . Pamela Clare is a remarkable storyteller."
—*Fresh Fiction*

"This is an exciting fast-paced romantic suspense thriller . . . Action-packed."
—*Midwest Book Review*

"A romantic suspense that has it all: gritty realism, edge-of-your-seat action, dynamic characterizations, surprising plot twists, and a scorching romance between two leads you won't soon forget."
—*BookLoons*

"A gripping and emotional story . . . An engaging tale that will have readers on the edge of their seats."
—*Romance Reviews Today*

"A thrilling, captivating suspense novel . . . It has great characters, a wonderful story line with different connecting plots, and a happy ending for a couple that has many obstacles that they must surmount together."
—*Romance Reader at Heart*

"Clare's impressive novel is rife with gripping suspense, secrets masterfully revealed, and characters in whom readers can become emotionally invested. The sexual tension between the protagonists is deliciously steamy, and the skillful plotting makes this thrilling book one readers won't be able to close until the final page."
—*Romantic Times* (4½ stars)

continued . . .

HARD EVIDENCE

"A page-turner, a pulse-pounding thriller . . . Whether she is writing her incredible historicals or these great contemporaries, Ms. Clare proves, once again, she is one of the best storytellers today . . . It is a thriller, it is a treasure, and it is tremendous."
—*Fresh Fiction*

"Superb romantic suspense . . . Fans will appreciate this strong thriller."
—*Midwest Book Review*

"I cannot recommend this book highly enough. Pamela Clare's *Hard Evidence* is a powerful and, dare I say, flawless book, in my opinion. For those who love a good suspense or even just a good, satisfying read, it's a 'don't miss.' "
—*Romance Reader at Heart*

"This was a hard-to-put-down book with an exciting story line."
—*MyShelf.com*

"Clare adds a realistic edge to her suspenseful writing . . . [A] tight, gritty thriller . . . Clare definitely seems to have found her niche."
—*Romantic Times*

EXTREME EXPOSURE

NAKED EDGE

PAMELA CLARE

BERKLEY SENSATION, NEW YORK

THE BERKLEY PUBLISHING GROUP
Published by the Penguin Group
Penguin Group (USA) LLC
375 Hudson Street, New York, New York 10014

USA • Canada • UK • Ireland • Australia • New Zealand • India • South Africa • China

penguin.com

A Penguin Random House Company

NAKED EDGE

A Berkley Sensation Book / published by arrangement with the author

Berkley Sensation Books are published by The Berkley Publishing Group.
BERKLEY SENSATION® is a registered trademark of Penguin Group (USA) LLC.
The "B" design is a trademark of Penguin Group (USA) LLC.

For information, address: The Berkley Publishing Group,
a division of Penguin Group (USA) LLC,
375 Hudson Street, New York, New York 10014.

ISBN: 978-0-425-21976-8

PUBLISHING HISTORY
Berkley Sensation mass-market edition / March 2010

PRINTED IN THE UNITED STATES OF AMERICA

10 9 8 7 6 5 4 3 2

This book is humbly dedicated to the Diné people of Black Mesa for opening their hogaans to a lost *Bilagáanaa* journalist, feeding her roasted corn, frybread, and mutton stew, and sharing their troubles and joys and prayers with her. I came to the *dinetah* to help you, and in the end it was you who helped me. *Ahéhee'*.

ACKNOWLEDGMENTS

With love and deep gratitude to Ray James (Salt Clan) and to Kat Kozell-James for their endless support, love, and friendship. You are always in my prayers and in my heart. You reached out to me when you didn't even know me and turned my face to the East so that I could start again. *Ahéhee'*.

Special thanks to Rick Hatfield for sharing his expertise on the duties, challenges, and gear involved in being a mountain ranger.

Additional thanks to Teresa Robertson, RN, CNM, for sharing her experiences of working as a midwife among the Diné; to Sgt. Gary Arai for his gun expertise; to my mother, Mary White, RN, for her input on the medical scenes; and to my brother Robert for his help with the technical climbing aspects of this story.

A lifetime of thanks to Robert White, my father, for instilling in me a deep love of the mountains and the life within them and for sharing his knowledge of astronomy; and to my brother David for *living*—and for sending me all the beautiful photographs from his hikes.

An enormous thank-you to my editor, Cindy Hwang, for her understanding and patience as I worked for more than a year to write this book. Thanks, too, to Natasha Kern, my agent, for (yet again) helping me through my midmanuscript jitters.

Love and thanks to my beautiful sister, Michelle, for reading every word I write and re-write; to my beloved

Gangstas—Sue, Kristi, Libby—for holding my hand and helping me breathe through the rather painful birth of this book; and to my dear, sweet FOPs for always being there for me.

And as always, thanks to my sons, Alec and Benjamin, for their help, love, and encouragement. You are what I cherish most about being me.

PROLOGUE

THE COYOTE CAME out of nowhere. It streaked across four lanes of traffic directly in front of Katherine James's pickup truck, ears back, head down, tail tucked between its hind legs, then disappeared in the prairie grass to her right. Kat's foot jerked off the gas pedal, but it was already too late. At fifty-five miles an hour, she'd already blown past the spot where it had left the road.

Whenever the Ma'ii crosses our path, we stop and make an offering to show our respect. If we don't, our lives might be thrown out of balance, and bad luck might come upon us.

Grandma Alice's voice sounded clear in her mind, accompanied by an image of gentle, old hands sprinkling yellow corn pollen on red earth. But the rutted, dirt roads of K'ai'bii'tó on the *dinetah*—Navajoland—were far removed from the traffic of Colorado's infamous Highway 93. If she stopped now, bad luck would immediately come upon her in the form of a ten-car pileup.

Pray for me. I drive 93.

The slogan on a popular bumper sticker popped into Kat's mind as she glanced at the SUV in her rearview mirror and pushed on the gas. And then she did pray, muttering a few words in her mother tongue, thanking Coyote.

But a sense of uneasiness had already settled on her skin, and it stayed with her despite the bright morning sky and the deep green beauty of the forested foothills. It was still with her when she turned off the highway and headed west on CO-170 toward Eldorado Canyon State Park. Only when she'd parked her pickup and gotten her first good breath of mountain air did the feeling begin to fade.

Leaving her cell phone in the glove box, she grabbed her backpack from the passenger seat and slipped the straps over her shoulders. Packed with just enough to see her through a midmorning hike—a sweater, a pair of binoculars, her pouch of corn pollen, water, and frozen grapes—it wasn't heavy. She locked the truck, zipped her keys in the front pocket of her pack, and started up the dirt road toward the trail.

The summer sun shone warm and bright, her shadow stretching out on the road before her. Thickets of tall choke-cherry bushes lined the trail, their branches laden with clusters of wine-red fruit, food for hungry bears trying to fatten up for winter. Broad-tailed hummingbirds buzzed through the limbs of a nearby ponderosa pine, so quick and tiny they were almost impossible to spot. White butterflies gathered at the edges of mud puddles left by last night's downpour, the scent of water calling them to drink.

Grandpa Red Crow had been right. "What you need, Kimímila," he'd said, calling her by the Lakota nickname he'd given her, "is a chance to be alone with the sun and the wind and the sky."

Not that she was actually alone. The road was lined with Subarus and Jeeps and SUVs of all kinds, transportation for those who'd come to the canyon to climb the cliffs for which it was famous. People drove in by the hundreds to crawl up the rocks like four-legged spiders, ropes trailing like webs behind them.

But the climbers didn't bother her. Growing up in a two-room hogaan with seven brothers and three sisters, her aunt Louise, her mother, and her grandparents, she'd long ago learned to turn inward when she needed privacy. Besides, she hadn't come here to get away from people. She'd come to get away from the concrete and neon of the city, to breathe clean air, to feel earth beneath her feet.

It had been three years since she'd left the reservation, perhaps the best and toughest decision of her life. It wasn't that she didn't like living among other Navajo, or Diné. In fact, there'd been a time in her life when she'd vowed never to do what so many young Diné people did—grow up, go to college, and then leave for high-paying jobs far away from the parents and elders who'd raised them. She hadn't been able to keep that vow, but not for lack of trying.

She'd gotten her journalism degree at the University of New Mexico, then come back to the rez to work at the *Navajo Times*, hoping to use her skills to help give a voice to the voiceless among her people. At first, she felt she'd found her place in the world. In her first year as a reporter, she'd broken a story about families growing sick after being relocated from traditional homesites to government housing that had been built on the radioactive mine tailings. She'd won awards for her work, but the greatest reward had been the satisfaction she'd felt at helping Diné families.

She'd lived in a trailer in Tségháhoodzáni—known to the outside world as Window Rock—during the workweek, making the long drive home to K'ai'bii'tó each Friday night, her truck filled with food and water she'd bought with her paycheck. Her grandmother would wait up for her, welcoming her home with warm frybread, a hot bowl of mutton stew, and a strong cup of coffee, asking her to sit and share the news from the Earth's Center—the ceremonial name for the Navajo Nation's capital. But her mother had made it clear that she'd have been happier had Kat stayed away.

That's how it had always been—love from her grandmother, loathing from her mother. Though Kat had hoped her mother would at least come to respect her for the work she did at the newspaper, nothing had changed. No matter what Kat might become, no matter what she might accomplish, she had done her mother unforgivable harm. She'd been conceived of a man who wasn't her mother's husband—a *Bilagáanaa* man.

A white man.

The only thing Kat knew about her father was the color of his skin—and the fact that he'd gotten her mother pregnant, then left her to deal with the consequences alone. He hadn't even stayed on the rez long enough to put his name on Kat's birth certificate.

"Every time I look at you, I see him," her mother had told her more times than Kat cared to remember. "Your green eyes, your light hair, your white skin. Why did you have to be born?"

Kat's eyes were hazel, not green. Her hair was dark brown, and her skin was more caramel than peaches and cream. But there was no denying that she was fathered by a different man than her brothers and sisters, a fact that they refused to forget, calling her a "Half-ajo," instead of Navajo, and teasing her about her eyes. And so, faced with her mother's resentment and the indifference of her siblings, she'd piled everything she owned in her pickup truck and left K'ai'bii'tó behind. It was the only time in her life she could remember seeing tears in her grandmother's eyes.

"Don't forget your Diné tongue," her grandmother had said, before turning back to her weaving, too upset to watch Kat drive away.

Kat had driven north to Denver, winning a coveted seat on the Denver Independent's Investigative Team—the I-Team—as its environmental reporter. Although she missed her grandmother and the wide-open beauty of the desert with all of her soul, she loved her job and had grown to care for her fellow I-Team members. And if the city sometimes seemed to press in on her, making her feel shut off and alone?

Well, that's why there were mountains.

She came to the trailhead and left the dirt road behind, ducking beneath pine boughs and following the steep trail uphill. From somewhere overhead came the cry of a prairie falcon, followed by the chatter of a nervous squirrel. Falcons nested in these cliffs, as did golden eagles. Kat had been coming up here all summer to observe the nests from a distance, watching the young grow from fuzzy hatchlings to sharp-eyed hunters. The nests were now empty, but she still loved to hike to the top of the ridge and look out over the valley to the east and the high, snow-capped peaks to the west. Somehow, the vastness of the landscape made her problems seem small.

She hiked on, losing track of time, thoughts drifting away amid the scents of growing things until her mind was empty and free. The muscles in her thighs burned, her heart pumping, her lungs drawing in breath, the rhythm of footsteps, heartbeat, and breathing seeming to flow together like a song. When at last she gained the top of the ridge, the sense of uneasiness was gone, replaced by a feeling of contentment.

She walked to her favorite spot—a rocky outcrop at the top of the ridge. There, she shrugged off her backpack and looked out over the land—distant city to the east, a sea of mountaintops to the south and west and north. Far below her, cars and trucks looked like toys parked along a ribbon of road. Above, there was only sky.

She unzipped her pack and was about to take out her water bottle when she heard a crack and then a strange scraping noise, like stone rubbing stone. Then the rocks beneath her feet gave way—and she fell.

She screamed, reached, but there was nothing to grab. The world swirled gray around her—no up, no down, only motion. She hit something, kept falling, then hit again, bone snapping painlessly, the breath knocked from her lungs.

I didn't want to die today.

She remembered the coyote, an image of it darting in front of her truck flashing through her mind.

And then there was nothing.

GABRIEL ROSSITER CRIMPED the chalked fingers of his right hand around the small handhold, then carefully shifted his weight onto his fingertips, drawing himself to the right. He didn't notice his skinned shin or the people far below taking pictures of him and pointing, or the sweat trickling down his temples, his mind focused entirely on the rock as he worked the arête on a bad-tempered geological accident known as the Naked Edge. Scraped fingers reached again, caught rough stone, and held. He maneuvered his way around the jutting, razor-sharp edge for which the climb was named—no ropes, no cams, nothing beneath him but six hundred feet of air.

Some people needed heroin. Gabe preferred adrenaline.

He looked up and picked his way up the rock face with his

gaze, thinking his way through his next move in a language without words. This was what he needed—internal silence, emptiness, oblivion. He needed to forget.

He reached with his right foot . . . And then he heard her scream.

He caught just a glimpse—rocks spilling down the side of a nearby slope, a woman falling with them—and felt a moment of vertigo as she tumbled out of sight. And then a decade of experience kicked in.

So much for your day off, buddy.

He fired himself around the arête and thrust his fist into an overhanging hand crack, liebacking his way on hand jams to the final pitch and an easy finish. Then, with no ropes or gear to pack up, he was off.

It was a long, exposed scramble down the Eastern Slabs, but the rock was dry, enabling him to move quickly. He knew the terrain as if it were his own backyard—and really, it was. He'd been climbing here since he was sixteen, and he'd been a Boulder Mountain Parks Ranger since he was twenty-four—eight years. He'd spent almost every waking moment of his adult life in these mountains. He'd done his fair share of rescues over the years—and had helped bring down his share of bodies.

And that's what you're going to find today, Rossiter—a body.

He didn't let the thought slow him. If by some miracle she had survived, she was going to need his help.

He moved down the steep rock face, his cell phone out of his pocket and in his hand the moment his feet hit dirt. He dialed 911. "Sixty-forty-five, off duty."

"Go ahead, sixty-forty-five."

"Rockslide in Eldorado Canyon State Park approximately one half-mile north of Redgarden Wall. Saw a woman go down with it. I'm en route, but I don't have a damned bit of gear with me. I'll call again when I have her location."

"Copy, sixty-forty-five—"

That was all he needed to hear.

He hung up and took off through the trees at a run.

* * *

IT TOOK GABE almost ten minutes to reach the base of the rockslide area. Sucking wind, his heart pounding from exertion, he searched for her amid the rubble—boulders as big as trash cans, smaller rocks, mangled tree branches. He found a lone turquoise earring and a backpack that must have belonged to her. But he didn't find her.

There was really only one possibility.

She was dead and buried, crushed somewhere beneath all that rock.

"Dammit! Goddamn it!" He pulled his cell out and dialed 911 again. "Sixty-forty-five, at the site."

"Sixty-forty-five, can you repeat? You're breaking up."

"At the site. No sign of the victim, but there's no way she walked away from this. She's probably buried. There's a good ton of rock here. We're going to need—"

A cry.

Stunned, he stopped midsentence.

Another cry—the sound of a woman in pain.

"She's alive! Are you getting a lat and a long on me?" Gabe hoped the signal from his phone was strong enough to give dispatch a solid GPS reading.

The answer came in a burst of static—and then the call disconnected.

Damned cell phones.

He pocketed the phone, hitched her pack over his shoulder, and ran uphill through the trees toward the sound.

She screamed again.

He adjusted his direction, quickened his pace.

And then he saw her.

Her jeans torn and muddy, she was crawling, or trying to crawl, her right leg dragging behind her, probably broken. She inched forward, crying out as her injured leg dragged across the damp forest floor. Then she sank onto her belly, whimpering. But before he could call to her to let her know help had arrived, she pushed herself up again and struggled forward another few inches, her scream catching behind clenched teeth.

She was heading toward the trail, he realized. She was trying to rescue herself, trying to get to where help could find her. Lucky for her, it already had.

He hurried toward her. "I'm Gabe Rossiter with Boulder Mountain Parks."

She looked over at him with a startled gasp, turning over as if to sit, the movement making her moan in pain. She sank onto her back, breathing hard.

"Easy, there." He walked to her side. "Just lie still. I'm here to help you."

The first thing he noticed was her eyes. An unusual shade of hazel green, they watched him warily as he knelt down beside her. Agony was etched on every feature of her pretty face, a streak of mud on her bruised cheek, pine needles in her long, dark hair, the other turquoise earring dangling from her left earlobe. She looked to be in her mid-twenties, no taller than five-five and small-boned—a red flag when it came to fractures. There were deep scratches on her arms and hands, but no obvious bleeding.

"The rocks . . . They fell." She spoke with just a hint of an accent.

American Indian?

"I saw. Last night's rain must have eroded the ground beneath them." Because he couldn't seem to help it, he looked into her eyes again, relieved to find that her pupils weren't dilated. "What's your name?"

"Katherine James."

"How old are you, Katherine?"

"Twenty-six."

"Do you know today's date?"

She shivered, cold sweat on her forehead. "It's Sunday . . . August twenty-sixth."

In shock, but coherent. Probable broken leg. Scrapes and bruises.

"Help is on its way." He kept his voice soothing. "In the meantime, I'll do what I can for you. Can you tell me where you hurt?"

"Everywhere."

"I'll bet." He dug into her pack. She wasn't carrying a first-aid kit, but she had brought a sweater. He draped it over her. "I'm a paramedic and a park ranger. If it's okay with you, I'm going to check you to see how badly you're injured."

She eyed him suspiciously, still shivering, her gaze dropping to his bare chest, with its chalk marks, to the chalk on his hands, to the climbing shoes on his feet.

Okay, so he looked like some kind of half-naked freak to her. Fair enough. "I'm off duty. I was rock climbing nearby and saw you fall. Let me help you."

She seemed to measure him, then nodded, wincing slightly with her next breath.

Broken ribs. Possible internal bleeding.

He put his hand on her shoulder, tried to reassure her. "I'm going to feel on the outside of your clothes, and you tell me where it hurts, okay?"

"O-kay."

He stood, walked around to her other side and started with the obvious, sliding his hands over her jeans along the length of her right thigh. "Does it hurt here?"

"No."

Thank God it wasn't her femur. He'd seen more than one woman bleed out from a severed femoral artery, dead before help could arrive.

He slid his hands past her knee and heard her gasp just as he found the bulge on her shin. "Your tibia is broken."

Not quite a compound fracture, but bad enough.

Her right ankle was tender and swollen, as well, either broken or sprained.

But of more concern to him than the broken bones was the fact that she was beginning to fade, slowly lapsing into unconsciousness, her dark lashes now resting on her cheeks, her eyes closed. A few times she'd muttered something in a language he didn't understand, and once she'd asked him something about a coyote. He'd bet his ass she had some kind of head injury. With a fall like that, she wouldn't need to hit her head to injure her brain.

"Stay awake, Katherine. Stay with me."

* * *

STAY WITH ME.

Kat thought time was playing tricks on her. He'd just spoken those words a moment ago, and yet it seemed like hours. She forced her eyes open, saw him watching her, a worried look on his face, his hands moving gently over her, seeming magically to find all the places she hurt most—her right leg and ankle, the ribs on her left side, the deep scratch on her left arm.

As if through a fog, some part of her noticed that he was a very attractive man, rugged and tall, with deep blue eyes. His square jaw was covered with dark whiskers, his temples trickling sweat, his thick, dark hair curling at his nape. There were calluses and chalk on his fingers and scrapes on his knuckles and his left shin. He was wearing only shorts and strange shoes, and although Kat had seen many men without their shirts, she'd seen very few men who looked like he did—all lean muscle from head to toe, as if an artist had carved him from marble and then brought him to life.

Strange that she should notice such an unimportant thing right now.

His callused fingers worked their way gently along her collarbones, over her shoulders and into her hair. "Did you lose consciousness when you fell?"

She tried to think. She'd heard the rocks scrape, felt the ground give way, felt herself falling, and then . . .

The next thing she remembered was looking up at the sky, her right leg hooked over a rock, her entire body wracked with pain. "I think . . . I must have."

Apparently done checking her, he sat back on his heels, looking down at her. "You are one amazing woman, Katherine James. I don't know many people, men or women, who would have been tough enough to do what you just did. You crawled the length of a football field, dragging that broken leg behind you."

But Kat hadn't been brave. She'd been terrified. Once she'd come to herself, she'd realized that no one knew where she was and that unless she could make her way back to the trail where hikers could discover her, she would die right where she lay. Fear had gotten her onto her hands and knees, driving her forward each unbearable inch, the pain excruciating.

Without warning, the full weight of what had just happened hit her. Tears burned her eyes, spilled down her temples, her body shaking uncontrollably.

You almost died, Kat.

The ranger took her hand, held it, his fingers warm. "It's going to be all right. I know it hurts, but they'll be here soon."

She looked up at him. "Y-you saved my life."

He shook his head. "You'd have been all right without me. You'd have made it to the trail eventually. It wouldn't have been fun, but you'd have made it."

But she wasn't so sure.

SHE LOST TRACK of time after that.

The park ranger telling her to stay awake, stroking her cheek, telling her everything was going to be all right. People crowding around her. An oxygen mask over her mouth. The prick of a needle in her arm. A warm blanket.

There was a moment of terrible, sharp pain when they put a splint on her leg, and she heard herself cry out. The ranger's warm hand squeezed hers, his voice deep and soothing. Why couldn't she remember his name?

"It's almost over, Katherine. In twenty minutes you'll be in Denver, and St. Anthony's will take good care of you."

Was he coming with her? A part of her hoped he was.

She didn't really know him at all, but somehow she trusted him.

"She fell from there?" a man's voice said. "Holy shit! Why is she still alive?"

"I can't believe she crawled all that way with a badly broken leg," said a woman. "Just the thought makes me queasy."

"So, you were free-soloing the Naked Edge when you saw her fall. Gee-zus! You have a death wish, Rossiter. One of these days we're going to be rescuing you, only there won't be anything left of you to save."

And then Kat was bouncing along as they carried the stretcher out of the trees toward a helicopter, the ranger walking beside her, his voice her anchor.

"Stay awake, Katherine."

Only after the helicopter had lifted off did she realize that he was gone.

And she hadn't even thanked him.

CHAPTER 1

Three months later

GABRIEL ROSSITER UNZIPPED his pants only far enough to free his cock, then bent her over the back of her sofa and pushed her skirt up over her hips, rubbing his hands over her smooth, round ass, her impatient whimpers urging him on. He slipped on a condom, then grabbed her hips, forced her legs wider apart—and filled her with a single thrust.

Oh, hell, yeah.

It felt so good, so damned good. He let his mind go blank and drove into her hard, allowing himself to feel only the pulsing ache in his cock, holding back just long enough to hear her scream. Then he fell over the edge, orgasm washing through him in a white-hot rush. And for a few blissful seconds, he forgot himself.

But the oblivion didn't last. It never did.

"God, Gabe, you are the best."

He gave himself a moment to catch his breath, her muscles still pulsing around him, the musky scent of sex filling his head. Then he slowly withdrew, walked to the bathroom, and tossed the condom in the trash. He wiped himself off with a tissue and had just started to wash his hands when he heard her footsteps. He looked up to find her blocking the bathroom doorway, wearing nothing but spiked heels and a smile.

Samantha Price had the best body money could buy, from her surgically enhanced tits to her Brazilian wax job to the tips of her red toenails. She ran her pretty fingers through her dyed red hair, her gaze on his chest. "Why don't you stay?

We can do that all night long—as many times as you like. I'll even let you tie me up."

He supposed he should take it as a compliment. He doubted Samantha, one of Boulder's most expensive criminal attorneys, invited many men to dominate her. At another time in his life, he'd have been only too happy to oblige. Instead, he felt annoyed. "That's not how it works, Samantha. You know that."

She tilted her head, an attempt at being seductive. "Things can change. We've been together for almost six months now."

"Together?" He turned off the faucet and dried his hands. "Hooking up for a quick fuck now and again doesn't mean we're 'together.'"

He zipped his pants, buckled his duty belt, and pushed past her, adjusting the weight of his sidearm as he went. He'd known it was going to come to this. It always did—the mutual exchange of physical pleasure ruined by delusions of attachment. Sex was just a chemical reaction, love nothing more than a hormonal haze in the brain. Why did so many people try to turn it in to something more than that?

You used to believe in love, Rossiter.

Yeah, and he'd learned his lesson the hard way.

"It doesn't have to be just sex. I know that's what I said at first but—"

"Forget it, Samantha." He retrieved his undershirt from the floor where she'd dropped it, slipped it over his head, then reached for his shirt, buttoning it and tucking it into his pants. "It won't work."

"What makes you so sure?" She picked up his winter uniform jacket, traced a finger over the badge pinned to the front, then began to search the pockets in a cloying display of female nosiness.

"Because I'm sure."

She drew something out of his pocket and held it up. "What's this?"

It was Katherine James's turquoise earring.

Gabe had forgotten to give it to her before the chopper had taken off. He'd meant to track down her address and mail it to her afterward but hadn't. Even he couldn't explain how it had ended up in his coat pocket—or why it had stayed there. Of course, he wasn't about to tell Samantha any of this.

"Is she your next destination?"

He didn't bother to dignify Samantha's prying question with an answer. "We never agreed to be exclusive, Samantha—only safe."

She shoved the jacket against his chest, the earring still in her hand. "You're an asshole, you know that?"

"Did you enjoy what we just did?" He held out his hand for the earring.

"Yes." She dropped it onto his upturned palm. "You know I did."

"Then what more do you want from me?" He tucked it back in his pocket.

"More. Just more."

Hell, were those tears in her eyes?

"Sorry, Sam, but I don't have anything more to give you." He turned and walked out of the living room and down the hallway toward the front door.

"I know about your fiancée," she called after him, an edge to her voice. "I know what really happened."

Gabe felt his stride falter, but he didn't look back. He opened the door and stepped into the night, knowing he'd never come here again.

A cold wind hit him in the face, carrying away Samantha's scent, taking the hottest edge off a sudden surge of temper. He filled his lungs, walked down the icy sidewalk to his service truck, trying to put Samantha and her last salvo out of his mind and ignoring the pricking of his own conscience.

Why in the hell should he feel guilty? Samantha was an adult. She knew what she'd signed on for. He'd told her right up front that he wasn't interested in a relationship, and she'd told him all she wanted was good sex. So now she'd changed her mind and he was supposed to feel bad?

Well, he'd never liked breast implants anyway.

He climbed in behind the wheel, adjusted the gear on his duty belt so that it wouldn't jab him in the back, then shoved his key into the ignition. The digital clock on the truck's dash read 8:45—enough time to get in a few routes at the rock gym before it closed. He'd just turned onto Baseline Road when his pager went off. He pulled it out of its holster and read the LED display.

Flames on Mesa Butte. On-call officer please respond. Police request backup.

On-call officer. Tonight, that was Gabe. But what were the cops doing at Mesa Butte? That was Mountain Parks's jurisdiction.

He flipped on his overheads, pulled a U-turn, and sped east toward the butte.

KAT STARED IN disbelief and shock toward the open sweat lodge door, only to be blinded by a flashlight.

"Police!" a man's voice shouted. "Everyone out!"

Stunned, she shielded her eyes and looked to Grandpa Red Crow, who sat on her left closest to the door. He looked amazingly calm, beads of sweat on his wrinkled face and bare chest, an eagle-bone whistle in his hand, its piercing song abruptly silenced.

"Come on! Move it! Out!"

Grandpa Red Crow leaned toward the door, spoke to the man outside. "You are interrupting the *inipi*, a sacred Indian ceremony—"

The police officer reached in and grabbed Grandpa by the arms. "Come on, old man. Out!"

Wearing only gym shorts, a towel wrapped around his waist for modesty's sake, Grandpa was hauled roughly forward, whistle clutched tightly in his hand.

"No!" Kat shouted, her cry echoed by the dozen women who'd come to Mesa Butte to pray.

This can't be happening!

Oh, but it was.

No sooner had Grandpa Red Crow been dragged through the small opening, than the same cop ducked down and took hold of Glenna, an Oglala Lakota elder from Denver who was sick with ovarian cancer. Her eyes wide in her thin face, Glenna cried out in her native tongue, her towel slipping from her shoulders, exposing her damp T-shirt and skirt, as the officer pulled her through the doorway. *"Hiyá! Hiyá!"* No! No!

Then the cop ducked down and shined his flashlight into the lodge once more. "Are the rest of you going to come out, or do we have to drag you out one at a time?"

Pauline, a young Cheyenne woman and next in line to the door, looked to Kat, panic in her eyes. "What should I do?"

Kat swallowed her own fear. "I'll go, and you follow me."

She crawled around the edge of the fire pit toward the door, feeling trapped in some kind of nightmare. When she reached the doorway, she spoke the Lakota words she would have spoken when leaving the lodge at the end of the ceremony had it not been interrupted. *"Mitakuye Oyasin."* All my relations.

"Come on! Hurry it up!" the officer shouted.

She lifted her head and crawled forward another step, only to feel a fist close in her hair, the cop yanking her painfully upright, her towel falling into the mud. She tried to stand, but her weight came down on her right leg, which had been out of its cast for only a few days and was still weak. Her ankle twisted, and she lost her balance, falling forward, clutching at the hand that held her hair, trying to keep it from being ripped out by the roots.

"What the hell are you doing?" A familiar voice, footsteps. "Let go of her! You can't just manhandle people like that!"

"They're resisting." The cop released her.

Scalp still burning, Kat landed on her hands and knees in cold mud, her heart slamming, tears of shock and rage and pain blurring her vision. Unable to stop her trembling, she looked up—and felt as if the breath had been knocked from her lungs.

There, striding toward her, was Gabriel Rossiter, the park ranger who'd saved her life. This time he was dressed in his full ranger uniform—dark jacket with a silver badge on the front, gun on his hip, heavy boots on his feet. From the way he walked, she could tell he was angry.

"It looks to me like they're doing what you asked them to do, so why don't you stand back and give them some room?" He knelt down before her, his face cast half in golden light from the fire and half in shadow. "How's your leg? Are you able to stand?"

Kat nodded, confused to see him here, horrified to think that the man who'd saved her life, the man she'd thought about every day for the past three months, the man she'd just remembered in her prayers, could be a part of this . . . this desecration.

"You know her?" the cop asked. Lantern-jawed and clean-cut, he had a military look about him. "Better get her out of here before she gets herself arrested."

The ranger didn't answer. "I'll help you up."

Strong hands grasped her arms, lifting her out of the mud and holding her steady until she got her footing. Her gaze met his, and for a moment all she could do was stand there, looking up at him. He was taller than she remembered, her head only reaching his chest. And he was a lot angrier.

He picked up her muddy, wet towel and handed it to her. "I'm sorry, Katherine, but we have orders to put out the fire and clear the butte."

"Why?" Icy November wind blew through her damp hair, piercing the wet cloth of her skirt and T-shirt, chilling her to the bone.

"I'm not exactly sure why." He glanced about. "Apparently, the fire violates land-use codes that the city has suddenly decided to enforce."

Land-use codes?

She started to tell him that federal laws protecting Indian religious freedom trumped city land-use codes, but the cop had knelt down before the sweat lodge again.

"I guess all we got here are squaws," he said, panning his flashlight over the women inside, a degrading tone to his voice. "Must be the braves's night off. Either that or the old guy has himself a harem. Come on! Move it!"

Inside, Pauline sobbed.

"No! Let me! She's afraid of you!" Outraged by the cop's insulting comments and his bullying manner, Kat turned to help, but the ranger caught her with a strong arm around her waist and drew her back against him, the contact startling.

He spoke quietly, his breath warm on her chilled skin. "You'll only get yourself arrested. Let me handle it. Go back to your car and warm up."

But right now Kat didn't care about being cold, and she wasn't about to leave the other women behind. Shivering hard, she wrapped her wet, muddy towel around her shoulders, stepped back and watched as the ranger bent down and spoke to the cop.

She couldn't hear what he was saying, but after a moment, the cop stood, glaring at him. "Fine. Do it your way, Rossiter, but it's on your head."

Then the cop stepped away from the sweat lodge, making room for the ranger, obviously furious at him for interfering.

The ranger squatted down before the sweat lodge door, hands in his pockets. "It's all right. No one's going to hurt you. Come on out."

Kat recognized the soothing tone of his voice, and despite her anger, she knew he meant what he said. She leaned nearer to the sweat lodge door and called out. "It's okay, Pauline. You don't have to be afraid. This one won't hurt you."

She saw the top of Pauline's head and stepped back to make room for her and the other women, looking beyond the firelight, searching for Grandpa Red Crow and Glenna. And then she saw.

A dozen squad cars were parked down below on the access road, lights flashing. Three fire trucks stood nearby. The butte seemed to swarm with law enforcement, two officers holding German shepherds on leashes.

Police? Firefighters? K-9 units?

All of this—to stop an *inipi*?

Everything but the cavalry.

Fighting tears of rage with every breath, she spotted both Grandpa Red Crow and Glenna just beyond the firelight, talking with a uniformed officer. She might have walked over to them and tried to help, but then Pauline was there, trembling and crying, soggy towel around her shoulders, the other women emerging one by one behind her, their faces pinched with fear.

"Come." She met the ranger's gaze, then turned away, wrapping her arm around Pauline's shoulder. "Let's get dressed."

GABE WATCHED AS Katherine limped, soaking wet and barefoot, through the snow, shepherding the other women around to the other side of a blanket that had been strung up between two saplings, her quiet dignity an indictment.

He'd arrived to find three fire trucks and most of the cops in the city parked along the access road to the butte, lights flashing. With that kind of response, he'd expected to find a frat party turned homicide or perhaps even arson. Instead, he'd found nothing more threatening than an *inipi*—the same kind of ceremony that had been going on up here every Saturday night since before Gabe had become a ranger.

He'd hiked up the butte in search of the officer in charge of this clusterfuck to try to minimize the damage, only to see Sgt. Frank Daniels—one cop he'd never liked—dragging a woman out of the lodge by her hair. In a heartbeat he'd gone from irritated to fucking pissed off. And then he'd recognized her.

Katherine had fallen to her hands and knees, her long hair wet and hanging to the muddy ground, tears on her pretty face, the shock and fear in her eyes making him want to punch Daniels in the face, to kick his balls into his throat, to drag him around by the short hairs and see how he liked it.

He turned on Daniels. "Do you want to tell me what in the hell you were doing?"

The son of a bitch shrugged, as if he had no idea why Gabe was angry with him. "We got an anonymous complaint that someone had seen flames up here and—"

"I know that!" Gabe glanced toward the blanket, making sure no gung-ho cop was about to intrude on the women as they changed into dry clothes. "What I want to know is why having a campfire without a permit merits the use of physical force. These aren't drug dealers, Daniels. They're unarmed, terrified women."

"I'm under orders to vacate that little hut—whatever they

call it." Daniels jerked a gloved thumb in the direction of the dome-shaped sweat lodge. "If they resist, we have to take it to another level."

"It didn't seem to me that anyone was resisting, least of all the woman whose head you nearly yanked off." Gabe bent nearer, no longer masking his anger, his face inches from Daniels's. "This land is under Mountain Parks's jurisdiction. Knock off the Rambo act, got it? Now who the fuck is responsible for this mess?"

GABE PUT IN a call to his supervisor, Chief Ranger Webb, then spent the next ten minutes trying to undo as much of the damage as he could, assuring Police Chief Barker that Indian people had always used Mesa Butte for ceremonies with the knowledge of Mountain Parks. No, Mountain Parks had never required the medicine men who ran the sweat lodges to pay for a permit because sweat lodges constituted a traditional use of the land and were religious in nature. Yes, they occasionally got phone calls from concerned citizens who saw the fires and didn't know what was going on, but no one had ever filed a formal complaint. No, there had never been any problem with litter or property damage because the participants had always been careful to clean up after themselves.

Then Chief Barker fell back on city land-use codes, reading from his notebook. "It says here, plain as day, 'No open fires on city open space without a permit.' Do you boys over at Mountain Parks enforce the law or—"

But Gabe didn't hear another word. "Excuse me."

Katherine stepped out from behind the blanket, now bundled in a heavy fleece-lined denim jacket, hiking boots, and jeans, her towel rolled up and tucked beneath her arm, her wet hair hanging down her back. She walked with the other women toward several parked vehicles at the top of the access road, then split off on her own, heading toward a big, black Dodge Ram pickup.

He came up behind her. "Katherine."

She ignored him, unlocked the door to her truck.

"Katherine, I'm sorry. This wasn't supposed to happen."

She looked over her shoulder at him and jerked her door open. "No, it wasn't."

"Someone must have called in a complaint. For some reason, dispatch routed it to the police instead of to Mountain Parks. If the call had come to us, it never would have come to this. The land is under Mountain Parks's jurisdiction, so I expect there will be some shouting on Monday morning. We'll get it sorted out."

She tossed her towel across the seat, then turned to face him, a streak of mud on her cheek making his fingers itch to brush it away. "While you're sorting it out, think about this: tonight was a special women's lodge, called so that we could pray with a friend of ours who's sick with ovarian cancer. The police brought men with guns and dogs to stop our prayers. How would you feel if you were in church praying for a sick friend and got dragged out by your hair?"

"I'd be angry as hell." He didn't say that he hadn't set foot in a church since grade school. "I'm sorry. I really am. But I'm not your enemy."

"Then why are you here?" She crossed her arms over her chest.

"It's my night on call"—*lucky me*—"and I was paged. I had no idea what was happening until I got here. By then it was already too late to do anything beyond damage control. I'm trying to find out how this happened, and I promise I'll do everything I can to keep it from happening again."

She seemed to consider this, some of the anger leaving her face. "Thanks for getting that cop to back off."

"I'm sorry he hurt you. I'm going to report it, and you should, too."

"I will." She started to turn away, then seemed to hesitate. "And thanks again for saving my life."

Around them, the other cars were backing up, turning, driving away, their tires crunching on the snowy gravel road.

"Hey, I told you. You saved your own life." Then he remembered. "I have something that belongs to you."

He felt in his pocket for the earring, held it out for her.

For a moment she stared at it as if she didn't know what

it was. Then her eyes went wide, and she took it from him. "Thank you."

"Have dinner with me."

What the hell? Have you lost your fucking mind, Rossiter?

Apparently, he had. Not only had he asked her out—when was the last time he'd asked a woman to have dinner with him?—but he also seemed to be holding his breath, waiting for her answer as if it mattered.

"I'm sorry. I . . . I couldn't." She looked toward the line of red taillights heading down the road. "I need to go. We're meeting at Grandpa Red Crow's house to finish our prayers and talk about this."

"Then how about lunch, something really informal?"

She climbed into her truck, slid behind the wheel, the vehicle seeming almost too big for her. And for a moment she said nothing, obviously thinking it over—not the reaction Gabe was used to getting from women.

Watch the ego, dumbass.

She turned to look at him at last. "Okay, but only if you agree to share everything you find out about why this happened."

Having conditions placed on an informal lunch date felt like more of a smack in the face than an outright rejection. But that didn't stop him from agreeing to it. "All right. It's a deal. How about the South Side Café at noon on Monday."

"Noon on Monday." She closed the door, and the truck's engine roared to life.

As Gabe watched her drive away, he wondered what the hell was wrong with him.

CHAPTER 2

KAT SPENT MOST of Sunday at Grandpa Red Crow's house, helping the other women in the kitchen while men held a talking circle and discussed how to respond to this violation of the people's rights and how to make sure it never happened again. Pauline kept teasing her about the ranger—Ranger Easy-on-the-Eyes, she called him—making the other women curious until Kat was cornered into telling about the two times he'd helped her, first saving her life after the rockslide and then stopping the other officer from hurting her at the desecrated *inipi*.

"And she's going out to lunch with him tomorrow," Pauline added.

"Yáadilá!" Good grief! Kat tried not to grow annoyed, keeping her voice even, her hands busy drying dishes. "I'm not going out with him. It's a business lunch. I asked him to find out whatever he could about what went wrong Saturday night. He said the complaint should have been sent to Mountain Parks. I want to know why it wasn't."

The ranger's dinner invitation had taken her by surprise. A part of her—the same part of her that had spent the past three months thinking about him, remembering how it had felt when he'd comforted her and held her hand—had wanted to accept his invitation just to get to know him better. But she didn't date casually.

It wasn't that she felt no need for a man or a sex life. She was as red-blooded as the next woman. But she believed what Grandma Alice had taught her—that the joining of male and female was sacred and meant to be treated as such. Besides, she'd seen what happened when a woman trusted the wrong man. She didn't want to make the same mistake as her mother, who'd betrayed her husband only to be betrayed herself in the end. Nor did she want to end up like so many other young Diné women, abandoned to raise a child alone on commodities and welfare.

Long ago, she'd promised herself she wouldn't sleep with a man until she met her true half-side—her perfect, matching male half. She would wait for the one man who was meant for her, the man who was worth it, the man she loved so much that going without him felt unthinkable. And if at age twenty-six she'd begun to fear she would dry up and blow away before she met that man?

No one had ever said that walking a good path was easy.

She and the other young women had just finished washing the supper dishes when Glenna came and took her by the arm.

"The old man wants you," she said, a slight smile on her lips.

Damp dish towel in hand, Kat followed Glenna, surprised to find the living room silent, all eyes turned her way. She stood there, waiting for Grandpa Red Crow to speak and wondering if she should make more coffee.

He stood, his face grave, one hand raised. "Not all of you know Katherine James, so I will tell you about her."

Speaking slowly in heavily accented English, he told them how she'd come to Denver from Navajoland to work at the paper and had met him at the Denver March Powwow, where she'd gone in search of decent frybread. This, of course, made everyone laugh. When it grew quiet again, he told them how he'd invited her to an *inipi* and how she'd soon become a regular at the Saturday night sweats on Mesa Butte. Then he told them how she'd tried to protect the other women when the *inipi* had been disrupted, taking the *wasicu* policeman's violence onto herself.

"I call her Kimímila—Butterfly," he said, "but that was the act of a warrior."

"Aho!" the men called in near unison, voicing their agreement.

"Now, the people need her to fight for them again—but in a different way."

Amazed to find herself singled out for such recognition, she saw Grandpa Red Crow pull something out of his pocket.

A pouch of tobacco.

Stunned, all she could do was stare.

He took her hand, pressed the tobacco into her palm, his dark eyes—eyes that had seen so much—looking into hers. "We need your help to get to the bottom of things, to find out why the *inipi* was stopped last night. We need the world to know what happened so that good-hearted people of all nations can help us to protect our ceremonies and ways of life. The people need you to be a journalist for them."

Kat closed her fingers around the tobacco, touched beyond words that the elders should ask for her help in such a respectful way. But there was no question as to whether she would do as they'd asked. That's why she'd become a journalist in the first place—to protect Native people and the Earth.

Grandpa Red Crow knew that, of course. He seemed to know more about Kat than she knew about herself, having taken her under his wing when she'd first moved to Denver. A Hunkpapa Lakota medicine man whose ancestors had walked with the great leader Tatanka Iyotake—Sitting Bull—he'd accepted her without question, introducing her to Lakota ceremonies, helping her to adjust to her new home, becoming the father she'd never had. To know that he had faith in her abilities, to see the trust on his face . . .

She swallowed the lump in her throat. "I'm humbled by your words and grateful to have the chance to help in a meaningful way."

He didn't smile—the moment was too serious for that—but she could see the gleam of approval in his eyes.

KAT ARRIVED AT the office early on Monday morning, a plan of action outlined in her mind, her determination to expose this injustice strengthened by the trust Grandpa Red Crow and the other elders had placed in her, their prayers for her echoing in her mind. She doubted most people in Denver would understand what it meant to have an *inipi* interrupted, but explaining it to them would be her job.

Of course, there was the possibility that Tom would refuse to let her set aside her investigation of the county's proposed solar-energy program to cover it. Tom Trent was the best editor she'd ever worked for, which helped make up for his terrible temper. But he was also meticulous in matters of journalistic ethics. Would he view Kat's presence at the *inipi* as a conflict of interests and give the story to someone else? Would he understand that she, as an Indian woman, could bring knowledge to her coverage of the story that no one else on the I-Team could?

She settled in at her desk, then called the Boulder Police Department and asked for a copy of the police report from the raid. When that was done, she typed out an open-records request demanding the police dispatch logs from Saturday night, as well as all documents and e-mails in the city's files pertaining to Mesa Butte. Though that was probably casting her net a bit wide, it didn't hurt to be thorough.

Focused on her work, she barely noticed her fellow I-Team members drift in or heard the greetings they called out to her. She had just faxed off the request to the police department and Mountain Parks when she realized that it was already time for the daily I-Team meeting.

"Coming, Kat?" Sophie Alton-Hunter, the I-Team's prison reporter, waited for her, notepad and pen in one hand, water bottle in the other.

One of the most courageous women Kat had ever met, Sophie had nearly been killed two years ago while trying to bring justice to abused female inmates. Now she was married to her high school sweetheart and mother to an adorable one-year-old boy. Three months along with her second baby, she seemed to glow with such happiness that Kat was surprised no one else had figured out she was pregnant yet.

Kat grabbed her notepad and hurried over to Sophie, the two of them lagging behind the rest of the I-Team. "How are you feeling?"

"Better, thanks." Sophie gave her an easy smile. "The morning sickness is fading, and I'm less tired than I was.

Hunt has been keeping an eye on Chase so I can take lots of naps on the weekends. He's so excited about this baby. He missed out on this part of the pregnancy last time because he was still behind bars."

Kat remembered those days, remembered how rough it had been for Sophie not knowing whether the man she loved would be a part of her and her baby's life or whether he'd spend the rest of his life in prison. "When are you going to tell Tom?"

Tom seemed to disapprove of pregnancy, begrudging his female employees their eight weeks of maternity leave, as if a woman's bringing a new life into the world were more of an inconvenience than a cause for celebration.

Sophie gave a sigh. "I haven't decided yet."

In the conference room, they found Tom poring over the newspaper, one pencil tucked behind his ear, another in his hand. Built like a bull, he could be just as stubborn and intimidating. And yet, despite his temper, Kat had come to respect him as a journalist. In his own way, he was a warrior, using ink and paper to fight on behalf of those who had no voice.

He looked up, pushing a shock of curly gray hair out of his eyes with a beefy hand, his gaze coming to rest on Sophie. "Alton, since you were the last through the door, you can be first in the hot seat. What've you got?"

Sophie tucked a strand of strawberry-blond hair behind her ear and glanced down at her notes. "A prison-reform group released a study showing that most Coloradans oppose incarcerating people for nonviolent drug crimes like possession. I can look at our prison population, figure out how many beds it would free up and how much money the state would save if we put nonviolent drug offenders into treatment instead of behind bars. I'm guessing a solid ten inches."

Syd Wilson, the managing editor, tapped the numbers into her calculator, doing the magical math that made the news fit, her short salt-and-pepper hair streaked with bright purple this morning. "Photos?"

Sophie shook her head. "We might be able to work up a graph. I'll see what kind of data I can find."

Tom turned to Natalie. "Benoit?"

Natalie Benoit had come to Colorado from New Orleans after losing everything but her life in Hurricane Katrina. Her eyewitness coverage of the tragedy at a New Orleans hospital had made her a Pulitzer finalist, and Tom had hired her on the spot. With long dark hair, big aqua eyes, and a charming New Orleans accent, she was pretty in a way that drew people to her. Yet she didn't seem to date and rarely socialized with the rest of the reporters. Some people thought she was stuck up, but Kat knew that wasn't true. There was something tragic about Natalie, a grief that she kept hidden. Kat didn't know what it was, and it wasn't her place to pry. But she sensed it all the same.

Natalie flipped through her notes. "A rookie cop got shot early this morning responding to a domestic-violence call. He has a wife and a new baby. Right now he's still critical. I thought I'd look into it, talk to his family, get the latest stats on domestic violence. Probably a good fifteen to twenty inches."

Tom turned to his left. "Ramirez, isn't that what you shot this morning?"

Joaquin Ramirez, the photographer assigned to the I-Team, nodded. Usually the most cheerful person in the room, his face was lined by fatigue, his dark eyes full of shadows. "It was down the street from my house. I got pretty much the entire thing. The bastard shot him from the upstairs window when the officer was walking up to the door. Didn't even warn him."

"The shooter turned the gun on his wife and then himself a short time later," Natalie said. "He died. His wife is going to make it—thank God."

Syd punched in the numbers. "Front page?"

Tom nodded. "Let's start it below the fold and jump to a photo spread on page three. Nothing too graphic. People need to be able to read the paper while they eat their cornflakes. Harker, what's going on downtown?"

Matt Harker, the city reporter, sat up straighter and smoothed his wrinkled tie—the same wrinkled tie he'd worn every day since Kat had come to work at the paper. With freckles on his face and reddish hair, he had a boyish look that seemed to contradict his abilities as a serious reporter. "I got a tip over the weekend that the city's finance director has been embezzling the employee pension fund."

Joaquin gave a low whistle. "That's big."

"I spent most of yesterday with some leaked records and a forensic accountant, and it seems the tip is solid. I need to make a few calls, talk to the city attorney, but I think we can run with it today. Fifteen inches maybe?"

Syd tapped her calculator. "Photos?"

"A couple of head shots."

Tom's gaze fixed on Kat. "How's the solar-energy story coming, James?"

"I need to put it on hold." Kat drew a steadying breath. "On Saturday night, Boulder police raided an *inipi*—a sweat lodge ceremony—that a group of Indian people were holding on Mesa Butte just east of Boulder. Native people have been using the site, which is considered sacred, for hundreds of years. The city has long known that Indians hold ceremonies there, but they've suddenly decided to enforce land-use codes."

"That sounds like it could be a violation of the American Indian Religious Freedom Act," Tom said, a frown on his face.

"Yes, it is." Some of Kat's nervousness slipped away. At least Tom was familiar with the law. "Indian people from across the region are gathering in Boulder today to protest the raid and to demand both an apology and changes in the city's land-use codes. I know it's not my beat, but this is an important issue to Indian people all over the country, and . . . And I was there. A police officer dragged me out of the *inipi* by my hair because he felt I wasn't moving fast enough. They had dogs."

And suddenly Kat couldn't say another word, her throat too tight.

"Oh, Kat, I'm so sorry! Why didn't you tell me?" Sophie reached over and took her hand. "I can't imagine how terrible that must have been."

"I'm sorry you had to go through that." Natalie met Kat's gaze, her eyes full of sympathy. "Can you imagine if the police had dragged a bunch of Catholics or Baptists out of church by their hair? It would've made CNN, and people would be raising hell."

Matt looked genuinely angry, his freckled face flushed. "Don't they know the law? Aren't they supposed to enforce it?"

Kat swallowed—hard. "I'd like to cover the protests and follow this as it unfolds. With photos and eyewitness interviews, I could easily have twenty inches. I know it's not my beat and that it might seem like a conflict of interests but—"

"No one can bring to this story what you can." Tom stood. "Do it."

And the meeting was over.

KAT HEADED NORTH to Boulder on Highway 36. The sky was bright blue, the mountains gleaming white in the sunshine. She parked downtown and walked through an icy wind toward the municipal building where protesters had been asked to gather, her right leg aching from the cold. She heard the protest before she saw it, the big drum beating like a heartbeat, men's voices rising above it, singing sacred songs.

The sight that greeted her put a warm lump in her throat. More than a hundred American Indian people stood together in front of the entrance to the municipal building, the drum in the center, elders given a place of honor beside the singers, younger people standing on the periphery holding protest signs so that passing motorists could see them. Glenna, pale but smiling, was there with Pauline, who looked proud now, not afraid. They saw her, smiled, and waved.

Grandpa Red Crow stood off to one side in his best blue jeans, a red shirt, a black leather bolo tie, and a black vest, an eagle feather in his hair, his forehead and the part in his hair painted red to show he was a warrior. He was speaking to a news crew together with Robert Many Goats, a Diné attorney from the First Nations Rights Fund, and Adam Caywood, the Creek/Choctaw actor Kat had had a crush on—until she'd learned he was Two Spirit and preferred men.

She waved to Joaquin, who'd beaten her there as usual and was busy snapping away, then drew out her digital recorder and joined the other reporters, the words of the Lakota song that was being sung running through her mind.

Our grandfather's drum is beating/Our grandfather's drum is beating/Hear, our grandfather's drum is beating/His drum beats/Our hearts beat/And our ancestors walk strong beside us.

Behind her a man spoke in Lakota. "She's the Navajo journalist who was there."

Kat felt a swell of pride. Her mother might not have appreciated what she did for a living, but these men and women did.

"Mesa Butte has long been sacred to Indian people," Grandpa Red Crow was saying. "My ancestors have prayed there and held their ceremonies there since long before European settlers came to this land. Now the police come to stop our prayers and drive us away. Where is the justice in that?"

"The city says you didn't have a land-use permit," one of the reporters said, the tone of his voice indicating that he thought this justified everything. "Is this true?"

Robert Many Goats ducked his head toward the mic. "Do you need a permit when you pray at your church? The American Indian Religious Freedom Act of 1978 guarantees Indian people access to their sacred sites and protects our right to pray in the traditional way. When the police broke up the sweat lodge, frightening and manhandling our sisters, they broke the law."

Then it was Adam Caywood's turn. "Native people are losing sacred sites across the continent. What happens to Indian people, especially urban Indians, when these places are turned into strip malls and parking lots? If our ways of life are to survive, these sites, and our access to them, have to be protected."

Grandpa Red Crow nodded. "The land is our bible. How can I teach my young people if our ceremonies are interrupted and we are driven off the land?"

The look on his dear face told Kat that he was trying desperately to communicate what for him was a profound and important truth, but it was clear the reporters didn't understand.

"Did you have a permit or not?" the reporter asked again.

Kat bit her tongue.

CHAPTER 3

GABE SAT AT the corner table with his back to the wall, watching the restaurant's front door as a couple of silver-haired seniors in jogging suits entered and were seated. He glanced up at the clock. It seemed that Katherine James had stood him up. It was only lunch—lunch with conditions tacked on to it—but she'd stood him up.

What in the hell had he been thinking when he'd asked her out? Or maybe it was less a question of what he'd been thinking and more a question of which part of him had been doing the thinking.

Your dick getting you into trouble again, Rossiter?

Except that he hadn't been out of Samantha's house—or, for that matter, out of Samantha—for an hour yet when he'd asked Katherine to go out with him. It's not like he'd gone without sex for a month and had been desperate to get laid. In fact, the more he thought about why he'd asked her out, the less it made sense to him. One moment he'd felt perfectly sane, and the next his mouth had started talking.

He supposed he ought to be grateful that she was a no-show. It might bruise his ego, but it helped make up for whatever had gone wrong with his brain Saturday night when he'd—

The restaurant door opened, and she walked in, the wind catching her dark hair for one last moment before the door closed behind her.

Gabe felt a little hitch in his chest.

Okay, he could cut that shit out right now. He was not going to get tangled up in her. He didn't even know her—where she was from, what Indian nation she was a member of, whether she was even single. Hell, yeah, she was pretty—okay, more than pretty. And, true, he respected her for the strength she'd shown after she'd fallen. And, sure, he supposed he felt a certain protectiveness toward her, but that was probably just the Neanderthal part of his brain stuck in rescue mode or some shit.

Have you ever felt protective of the other people you've rescued?

Ignoring the question, Gabe stood, watched her scan the crowded eatery, her gaze finding him. She threaded her way through the tables, her limp still noticeable. She wore a gray boiled-wool coat with Indian designs on it, a long denim skirt and brown leather boots, a brown leather purse hanging from one shoulder. As she drew closer, he saw that her cheeks were rosy, as if she'd been outdoors all morning, her hair tousled by the wind.

"Sorry I'm late." She set her purse on the chair beside her, sat, and slipped off her coat. She was wearing a shirt the same rosy color as her cheeks, a turquoise and silver bear claw hanging from a slender silver chain to nestle distractingly between her breasts. "I hope you weren't waiting long. I've been covering the protest at the municipal building and was about to leave when the mayor came out for an impromptu press conference."

"Covering it? So you're . . . a reporter?"

She nodded. "I'm part of the *Denver Independent*'s I-Team."

That's why she'd made him agree to share everything he learned. She was a journalist, and she was covering this as a story. For her, this was nothing more than a business lunch, and he was nothing more than a source.

Now do you feel like an idiot, idiot?

Thrown off balance, he tried to cover his surprise and irritation. "How's the protest going?"

She unfolded a paper napkin and put it in her lap, looking down at her hands. "So far the mayor and a few city council members have promised to look into what happened, but there's been no official apology from the city yet."

He was about to warn her not to hold her breath when their
server came to take their drink order. Gabe asked for water,
Katherine a cup of black coffee. And for a moment, they sat
in silence.

A damned reporter!

"How's your leg?"

"It still hurts sometimes, but it's getting stronger. They
had to put pins in it, so I haven't been walking on it for long.
Thanks for asking." Her gaze skimmed lightly over him. "I
thought you'd be in uniform."

"I work weekends, so today's one of my days off."

She looked away, tucking a strand of hair behind her ear, a
familiar turquoise earring dangling from her pierced earlobe.
"Grandpa Red Crow wanted me to thank you for getting that
officer to back off and for being respectful of the women."

As his surprise lessened, Gabe found himself watching
her, just taking her in—the strange color of her eyes, the
gentle movements of her hands, the almost shy way she tilted
her head as if unable to meet his gaze. He knew some Indian
cultures felt it was rude to look people directly in the eye
unless you knew them well, so it might have been a cultural
thing. Even so, it struck him as sweet.

"Did you report Officer Daniels?" It was then he realized
she wasn't wearing any makeup, her caramel skin smooth
and luminous and clean, her dark lashes thick and long, her
fingernails neat and free of polish. He'd bet the curves under
her sweater were real, too. She was the opposite of Samantha
Price—no artifice, nothing artificial.

"Yes," she said, still not looking at him.

"Good. So did I." He hoped the bastard got demoted to
meter maid. "If I'd been the first one to show up at Mesa
Butte, none of this would have happened."

Kat could hear in Gabe's voice that he meant what he said,
and she regretted being so harsh with him Saturday night.
He'd saved her life, protected her from an overzealous cop,
and offered to help her get to the bottom of the whole mess.
So why did she feel so ill at ease around him, this man who
had twice come to her rescue? She glanced up at him—and
the answer hit her.

You're attracted to him.

She wanted to deny it, but couldn't. Not that she blamed herself. Any living, breathing human female would be. He was one of the most attractive men Kat had ever met, more handsome even than Adam Caywood—and definitely more virile. Sitting across from her, his arm stretched over the back of the chair beside him, he seemed so big and broad-shouldered, his gray cable-knit sweater, tanned skin, and dark, windblown hair adding to the masculinity he exuded. She had some recollection of what he looked like beneath the sweater—all lean muscle and smooth skin. And those blue eyes . . .

Ranger Easy-on-the-Eyes.

That much was certain.

She willed herself to meet his gaze, determined to let none of what she was feeling show on her face. Like she'd told Pauline and the others, this was strictly a business lunch. She'd come here for information, not to flirt. Besides she wasn't sure she really knew how to flirt. She'd never tried.

She took a sip of her coffee, its warmth seeping slowly into her bones. "Most people call me Kat."

He grinned. "Okay, Kat. But I think Katherine fits you better. It's prettier, more feminine."

"What were you able to find out?" Disturbed by the way his smile and words affected her, she switched into a business tone of voice, her question coming out colder and more abruptly than she'd intended.

He arched an eyebrow, as if wondering at the change. "I paid dispatch a visit Saturday night. It turns out that there was no complaint. According to the supervisor, Daniels saw the fire and took it upon himself to act. Dispatch heard about it when he called in for reinforcements, and that's when they paged me."

This wasn't what Kat had expected to hear. "So he saw the fire, and rather than contacting Mountain Parks to find out what was going on, he just decided to break it up? Why would he do that?"

"Who knows? Daniels has always struck me as one of those cops who enjoys busting people."

"And hurting them." Kat's scalp seemed to tingle where Daniels had pulled her hair. "So if there was no complaint, then Daniels lied. Why?"

Gabe shrugged. "No mystery there. It's just standard CYA. He's trying to avoid getting in trouble for ignoring jurisdiction and getting the city into this mess."

"What's 'standard CYA'?" Kat hadn't heard the term before. "Is that a city policy or something?"

Gabe laughed. " 'CYA' means 'cover your ass.' "

GABE FINISHED HIS burger and fries, watching the subtle changes in Kat's expression as she told him about the Native community's response to the raid on the *inipi*. His own thoughts were far from Mesa Butte, his mind full of illicit images. Kat kissing him as he tore off her clothes. Kat lying naked on his bed, twisting and turning while he kissed and licked and sucked her nipples. Kat spreading her thighs for him as he nibbled his way down her belly and then took her with his mouth. Kat arching beneath him as he drove into her, fucking her hard, sending them both over the edge.

What would she taste like? What would she feel like beneath him? And what would the reserved Ms. James do when she came? Would she shiver and sigh, or would she dig her nails into his back—and scream?

You'd just love to find out, wouldn't you, Rossiter?

Hell, yeah, he would. His cock had gone rock solid just thinking about it and now strained uncomfortably against his jeans.

Kat dabbed her lips—lips he'd love to taste. "I don't know how to thank you for looking into this for me."

Emboldened by her gratitude, he decided to go for it. "Have dinner with me Friday night."

She eyed him warily. "I . . . I don't date men."

Gabe stared at her for a moment. *What the hell?* The male race had to be doing something terribly wrong if women like Kat were playing for the other team. "So . . . you prefer women then?"

Her eyes went wide, her face flushing pink. "No! No, no! I

like men. I mean . . . What I meant to say was . . . Oh, no, that didn't come out right."

Both amused and relieved, he leaned back in his chair and crossed his arms over his chest, unable to hold back a grin. "Want to try again?"

Kat drew a deep breath, felt her cheeks burn, both embarrassed by what she'd said and uncomfortable with what she saw in Gabe's eyes—blatant male interest. If he were like other men, his interest in her wouldn't last once he understood that she wasn't going to topple into bed with him. That seemed to be the only thing most men cared about. They weren't interested in having a family, being husbands and fathers.

She willed herself to meet his gaze straight on. "I decided a long time ago that I would never be any man's conquest, so I don't date. I've never been . . . with a man, and I won't be until I find the one who wants to be a part of my life and isn't just looking for a one-night stand. So unless you want lots of children, love mutton stew, and enjoy spending your summer vacations in one-hundred-fourteen-degree heat in a two-room hogaan without electricity or running water, we shouldn't even start down that road."

He seemed to consider what she said, a look of confused concentration on his face. "So . . . what you're saying is that you're saving yourself for Mr. Right and that if all I want is to get inside you, I can forget taking you out to dinner, because you want happily ever after and not just sex. Did I get that right?"

"Something like that." She felt her cheeks burn.

"You're a little too old to believe in fairy tales, aren't you?"

She'd known he would find a way to ridicule her. They all did. And yet she couldn't help but feel let down. After the compassion he'd shown her, some part of her had hoped he'd be different. "You think love and commitment are just for fairy tales?"

"People fall in and out of love faster than the wind changes. There's no such thing as 'happily ever after.' Commitment only lasts as long as the hormones hold out. Love, romance, sex—it's nothing more than chemistry."

Her disappointment grew. "That's an awfully cynical point of view."

"It's reality." He glanced out the window at a young couple walking hand in hand. "People try to make sex into more than it is, and they end up getting hurt."

Kat couldn't believe he truly meant what he'd said. "Don't you hope to get married one day and be a father?"

A muscle clenched in his jaw. "No. Not interested."

The tone of his voice was starkly final.

He drew his gaze from the window. "Man, I bet it scares the shit out of most guys when you say that stuff."

Yes, it did. "Most guys just want to play around, but women aren't toys."

His gaze hardened. "Are you saying that most women don't play around, that women don't use men?"

"Not in the same way." Not the women Kat knew, certainly.

"If you say so." He gave a bitter laugh. "Thanks for being so direct. But when I asked you to dinner, I wasn't asking you to have sex with me. I just wanted to get to know you better."

Kat stared at him, astonished and mortified. Could she have misjudged him? Could she have been wrong about the look she'd seen in his eyes? She'd thought for certain that he was coming on to her, but . . .

Wishing she could hide under a rock, she looked away, cleared her throat, and changed the subject, her cheeks burning even hotter. "Is . . . Is there any chance you could get into trouble if I use the information you gave me about Officer Daniels in my interviews and my article?"

After all he'd done to help her, she didn't want to get him fired.

He seemed to consider the possibility for a moment, then shook his head. "It will become public record soon enough. Just don't attribute it to me."

"Do you have a number I can reach you at if I have any questions?"

He reached into his pocket, took out his wallet, and wrote his number on the back of a business card. "It's best if you call my cell."

"Thanks." She gave him her card, then took one last sip of her coffee. "We're hoping the city will apologize and then amend its charter to guarantee us access to Mesa Butte. If only we could make the public understand . . . But then I guess it's impossible for anyone who wasn't brought up with the Native way of life to see the land the way we do and understand why the butte is so important to us."

He raised a single dark brow. "Is that so?"

The note of challenge in his voice made it clear he wasn't convinced.

She stood her ground. "Of course, it is."

"Well, then how about this? Meet me up there on Saturday at four. My shift will be over, and it will still be daylight. You can show me what the land looks like through your eyes, and I'll tell you how I see it through mine."

KAT'S ARTICLE HIT the street the next morning, her version of the story so much more complete that the other news outlets were now scrambling to catch up. She'd gone to print with the tip about Daniels she'd gotten from Gabe, a tip she'd verified using transcripts from police dispatch. She'd also included the Native community's demand for a formal apology and guaranteed access to Mesa Butte. A radio station in Boulder had asked her to come on the air this evening to talk about what had happened at the butte. But best of all, Grandpa Red Crow had already called her to tell her how much he appreciated the article.

"It's good to read our side of the story for once, Kimímila," he'd said.

She'd promised to stop by with a few extra copies of the paper after work, his praise touching her deeply, some part of her wishing her mother could hear him.

Of course, hers wasn't the only I-Team article making waves this morning. Matt's story about the embezzled pension fund was a scoop, the clamor from city hall deafening as city council members demanded answers from the confused mayor, who knew nothing about it and had to defer to Matt's article. Because Tom had taken the time to copyright both stories, the TV networks were forced to credit the *Denver Independent* with breaking the news.

"Find the bastards, and nail 'em to the wall. That's what we do." Tom was in a very good mood.

Kat should have been in high spirits, too, but her thoughts kept drifting to Gabe. She shouldn't be thinking of him at all. He was exactly the kind of man she'd spent her adult life avoiding, the kind who made love to lots of women without loving any of them, who couldn't be burdened with something as inconvenient as monogamy or family and saw sex as nothing more than recreation.

What had he called it? Chemistry.

How could a man who cared enough about people to save the lives of strangers have such a cynical view of love and human relationships?

Kat didn't know. But she did know that she wasn't willing to settle for random hormonal impulses. She wanted love. She wanted "happily ever after."

You're not going to find it with him.

No, she wasn't.

And with that realization, her day became a bit grayer.

Forcing her emotions aside, she followed the rest of the I-Team to the conference room for their morning meeting. Matt was doing a follow-up to yesterday's article, hoping to be present for the embezzler's arrest. Natalie wanted to write a follow-up about the wounded officer, who had been moved out of intensive care this morning. Sophie was researching the lack of community corrections programs for women and how that meant more time behind bars for them.

"Also," she said, meeting Kat's gaze in an unspoken plea for support, "I wanted to share some exciting news. Hunt and I are expecting another baby in May."

Natalie gave a little squeal. "That's wonderful! Congratulations!"

"I'm so happy for you!" Kat reached over and gave Sophie's hand a squeeze.

"You know, they've figured out what causes that," Matt said with feigned seriousness. "You might want to research it."

Sophie smiled. "Research it, Matt? Obviously, I'm an expert."

Matt turned red.

"Do you know if it's a boy or a girl yet?" Syd asked.

Sophie shook her head. "Either way I'm happy."

Then the room fell silent, everyone seeming to hold their breath, waiting for Tom's reaction. But Sophie had timed her news well.

"Congratulations, Alton." He gave Sophie a nod, then turned to Kat. "James, what have you got?"

GABE PARKED HIS service vehicle, then headed inside Mountain Parks headquarters, leaving his copy of the *Denver Independent* on the truck's seat. He'd already read through Kat's article twice, impressed by the way she'd put it together, explaining what had happened and asking the tough questions about the city's land-use policies. It felt fair, and yet, at the same time, it did a much better job of explaining the Native perspective than the other papers had done. And he was in it, right there in the fourth paragraph: "according to a source close to the investigation."

He'd bet that had made the suits at city hall shit their pants.

He drew his key card from inside his coat and scanned it, entering through the back door and heading straight to the john, where he washed the dried deer blood off his hands. Then he walked toward the break room, stripping off his coat and his heavy Kevlar as he went, his mind on what had already been a busy day.

Just after sunrise, he'd found a vagrant frozen half to death in the parking lot at the mouth of Gregory Canyon and had had to call an ambulance. He recognized the man, an old guy who drifted through town every so often. The man had apparently gotten kicked out of the homeless shelter late last night for being drunk and had tried to sleep it off in an old sleeping bag beneath a picnic table. Not the best decision he'd ever made.

Then a call had come in from a couple of hysterical cross-country skiers who said they'd seen a mountain lion. The lion hadn't attacked them; in fact, it had done what mountain lions were supposed to do. It had taken one look at their shocked faces and had run the hell away. But Gabe had gone up to check it out. He'd found a freshly killed doe about ten feet off the Lost Canyon Trail, mountain lion tracks all around it. He'd called for backup, and then, with Hatfield watching to make sure he wasn't jumped from behind by a pissed-off cat, he'd moved the half-eaten carcass deeper into the forest where the mountain lion could feed in peace.

Of course, the whole time he'd been thinking about Kat. He'd found it almost impossible not to think about her, even though thinking about her only made him want what he couldn't have. She'd made it good and clear that she wasn't going to get naked with him, not without a ring. But Gabe no longer did rings. He'd buried the only one he would ever buy with Jill.

It was probably for the best that Kat had made her position clear. It would save them both time. He preferred his sex straight up—no illusions, no attachments, no complications. She was a virgin who believed in happily-ever-afters. A virgin! When was the last time he'd used that word to describe anything other than olive oil?

I bet it scares the shit out of most guys when you say that stuff.

It had certainly scared the shit out of him. But what freaked him out the most wasn't the idea that she was keeping herself for one man, but the realization that some deluded part of him actually respected her for it. What was that about?

I decided a long time ago that I would never be any man's conquest.

She'd looked at him, had seen the horn dog lurking inside him, and had handed him his ass. And how had he reacted? Like a jerk, of course.

You're a little too old to believe in fairy tales, aren't you?

The moment the words had left his mouth, he'd wished he could take them back—and not just because he'd ruined his chances of ever having sex with her. He'd seen the disappointment in her eyes, and it had made him feel lower than dirt. So, naturally, he'd dug himself in deeper.

I wasn't asking you to have sex with me. I just wanted to get to know you better.

What a fucking liar he was. He'd wanted to take her to dinner, but he'd hoped to have her for dessert. Rather than admitting that he was guilty as charged, he'd embarrassed her by acting like she was the one who was assuming too much. And still she'd reacted with dignity, taking a deep breath and changing the subject, her cheeks flushing bright pink.

Proud of yourself, dickhead?

In the break room, he poured himself a cup of coffee, then grabbed a couple of burritos out of the freezer, dumped them on a plate, and popped them in the microwave to nuke for three minutes. At the table, rangers Rick Sutherland and Dave Hatfield were already stuffing their faces—and reading Kat's article.

"There's a message for you." Hatfield pointed toward the counter. "A woman from some law firm. Said she's been trying to reach you and leaving voice mails but hasn't heard back. She sounded pretty desperate."

Samantha. Cursing under his breath, Gabe grabbed the scrap of paper, crushed it in his fist, and tossed it into the recycling bin. It was one of at least a dozen messages she'd left him since Saturday night, apologizing for how she's acted, promising never to do it again, and pleading with him to call her.

When hell freezes over.

Sutherland looked at him from behind the newspaper and spoke with his mouth full of sandwich. "The city is up to its chin in shit this time. You read this?"

"Yeah." Gabe grabbed the salsa out of the fridge. "I was on call that night."

"Was it as bad as it sounds?"

Gabe nodded, searching for a clean fork. "I reported Frank Daniels. He tried to drag one of the women out of the lodge by her hair."

Sutherland shook his head. "Fucking idiot. Why didn't the call come to us?"

"Daniels was on patrol, saw the fire, and decided jurisdiction didn't matter."

"I wonder if this is why Webb's been in such a bad mood." Hatfield brushed crumbs from his shirt to the floor. "He had suits from the city in his office earlier this morning. There was some yelling behind closed doors."

Gabe kept his voice neutral, pretty sure he knew what the yelling had been about. "I wonder what's up."

The microwave beeped.

He retrieved his plate, dumped salsa on his burritos, and dug in.

"Me and some friends are planning some hut-to-hut skiing next month, Rossiter." Sutherland was the newest addition to the department and was always inviting Gabe to join him. "You should come along. I hear you're a badass."

Hatfield gave a snort. "Rossiter here skis shit no one should even try to ski, but forget about him joining the likes of us. He prefers to do everything solo."

Mouth full, Gabe gave Hatfield a quelling look. Hatfield had once been one of Gabe's closest friends and knew damned well he was treading on thin ice. "Thanks, Rick. Maybe some other time."

It was the answer Gabe always gave.

Chief Ranger Webb popped his head into the kitchen, a frown on his tanned face. "Rossiter, can I see you in my office?"

Shit.

"That depends. Can I bring my lunch?"

"Yes, for God's sake!"

Gabe stood and followed his boss down the hallway, Sutherland and Hatfield's chuckles following after him.

CHAPTER
4

ON FRIDAY, KAT found herself feeling unusually out of sorts. This she blamed on the whole Mesa Butte controversy. She'd had nothing new to report on it since the beginning of the week. The city still hadn't responded to her request for files on Mesa Butte, which meant the city had broken the law. The paper's legal team had opted to send a reminder rather than take the city to court. Meanwhile, the Boulder city council and mayor were still publicly promising to "look into" the incident, but were vague as to how or when, exactly, this would happen or when an apology might be forthcoming. And, of course, the complaint she'd filed against Officer Daniels for excessive use of force had resulted in a letter from Boulder's chief of police promising an internal investigation.

Lots of promises, no action.

Of course, the real reason for her bad mood was a certain mountain ranger who couldn't seem to leave her alone, intruding into her thoughts, pestering her even in her sleep. Why, oh, why had she agreed to meet with him tomorrow? Maybe there was still time to cancel. She could call his cell phone and . . .

Are you that afraid to be around him, Kat?

She was still trying to answer that question at five o'clock when Sophie stopped at her desk to remind her that it was the second Friday of the month and therefore Girls' Night Out—a tradition that had evolved out of weekly I-Team get-togethers in the nearest brewpub. With so many of the women now married with small children, they'd had to become more organized about their time together.

"I think both Kara and Tess will be there tonight." Sophie fished her keys out of her briefcase. "They read your article about what happened Sunday at the sweat lodge, and they both asked about you."

Kara McMillan and Tessa Darcangelo were former members of the I-Team who now worked as freelance journalists and nonfiction authors. It was Kara's departure from the paper that had opened up a position for Kat. Kara had married a state senator and was now the mother of three, while Tessa, whose courage had so impressed Kat during her first year at the paper, had married a former FBI agent turned cop. The two of them were parents to an adorable little girl who wasn't yet two. Kat admired both women and their husbands greatly and considered them friends.

And she felt her spirits lift. "Yes, I'll come."

THEY MET AT the Wynkoop—Kat, Sophie, Natalie, Kara, Tessa, and Holly Bradshaw, one of the paper's entertainment reporters—and claimed the big round booth in the back corner. Kara, Tessa, Holly and Natalie ordered martinis, while Kat, who didn't drink, and Sophie, who couldn't drink, ordered Italian sodas.

Kara shared the news about Reece's decision not to run for Congress. "He's term limited, so after May he'll be out of office and done with politics."

Sophie nibbled her cherry. "How does he feel about that?"

"I think he's relieved." Kara took a sip of her martini and tucked her long dark hair behind her ear to reveal a smooth pearl earring. "Neither of us liked the thought of having to commute between Denver and D.C. He's looking forward to teaching again."

Sophie shared the names she and Marc had picked out for their baby. "If it's a girl, we've agreed on Addison Lyra, and if it's a boy, he'll be Elijah Phoenix."

Everyone laughed except Kat, who didn't understand what was funny.

"Chase Orion, Addison Lyra, Elijah Phoenix—they all

have constellations as middle names," Tessa explained, smiling, her blond curls spilling over her shoulder.

It struck Kat as wonderful that parents would name their children after stars. "I think that's beautiful, Sophie."

"The three of you are so lucky." Natalie smiled—a sad smile, Kat thought. "You have it all—wonderful husbands, successful careers and beautiful kids."

"I'm sure you'll meet the right guy one of these days," Sophie reassured her. "Half the men at the paper think they're in love with you."

"Only half?" Natalie joked.

But Kat could see in her eyes that she wasn't really laughing.

Then Holly told them all a story that started with how her neighbor was pregnant with in-vitro twins and ended with how a local painter had asked Holly to pose for him in the nude. Platinum blond and stunningly beautiful, Holly lived on the light side of life, seeming to take nothing but her appearance and her sex life seriously. Though that often led her to say things that others found insensitive or superficial, Kat found her lightness to be a gift. No matter what was happening around them, Holly always made them laugh.

"So, are you going to do it?" Kara asked.

Holly took a sip of her martini, a thoughtful frown on her face. "Do you think people will assume he and I are lovers if he paints me naked? I mean, the guy isn't sexy in the least, and I would never want people to think I'd slept with him."

The others debated this while Kat tried to imagine how any woman could be so bold as to pose naked for paintings that would be displayed in public art galleries.

It was Kara who finally changed the subject. "I read your article about the trouble up on Mesa Butte last weekend. I learned a lot from it. I thought you did a really good job of explaining to your audience what this meant to Indian people."

Kat met Kara's gaze and felt something in her chest swell at the compliment. "Thank you. That means a lot to me."

"What about this officer who pulled your hair?" Tessa asked. "You said in the article that you had filed a complaint against him. Any word on that?"

"They've promised to look into it. Gabe filed a complaint against him, too, so I hope that means they'll take it more seriously than they otherwise might."

Four pairs of eyes looked at Kat—and blinked.

"Gabe?" Sophie asked. "Who exactly is Gabe?"

"Gabe Rossiter. He's the park ranger who intervened. It turns out he's also the ranger who saved my life last summer."

Holly made a little sound in her throat like a purr. "Is he single?"

TALKING WITH HER friends about Gabe only made Kat think about him more. She thought about him on her way home. She thought about him when she brushed her teeth. She was still thinking about him the next morning—and thinking about how she might be able to get out of meeting him—when Grandpa Red Crow called to tell her there would be an *inipi* on the butte tonight in defiance of the unjust law.

When she told him how frustrated she felt about her progress on the Mesa Butte investigation, he urged her to be patient. "This problem is more than five hundred years old. You can't expect to solve it in five days, my Kimímila."

Then he changed the subject. "When are you seeing your ranger again? I think he is a good man, a man you can trust."

Kat suppressed an exasperated groan. Two minutes had gone by when she hadn't been thinking of Gabe, and Grandpa Red Crow just had to bring him up. "I'm meeting him at the butte this afternoon. I'm going to try to explain why it's sacred to us."

So much for canceling.

Grandpa chuckled. "Good. That's good. Maybe he can join us in the lodge. If he is with us, perhaps we can pray in peace."

The offer took Kat by surprise. It wasn't often that one of the elders asked an outsider to participate. Did Grandpa trust him that much? "I'll ask him."

She spent the morning cleaning her condo, then clipped last week's articles and mailed them to her grandmother,

knowing that her mother or one of her sisters would be given
the job of translating them and reading them aloud. Then she
ran a few errands, buying groceries, getting gas, picking up
her dry cleaning. When she got back, it was already time to
get her things together for the *inipi*—towel, skirt, old T-shirt,
prayer ties, food for sharing afterward—and drive to Boulder
to meet Gabe.

She loaded her things into her truck, climbed in, and had
just opened her garage door to back out when she saw it.

A coyote.

The hair on her nape rose.

It stood at the end of her driveway, staring at her, its tail
full and bushy, its dull brown fur almost a match for the
winter brown of her front lawn. She got out of the truck and
slammed the driver's side door, certain her movements and
the noise would frighten it away. But it only shifted on its
front paws, its gaze still on her.

She opened the truck door again and grabbed her pouch
of corn pollen out of the glove box. It's not that she truly
believed crossing the coyote's path might throw her life out of
balance. Sprinkling corn pollen in its footprints was a Navajo
tradition, and she was just observing that tradition. That's
what she told herself, anyway.

She turned toward it to find it walking lazily across her
yard toward the park, looking over its shoulder back at her.
Slowly, she walked to her yard where it had crossed her path
and knelt down. Then she did what her grandmother had
taught her to do, sprinkling yellow pollen onto its paw prints.

Two kids on bikes stared at her as they passed.

Now, do you feel silly?

Yes, she did. It's just that the last time a coyote had crossed
her path . . .

Last time one crossed your path, you almost died.

SHE'D ALL BUT forgotten about the strange encounter with
the coyote by the time she reached the outskirts of Boulder,
her mind filled with new resolve. She would meet with Gabe
as she'd agreed to do, sharing what she knew about Mesa

Butte with a man who played an important role as a guardian of the land. She would invite him to the *inipi* as Grandpa Red Crow had asked. And then, whether he attended or not, she would sweat him out of her system, refocusing her energy on things that mattered.

By the time she reached the butte, she had almost convinced herself that this would work. Then she turned the corner onto the access road—and she saw him.

Wearing only his dark green uniform trousers and those strange shoes he'd been wearing the day he'd rescued her, he was climbing along on the underside of an overhanging lip of rock, perhaps thirty feet above the ground. She couldn't see any ropes, which meant that if he fell . . .

What did he think he was doing?

She parked her truck, jumped out, and stared, half in awe and half terrified that he would slip. His body moved like she'd never seen a man's body move before, powerful arms reaching for handholds, fingers gripping holds she couldn't see, his feet finding their own invisible purchase. His body seemed weightless, muscles bunching and shifting in their own rhythm as he worked his way along the length of the overhang, his motions strong and . . . beautiful.

Oh. My.

Her fear now pushed aside by an entirely different emotion, Kat couldn't take her gaze off him, the sight of him making her feel warm, stirring longings she'd ignored for years. She found herself wishing she felt as sexually free as Holly. What it would feel like to touch that body, to have those arms hold her, to be—

One of his feet slipped—and then the other.

Her stomach in free fall, Kat grabbed on to the open driver's side door as he hung suspended by only his fingertips, his arms stretched over his head. Then with strength that amazed her, he drew himself upward, the muscles of his bare arms, chest, and abdomen straining with the effort until his feet met rock again. Only when he reached the other side and began to climb down did Kat realize she'd been holding her breath.

His feet met the earth, and he walked over to her, grinning. "Sorry. I got here early and thought I could get some climbing in before you showed up."

But Kat was still clutching the door, fighting the falling sensation that had overwhelmed her the moment he'd slipped, her heart thudding, her legs shaky.

GABE SAW KAT's bloodless face, her wide eyes. She looked like she'd just been frightened out of her skin. "Are you okay?"

Her gaze met his, the fear in her eyes transforming to anger. "You . . . You could have gotten yourself killed!"

"You were afraid for me?" Something warm spread inside his chest.

She glared up at him. "You almost fell!"

He heard the slight tremor in her voice, and then it came to him. It'd been only three months since her fall, and the experience was probably still visceral for her. "It's still with you, isn't it—the feeling of falling?"

She nodded, then looked down at her feet, her lashes dark against her cheeks.

He tucked a finger beneath her chin, lifted her gaze to his, unable to keep himself from running his thumb over the softness of her cheek. "I do this for a living, Kat. What you saw— that's nothing. It's just me relaxing after a day's work."

She let out a breath, stepped back from him, clearly still angry. "I guess that's the first difference in how we view the land. It's not just a big playground or something to be conquered. No Native man would ever climb here. Mesa Butte is for prayer."

Too touched by her concern to feel truly irritated, Gabe walked over to his truck, opened the door, and grabbed his T-shirt off the front seat. "Or maybe climbing is for me what the *inipi* is for you or what Sun Dance is for a Sun Dancer."

He'd never thought of it as prayer, exactly, but now that he'd said it, he supposed climbing was the closest he came to communing with any higher power.

"A Sun Dancer suffers for the sake of others, not for his own fulfillment."

Well, she had him there. And then again . . . "When my ability to climb enables me to save someone's life, is what I do still selfish?"

She said nothing this time.

Aware that she was watching him, he drew the shirt over his head, then reached for his duty belt and strapped it into place. Although he was off duty, he was unwilling to leave his sidearm unattended in his truck. He took off his climbing shoes and grabbed his socks and boots, then turned and sat facing outward on the driver's seat to put them on, his gaze drawn back to her.

The apology was in her eyes before she spoke. "I'm sorry. I . . ."

"You saw me slip, and it brought back the day you fell. I understand." He finished tying his boots, then reached for his coat, letting the subject drop. "I read the article, by the way. Great work."

The color was coming back to her cheeks. "Did I get you into trouble?"

"Nope." Webb had been more worried about possible blowback because of the complaint Gabe had filed against Daniels.

"Daniels claims you're connected to this woman and that's why you're supporting her complaint," Webb had said. "He says you seemed to know her."

"She's the woman who got caught in the rockslide at Eldo, so, yes, I recognized her," Gabe had answered. "But other than that, Daniels is full of shit, sir."

And that had been the end of it.

Gabe zipped his coat. "Can your leg handle hiking up, or should we drive?"

"It will be good for my leg to hike, but I probably won't be very fast."

"I'm in no hurry." He waited for her to reach his side, unable to help noticing how good she looked in jeans, the motion of her hips as she walked undeniably female despite her limp, her long hair drawn back from her face by a silver barrette, her hands tucked in the pockets of her fleece-lined denim jacket.

They walked for a moment, no sound but the distant drone of cars and the crunching of gravel beneath their boots.

She spoke first. "I've never understood whether park rangers are like police officers or whether they're something completely different."

"We're like cops in every way. We have badges, carry firearms, wear Kevlar, have the full authority of the law. We arrest our share of drunk drivers, drug dealers, and fugitives, too, but we do it in the mountains. That brings its own challenges. Try chasing some armed lunatic uphill through dense undergrowth. We also deal with wilderness rescues and wildlife, something city police aren't trained to do."

"Is that what you always wanted to be—a mountain ranger?"

"I grew up here and spent all my spare time in the mountains, hiking, climbing, skiing. I got a degree in biology thinking I might become a wildlife vet, but when it came time to get a job, all I wanted to do was be outdoors. So I went through the police academy, trained as a paramedic, and then volunteered for some technically difficult search and rescue. I guess they figured I wasn't going away, so when a position opened up, they gave it to me."

She laughed. It was the first time he'd heard her laugh, and the sound of it warmed him like sunshine.

GABE HIKED SLOWLY up the access road, allowing Kat to set the pace. It was clear that every step hurt her, the muscles of her leg probably atrophied from three months of immobility, her tibia almost certainly still sore from whatever hardware the surgeon had used to bolt it back together. But she didn't complain or even ask him to rest, still every bit the woman who'd crawled away from the rockslide, dragging that leg behind her.

The sky was wide and blue, the sunshine warm, a brisk breeze blowing from the west, carrying the promise of snow. And as they walked along, Kat asking him questions about his job, Gabe felt some part of him letting go, a feeling of release he usually only got when he was alone in the mountains.

"What do you deal with most—animal problems or people problems?" She looked over at him, her cheeks pink from exertion.

"People problems—without a doubt. Even most animal problems are caused by people—people who leave garbage where it can attract bears, people who get too close to wildlife, people who let their dogs run off leash."

"What's the most common crime you see?"

"I'd say half of what we deal with are alcohol-related crimes or people having sex in public. If I had a dollar for every bare ass I've seen on the job . . ."

She looked up at him, surprise on her face. "You're kidding me!"

A virgin, Rossiter.

"No, I'm not. People get into the mountains and start feeling their animal instincts or something." Gabe understood that. Being outdoors stirred a person's senses—all of them. Walking beside Kat with his lungs full of fresh air certainly had Gabe's senses going, her femininity teasing him, the honey-sweet scent of her skin filling his head, the gleam of her dark hair making him want to run his fingers through it. "I'll be walking along through the trees and see a man and woman jump up and start running with their pants around their ankles."

She laughed. "Do you arrest them?"

He shook his head. He'd done his share of fucking al fresco and would have felt like a hypocrite if he'd cited anyone else. "No. I figure they're humiliated enough as it is. If I find people having sex in a parked vehicle, I make sure it's consensual and then send them on their way."

"I can't imagine why anyone would want to risk getting caught like that."

"Crazy, huh?" Gabe had to fight back a grin, her naiveté amusing.

They were about halfway up by now, the plains stretching to the east, the basalt dike that formed the backbone of the butte rising to the north, Boulder Valley stretching out behind them and, beyond it, the high peaks. A red-tailed hawk circled slowly above them, its rust-colored tail feathers catching the sunlight.

"So if I were a new volunteer for Mountain Parks and you had to explain to me the significance of Mesa Butte, what would you say?"

And now came the test.

"I would first explain its geological significance as evidence of earlier volcanic activity and talk about how erosion from the melting of the last ice age had washed the earth away, exposing the rock. Then I would talk about the importance of riparian habitat, which offers an especially rich environment for plants and animals. Because two rivers converge here, there's almost always water, even during the driest times. I would explain how essential the butte is for raptors, which use the crags for perching and nesting sites. I would point out that the butte provided food, water, and shelter for the Arapaho, Cheyenne, and other Plains nations, who hunted bison and antelope nearby, camped by the rivers, and used the butte for ceremonies."

Kat listened as Gabe went on, impressed by his understanding of the land. It wasn't the same as hers, exactly, but it wasn't terribly different, either. He saw how it all fit together—the land, the plants, the animals, the people—but his knowledge was scientific instead of spiritual. At the same time, she could tell it truly mattered to him. The land, the plants, the four-legged creatures, the winged ones—they mattered to him.

"You really love it out here, don't you?" she asked when he had finished.

"Why else would I choose to be a ranger when I could sit at a nice desk all day playing with paper clips?" He grinned, making her pulse trip.

She was surprised how comfortable she felt being out here with him. There was an easiness to it, something she certainly hadn't expected after their last meeting in the restaurant. He seemed to belong here as much as she did.

The wind knows him.

The truth of that realization startled her. Then she thought of Grandpa Red Crow, who, for some reason, already trusted Gabe. He'd always had a sixth sense about people.

"So how'd I do? Better than the average *Bilagáanaa*?"

Kat couldn't help but smile at his use of that Navajo word. "How did you know I'm Navajo? Is it the earrings? And how do you know so much about Indian culture, like the Sun Dance and the *inipi*?"

He chuckled. "All rangers are required to undergo training in local history and indigenous culture. As for how I knew you were Navajo, you told me in the restaurant. You said your family lived in a hogaan, remember?"

"Yes, I remember." So he was a man who listened. She liked that.

"What clan are you?"

"I was born to the *Ashiihi*—Salt Clan." If she'd had a Navajo father, she'd have been able to tell him what clan she'd been born for—one was born *to* the clan of one's mother and *for* the clan of one's father—but she didn't even know who her father was. She wondered if Gabe would be able to tell that she was fatherless. If so, he said nothing, so she changed the subject. "You did very well—much better than the average *Bilagáanaa*. But let me explain what we know."

She told how any place where two rivers came together was believed to be sacred by itself and how two rivers at the base of a high place like Mesa Butte marked it as special, a place set aside by Creator for people to pray. She told him how the Old Ones would have found everything they needed right here—wood from the river valley below, stones that retained heat well, deer, bison, and antelope for food and clothing, and a clear view in all four directions should enemies approach.

They were near the top now, the access road widening as it came to its end. And there up ahead she saw a familiar pickup truck, the driver's side door open.

"Grandpa Red Crow is here."

"He's the old guy who was pouring water for the *inipi* that night, right?"

Kat nodded. "He's one of our most revered elders, a Hunk-papa Lakota medicine man from Rosebud. He wants me to invite you to tonight's *inipi*."

"He's holding an *inipi* up here tonight?" The tone of Gabe's voice told her he didn't think this was a great idea.

"Yes. Now that we know what happened, he says he sees no reason why we can't go on as we did before. Besides, he refuses to be driven off the land. He wanted me to invite you to join us. He thinks we might be left in peace if there's a ranger with us."

"Oh, I see. He just wants me there for my badge—is that it?"

Realizing what she'd said—or, rather, how she'd said it—Kat rushed to explain, afraid she'd hurt his feelings. "Oh, no! No! That's not what I meant. He—"

A grin spread across Gabe's face, and Kat realized he was teasing her. "I'm honored by the invitation. Still, it might not be such a great idea to hold another ceremony here until the city clarifies its position on the land-use code."

"Why should we wait when we have a right to be here?"

The butte leveled out, the sweat lodge standing off to their left, a pile of firewood beside it, waiting to be split. Grandpa Red Crow's ax was there, but he wasn't.

"Does he usually arrive this early?" Gabe asked, turning and glancing about them.

Kat nodded, expecting to see Grandpa Red Crow any moment. "He cleans the lodge and splits wood for the fire chief to use."

They stood there for a good fifteen minutes, debating whether it was wise to hold another *inipi*, but still Grandpa Red Crow did not appear. Kat began to worry about him. He wasn't a young man. If he'd twisted his ankle on the steep terrain or gotten sick . . .

"Have you ever been to the top?" Gabe asked, looking up at the flat, rocky crown that formed the butte's summit.

Kat shook her head. "It's almost always dark when I'm here."

"Come on. The view is amazing."

"I . . . I don't know if I should."

His brows knitted together in a frown. "Is it against your beliefs to go up there?"

"No. Nothing like that. It's just . . ." How was she going to explain this to a man who hung upside down from cliffs for fun? "Ever since I fell, I've had a bad fear of heights. I . . . I get dizzy and . . ." She willed herself to meet his gaze, expecting to see disappointment in his eyes, but finding understanding.

"I'm not surprised. You took one hell of a fall. But that's a solid basalt dike. It's not going to disappear from beneath your feet." Then he looked straight into her eyes. "And I promise I won't let you fall."

She followed him up the rocky, winding trail to the top, listening as he told her about the great surge of hot, volcanic rock that had created the butte, the wind picking up and tousling her hair as they neared the summit.

And then she was there on the highest point of Mesa Butte, the four directions stretching out before her. The summit was flat. No plants. No trees. Nothing but an empty liquor bottle. She took one step forward—and regretted it.

The dizziness hit her, making her head spin. Trying to shake the feeling, she drew air into her lungs, reminded herself that the rock beneath her boots was solid. But it didn't seem to help. Her stomach sank toward the ground, her knees turning to rubber, her lungs too constricted to draw breath.

Gabe caught her around the waist and drew her up against the hard wall of his chest. "Easy, Kat. Open your eyes."

She hadn't realized she'd closed them. She did as he'd asked and found herself looking up into his eyes.

"Now breathe. Slowly. That's the way." After a moment he moved to the side, the view opening before her once more.

"Don't—!" She grabbed for him.

Warm fingers clasped hers. "I'm not going anywhere."

Reassured by his presence, she looked at the chain of white-capped mountains that stretched as far as the eye could see to the west, then she turned in a slow circle, seeing the sweat lodge and Grandpa Red Crow's pickup below to the south. Open prairie spread like an undulating sea of grass to the east and beyond that the skyscrapers and brown cloud of Denver. To the north stood a cluster of farmhouses separated from the road by the conjoined rivers. What she didn't see was Grandpa Red Crow.

"Are you up for a view off the edge?"

Kat shook her head. "No, I don't think I . . ."

"I bet you can." He drew her forward, stepping over the whisky bottle. "Just try. Trust me. Keep your eyes on me if you have to."

Holding fast to his hand, she followed, a feeling of exhilaration sweeping through her as, step by baby step, her fear began to lessen.

An arm's length ahead of her, Gabe stopped at the very edge and looked down. Something—surprise?—flashed across his features, then a muscle clenched in his jaw. He turned to her. "We're going back to my truck—now."

Something in his voice, something in the hard look on his face, set her heart to pounding. She stepped forward, felt his arm catch her around the waist, holding her back from the edge—but not so far back that she couldn't see.

There, two hundred feet below, dressed in his red shirt and black vest, lay Grandpa Red Crow, shattered upon the ground.

Her knees gave way, the world spinning beneath her feet, and her heart seeming to burst in her chest. Strong arms held her fast, drew her back from the precipice. As if from far away, she heard herself scream "No!"

CHAPTER
5

GABE KNELT BESIDE the old man, knowing before he checked for a pulse that he wouldn't find one. No one could fall that far and survive. Cold to the touch, Grandpa had been dead for a while, his head at an unnatural angle to his body, his eyes staring unseeing at the sky.

In the distance Gabe could hear the approaching wail of sirens. But there was nothing anyone could do for the old man now, except try to figure out how this had happened. Had he fallen—or had he been pushed?

Gabe's instincts told him it was the latter.

He stood and took a step back from the body, not wanting to disturb a potential crime scene more than he already had. Then he saw it.

A potsherd.

The same reddish color as the soil and painted with black lines, it lay in pieces beside the body. Though Gabe was no archaeologist, he'd bet his ass that it was an American Indian artifact, part of a small bowl judging by the curved shape of the pieces.

What the hell?

This could not mean what he thought it meant.

From behind him, he heard the soft sound of Kat's weeping. He turned to find her walking slowly toward him, her face wet with tears and lined with grief, her gaze averted from the body. He'd told her to stay in the truck, not sure how much of a mess he'd find and hoping to spare her memories she didn't need. Falling two hundred feet could do serious damage to the human anatomy.

"You don't have to see this, Kat."

But she didn't seem to hear him, sinking to her knees in the dirt near the old man's feet. "H-help h-him! L-like you helped m-me."

"There's nothing I can do, honey. It's too late."

She squeezed her eyes shut, pressed a hand to her mouth, clearly struggling to believe that someone she loved was gone forever.

Gabe knew only too well what that was like—disbelief, shock, grief so strong it ripped through you. He walked over to her and knelt beside her, then, unable to do anything else, drew her into his arms and held her. "I'm so sorry."

She was trembling, probably as much from shock as from grief, her hair soft against his cheek, her fingers curling into the fabric of his coat, her quiet sobs tearing at him. "I-I t-talked to h-him just a f-few hours ago. H-how could he be d-dead?"

"It doesn't make sense, does it?"

"Why w-would anyone want to k-kill him?"

"We don't know for sure that's what happened. It could be an accident of some kind. Maybe he got too close to the edge and slipped." Strictly speaking, what Gabe said was true, and yet his gut told him she was right.

The old man had been murdered.

The fire truck arrived first, the approaching sound of its siren seeming to bring Kat back to herself. She stiffened, drew away from him. "I-I'm sorry."

Gabe cupped her tear-streaked cheek, forced her to meet his gaze. "You have no reason to apologize. I only wish I could have done something for him."

She sniffed. "Thanks."

He drew her to her feet, watching as she wiped the tears from her eyes and somehow found the inner strength to put her grief aside. By the time the fire truck had arrived, the haunted look in her eyes was the only sign of the anguish she was feeling, her courage making him want to protect her all the more.

Two firefighters took in the situation at a glance, realized there were no lives to save, and giving Gabe a nod, went to stand by the truck, waiting for law enforcement.

Hatfield and Chief Ranger Webb were the first on the scene. Webb drew Gabe aside. "Want to tell me what the hell you're doing out here with her, Rossiter?"

Gabe filled his boss in, watching as a sympathetic firefighter brought Kat bottled water and a blanket. He'd just finished bringing Webb up to speed when a squad car pulled up and Frank Daniels got out, all blond crew cut and Kevlar.

Gabe saw Kat tense, her body going rigid as she recognized the bastard. Then he met Webb's gaze. "He *is not* going to question her. He's not going anywhere near her. He's already brutalized her once, and that was before she ripped him a new one in her news article."

Webb leaned in, his voice dropping to a pissed-off whisper. "Do you know how bad this looks—the two of you together? It's damned hard for me to argue that your complaint against Daniels is legit when you're fraternizing with her and watching over her like a guard dog."

"We're not fraternizing. I told you—"

"You met her here for a nice afternoon of cultural exchange. Yeah, you told me." Webb rolled his eyes, obviously not believing it. "You let me deal with Daniels, got it? If this is ruled a homicide, BPD is going to claim jurisdiction, and the last thing we need is you turning this into some kind of interdepartmental dick fight."

"Me? He's the asshole who ignored our jurisdiction and—"

"Stay away from him, got it? And if you can manage it, stay away from her, too!" Webb jabbed a finger in Kat's direction.

But Gabe had no intention of leaving Kat to go through this alone.

IT DIDN'T SEEM real.

None of it seemed real. Not the police cars and flashing lights. Not the gloved officers going inch by inch over the ground. Not the yellow crime-scene tape.

Faces swam in and out of her vision. Sirens wailed and fell

silent. Snatches of conversation drifted just beyond reach of her conscious mind.

"You think it was someone stealing artifacts?"

"We'll see what the autopsy and toxicology results say."

"Did she identify the body?"

He was dead. Grandpa Red Crow was dead.

She knew she ought to find her cell phone and call Glenna or Uncle Allen so they could let everyone else know. She ought to call the paper and get a reporter and photographer out here. But she couldn't seem to think straight long enough to figure out where her cell phone was. And then an officer started asking her questions.

How did she know the deceased? How had she spent her day? When had she arrived at the butte? Why had she come here? What had she done once she'd arrived at the butte? When had the body been discovered? Who'd found it?

Gabe came up from behind, his nearness and the sound of his voice more reassuring than she could have imagined. He stayed with her as she answered the officer's questions, his presence steadying her, holding her together.

And then she saw Officer Daniels walk over to Grandpa Red Crow's body, a large black plastic bag under his arm, an EMT following behind him with a gurney. He dropped the bag on the ground and unzipped it.

A body bag.

"No!" She hadn't realized she'd shouted until she heard her own voice.

Everyone fell silent, staring at her.

Gabe whispered in her ear, a warning tone to his voice. "Kat, you can't—"

On a surge of anger and grief, she pulled away from him, ducked beneath the yellow tape, and went to stand over Grandpa Red Crow's body. "Not you! I don't want you touching him! I don't want you near him, not after what you did!"

Daniels glared at her, clearly recognizing her. Then his gaze flicked nervously toward Gabe and the other police officers, a mask of indifference sliding over his face. "Are you trying to get yourself arrested? Interfering with a police officer is a crime."

Her heart pounding, her rage moving toward tears, she met his gaze straight on, forcing words past the lump in her throat. "He was *wicasa wakan*, a holy man, and you treated him like garbage! You will not touch him!"

For a moment she thought Daniels would arrest her. Then he stepped back, jerking the gloves off his hands. "Have it your way."

"I'll do it." An EMT stepped forward. "If that's okay with you."

Kat nodded, turned to Gabe. "He trusted you. Could you . . . ?"

But she couldn't say it, her throat suddenly too tight to speak.

She saw in Gabe's eyes that he understood. "Yeah, I'll help."

Shaking his head and laughing, Daniels walked away.

Kat watched as Gabe put on gloves and, with the help of the EMT, carefully placed Grandpa Red Crow in the body bag and zipped it shut, cutting off the old man's last view of the sky, the ripping sound of the zipper so painfully final.

"Hágoónee'" She whispered farewell to him in Diné and then repeated it in his language, tears blurring her vision. *"Toksa ake."*

She watched until his body was loaded into the waiting ambulance, then turned and started walking, needing to get away from here.

"Where do you think you're going?" Gabe overtook her with his long strides.

She tried to think. "Home."

"You're not driving anywhere, honey, not like this." He stepped in front of her, blocked her path, one big hand on her shoulder. "You're too upset. Give me your keys. I'll have Hatfield drive your truck to my place."

It was a measure of how upset she was that she did as he asked, fishing her keys out of her pocket and putting them in his upturned palm. "Where will I go?"

"You're coming home with me."

* * *

IT WAS DARK and snowing by the time Gabe pulled into his driveway, small, icy flakes blowing on a frigid wind. He parked in the garage and looked over to see Kat with her hands folded in her lap, her gaze focused on nothing, a look of devastation on her sweet face. He wished there were something he could say or do to make this easier for her, but he knew from experience that there wasn't.

He reached over, brushed a strand of hair from her cheek. "Hey, we're here. Let's get you inside."

Once indoors, he lit a fire in the fireplace and told her to make herself at home, then headed into the bathroom to wash up. Hands and face clean, he crossed the hall to his bedroom and found it exactly as he'd left it—buried in dirty clothes, his bed unmade, climbing and ski magazines strewn across the floor.

You're a pig, Rossiter.

Yes, he was, but most of the time it didn't matter. In the three years he'd lived here, he'd never once brought a woman home. He'd bought the house with the money he and Jill had set aside for a climbing trip to Everest, needing to escape their old condo and anything that reminded him of her. Since then, whenever he'd been with women, it had always been in their space. He preferred it that way because it meant he could leave whenever he chose.

Knowing he'd left Kat alone, he quickly changed into jeans and a T-shirt, picked up his climbing and ski porn, then gathered up every piece of putrefied clothing he could find and carried it all downstairs to the laundry room, where he unceremoniously dumped it on the floor. He'd do something about clean sheets later. She could have the bed, and he would sleep on the couch.

His mind on dinner, he walked back into the living room and found her sitting on the couch in front of the fire, still wearing her coat and looking as if her entire world had come crashing down. He reached for her jacket. "I'll take that."

Her motions wooden, she stood, took off her jacket, and

handed it to him, revealing a silky lavender sweater that clung a little too nicely to her curves. Without speaking, she sat again, her hands in her lap, her gaze on the fire.

He hung her coat, then walked over to his entertainment center, which acted as a sort of bar, and poured her a double Bushmills, figuring that the best and perhaps only answer to a moment like this was twenty-one-year-old Irish whisky.

He walked over to her, sat beside her, and pressed the tumbler into her hands. "Drink. It will help clear your head."

She looked at him, then looked at what he'd placed in her hands and shook her head. "I don't drink. Grandpa Red Crow says . . ."

Tears filled her eyes as she realized what she said, her chin quivering, her grief palpable.

"The rules don't apply tonight, Kat. Even nice Navajo girls get to sip a little whisky when they've been through what you've just been through. I'm sure Grandpa Red Crow—"

She raised the tumbler to her lips—and tossed back almost the entire drink.

"—would understand."

Her eyes went wide, a shocked expression on her face, her entire body shuddering. She gasped, coughed, gaped up at him.

He took the tumbler from her hands. "I said sip, honey."

KAT TOOK ANOTHER sip. How could anyone drink this stuff? It was like swallowing fire, the whisky burning its way down her throat and into her stomach, where it smoldered. She shuddered, her eyes watering.

Now you know why they called it firewater.

She'd just gotten off the phone from telling Glenna the bad news—as if the poor woman needed more bad news. Glenna had at first refused to believe it. Then she'd burst into tears, thanking Kat between sobs for calling and promising to spread the word, her grief making the horrible events of this day inescapably real.

From the kitchen came the sound of Gabe's voice as he

ordered pizza. She'd told him he didn't need to worry about feeding her, but he hadn't listened.

"You need something in your stomach to soak this up," he'd said, pouring her a second, smaller drink. "Just sit back and try to relax. I'll be in the next room."

Feeling almost numb, Kat glanced around, seeing her surroundings for the first time. She sat on a blocky sofa of brown leather, a matching ottoman in front of her. An enormous plasma screen TV hung on the wall across from her, liquor bottles and glasses sitting on top of the wooden entertainment center beneath it. Beside them sat a little stereo into which Gabe had plugged his iPod. CDs and DVDs stood in rows on the shelves below, spilling onto the floor. A stack of magazines with names like *Ski*, *Outside*, and *Rock and Ice* sat on the polished wood floor on the left end of the sofa, while a fireplace stood to the right. The walls were bare—no art, no family photos, no pictures of friends.

Feeling a little dizzy, Kat relaxed into the sofa cushions and took another sip. Maybe it was the heat of the fire, but she felt flushed, the tension inside her slowly melting away—but not the sadness. It was still there, sharp and aching.

He's gone. Grandpa Red Crow is really gone.

With no warning, it hit her, a wave of grief so strong it seemed to tear out her heart. Tears blurred her vision, spilled down her cheeks, a torrent of pain washing up from inside her, cutting off her breath.

She didn't know Gabe was there until he took the drink from her hand, set it down on the floor, and sat beside her. "I know there's nothing I can say that makes this any easier, but I want you to know that I really am sorry."

She could hear in his voice that he meant it, but she closed her eyes and turned her face away from him, not wanting him to see her come apart. "H-he was a father to me. He was the only m-man who . . . When I first came to Denver . . . he w-was there for me. He taught me so much. H-he called me Kimímila. That m-means Butterfly."

Then Gabe's arms went around her, and he drew her against the hard wall of his chest. "It's okay, Kat. Let it out."

And she broke.

Holding on to Gabe as if to save herself from falling, she wept as she'd never wept before, her heart seeming truly to shatter. She would never see Grandpa Red Crow again. She would never hear him sing the songs or play his flute in the *inipi* again, or listen to his stories, or turn to him for advice. She would never be able to tell him how much he meant to her or thank him for all he'd done.

Everything he was, everything he knew, was gone.

She had no idea how much time had passed, but slowly her tears subsided, the sharpest edge of her grief blunted. Gradually, she became aware of other things. The strength of Gabe's arms around her. The steady thrum of his heartbeat against her cheek. The hard feel of his chest. The warmth of his body. The scent of the outdoors that seemed to cling to his skin. The gentleness of his hand as it stroked her hair. The rhythm of his breathing.

She'd never been held like this by a man—or anyone, for that matter. Apart from rare hugs her grandmother had given her, she'd grown up without physical contact. She was surprised to find that she liked it. It felt good, warm, soothing.

More than that, it felt right.

The wind knows him.

She drew back only far enough to look up at his face. He was watching her, his blue eyes filled with concern, his lashes dark, his brow furrowed. His skin was brown from the sun, his jaw shadowed by a new growth of stubble, and his lips . . .

She found herself wondering again what it would be like to kiss those lips. She'd been kissed before, once in middle school by one of the Benally brothers and twice in high school by Willie Tsosie—and she hadn't been impressed. But somehow she didn't think Gabe would lose his gum in her mouth or slobber on her.

As if of their own will, her fingers found their way to his mouth, tracing the curve of his lower lip, exploring its fullness.

He tensed, and his eyes went dark. "Kat . . ."

She knew there were reasons why she shouldn't be touching him like this, but she didn't really care, his words echoing through her mind.

The rules don't apply tonight.

She sat up higher, took his face between her palms, and pressed her lips to his.

CHAPTER 6

Geee-zus!

Gabe sucked in a breath, shocked by the blistering impact of Kat's unexpected kiss, heat shearing through his gut at the first clumsy press of her lips against his. Even as his body responded, some part of his brain knew this shouldn't be happening. "Kat, you're upset and tipsy and—"

She kissed him again, tilting her head to better slant her mouth over his.

Christ!

He turned his face away, felt her lips brush his jaw. "Honey, you don't really want this. You've just lost—"

She made a little sound of protest, her arms sliding behind his head, drawing his lips closer to hers, as if to show him that she *did* really want it.

Good. So did he.

Ignoring the pathetic warnings of his conscience, he took control of the kiss, drawing her tight against him, capturing her mouth with his.

God, she tasted sweet! She smelled sweet, too—like honey and woman. She gave a little whimper, melting against him in a way that was utterly feminine, every inch of her soft body molding to his, her breasts pressing against his ribs, her lips parting to give him access. He swirled his tongue over hers, felt her body tense. And through a pheromone fog, he realized she wasn't just a virgin between her legs.

Kissing—real kissing—was new to her, too.

Not just virgin, buddy—extra virgin.

He reined himself in, gentled the kiss, slowed it down,

brushing her lips lightly with his, teasing their outline with
the tip of his tongue, nipping their fullness, his lust for her at
war with some strange urge to protect her from himself. In
his world, any night that started with kissing ended soon after
with fucking. His cock had already risen to the occasion and
strained painfully against his fly, looking for the surest route
out of denim and into her. But that couldn't happen—not
tonight, not when she was vulnerable and afraid and hurting,
probably not ever. She wanted happily ever after, and all he
could give her was sex. Still, he could keep kissing her . . .

Hell, yeah.

He claimed her mouth in a no-holds-barred kiss, pene-
trating deep, taking her tongue with his, sucking it into his
mouth, biting down. She whimpered, kissed him back, meeting the strokes of his tongue with her own, her fingers curled
in his hair, her body almost undulating against his, commu-
nicating in a primal language of its own, one Gabe's body
understood only too well.

Katherine James might want to save her virginity, but her
body had other plans.

With a groan, he drew her beneath him, testosterone shorting out his brain, his body taking over, his blood running hot
and fast. He found her throat and pressed his lips against the
rapid beating of her pulse, kissing a path over soft, sweet skin,
tasting her, nibbling her earlobe. And he wasn't finished—not
by a long shot.

"Oh!" Kat heard herself whimper and turned her head to
the side, surrendering her throat to Gabe, the heat of his lips
raising goose bumps on her skin, his male scent filling her
head, the hard press of his body on top of hers making her
belly flutter.

She'd never felt anything like this, never even imagined
it—the heat, the intensity, the overwhelming physical force
of it. Her body trembled, and her heart raced, her breathing
uneven as if she'd been running. And she *was* running—from
her grief, from her fear, from everything that hurt. Some part
of her knew this, but that only made her run faster.

The rules don't apply tonight.

She didn't stop him when he slid a callused hand beneath

her sweater to trace tiny circles up her rib cage. She didn't object when his clever fingers found the clasp of her bra between her breasts and unhooked it. And when he cupped her left breast, when his thumb flicked her nipple . . .

She gasped, stunned, the sensation too astonishing, too arousing, too wonderful to be real. Jagged shafts of heat seemed to shoot straight from her breast to her belly, turning to liquid between her thighs.

"You like that, don't you?"

At the husky sound of his voice, her eyes flew open. She found him looking down at her, his breathing as rough as hers, his blue eyes burning, a smile on his wet lips. She forced herself to hold his gaze, shocked by the intimacy of watching him as he watched her, as he watched the effect his touch had on her, his hand still cupping and shaping her breast, his thumb tracing lazy circles over its aching crest.

And the heat in her belly became a wildfire.

Then he pushed her sweater up, baring her breasts, his gaze raking hungrily over her. "God, Kat, honey, you've got beautiful breasts. They're so . . . Mmm."

Whatever he'd been about to say became a moan as he ducked down and drew one of her nipples into the scorching heat of his mouth.

"Gabe!" Kat's body jerked at the initial shock of it, the pleasure staggering as he suckled first one nipple and then the other, tugging at her with his lips, teasing her with velvet strokes of his tongue, tormenting her with nips of his teeth. It was sweet, so sweet, and terrible, too, the fire between her thighs now a throbbing ache. She heard herself calling his name, felt her hips lifting toward him, wanting, wanting . . .

Wanting *him*.

He groaned, settled his weight between her thighs, and answered her need, grinding what could only be the thick ridge of his erection against her . . . *there*. Slowly, so slowly he moved against her, taking the edge off the ache, only to make it so much worse. She was wet, the emptiness inside her burning, her inner muscles clenching around nothing. And she knew.

If he kept going, if he pressed her, she wouldn't be able to stop him. She wouldn't want to.

Gabe's body was strung so tightly he thought it might snap. He'd been a damned idiot to take it this far. He'd wanted to give her the comfort she so obviously needed, and one thing had led to another. Or that's what he'd told himself. In truth, he'd wanted to kiss her and hold her—and so he had.

He needed to stop. But how could he when Kat was coming apart in his arms, her response burning him up? Her little mewls and whimpers were driving him out of his mind, her wine-dark nipples drawn into tight buds that begged for his mouth, her hips moving in a way that was both feminine and undeniably erotic. He didn't want to stop—oh, hell, no! He wanted to fuck her long and hard. He wanted to make her come again and again. He wanted to forget himself inside her.

And then what, buddy? You'll pluck her sweet cherry and show her the door? She deserves better than that, and you damned well know it.

Gabe dragged his lips from hers, forced his hips to hold still, sexual need grinding in his gut, blood pounding through his veins. "*Kat.*"

She looked up at him, so beautiful it made his chest ache, confusion and longing in those hazel green eyes, tear stains on her cheeks, her lips red and swollen, her delicious breasts rising and falling with each rapid breath—no makeup, no silicon, nothing but sweet, soft, sexually aroused woman.

He fought the urge, so elemental, to kiss her again and settled for running his knuckles over her cheek. Somehow, he managed to string a few words together. "If I don't stop now, honey, we're going to be at this all night."

She squeezed her eyes shut, turned her head to the side, and nodded, her breathing still erratic, her body shaking.

Not sure what to do at a moment like this, he lifted his weight off her, sat back on the couch, drawing her up with him, settling her beside him, her back to his chest. And for a moment he just held her, his cheek resting against her hair, his arm around her waist, waiting for his head to clear and her trembling to subside. It was strangely satisfying, holding her like this. Not as gratifying as sex would have been, but far better than not holding her—as he discovered a moment later, when she scooted forward, away from him.

She fastened her bra and let her sweater fall into place. "I . . . I'm sorry. It's my fault. I shouldn't have—"

"Hey, don't." He'd be damned if he'd let her turn a little R-rated make-out session into a reason to feel guilty. He sat forward and cupped her cheek, turning her head, forcing her to meet his gaze. "You have no reason to apologize. You've had one hell of a day. It's only natural that you'd try to find some comfort. Combine that with a couple shots of whisky and compatible chemistry and—"

The doorbell rang.

"Pizza." Gabe stood, ran a finger over Kat's cheek. "You just hang tight, and we'll finish this discussion in a minute."

His heart still pounding, his cock half hard, he walked down the hallway to the front door, opened it—and felt his teeth grind.

Not pizza.

Dammit!

He lowered his voice. "Samantha. What the hell are you doing here?"

BOTH RELIEVED AND disappointed to find herself alone, Kat hugged her arms around herself, closed her eyes, and drew several shaky breaths, trying to slow her racing heart and stop herself from trembling. Her lips still tingled from his kisses, her breasts heavy and aching, raw arousal pulsing between her thighs.

What have you done, Kat?

What she'd done was kiss him. He'd tried to warn her, had given her a chance to stop, and still she'd kissed him. Over and over again.

It must have been the whisky. She'd never had so much as a sip of alcohol before tonight. Although she knew alcohol made people do things they wouldn't ordinarily do, she hadn't realized it was affecting her. It had lowered her inhibitions and . . .

Even as she grasped for that excuse, she knew that's all it was—an excuse. Yes, she'd had a little whisky to drink, but not so much that she hadn't known what she was doing. If she'd been that drunk she wouldn't be sitting here having a rational conversation with herself. No, she'd known what she was doing. She'd chosen to do it.

Kat, you're upset and tipsy and—

Yes, she'd been upset. She'd been more than upset. She loved Grandpa Red Crow like a father, and now he was gone. Senselessly, needlessly gone. To have seen the way he'd died, to have seen the light gone from his eyes . . .

Tears blurred her vision, grief rising thick and hot in her throat.

Yes, she'd been upset, and in the wake of Grandpa Red Crow's death, she'd reached for comfort, for life, for Gabe. And he'd understood, at first trying to stop her.

Honey, you don't really want this.

But she *had* really wanted it. In that moment she'd wanted it more than anything. She wondered for days what it would be like to be kissed by him. Now she knew.

And now she needed to forget. Because kissing him had made her want to forget every promise she'd ever made herself.

And where would that leave you, Kat?

No place she'd want to be. She wanted love. He wanted a good time. He'd made it clear in the restaurant on Monday that he wasn't interested in a relationship. For him, sex was nothing more than a physical thing. How had he put it?

There's no such thing as "happily ever after." Love, romance, sex—it's nothing more than chemistry.

Chemistry.

He'd used that word just now, too.

You've had one hell of a day. It's only natural that you'd try to find some comfort. Combine that with a couple shots of whisky and compatible chemistry and—

So that's how he saw it—a mere matter of physiology, psychology, and biology. Like the confluence of geology, geography, and biology at the butte, it could be studied, classified, and explained by science. But science merely revealed the "how" of things, never the deeper "why." And Kat desperately needed that "why."

Why, oh, why was she so drawn to a man who might want her in his bed but would never want her in his life?

She wiped the tears from her cheeks, wondering what was taking Gabe so long with the pizza. Not that she was hungry . . .

Then she heard voices—his and a woman's. It sounded like they were arguing. But why would he be arguing with the pizza driver?

She stood and walked toward the sound, only to find him blocking the doorway with his body, keeping a much smaller and very beautiful red-haired woman from coming inside. The woman shoved against him, tottered on her heels, failing to budge him even an inch, her short, black dress and jacket at odds with the snow that fell behind her.

"You can't just sleep with me and then ignore me!" she hissed in his face.

So this woman and Gabe are involved.

A heaviness gathered in Kat's chest.

"You don't have a shred of dignity, do you? Go home, Samantha."

And now Gabe wants nothing to do with her.

That strange heaviness sank right into Kat's stomach.

The woman caught sight of Kat, and her expression changed from despair to loathing. "I see why you won't let me in. You're busy."

Gabe's head jerked around, the surprise on his face telling Kat that he hadn't known she was standing there. He closed his eyes for a moment, drew a deep breath, then turned back to Samantha. "Leave her out of this. She's none of your—"

"You asshole!" The woman slapped Gabe hard enough to turn his head, the blow making Kat gasp. Then she glared at Kat. "You must give really good head, bitch, because I'm an expert, and he never once brought me here. I had to get his address from the DMV!"

"Samantha!" Gabe's shout made Kat jump. He took a step forward, forcing Samantha back. "Get the hell off my doorstep and out of my sight!"

"Or what? You'll call the police?" Samantha's nostrils flared, and she shot Kat one last venomous look, before glaring up at Gabe again. "Go to hell, you jerk! Your bitch of a fiancée, Jill, is there waiting for you."

Then the woman turned on her heels and stomped off through the snow, Gabe closing the door behind her.

Fiancée? Had Gabe been engaged? And why would his fiancée be waiting in hell, unless she was . . . unless she was dead.

For a moment, this revelation seemed terribly important to Kat. If she hadn't had that whisky, if she weren't already emotionally overwhelmed, she might have been able to work it out. But then Gabe turned toward her, his expression hard, a muscle clenching in his jaw. He met her gaze, and his expression softened.

"I'm sorry you saw that. She's a . . . She's just a . . ."

Feeling hollow, Kat finished for him. "A failed chemistry experiment?"

THIS WAS JUST great. This was goddamned great!

"You don't have to go." Gabe watched Kat search her purse for her cell phone, wishing he could wring Samantha's neck. Leave it to Sam to go *Fatal Attraction* on him . . . "You can have my bed. I'll take the couch."

"No, thank you." Kat drew her cell phone out, flipped it open, tapped in a number with her thumb. "I need to get home. I'll come for my truck tomorrow."

The doorbell rang again.

Gabe paid the pizza delivery kid and carried the box to the kitchen, half listening while Kat told someone named Sophie about Grandpa Red Crow and asked if someone could pick her up, her voice choked with tears, her grief stirring something inside him he didn't want to feel.

Go to hell, you jerk! Your bitch of a fiancée, Jill, is there waiting for you.

He ruthlessly quashed the unwanted emotion, willed himself not to think of Jill or Samantha or to waste a single moment wondering how Samantha knew about Jill. She'd probably slept with one of his old climbing buddies. They were the only ones who'd known the truth—which is why he hadn't spoken to them in three years.

"What's your address?" Kat called to him.

He ground it out, trying not to grit his teeth. "Nine-forty-five Tenth Street."

"Thanks." She repeated it over the phone.

He dropped the pizza box on the table, set two paper plates and a small stack of paper napkins down beside it, the night having officially gone to hell. Why should he care if Kat wanted to head home? If that's what she needed, that was fine by him. It's not like he'd planned to have her spend the night. And if the thought of her sleeping in his bed—without him—had pleased him in some strange way?

It only proved that she was right. It was best if she left—best for both of them. He was getting way too caught up in her.

She appeared in the kitchen doorway. "Her husband, Marc, is at a regional drug task force meeting in Broomfield. He'll be here in about twenty minutes."

Twenty minutes.

Why do you care, Rossiter?

He ignored the question.

"That gives you plenty of time to get something in your stomach." He pulled out a chair for her. "I hope you like pepperoni. Pizza Hut was clean out of mutton."

AN AWKWARD SILENCE stretched between them while they ate, Gabe unable to take his gaze from her. She made what she called a Spirit Plate, putting a bit of her pizza on it and asking him if she could set it outside his back door. He thought he knew what it was for—an offering for the spirit of Grandpa Red Crow. He opened the back door for her himself and watched as she set it on the ground in the inch or so of snow that had gathered, speaking words he didn't understand.

But it looked like Red Crow's spirit was getting more pizza tonight than Kat. She nibbled at it, obviously too upset to be hungry. And he had to blame himself for part of that.

He'd brought her here to give her a quiet place to rest and recover from the shock of Red Crow's death. Instead of peace and quiet, she'd been pawed and verbally harassed. No wonder she wanted to get the hell home.

He raised his beer, took a swallow, set the bottle down again, his conscience refusing to leave him in peace. "I'm sorry, Kat. I had no idea she was going to show up here like that. What she said to you—she was way out of line."

Back to avoiding eye contact with him, Kat dabbed her lips with her napkin. "She seemed very upset that you'd broken up with her."

"I didn't break up with her. We were never together—not like that. We had an arrangement. She wanted more than I could give her. I ended it. She doesn't mean anything to me. Hell, we barely know each other."

His words sounded incredibly shallow, even to his own ears.

Could you have possibly said anything more crass, dumbass?

Kat met his gaze, her hazel eyes seeming to see through him. "So you slept with her, but she doesn't mean anything to you?"

"That's not what I meant." *Yeah, it is. That's exactly what you meant.* "We did not *sleep* together."

"I saw how it was when she was here." Kat put her napkin down and stood. "I guess I should thank you for stopping when you did. I'd be devastated if I'd made love with a man and he treated me that way. Thanks for supper."

She turned to leave the kitchen.

"Kat!" Gabe was on his feet, blocking her path, drawing her into his arms, relieved when she seemed to come willingly. He ran a finger over the curve of her cheek. "It wouldn't have been like that, not with you. If we'd had sex—"

The doorbell rang, stopping him from saying God only knew what.

"That must be Marc." She drew away and hurried off to get her things.

Gabe opened the door and found a man about his own age. With shoulder-length brown hair and wearing a faded denim jacket, the man stood tall enough to look Gabe straight in the eye, and Gabe was certain he'd seen him somewhere before.

"I'm guessing you're here for Kat." Gabe moved aside to let him in.

The man stomped the snow off his boots and stepped inside, sizing Gabe up like a big brother who'd found a stranger sniffing around his little sister. It made Gabe wonder whether Kat had mentioned their little make-out session when she'd spoken with her friend. And why did the bastard look so familiar?

The man held out his hand. "Marc Hunter, Denver PD."

And then it clicked. This was the son of a bitch Gabe had spent three weeks chasing through the mountains in the dead of winter, the son of a bitch whose face had spent the better part of a month hanging on Gabe's office wall—on a wanted poster.

"Gabe Rossiter, Boulder Mountain Parks." Gabe shook Hunter's hand, giving back as good as he got. "I busted my ass trying to bring you in."

"It's lucky for both of us that you didn't find me." Hunter glanced about, obviously looking for Kat, his gaze falling on a climbing harness that Gabe had overlooked on the hallway floor. "You're a rock jock, huh? I bet that helps you out when it comes to scrambling up the east face of the Third Flatiron and shit."

"No, not the east face of the Third." *You prick.* "But it did come in handy when a couple of guys got stuck in a freak blizzard climbing the Diamond on Longs Peak not too long ago."

Hunter's eyebrows rose a notch, and he nodded. "Thanks, by the way, for saving Kat's life this past summer and for stopping that son of a bitch who pulled her hair. I'd like to kick his ass."

"That makes two of us."

And then Kat was there, already wearing her coat and ready to go. She looked up at Gabe, tears shimmering in those guileless eyes of hers. "I'll never be able to thank you enough for what you did to help Grandpa Red Crow today—

and for being there for me. Walk in beauty, Gabe Rossiter. *Hágoónee'*."

As Gabe watched her climb into Hunter's Jeep Cherokee and disappear down the snowy road, he wondered how long it had been since he'd walked in any way that even remotely resembled beauty.

CHAPTER 7

KAT WATCHED THE lights of the city glide past the window, as if in a dream, Marc driving in silence, seeming to understand that she didn't have the energy just now to talk about what had happened. He'd already made it clear that he and Sophie expected her to spend the night at their house.

"You shouldn't be alone tonight," he'd said. "No arguments. Got it, kiddo?"

"Got it." She'd smiled at the no-nonsense tone in his voice, his words more protective and brotherly than anything any of her brothers had ever said to her.

Sophie had married a good man.

Sophie was waiting for them at the front door. She greeted Kat with a silent hug, then settled the three of them in the family room with cups of steaming hot tea, little Chase already fast asleep in his crib. Then she and Marc listened while Kat told them about meeting Gabe at Mesa Butte, hiking up the butte and finding first Grandpa Red Crow's truck and then his body.

As the words poured out of her, she found herself telling them things she'd never told any of her I-Team friends before—how her mother, brothers, and sisters had rejected her almost from the moment she was born, why she'd left the *dinetah*, how much Grandpa Red Crow had done to help her adjust to life off the rez, introducing her to Lakota ceremonies and ways of life, bringing her into his family, helping her to make peace with the life she was living—and the life she'd left behind.

"He was like a father to me," she told them, unable to hold back her tears.

"I'm so sorry, Kat!" Sophie hugged her tight.

"If you'd like Darcangelo and me to look into it, to stay on top of the Boulder cops, we'll do it," Marc offered, something in his eyes telling her they would do it whether she asked it of them or not.

"Thanks. I'd be very grateful."

Of Gabe and her confused feelings for him, she said nothing. She'd reached a decision tonight—a decision to let him go from her life. He didn't want the same things she wanted, so there was no point in spending time together and letting their mutual attraction, or "chemistry," confuse matters. When she'd told him farewell tonight, she hadn't meant farewell only for now.

Sophie settled her in their guest room for the night. "If you need anything, please don't hesitate to come wake me, okay?"

"Thanks, Sophie."

The moment Kat's head hit the pillow, she was dreaming. In her dream, a coyote ran loose circles around her, now in the distance, now close behind her, yipping and howling as if trying to tell her something. But when she awoke the next morning, she'd forgotten the dream.

THEY MET WHERE they always met—on the edge of town in the parking lot at the baseball fields. This time of year, the place was deserted, especially in the middle of the night. For a moment, they stood in silence.

"Tell me you had nothing to do with that man's death."

"It couldn't be helped. One minute I was digging hard, the next he was just there. It was like he knew where to find me."

"You imbecile! Murder was never part of our deal!"

"What the hell was I supposed to do? Ask him to please keep a secret? I don't know about you, but I am not going to prison. And if they catch me, they catch you."

"Is that a threat?"

"Take it however you want."

"You know, a dead body is going to attract a lot more attention to that place. At the very least, you should have dumped him somewhere else."

"For someone who claims to be the brains of our operation, you're a fucking idiot. If I'd moved his body, they'd know for sure it was homicide. The way I did it, I bet they'll rule it an accident and maybe even blame the old man."

"It's not that simple. Katherine James from the I-Team is going to be all over this. She's one of them, you know—an Indian. If she finds out—"

"If she finds out, one of us is going to have to deal with her."

"What? You mean kill her? Is that your answer to everything?"

"Either scare her into backing off or kill her."

"I won't have anything to do with it."

"That's what you think."

NEWS OF GRANDPA Red Crow's death raced through Indian country. By the time Kat had retrieved her truck from Gabe's house—he was already at work—and made the drive back to Denver, she had sixteen messages on her voice mail. By noon, her living room was filled with people who'd come to hear from her what had happened and to pray, pickup trucks parked along both sides of the street for a city block.

Everyone brought food, Pauline taking charge in the kitchen because Glenna was too weak and upset. Nathan Spotted Eagle brought his drum. And Allen Lemieux, called "Uncle Allen" because he was Grandpa Red Crow's cousin and a spiritual leader in his own right, brought his *chanupa*—his sacred pipe. Everyone listened while Kat told the entire story, silent tears running down the women's faces—and some of the men's, too—when she described how he'd died.

A long moment of silence passed when she had finished.

Then Allen spoke. "I want to thank our sister Kat for her courage and for watching over Grandpa Red Crow's body."

"Aho!" several men called.

Allen went on. "It's a terrible thing to lose our grandfather at this troubled time. Our *inipi* was interrupted. Our women were harassed. Now Grandpa Red Crow is gone from this earth. But we Indian people know that you can kill a man's body, but you cannot kill his spirit."

"*Aho!*" More shouts.

Glenna's quiet weeping.

"Whoever pushed Grandpa Red Crow off the butte doesn't know that he sent our grandfather to a place where his spirit can watch over us. Our prayers are stronger than any man's hatred. We'll hold an *inipi* for Grandpa Red Crow at the lodge up above Conifer tonight. But first I think we should ask this ranger who protected our Kimímila and who cared for our grandfather's body to join us. If you can tell us how to find him, Kat, Nathan and I will go and ask him respectfully—in person."

Kat's pulse skipped. She hadn't thought to see Gabe again. She'd known she might have to speak to him again in a professional capacity one of these days, but she hadn't thought to see him in a personal way again. She hesitated.

Around her, heads nodded in approval.

It seemed fate wasn't going to let Gabe go from her life quite so easily.

GABE GOT THE call around two, just moments after he'd finished helping Rocky Mountain Rescue bring down a couple of drunk college kids who'd gotten themselves stranded at the top of the Third Flatiron, too stupid and drunk not to keep their feet on the ground but not stupid or drunk enough to attempt to climb down. That was the problem with the Third Flatiron. Any idiot could make it up the east face. Gabe could probably climb it in roller skates. But getting down the three deadly hundred-foot pitches of the rappel on the west face was enough to make even seasoned climbers piss their pants.

"There are a couple of Native American men here, who say they want to talk to you," Webb's voice said over Gabe's cell phone. "Know anything about this?"

Damn!

"Nope," Gabe lied, certain this had to do with Kat—whom he absolutely should not have been kissing last night or thinking about today.

They've come to kick your ass, buddy. And guess what? You deserve it.

Yeah, he deserved it. He'd listened to her virginity speech at the South Side Café and had understood clearly that she would only give it up for Mr. Right, whom he most certainly was not. He'd known she was upset and tipsy and not herself last night. And he'd gone ahead and gotten beneath her lacy bra anyway.

If that hadn't been enough, he'd opened the door and given Samantha the chance to spew her jealous bullshit at Kat, then tried to explain Samantha away, shoving both feet in his mouth in the process.

I'm sorry you saw that. She's a . . . She's just a . . .

A failed chemistry experiment?

He'd seen the disappointment in Kat's eyes, those eyes that seemed to see right through him. So he'd gone and made it worse by telling her that Samantha hadn't meant anything to him. And wasn't that just the way to impress a woman?

Yeah, he deserved it.

Be happy it isn't Marc Hunter.

Yes, Gabe was happy about that, all right. If he remembered correctly—and he was pretty sure he did—Hunter had served in Special Forces, fighting in Afghanistan before honing his ass-kicking skills over six years in prison. Gabe would hate to go up against Hunter, for damned sure.

"Tell them I'll be there in about a half hour if they feel like waiting."

He was pretty sure they'd wait.

And they did.

Gabe pulled into the parking lot at Boulder Mountain Parks to find them leaning up against a battered blue Ford F-150 four-by-four. He parked beside them, got out of his service truck, and walked around to meet them. They were both shorter than he was, and he had them in weight, too. But there were two of them.

He held out his hand, testing the waters. "Gabe Rossiter."

The older of the two men studied him through eyes that

gave away nothing, then took his hand and shook it, pressing something into his palm.

A pouch of tobacco.

"I'm Allen Lemieux, Old Man Red Crow's cousin. This is Nathan Spotted Eagle. We came to thank you for watching over our sister Kat James and for tending to my cousin's body last night. We'd like you to join us tonight at an *inipi* in his memory."

Gabe stared at the tobacco in his palm, recognized it as the sign of respect that it was. Well, he'd be damned.

He met Lemieux's gaze. "I'd be honored."

KAT STOOD WITH the other women outside the sweat lodge, her towel wrapped around her shoulders, waiting for Uncle Allen to enter first. She was barely aware of the cold wind that whipped her skirt about her legs or the icy snow beneath her bare feet, her gaze fixed on the man who stood on the other side of the altar beside Nathan. Like the other men, Gabe wore a towel low around his hips, his legs and feet bare, shorts or swim trunks presumably hidden beneath the towel. The tallest man present, he towered over Nathan. Golden firelight played off his body, emphasizing the ridges and valleys of his chest and abdomen.

Kat looked away, alarmed to find that she responded even to the sight of him. He wasn't touching her, wasn't even looking her direction, and yet her heart was beating faster, memories of last night playing through her mind, his lips all over her, his hard body pressing her down into the cushions, his thumb teasing her nipples.

"Ranger Easy-on-the-Eyes," Pauline whispered in her ear.

Yes, he was that.

Then it was time for the *inipi* to begin.

Kat followed Allen out of the wind and inside the lodge, her position beside him a mark of honor. She kept her eyes downcast, resolved to keep her mind on Grandpa Red Crow and the ceremony and not the man who'd just crawled through the door and now sat directly across from her.

Hot stones. Sage. Cedar. Sweetgrass. Smoke.

Then the door went down, and darkness enveloped them.

She gave herself over to the familiar rhythm of the *inipi*, her prayers and tears mingling with those of her friends, scalding steam, songs and prayers purging their sorrow, cleansing away their grief, voices raised in unison for a man who had done so much for each and every one of them, a man they had all loved—and lost.

GABE HAD DONE a sweat lodge once during his ranger training. He'd known to expect the pitch black, the blistering heat, the thick, steamy air. It hadn't bothered him before. So why was his heart pounding now? Why had his mouth gone dry the moment the door had come down? And why was it taking all of his strength to keep himself from crawling over the other men in a panicked rush to get the hell out? He wasn't claustrophobic or afraid of the dark.

Get a fucking grip, Rossiter!

He tried to focus on his breathing, on the cool, solid earth beneath him, and still he couldn't make the panic recede. He forced his mind onto other things—the beating of a drum, the hiss of water against heated stones, the sound of both men and women weeping as they sang. Their grief tugged at him through the darkness, permeating him, threatening to open that abyss inside him that he'd fought so hard to close off, to ignore, to forget, every moment drawing him nearer to that perilous emotional edge until there was simply no escaping it.

Jill. God, Jill!

No! No!

He wouldn't go there. He couldn't go there. Not now. Not ever.

Heart thrumming, adrenaline shooting through his veins, he reached out for the reassuring sound of Kat's voice and held on to it with all of his might.

SINGING WORDS SHE knew by heart, Kat let her tears flow, her thoughts drifting like clouds across the sky as they often did during the *inipi*. But now that sky was clouded by unwanted images, memories made more vivid by the darkness of the lodge. Grandpa Red Crow dragged from the sweat lodge, eagle bone whistle in his hand. Grandpa Red Crow lying on his back at the base of the butte. Grandpa Red Crow staring sightless at the sky as the zipper closed over his face.

A loud hiss. A burst of steam against hot stone. Scorching heat.

Like Kat, Grandpa Red Crow had fallen. Had he known he would die? Had he gotten the same terrible free-fall feeling in the pit of his stomach as she had when she'd fallen? Had he seen her weeping over his body? Did he see her now?

One song ended. Another began.

Drums beating, beating like a heartbeat.

Gabe Rossiter. Gabe. Gabriel. One of the archangels from the Judeo-Christian tradition. And hadn't he been her angel?

He'd saved her life when she'd been caught in the rockslide. He'd protected her and the rest of the women when Officer Daniels had dragged her by her hair. And he'd been there for her yesterday, shielding her as best he could from the horror of Grandpa Red Crow's death, watching over her, caring for Grandpa Red Crow's body.

Then later, when she'd kissed him, he'd tried to warn her, tried to stop her, but she'd done it anyway. That had been too much for him, and he'd given in and kissed her back, touching her in ways no man had ever touched her, the pleasure of it more than she'd imagined. And when she hadn't found the strength to stop, he had.

He was a good man. He'd proved that to her more than once. The wind knew it. Grandpa Red Crow had known it.

Another hiss. More steam.

But Gabe had his dark side, too, and the woman at his door had shown that he was as capable of hurting women as he was of saving them. Kat pitied that woman. She knew that, had Gabe not stopped last night, she might have become that woman—discarded, desperate, and beyond dignity.

And then Kat remembered what the woman had revealed about Gabe, its significance now clear to her. She hadn't been able to sort through it at the time, but here in the dark she understood.

He'd once been engaged. The man who'd told her that love and marriage were just for fairy tales had once been engaged. He had once proposed to a woman named Jill, had been ready and willing to bind himself to her, to throw his future together with hers. But she had died somehow, and now he lived his life as if he no longer believed in love at all, as if one woman met his needs as well as the next.

People fall in and out of love faster than the wind changes. There's no such thing as "happily ever after." Love, romance, sex—it's nothing more than chemistry.

What had happened? What could shut down a man's heart like that?

His fiancée had died and . . .

The last song came to an end. The door went up, firelight flooding the lodge, steam billowing out, cold night air rushing in. Kat found herself looking across the lodge into Gabe's eyes. And the shadows she saw there made her heart ache.

GABE CHANGED AS quickly as he could, needing desperately to get away from here, to get home and get his hands on that bottle of whisky. Barely remembering to thank Allen and Nathan for inviting him, he tucked his soggy towel under his arm and headed straight for his SUV. But Kat was already waiting for him.

So much for a clean getaway, Rossiter.

Dammit!

She hadn't changed yet, her hair damp, the wet folds of her skirt stiff as they froze in the night air, her teeth chattering. "I w-wanted to talk to y-you. I have s-something I n-need to say."

Gabe could only imagine what that was. "Say it inside the Jeep, or you're going to become hypothermic."

He jerked open the door, let her climb in first, then followed her. He stuck the key in the ignition and, leaving the headlights off, turned on the engine, cranking the heater. Then he reached behind his seat, grabbed an emergency blanket, unfolded it, and wrapped it around her. "Why didn't you change into something dry?"

"Y-you seemed in a h-hurry."

Yeah, he had been. He'd been desperate as all hell to get away from whatever had happened in that lodge. "So what is it?"

She didn't answer but sat there shivering. He gave her a moment to warm up, then when it was clear that wasn't going to happen quickly, took her ice-cold hands and rubbed them between his.

"What did you think of the *inipi*?" she asked at last.

"It wasn't my first. I knew what to expect." An answer that wasn't an answer.

"When I came to my first lodge, I panicked. The only thing that kept me from begging to be let out was knowing how disappointed Grandpa Red Crow would be."

Why was she saying this? Had she somehow read his mind in there? Or had his heart been pounding so hard that she'd heard it?

"He told me that the darkness of the lodge is a darkness that reveals things, rather than hiding them. He told me that nothing happens during the *inipi* that we don't take in with us. Sweat lodge helps to make us right with ourselves and with Creator." She watched him through those big eyes of hers, looking beautiful and vulnerable and intimidating as hell.

"Hmm," he said, trying to sound mildly interested.

What did this inipi *just reveal about you, Rossiter?*

He didn't want to think about that.

"I wanted to tell you that yesterday morning, the last time I spoke with Grandpa Red Crow, he asked about you. He told me he thought you were a man I could trust. He was right. Last night, I . . ." She seemed to hesitate. "I wanted you so badly that, if you hadn't stopped, I'm not sure what would have happened."

Suddenly Gabe was no longer thinking about the *inipi* and how he'd freaked out over things that should no longer bother him. His gaze was fixed on Kat. He wasn't astonished to hear that she'd wanted him. He knew enough about women to have been certain of that himself. And there was no doubt about what would have happened. He'd have fucked her. All. Night. Long.

What astonished him was that she had admitted it. She'd admitted that she wouldn't have stopped him, admitted that she'd have let him peel off her clothes, admitted that she'd have let him take what she'd told him she wouldn't give away. He hadn't expected her to be quite so honest, painfully honest though she often was. Why was she telling him this?

She reached up and smoothed a stray lock of hair from his forehead, her cold fingers burning his skin. "What you did proved to me that you care more about me than you care about sex. A man who only cares about sex stops only if a woman asks him to stop. Thank you for caring about me, Gabe Rossiter. And thank you for being here tonight. Grandpa Red Crow was watching."

With those words, she rose up and kissed his cheek. Before he could think of a single word to say, she'd climbed out the passenger door and walked off through the snow, still barefoot.

CHAPTER 8

KAT TURNED OFF her alarm and sank back into bed, wondering how it could possibly be morning already. She'd gotten home from the *inipi* shortly after midnight but had been too wound up to sleep, her thoughts and emotions running in circles from her investigation to Grandpa Red Crow's death to Gabe and back again. The last time she'd looked at the clock, it had been almost two in the morning—four hours ago.

She pushed herself up, feeling almost painfully tired. Last night, as she'd lain awake in the darkness, she'd considered calling Tom and asking for the day off. She'd tell him there'd been a death in her family, which from the Native perspective was true. But, as much as she felt she needed the time to herself—and the extra sleep—she had work to do.

She shuffled into the bathroom, flicked on the light, turned the shower on as hot as she could stand it, then stood under the spray, letting the water revive her. She didn't know how long she stood there—a minute, maybe two. Then she reached blindly for her shampoo and began to wash her hair, which was now about eight inches shorter, hanging to just below her breasts. She'd cut it last night, the custom when one was mourning the death of a loved one. She might not get her blood from Grandpa Red Crow, but he'd been family in every way that mattered.

As her mind nudged toward wakefulness, her thoughts picked up where they'd left off last night when she'd finally fallen asleep. The big question—the one that had refused to leave her alone even in her dreams—was whether Grandpa Red Crow's death was in some way related to the raid on the *inipi*. There wasn't a shred of evidence to suggest that one was related to the other. They'd both happened at Mesa Butte, of course, but that might just be coincidence. And yet she couldn't shake the suspicion that the two were somehow connected.

She rinsed away the shampoo, then worked conditioner through her hair, leaving it to soak in while she shaved her legs.

She hoped Tom would let her put the solar-energy story on hold again. She needed a couple of days to write a feature story about Grandpa Red Crow—his life and his death. She wanted to tell the world what he'd meant to Indians in the Denver metro area, how he'd created a community for Native people who'd never lived on the reservation and had lost touch with their roots, as well as for those like Kat who'd left their families behind in search of a better life in an unfamiliar world.

She would need to get a copy of the police report from Saturday, as well as the coroner's report. The coroner's report wouldn't be ready for a few days, depending on how long it took to get the toxicology tests back, but the police report should be on file. She would ask police records to fax one over as soon as she got to work. And then, of course, she needed the files on Mesa Butte that she'd requested last week.

She rinsed the shaving cream off her legs and the conditioner out of her hair, then turned off the water, grabbed a towel, and stepped out of the shower. She dried her hair first, then her body, and then used the towel to wipe the steam off the mirror, her gaze gliding over her reflection and catching a glimpse of her breasts.

God, Kat, honey, you've got beautiful breasts. They're so . . . Mmm.

She allowed her gaze to linger, a shiver running through her as she remembered the heat in his deep voice, the bliss of his mouth on her nipples, the hard feel of his erection as he'd ground it against her just where she'd needed it. He'd seemed to want her every bit as much as she wanted him. But had his passion been genuine, or was he like that with every woman?

Oh, Gabe.

All she had to do was think his name and her heart beat

faster. He was everything she'd always wanted in a man and everything she'd always sworn to avoid—a man with a warrior's heart and soul, but also a man who used women for sex. The gap between those two parts of him had seemed too wide to bridge, so she'd tried to put him out of her life, certain that it was best for both of them. But her people hadn't let that happen. They'd brought Gabe deeper into her world.

Then, in the darkness of the *inipi*, she'd realized that he hadn't always been the man he was now—a man who thought sex was a sport and love was for fairy tales. He might believe that's who he was, but it wasn't true. And that realization had complicated everything for Kat. If he'd been nothing more than another hot guy who liked to sleep around, she'd have had no problem turning her back on him. But he wasn't.

She'd seen the anguish in his eyes there in the sweat lodge, had seen it as plainly as if he'd cried out to her for help. He had once loved a woman enough to want to spend the rest of his life with her, and then she'd died, leaving him alone. No wonder he'd been so understanding about Grandpa Red Crow's death. He knew what it felt like to lose someone he loved.

I know there's nothing I can say that makes this any easier, but I want you to know that I really am sorry.

She didn't know how she'd found the courage to say what she'd said to him after the *inipi*. Talking to men about her personal feelings had never been easy for her, especially not *Bilagáanaa* men. Perhaps the words had come to her because it had seemed more about him in that moment than about her.

She'd tried to tell him that he wasn't the man he thought he was. She'd tried to show him that there was more to him than he remembered. Somehow, he'd forgotten a part of himself, or hidden it away, but it was still there. If he truly had become a man who only cared about sex, he wouldn't have stopped at kissing her that night. He'd have done anything, said anything, to get her to have sex with him. Then he'd have shrugged his shoulders and showed her the door in the morning.

Whether he'd understood what she'd clumsily tried to tell him or how he felt about it she didn't know. He'd barely uttered a word, his face expressionless apart from the shadows that lingered in his eyes. But one thing was for certain. He wouldn't be able to love anyone again until he healed from the loss of his fiancée.

The thought settled behind Kat's breastbone like a dull ache, and she realized that, despite her best intentions, she'd begun to have feelings for Gabe Rossiter.

Trying to put him out of her mind and focus on the day ahead, she finished drying off, then brushed her teeth and dressed. Fifteen minutes later, she was backing down her driveway, unable to keep her gaze from searching the street for that rogue coyote—or to hold back a sigh of relief when she didn't see it.

GABE TIED INTO his climbing harness, his fingers flying over the figure-eight retrace, as his gaze picked out his route up the rock wall. It was a damned tough route, opening with crimpers—holds so small that there was only room for the very tips of his fingers or the barest edge of his climbing shoes. It moved up to some long reaches, where he'd be dead-pointing to fingerlocks, then traversed a dihedral, before hitting a bulge that would require some major gription and going über-vertical for the crux move on the overhang. Yeah, a brutal route.

Good. That's exactly what Gabe needed—a little physical battering to clear his mind and get him thinking straight again.

He wasn't sure what the hell had happened to him in that sweat lodge, but he knew it had to do with Kat. He wasn't an open person. He kept his emotions and personal life guarded, but she seemed to read him like a book. She knew something had happened in the *inipi*. She'd looked into his eyes, and it had felt like she was looking into his soul. Then she'd come to him afterward, as if trying to help him sort it out.

Something about her got to him, stirring something inside him, and he didn't like it. He needed to get her out of his head—and fast.

He'd actually gone home from the *inipi* and pulled out the

one thing he'd kept from his life with Jill. A photo album that she'd put together, it held photos dating from the night they'd met at Camp 4 in Yosemite through that last backpacking trip they'd taken in the San Juan Mountains three weeks before she was killed. He hadn't looked at it since the day before her funeral, hadn't even opened it, needing to forget the past. But last night he'd sat there, turning the pages, looking at the photos, feeling . . .

Feeling what? Hell, even he couldn't say.

God, he'd loved Jill. She'd been the center of his life, the perfect partner, his lover, the woman he'd wanted to spend the rest of his life with—or so he'd thought. Beautiful, funny, smart, and one hell of a climber, she'd known his world, shared it, loved it as much as he had. He'd thought himself the luckiest son of a bitch in the world—until the day he'd found himself staring at her lifeless body in the morgue and the truth had come out. He'd never realized that the human heart could hurt so badly or feel so much rage. As he'd watched her casket being lowered into the ground one hellish week later, he'd tried to bury his pain and rage with her. And until he'd sat in the *inipi*, he'd thought he'd done just that.

Nothing happens during the inipi *that we don't take in with us.*

Last night, he'd found himself remembering things he'd tried so hard to forget. The warmth of waking up beside Jill every morning, bodies entwined. Her obsession with jalapeños— in omelets, in burgers, in beer. Her uninhibited laughter. The fruity scent of her favorite shampoo. The way she'd loved to fuck anytime and anywhere.

Three long years had gone by, but he could still remember her taste.

The old, familiar pain and rage had come rushing back, pushing past the whisky in his gut, fucking with his head. He'd shoved the photo album under the couch, then gone to bed, where he'd stared at his ceiling in the dark, his thoughts tormented by two women—one who'd hurt him more than he'd ever thought he could be hurt and one who seemed to think she was helping. But some shit was better left alone.

A man who only cares about sex stops only if a woman

asks him to stop. Thank you for caring about me, Gabe Rossiter.

God, Kat scared the shit out of him—Kat with her long dark hair, her hazel eyes, her sweet curves, her feminine strength, her unshakable dignity. He did not care about her—not like that. Never like that. Never again.

"It's a sick five-thirteen-B," Travis said from behind him, obviously admiring his own handiwork. The kid had worked late last night setting this route and had come back early this morning just to see how Gabe would climb it.

"Think so?"

"Dude, I know so."

Travis was, in Gabe's opinion, the best route setter in the known universe, an artist whose medium was little nubs spread over a vertical surface of artificial rock. The two of them had a symbiotic relationship. Travis tried to come up with moves that would force Gabe to stop and study the route or fall and hangdog, while Gabe tried to redpoint to the finish, climbing without pausing, getting stuck or falling. Each tested the other—which meant that they both kept getting better.

"On belay?"

"Belay on."

"Climbing." Gabe didn't bother to wait for the customary confirmation before edging his shoe against the first button-sized toehold of the new route.

"Dude, go for it!" Travis called after him, obviously not hung up on etiquette.

Gabe finessed his way past the crimpers, clipped into protection, then lunged upward for the first fingerlock, using it to draw himself quickly upward again to the next one, willing his mind to clear and his focus to go vertical.

"Who's the hottie?" a woman asked from below.

"That's Gabe Rossiter, local demigod," Travis answered.

"Sounds like you've got a man crush on him, Trav, but I can see why."

Their conversation barely registered with Gabe's conscious mind, his muscles already burning, his heart pumping, his lungs sucking wind as he worked his way steadily upward, his gaze a move ahead of the one his body was working through.

So you slept with her, but she doesn't mean anything to you?

He didn't need Kat's judgmental bullshit. She'd never even been in a sexual relationship. What the hell did she know about it?

Gabe dismissed the thoughts with a frustrated gust of breath, clearing his mind as he moved into the traverse. He edged into another toehold, stemmed his way to the right, and clipped into the next piece of protection, using his quads to push himself upward, his gaze sighting on the bulge.

Last night, I . . . I wanted you so badly that, if you hadn't stopped, I'm not sure what would have happened.

Gabe's hand hit the bulge wrong. He lost friction. His right foot slipped, and it was over. He fell, his weight jerking Travis forward before the kid got his shit together and caught the fall, stopping Gabe five feet short of the floor.

"Whoa, dude!"

Gabe bit back a stream of profanity. What the fuck was wrong with him today? He never had problems concentrating when he was climbing. If he'd been free-soloing on Redgarden Wall just now, he would currently be suffering from an incurable case of RDS—Rapid Deceleration Syndrome, the sudden, terminal illness that began at the end of a long fall.

"Thanks, man," he called down to Travis.

"No prob." There was a note of triumph in Travis's voice, a grin spreading above his goatee. "You want me to dirt you, or do you want to try again from there?"

Beyond Travis, Gabe saw Rick and Dave walk through the gym's front doors. In full uniform, they stopped at the front desk, then pointed up at him.

Not a good sign.

"Looks like I have company."

Slowly, Travis belayed him to the floor, still grinning.

KAT ARRIVED AT the paper to find her desk buried in white flowers, each bouquet accompanied by a small card expressing condolences. White winter irises from Kara and Reece. White lilies from Tessa and Julian. White mums and orchids mixed with sprigs of bright green boxwood from Sophie and Marc. And off to one side a big bouquet of white roses from the I-Team.

"We know he was family to you. Remember that you are family to us. We are so sorry for your loss and want to be there for you through this hard time," the card read, people's signatures squeezed into the remaining space.

Deeply touched, Kat stared at the card until she could no longer see it, tears blurring her vision, a hard lump in her throat. She blinked the tears back and looked up to find the other I-Team members gathered around her desk. "*Ahéhee'*. Thank you."

Natalie stood. "If there's anything we can do . . ."

"Thanks. You already have."

Sophie and Natalie gave her hugs, then went back to their desks, while Matt went off to buy her a cup of coffee, leaving her with Joaquin.

His dark eyes were shadowed by grief. "I only spoke with him once—at the protest last Monday—and it was only for a few minutes. But there was something special about him, something real, something holy. I don't know. I'm just sorry he's gone."

"He touched a lot of people." Kat rose up on her toes and kissed Joaquin's cheek.

"If you need anything—"

"Oh, look at all the flowers! Is it your birthday?" Holly walked up to the two of them, smiling. "And, hey! You cut your hair! I love the new length, but . . . Well, the ends are a little uneven. Where'd you get it done? I hope you didn't tip. I have the world's greatest stylist if you need a referral."

For the first time since Saturday, Kat laughed.

Joaquin stepped forward and wrapped his arm around Holly's shoulders. "Hey, Holly. Let's go have a little chat, okay?"

KAT LOGGED INTO NewsLink, her fingers hesitating above her keyboard. She really shouldn't do this. It was none of her business. If Gabe had wanted to tell her, he would have. Using the news database to pry into his past was wrong.

It's public information. It's already been published.

That was true. Every article listed in the database had already run in a newspaper somewhere in the United States. It wasn't as if she were requesting a criminal background check through the FBI or probing his tax records.

Bolstered by that thought, Kat typed "Gabriel Rossiter, Jill" into the search field and hit return. A moment later twenty or so references came up on the screen. There was a link for images, too. And before she could stop herself, Kat clicked.

A single color image filled the screen—an engagement photo. Gabe sat on a large boulder next to a beautiful blond-haired woman with sparkling eyes. A forest of ponderosa pines made up the background, a red sunset stretching behind them. But it wasn't so much the scenery that caught Kat's eye but Gabe himself.

He looked different—younger, happy, relaxed. He wore gray shorts and a navy tank top, his arm around Jill's shoulders, a wide smile on his face, a coil of orange and green rope at his feet. His hair was long, drawn back in a ponytail, a goatee on his chin. His love for the woman beside was clear to see in the way he held himself—and her.

Jill was the image of the all-American girl. Her wide smile told Kat she'd been laughing when the photo had been taken—laughing and loving life. She had a blue bandana tied around her forehead, her pink tank top and tiny black shorts revealing the well-toned body of an athlete. So, she'd been a climber, too.

Jill Chandler. Her name had been Jill Chandler.

An ache swelled in Kat's chest for the people in the photo, a man and woman who sat smiling and laughing together, clearly in love, unaware that their life together would soon be over.

How would Gabe feel if he saw you looking at this?

He would think she was prying. And she was. She was using a professional resource for personal reasons, trying to unearth the secrets he hadn't chosen to confide in her. It wasn't right, and the next best thing to having never done it in the first place was to stop. Now.

Kat closed the search window and logged off, still desperately curious as to what had happened to Jill. But if Gabe had wanted her to know, he would've told her. Besides, she had a lot of other things she could and should be doing now besides digging into his personal life—like checking in with the Boulder County Coroner.

She'd already read through the police report and had found it surreal to see one of the worst days of her life reduced to a few pages of choppy police jargon. Three lines of the report had been redacted, the words blacked out with a marker, not unusual when a case was still open and under investigation. Still, it caught her attention because it meant they'd found something at the scene, something crucial to the police investigation. She was both relieved and frustrated by this— relieved because it meant detectives had something to go on and frustrated because she'd been there. If there'd been something unusual at the scene, why hadn't she noticed it?

She stood and was about to head to the break room for another cup of coffee when Natalie called to her from across the newsroom. "I think you'll want to see this."

Kat turned to find the I-Team gathered in front of the bank of six television sets, where an image of news anchor Nell Parker flashed onto one of the screens, the sound muted, the closed captioning hidden by a row of heads. She grabbed her notepad and threaded her way through the desks just as Natalie turned up the volume.

"The Boulder County Coroner's Office has just issued a press release announcing that the death of a prominent local American Indian leader was an alcohol-related accident. The release states that George Red Crow died after getting too close to the edge of a cliff while intoxicated and falling two hundred feet. He is believed to have died instantly."

The blood rushed to Kat's head, thrumming in her ears, leaving her almost dizzy.

Alcohol-related accident?

That was impossible!

Shocked, for a moment all she could do was stare at the television. Then shock turned to rage. "That's a lie!"

She turned and took a step back toward her desk, some

half-formed thought of calling the coroner's office in her mind, then stopped in her tracks.

Tom stood there, blocking her path.

"In my office." He motioned with a jerk of his head, then walked off.

Her heart still pounding, Kat followed.

CHAPTER 9

"You ARE FUCKING kidding me!" Gabe met Webb's gaze, unable to believe what he was hearing. "You brought me in on my day off for this?"

Webb looked at him through weary brown eyes that said he'd already swallowed far more than his recommended daily allowance of bullshit. "Look, Gabe—"

"This is a serious matter, Mr. Rossiter." Ira Feinman, the city attorney, glanced at Gabe with a disapproving frown on his thin face, then brushed imaginary lint off the sleeve of his gray Gucci suit. The man had instantly gotten under Gabe's skin with his nasal voice, fussy manners, and condescending attitude. "Given the potential liability here, the city must do all it can to manage the risks."

"Manage the risks?" Gabe couldn't help but laugh. "The city wouldn't be in this mess if Daniels hadn't ignored jurisdiction, gone in like the marines to break up the sweat lodge ceremony, and dragged an innocent woman by her hair!"

Feinman gave a prissy little sniff. "Officer Daniels acted in the line of duty to protect the city's interests based on the information he had at the time. In his statement, he said that Ms. James became belligerent and that his hand got caught in her hair when she resisted. As I see it, she's lucky she wasn't arrested."

Anger flared white-hot in Gabe's gut. "Daniels's statement is pure bullshit. I saw him bend down, take a handful of her hair, and drag her. I stand by my statement."

Feinman looked at him through the soulless brown eyes of a man who'd spent his entire life twisting the truth. "You place the city in an awkward position, lending credibility to her complaint."

"So, you want me to withdraw my statement and lie about what I saw?"

"Rossiter!" The tone in Webb's voice told Gabe he'd crossed the line—again.

The skin on Feinman's throat turned a mottled red. "That's not what I said. The city simply can't afford to wage fruitless court battles against litigious people who try to line their pockets with taxpayer dollars. I was hoping you would understand."

"Oh, I understand all right." Gabe gave a snort. "You're trying to get Daniels and the city off the hook."

Feinman said nothing, but reached down, picked up a copy of a newspaper that had been lying on top his briefcase, then perused its front page.

The moment Gabe saw the paper's banner he knew what was coming. It was the *Denver Independent*, Kat's paper.

Shit.

"Here's the article she wrote last week about the unauthorized ceremony. It reads, 'According to a source close to the investigation, no complaints were filed with police about the ceremony that night. The raid was initiated by Officer Frank Daniels, an eight-year veteran of the Boulder Police Department, who saw the fire and took it upon himself to act, ignoring jurisdictional boundaries.' " Feinman looked over at Gabe. "I certainly hope you're not the source to which Ms. James refers here. If the city were to discover you giving information to the media without your supervisor's authorization, your employment would be terminated immediately. It's not part of your job description to respond to media requests."

Nothing subtle about it—that was an outright threat.

Before Gabe could get in a word, Feinman went on. "Nor is it your job to visit police dispatch asking questions. Yes, I know about that."

Okay, now Gabe was really pissed. "Did it occur to you that, as the ranger on duty that night, I might want to know how Daniels ended up on the scene instead of Mountain Parks?"

"Did it occur to you that Ms. James might be dating you just to get information from you for her articles?"

Gabe was on his feet. "Ms. James is not sleeping with me! Oh, don't look shocked. That's exactly what you meant. She doesn't have a deceitful bone in her body. And if she were sleeping with me, it wouldn't be any of your damned business!"

"Rossiter, sit down!" Webb glared at him, then rubbed his face with his palms. "The important thing to acknowledge here is that we're all on the same team. The city wants contact with the media to go through the proper channels. I've assured Mr. Feinman and the city manager's office that you had nothing to do with that news article and have no problem following policy."

So Webb was sticking his neck out to defend Gabe, probably knowing full well that Gabe was guilty as charged. Gabe owed him.

He sat, met Feinman's gaze unblinking. "No, I've got no problem with that. I just hope the city takes steps to make sure nothing like this happens again. We all know the city violated federal law that night. And guess what, lawyer man—it *is* part of my job description to uphold the law."

Feinman tucked the newspaper away in his briefcase and stood. "I think we've reached an understanding. I need to get back to the office. Ms. James has just arrived at city hall, threatening to sue unless we open our files to her."

Gabe gave a snort. "It sucks having to comply with the law, doesn't it?"

Give 'em hell, Kat.

Webb stood, shook Feinman's hand. "Thanks for coming."

Gabe kept to his seat.

Not bothering to acknowledge Gabe, Feinman walked out of the office and disappeared down the hallway.

Webb shook his head, dropped into his chair. "I hate that son of a bitch."

So did Gabe. "What a prick!"

"You're a pain in my ass, Rossiter. If you weren't so damned good at your job, I'd fire you myself." Webb pulled a roll of Tums out of his desk, tossed a few tablets into his mouth, and chewed. Then he pointed a beefy finger at Gabe. "You stay out of this and let the suits sort it out."

Gabe looked at his boss and saw a man he respected, a man whose weathered face was proof of the years he'd spent patrolling trails. It disappointed him to hear Webb say those words. "The city broke federal law when it sent cops to raid the *inipi*. Now Feinman is helping the city bury its shit, and you want me to look the other way? We're supposed to be the good guys, chief."

"We are the good guys, but we'll be good guys without jobs if you keep flipping off the city brass. That might not scare you, but I've got two kids in college and bills to pay." Webb washed down his antacids with a gulp of coffee. "Go home, Rossiter. And try to stay out of trouble—and away from Ms. James if you can."

"Yeah. Right." And as Gabe walked out the door, he told himself that's exactly what he planned to do.

KAT SAT IN the lobby outside the Boulder City Manager's Office, waiting to speak with him. Tired of playing games, she'd showed up without an appointment, refusing to leave until Mr. Martin met with her and handed over the documents on Mesa Butte that she'd requested more than a week ago. Mr. Martin's executive assistant had snippily informed Kat that Mr. Martin had an important job to do.

"That's fine," Kat had answered. "So do I."

Media all along the Front Range were now reporting that Grandpa Red Crow's death was likely an alcohol-related accident, something she knew in her heart could not be true. She'd known people on the reservation who'd let their addiction to alcohol kill them. Their lives had been marked by hopelessness and an inability to see the blessings and beauty around them. Grandpa Red Crow had always been full of hope for himself and others. If he'd had a drinking problem, he would have shared it with them and asked for their prayers, not kept it secret.

When she'd stood at the scene, she'd been certain Grandpa

Red Crow had been murdered. Why she'd felt so sure of that she couldn't say. She of all people knew how quickly the unexpected could happen. Maybe he'd gotten too close to the edge and had slipped or been blown off by a sudden gust of wind. But there was no way he'd stood atop that sacred place, drunk himself into a stupor, and fallen.

She'd bet her life on it.

Of course, that wouldn't matter if she couldn't prove it. She needed facts—the rock-solid kind that she could put into a news article, the kind that would refute the other news reports and set the record straight. There was so much more at stake here than Nell Parker or the other newspapers or even her I-Team friends understood.

Grandpa Red Crow had been the keystone for Denver's Native community. He'd given so many Native people hope, brought so many back from the brink of despair, giving them something to believe in, someone they could look up to. To lose him was bad enough. To lose him in a way that dishonored everything he'd claimed to believe, everything he'd taught them, everything he'd represented . . .

Kat didn't have to imagine the loss of heart and hope this would cause, because she felt it herself. She'd already gotten a call from Uncle Allen, who seemed as stunned as she by the news and who'd been flooded with calls from people seeking answers and reassurance that he desperately wanted to give them.

She could not let those news reports stand.

Tom had given her the rest of the week to look into Grandpa Red Crow's death, but he'd been clear that he had misgivings about it. He'd called her into his office, shut the door, and laid it on the line.

"Is there any chance this could be true?"

His question had hit like a fist to the stomach. "No! Of course not!"

"No chance at all?"

Even as her mind had objected again, the journalist inside her had taken over, and she'd found herself weighing the possibility. Grandpa Red Crow had once had an alcohol problem, but that had been long ago when he'd been young and angry.

He'd been sober for decades, working hard to help others stop drinking. She remembered seeing the empty whisky bottle on top the butte. Was it possible that he'd relapsed and had hidden his problem from them? As someone who knew Grandpa Red Crow well, someone who loved him, she had to say no. But as a journalist . . .

She'd met Tom's gaze, hoping Grandpa Red Crow would forgive her for what she had to say. "I can't imagine it, but nothing is impossible."

Tom had nodded, and she'd seen the approval in his eyes. "Don't let your emotions cloud your journalistic judgment. Got it?"

"Yes."

"Good. Now, get a hold of the autopsy report."

So Kat had driven to Boulder and stopped by the coroner's office to pick up a copy of the report, her mind still on the three lines of redacted text in the police file. What was so important that the police were keeping it from the public? Had there been something at the scene that night, something she ought to have noticed? She'd been so upset at the time that the details were hazy.

But, though she couldn't remember, she knew who would.

As soon as she had finished here, she would call Gabe and ask for his help.

A middle-aged man in an expensive gray suit stepped into the lobby, a scowl on his narrow face, his thinning brown hair out of place as if he'd been running. "Are you Ms. James?"

"Yes." Kat stood. "Mr. Martin?"

"I'm Ira Feinman, the city attorney. I understand you arrived without an appointment and have refused to leave even though you've been informed that Mr. Martin is unavailable today. Is that correct?"

Kat met Feinman's cold gaze. "The city has had ample time to fill the open-records request I filed last Monday. If you can't turn the documents over to me now, I'll be happy to wait until I can speak directly to Mr. Martin about the problem."

"The city has already filed a formal request for ten additional days with your newspaper's counsel. That's ten working days, which means we don't need to turn these documents over to you until the Monday after Thanksgiving." He handed her a document dated today, one he'd probably typed up and faxed five minutes ago. "As you've already been told, Mr. Martin is not available today. If you refuse to leave, you'll give me no choice but to call the police and have you arrested for trespassing."

Kat stood her ground. "Mr. Feinman, this is a public office. You can call the police if you want, but you and I both know the charge won't stick. In the end, you'll still have to give me the documents, and you'll be facing a lawsuit from the paper—as well as a lot of negative press."

Feinman opened his mouth to speak again, blotches of red appearing on his cheeks, but whatever he was about to say was interrupted by the appearance of another man. Tall with salt-and-pepper hair, he wore navy blue slacks and a blue-and-white-striped Oxford shirt with a black tie, gold wire-rimmed glasses framing warm brown eyes. "That won't be necessary, Ira. I've got a few minutes before my next meeting, Ms. James. Let's go back to my office."

Mr. Martin's office was bright and airy with a view of the Pearl Street Mall below. Photos of him shaking hands with various politicians hung in frames along the walls, marking him as a man who took his career seriously and perhaps had political aspirations of his own. He motioned her toward a plush leather sofa, then sat beside her, Mr. Feinman settling in a matching chair across from them. "How can I help you today?"

"I've come for the documents I requested a week ago or a truthful explanation as to why I don't have them yet."

He nodded. "As I believe I overheard Ira telling you, we're asking for another ten days to fill that request."

"Yes, I just saw the letter, which was written and faxed today." She wanted to let them know that she'd noticed—and that she didn't buy it. "What I don't understand is why it's taking so long to get the documents together. Surely, it would take staff only a matter of hours to find the files and photo-copy them."

Mr. Feinman butted in. "The city is perfectly within its legal rights to—"

Mr. Martin held up a hand. "Ira, there's no need to be confrontational about this. Ms. James, the problem we're facing is that you requested *all* documents pertaining to Mesa Butte, and we're trying very hard to meet your demands. We have files spread out across the city—in the real estate department, with Mountain Parks, with the police department, here in my office, with the surveyor's office—and it's taking us a bit of time to coordinate with everyone to gather those files and eliminate the duplicate documents. If you want to narrow the scope of your request, things might move more quickly."

Kat weighed what he'd told her, still skeptical that it could take more than two weeks for the city's staff to get the job done. "You do know, don't you, Mr. Martin, that it's against the law for the city to use these additional days to sort through those files in an effort to hide information?"

Feinman glared at her. "Are you making accusations, Ms. James?"

"If I were in Ms. James position, I'd probably be thinking the exact same thing, Ira." Martin gave Kat a lopsided grin. "And call me Paul. Yes, I'm aware of the law, Ms. James. We're just trying to be thorough."

Then Martin launched into a long explanation about how the city needed to invest in a citywide computerized records system, rather than relying so heavily on paper, which was not only less environmentally friendly but also less efficient. By the time he finished, much more than a few minutes had passed.

"We're late for our next meeting." Feinman stood and left the room.

"Story of my life. I'm late for everything." Martin rose, looking over his shoulder toward his open office door. Then he leaned closer to Kat and whispered. "Remember what Shakespeare said about first killing all the lawyers? He was right!"

With a wink, he led Kat out of his office.

GABE TOSSED BACK the rest of his whisky, savoring its heat. Yes, it was three in the afternoon, and he was drunk—fall-down, shit-faced, legless drunk. But not so drunk that he didn't notice the sexy brunette checking him out. She sat at a table off the end of the bar, sipping her wine, her gaze fixed on him. She was sending all the signals, giving him flirty smiles, licking her lower lip, stroking the stem of her wineglass with her fingertips. All he had to do to get inside her was walk over and say hello.

He should do it. Hell, yeah, he should. He should get off this bar stool and walk right over to her and say something romantic like, "Let's fuck." He could use a good orgasm a lot more than another shot.

So why was he still sitting here?

The answer had beautiful hazel green eyes, long dark hair, soft curves—and a frustratingly intact hymen.

Kat.

She'd come into his life, and now nothing made sense, most especially whatever was going on inside his head. He'd had it together before she'd come along, had his life just the way he'd wanted it, but now she was making him question everything. She was even affecting his ability to climb. And still he wanted her, wanted her in a way he hadn't wanted a woman since . . .

Well, that was too damn bad, really, because she didn't want him. She'd made that clear. No, that wasn't what she'd said. She wanted him, but she just wanted other things too, things he couldn't give her—rings, vows, happily ever after.

Last night, I . . . I wanted you so badly that, if you hadn't stopped, I'm not sure what would have happened.

At the echo of her voice, his cock—the same cock that ignored the brunette—began to get hard. He almost groaned aloud, aggravation and sexual frustration forming a volatile mixture with the scotch in his gut. What the hell was wrong with him? Had he gone insane? Why had he let himself get tangled up in a woman who was never going to sleep with him? That's right—Kat was never going to sleep with him.

Hear that, dick?

His dick got harder, clearly not buying it.

And then the absurdity of the situation struck him.

Man, you're a fucking mess—on the brink of losing your job, drunk in a bar in the afternoon, having a silent conversation with your own stiff cock.

Well, he supposed that was better than talking out loud to some other guy's wood.

Shit, yeah, he was drunk.

He forced himself to check out the brunette, tried to imagine undressing her, kissing her tits, burying his hard-on inside her—and felt a whole lot of nothing.

So you slept with her, but she doesn't mean anything to you?

It was true. The brunette meant nothing to him. Neither had Sam—or any of these random women he'd had sex with since Jill's death. As long as he was inside them, they filled the emptiness in his life. And then they became part of the emptiness. It didn't make one damned bit of sense, but it was true.

And suddenly, more than anything, he wanted to talk her—to Kat. He needed to hear her voice, needed to tell her . . .

He handed the bartender a fifty, took her business card out of his wallet, then fished in his pocket for his cell phone—only to discover that it was already in his hand. Then, ignoring the little voice in his head that warned him against drunk-dialing her, he punched in her number.

CHAPTER 10

KAT PARKED HER truck on the street in front of Gabe's house, then dug the police report out of her briefcase. Dropping her keys in her coat pocket, she stepped out into the cold wind and headed up the walkway toward his front door, trying not to notice the nervous flutter in her stomach. A part of her was excited to see him again, but a part of her wished she could climb back in her truck and drive away.

I wanted you so badly that, if you hadn't stopped, I'm not sure what would have happened.

She cringed inwardly at the memory of her own words, feeling exposed in a way she'd never felt before. But her feelings really didn't matter. Her people were depending on her. Grandpa Red Crow was depending on her.

She climbed Gabe's front steps, rang the doorbell, and waited.

And waited.

Disappointed that he wasn't home, she headed back down the walk to her truck, planning to call and leave him a message when she got back to the office. She unlocked the door, climbed into the cab, and was about to drive off when her cell phone rang. She dug her phone out of her purse and saw that the call was coming from a pay phone. Hoping Pauline's mother hadn't kicked her out of the house again, she answered. "Katherine James."

But the voice she heard was not Pauline's. It didn't even sound human.

Cold and mechanical, it sang in her ear. "Ten little, nine

little, eight little Indians/Seven little, six little, five little Indians/Four little, three little, two little Indians/One little Indian . . . *dead.*"

The last word lingered in a long, drawn-out exhalation that made Kat's pulse spike and the hair on her nape rise. Then there was silence.

"Who is this? Who's calling?"

But the caller had already hung up.

Kat drew the phone away from her ear and stared at it, stunned. Like any reporter worth his or her salt, she'd gotten death threats before, but there was something about this call, something malevolent . . .

One Indian *was* dead. Grandpa Red Crow.

Chills shivered down her spine.

Was someone claiming responsibility for killing him? Or was the caller threatening her?

Report it to the police.

That's what she needed to do. But not the Boulder police. She didn't want to have to deal with Daniels again. She'd wait to report it till she was home in Denver. She drew a breath and glanced around her but saw no one.

What did you expect to see, Kat? Some thug in a ski mask watching you?

Feeling silly, she stuck her key in the ignition and started the engine.

She'd just pulled out of the parking space when her cell phone rang again. Her foot slammed on the brake, and for a moment she froze. Then slowly she reached over and picked up the phone—relief rushing through her when she saw Gabe's name on the LCD display.

She answered. "This is Kat."

"Hey, it's me, Gabe. I need to see you. I need to talk to you." His words were slightly slurred, and there was an edge to his voice that she hadn't heard before. Was he drunk? "Can we meet someplace? I just really need to see you."

"Where are you?" It sounded like there was a party in the background.

"At the West End Tavern. Been here since they opened. It's

happy hour, but they won't serve me another drink. I guess they figure I'm happy enough."

So he was drunk.

"I'm in Boulder." She didn't tell him she was in the middle of the street in front of his house. "Stay there, and I'll meet you in a few minutes, okay?"

"You're coming here?" The surprise in his voice made him sound boyish and strangely vulnerable.

"I'll be there in about ten minutes." She took her foot off the brake and pressed on the gas. "And Gabe?"

"Yeah, honey?"

She'd be lying if she said that hearing him call her honey had no affect on her. "Ask the bartender for a glass of water."

"HERE WE ARE." Her arm around his waist, Kat leaned Gabe against the brick wall just outside his own front door, having maneuvered him out of her truck and up the walk—no easy task when he was almost a foot taller than she and outweighed her by at least eighty pounds. Not only did the extra weight hurt her right leg, but she was afraid she'd slip and they'd both fall. "Do you have your keys?"

"In my pocket." He made no move to get them, but ducked down and nuzzled her cheek, then buried his nose in her hair, breathing deep. "Mmm. God, you smell good—sweet and clean and good enough to eat. Do you know that?"

"Um . . ." Kat tried to stay focused on what she was doing, not what she was feeling, her skin burning where his lips had touched her. She reached inside his coat pockets but found no keys. "Are you sure you didn't leave your keys at the bar?"

"Back pocket." He shifted, drew her against him, almost tottering them both to the concrete as he nibbled her earlobe. "God, I want you! I want to kiss you until you can't think. I want to kiss those perfect breasts. I want to taste you everywhere. I want to fuck you so damn bad. You don't even know what I mean, do you?"

Kat was forced to press herself against him to reach his back pocket, her hand sliding over the worn denim of his jeans, only butter-soft fabric between her palm and the disturbingly hard muscles of his butt. "I . . . I think I do know what you mean."

He groaned, his breath hot, his hips flexing against her, giving away his erection, his tongue seeking and teasing the whorl of her ear. "You might know what I mean, but you can't really know what I mean. You're extra virgin, honey."

She retrieved the keys, twisting to her left so that she could unlock the door. She tried to change the subject, this one far too unsettling, especially when he nibbled the sensitive skin below her ear. "D-do you like your coffee black?"

"You have no idea what it'd feel like to have my mouth between your legs. I'd suck on your clit till you came. Then I'd slide my cock inside you, and you'd be so wet and so tight." He nipped her throat with his teeth, his big hand sliding up from her waist to cup her breast, the contact scorching even through her sweater and bra. "I'd make you come. I'd make the dignified Katherine James scream. Mmm, yeah."

His words drove the breath from her lungs, heat rushing into her cheeks. It took her a moment to realize she had no idea which key opened the door. She held the keys up with a shaking hand. "Which key . . . Which key is it, Gabe? Can you help me?"

"Have you ever had an orgasm? But you don't want . . . And I can't . . ." He dropped his forehead head against her shoulder, the hand that had touched her breast now balled into a fist as he drew it away. "Get a grip, Rossiter, you stupid fuck."

"Gabe?" If he passed out, they would both land in the snow. "Which key?"

GABE WOKE UP naked in his own bed, certain he was an inch from death. His head throbbed. His mouth was as dry as sand and thick with the sour aftertaste of single malt. And his stomach . . .

Oh, God!

His skull seeming to shatter, he sat, felt his stomach revolt, and made a staggering, stumbling dash to the bathroom, where he spent the next ten minutes puking his guts out like a frat boy. When he was reasonably certain it was over, he flushed and rested his cheek against the porcelain rim.

"Do you feel better now?" a feminine voice asked softly.

Kat?

What the hell was she doing here?

He opened one eye, saw her standing in the doorway. And then he remembered. He'd called her from the bar. She'd come for him, driven him home, and . . .

I'd make you come. I'd make the dignified Katherine James scream.

He closed his one eye, groaned.

You're lucky she didn't drop you on the concrete, dickhead!

Now, he was sprawled naked on his bathroom floor using the toilet as a pillow.

Yeah, well, if that didn't turn her on, nothing would.

He heard the sound of running water, and then she was there, kneeling beside him, wiping his face with a cool, damp cloth. "Oh, you poor, silly goat!"

Silly goat?

He sat up, wincing as his skull exploded, then felt her press a glass of cold water and two pills—Christ, he hoped they were aspirin!—into his hands. He opened both eyes and almost wept for joy when he recognized them as Excedrin. Then he popped the pills and washed them down with gulps of cold, wonderful water. "More."

FIVE MINUTES LATER, he'd traded slumping buck naked against the toilet to slumping over the kitchen table in a pair of jeans, a jackhammer pounding inside his cranium. The only thing he could say for himself in that moment was that he'd at least gotten off the floor, gotten his ass in pants, brushed his teeth, and made his way into the kitchen without her help. He raised his head enough to look at the clock and saw it was almost midnight. Had she been here this entire time?

Then he remembered seeing documents spread out on the living room floor just now—it seemed like an hour ago—and he guessed she'd had.

"Here." She came up behind him and draped something—the blanket from his bed—around his shoulders. "I'll make you some coffee."

"Thanks." An almost forgotten sense of warmth grew inside Gabe's chest. It had been a long time since anyone had shown this kind of concern for him. Then again it had been a long time since he'd let anyone get close to him. "Sorry about this."

"You've rescued me a few times, so I figure it's alright if I rescue you." She had her back to him, her hands busy measuring out coffee grounds.

It was then he noticed. She'd cut her hair, the dark strands hanging to just below her shoulder blades. He was about to say something about it when he remembered that it was a sign of mourning in some American Indian cultures.

She's grieving the death of someone she loved, but instead of being home, she's rescuing you—from a bottle of scotch. Could you be any more pathetic, Rossiter?

"So . . ." He wasn't sure how to ask this. "Did you undress me?"

He sure as hell hadn't left the bar naked.

She shook her head. "You . . . um . . . took off your clothes when we got inside. Then you got a glass of water from the kitchen, walked off to your bedroom, and passed out. I did pull the covers over you, though."

He wasn't body shy in the least, but if he was going to bare it all in front of her, why couldn't he have done it under more flattering circumstances? "I haven't been that wasted since I was in college."

"Do you want to talk about it?" She set the filter in the coffeemaker and then turned to the sink to fill the coffeepot with water.

"About what?"

"About whatever drove you into the bar in the middle of the day."

"Not particularly."

She got two clean mugs out of the cupboard but said nothing.

His brain must have still been pickled in booze, because

the next thing he knew his mouth opened and he found himself telling her how Webb had saved his ass when the city attorney had threatened to fire him today.

"Ira Feinman?" She set a cup of coffee in front of him.

He took a sip, almost groaned. "Yeah. You know him? The guy is a serious asshole. He wanted me to withdraw my complaint against Daniels. Then he told me that if he found out I was giving you information, he'd fire me."

She sat across from him, coffee mug in her hands, a troubled look on her face. "I'm sorry. I didn't want to cause problems for you."

"It's not your fault." Gabe reached across the table and took her hand, surprised by the current of awareness that passed between them.

She looked away—but she didn't withdraw her hand. "I had a confrontation with Mr. Feinman today, too. I went to the city manager's office and refused to leave until they gave me the files on Mesa Butte or the city manager himself explained why I haven't yet received them. He threatened to have me arrested if—"

On the other side of the wall, her cell phone rang.

She went rigid, her face suddenly pale.

"Kat?"

She stood, walked almost hesitantly into the living room. When she spoke, there was genuine fear in her voice. "Who are you? What do you want?"

When she returned moments later, phone in hand, he could tell she was shaken.

Instinct got him on his feet, the pain in his head forgotten. "What is it?"

"Would you mind if I stayed here tonight?"

KAT WATCHED GABE slam the magazine into his handgun and rack the slide, that same feeling of unreality she'd felt off and on since they'd found Grandpa Red Crow's body settling over her again. The moment she'd told him about the calls, he'd walked off to set the alarm system on his house, a grim look on his face. It both unsettled her—and made her feel strangely pleased. She wasn't used to men being protective of her.

"Do you know how to use a gun?" He turned to her, weapon pointed at the floor.

She nodded. "A shotgun. My grandmother made sure all of us knew how to fire it so we could protect the sheep."

He raised an eyebrow. "Ever actually point it at anything?"

"No."

He laid the gun flat across his palm, the barrel pointed to the side. "All you have to know with a Glock is not to put your finger on the trigger until you're ready to fire. The safety is built into the trigger. See? When you pull on the trigger, you compress it, and the weapon is then able to fire. It's simple. Point and shoot."

Point and shoot?

"Don't you think you're overreacting?" Talking about shooting people wasn't making Kat feel one bit safer. Instead, the idea terrified her and added weight to her own misgivings about the calls. "It was just a few prank calls."

He tucked the gun into the back of his jeans. "Those weren't crank calls, honey. Those were death threats—and five is more than a few."

"Whoever it is probably just wants to scare me." That's what she'd told herself as her phone had kept ringing and Gabe had slept off the worst of his drinking binge. "Most of the time, people who make threats don't carry them out."

He settled his hands gently on her shoulders and drew her into his embrace. "Not to frighten you, but it sounds to me that this bastard is trying to take credit for killing Red Crow. If he's killed once, he's capable of killing again. I understand why you don't want to report the calls to the Boulder police, but promise me you'll call the cops as soon as you get back to Denver tomorrow. I don't want you to get hurt."

Kat nodded, her stomach sinking as Gabe's conclusions about the calls reinforced what her intuition had been trying to tell her.

One little Indian dead.

He stepped back from her, dropped his gaze to the floor, a troubled frown on his face. "You know, it might not be a bad idea to call your buddy Marc and have him come get you. I'd take you to his place myself, but I'm pretty sure I'm still over the legal limit. Besides, I think my truck is still downtown, isn't it?"

"You . . . You don't want me here?" Her stomach sank even farther.

"No, it's not that. It's just that . . . I'm a park ranger. He's a Special Forces veteran, a SWAT sniper, and an ex-con. If he can't shoot this guy, he can beat the shit out of him in a hundred dirty ways you and I can't imagine. You'd probably be safer if you stayed with him."

The expression on Gabe's face told her it hadn't been easy for him as a man to say this. He was trying his best to keep her safe, even if that meant sending her away. How could she tell him that she was still here because she wanted to be here, because she wanted to be with him?

For the first time in her life, she wanted to be close to a man.

"I . . . I'd rather stay here—with you."

He watched her for a moment, the way he looked at her making her pulse race. Then he grimaced, as if in pain. "I'm sorry."

"Does your head still hurt?"

"It's my dignity that's killing me now." He reached out, brushed his knuckles over her cheek. "I'm sorry for all of it. I'm sorry about this afternoon—what I said, how I acted. I don't know what the hell I was thinking, drunk-dialing you like that. Thanks for getting me home. Thanks for everything."

Her mind flashed on the sight of him, walking unabashedly naked around the house, his penis and testicles bared to her view. She hadn't looked away. Oh, no, far from it. She had stared at him, taking in every detail from the thick glands half hidden inside its foreskin to the heavy weight of his testicles to the dark curls at his groin, amazed at her first sight of a real, live naked man—erotic, primal, arousing.

She felt heat rush into her cheeks. "I . . . I'm glad I was able to help. That's what friends are for."

Slowly, he drew her against him. "Is that what we are, Kat? Are we friends?"

Then he took her mouth in a kiss that was deep and passionate and hot—and, unfortunately, brief. But when he dragged his lips from hers, she saw that he was breathing as hard as she was, his heart pounding every bit as fast as hers. And what he'd said earlier came rushing back to her.

I'd make you come. I'd make the dignified Katherine James scream.

Something in her belly clenched.

"Ever since I met you, I . . ." He stopped before he finished the thought, his brows drawn together in a frown. Then he stepped back from her. "You sleep in my bed. It's more comfortable. I'll take the couch. We can talk in the morning."

GABE TURNED ONTO his side, rearranged the pillow beneath his head, jerked the blanket up to his chin, willing himself to sleep. It didn't work. The arm of the couch bent his neck at an unnatural angle. His feet hung off the other end. Worse, the seam of his boxer briefs cut into his nuts like piano wire.

He rolled onto his back, adjusted himself, his hand closing around his cock. And for a moment he considered jacking off. He could kill two birds with one stone—relieve the tension roiling inside him and make himself fall asleep. There was only one catch: what he wanted was in his bedroom, lying in his bed, wearing one of his T-shirts. Touching himself seemed pretty lame compared to touching her.

What would she do if he went to her, if he stretched himself out beside her and started kissing her? Would she tell him to get out, or would she kiss him back? And what the hell was wrong with him that he was even considering it?

He closed his eyes again, his head crowded by a jumble of thoughts, images, memories. Jill lying dead at the morgue. Red Crow lying dead at Mesa Butte. Kat crawling, dragging her broken leg behind her. Kat being dragged out of the sweat lodge by her hair. Her tears as she'd knelt at Red Crow's side. Her whimpers as Gabe kissed and sucked her nipples. Falling at the rock gym. Almost falling outside his own damn door, drunk on his ass.

Somehow it all boiled down to one thing: he wanted Kat.

He shoved the blanket aside and stood, glancing down at the Glock and deciding to leave it by the couch. The alarm would give him plenty of time to retrieve it if he needed it. Before he could think too hard about what he was doing, he crossed the room, walked down the hallway, and silently opened his bedroom door.

She lay on her side facing the door, her hair a dark halo against the white pillowcases. He moved closer and saw that she was sound asleep, her face relaxed, her breathing deep and even, her lips slightly parted. One slender arm rested on top of the comforter, his T-shirt slipping to reveal the soft curve of her shoulder.

For a moment, he stood there, watching her sleep, feeling oddly like a trespasser in his own bedroom. Then he reached out, brushed a lock of hair from her cheek, rubbing the strands between his fingers, feeling their softness.

What was it about her that got to him? If only he knew, he'd get vaccinated, find a cure, look for some way to stop it. Hell, he'd wear a rope of garlic around his neck if he thought that would do the trick. He didn't want to want her, didn't want to need her, didn't want to get any more tangled up in her than he already was. He didn't want to feel whatever it was she made him feel.

As if to prove to him how impossible that would be, she sighed in her sleep and nuzzled deeper into her pillow, and the feeling of protectiveness he always seemed to feel for her grew stronger.

Then something slipped from her hand onto the sheets.

Her cell phone.

The damned thing was still on.

He picked it up. Letting his gaze linger on her face for a second longer, he turned, walked out of his room, and closed the door behind him. When he was sure the sound wouldn't wake her, he flipped the little device open and turned it off. He'd be damned if anyone was going to scare her again tonight. Then, setting the phone beside his Glock, he lay down, stared up at the ceiling, and waited for morning.

CHAPTER 11

KAT WOKE TO the sound of the running shower, fragments of her dream still drifting through her mind. There'd been a storm on the horizon, clouds as black as ink rising up to blot out the sun, and at first she'd been afraid. But then she'd found Grandpa Red Crow and Gabe beside her, and her fear had vanished. For the first time in a very long time, she'd felt truly happy.

Still surrounded by a warm bubble of happiness, she closed her eyes, savoring the feeling, Gabe's scent all around her—in the air she breathed, in the sheets, in the T-shirt that lay against her skin. She stretched, imagined his big body filling the bed, and found the idea that he slept here somehow exciting.

You're not in bed with him, Kat. You're just in his bed.

Ignoring that nagging voice, she let herself drift, knowing she needed to get up, but not yet willing to leave the warmth of his bed, imagining that its embrace was his embrace, the sound of the shower like a distant rainstorm.

She must have fallen asleep again, for in the next instant she heard Gabe's voice.

"Kat?"

Her eyes flew open, and she saw Gabe silhouetted in the doorway, light flooding in from behind him, making her blink. He wore only a towel, which he'd wrapped around his waist, and she could tell his hair was wet.

He opened the door wider. "Sorry there's no prince here to wake you, Sleeping Beauty. Time to rise and shine."

And just like that, her bubble of happiness burst.

* * *

"THE CORONER RULED it an alcohol-related accident, and I know that can't be true."

Gabe had to admit the news surprised him, too. He'd thought for sure the old man's death had been a homicide, given what he'd seen at the scene.

Then again . . .

Still wearing only a damp towel, he poured freshly brewed coffee into two clean mugs and set them on the table. Then he sat, keeping his gaze on her face and not the curves of her breasts, so nicely outlined by the gray angora sweater he'd been too drunk to notice last night. "The coroner wouldn't make that kind of ruling without concrete evidence to back it up."

Kat's chin came up, her hair still tousled by sleep. "When you stood there at the scene and looked at his body, did it feel like an accident to you?"

"That wasn't my first thought, no." He hadn't even considered it. "Do you have the coroner's report?"

"Yes, but . . ." Her gaze dropped to her coffee mug, her lashes dark against her cheeks, her expression troubled. "I haven't been able to read it. I tried last night, but the details are too . . . I just can't read it."

Gabe understood. He'd forced himself to read every word of Jill's autopsy report, an experience that was as close to hell on earth as he ever hoped to come. There were some things a person wasn't meant to know.

He changed the subject.

"Maybe you didn't know Red Crow as well as you thought you did. Maybe there was another side to him, one he didn't let you see." Gabe knew firsthand what that was like, too— the shock, the sense of betrayal, the soul-deep disappointment of trusting someone, of believing in them, and then discovering you were so very wrong.

Her gaze met his once more. "I know what you're trying to say, and as a journalist I have to agree that it's possible he was hiding some things from us. But as someone who knew him, I will never believe that he caused his own death by drinking, especially not on sacred land."

Gabe wasn't about to argue with her. "So, you said you needed my help."

She nodded, opened the file folders and drew out what he recognized as a police report. "I got this first thing this morning, and I've read through it. They've redacted a few lines here. I keep feeling like I should remember everything from that night, but I don't. I was wondering if you had some idea what it might say."

Gabe read through the report, stopped when he came to the lines that had been blacked out, and almost groaned out loud, wishing now that he hadn't drunk-dialed her—for both of their sakes. He stood, walked a few paces, leaned against the counter, trying to figure out what the hell he should tell her, Feinman's threat echoing through his mind. "Are we on or off the record?"

"I guess because you ask that means we're off the record."

"You got that right." He turned toward her and met her gaze, running a hand over the jaw he hadn't had time to shave. "I really don't want to be the one to tell you this, so just be sure you want to hear it."

"Is this where you tell me I can't handle the truth?" Her voice was calm, but he could see the uncertainty in her eyes.

He sat again, took a sip of his coffee. "On the ground beside Red Crow's body were piece of what looked to me like a pot."

"A pot? You mean . . ." Her eyes went wide. "An artifact? That kind of pot?"

"Yeah."

She frowned. "Why would the police redact that?"

Clearly she wasn't putting and two and two together yet. "It's standard policy for the city to omit references to artifacts from public documents in order to discourage looting. When people find out that an area is rich in Native objects, we start seeing local artifacts turn up on the black market from here to Saudi Arabia. If the public knew that Mesa Butte was an archaeologist's paradise, the place would be crawling with looters."

A look of sudden comprehension crossed her face. "Grandpa must have caught looters in the act, and they killed him for it."

Gabe wasn't surprised she'd leapt to that conclusion. What else could she believe? "There's another possibility."

"What's that?" She watched him expectantly, her faith in the old man so strong that the obvious still hadn't occurred to her.

Oh, he so did *not* want to go here.

He steeled himself. "A part of the pot was in his pocket."

KAT'S PULSE THUNDERED in her ears as she struggled to grasp what Gabe had just told her. "No! No, he would never have stolen artifacts from the land! He always told us that pot pinching was wrong, no matter who did it."

"Maybe he felt guilty and tried to make up for it by speaking out against it."

"No!" She found herself on her feet, her face burning with anger. "I don't believe it. I won't believe it. Why would he go against everything he stood for?"

"I don't know." Gabe shrugged. "Maybe he needed the money."

The absurdity of the idea made a hysterical laugh bubble up inside her. She took several steps through his kitchen, then stopped, tears pricking her eyes. "He looted sacred land because he needed cash to fund his secret drinking habit. Is that it?"

"I have no idea. I'm just telling you what I saw."

She closed her eyes, drew breath into her lungs, trying to rein in her anger and her panic. "I know. I'm sorry. This isn't your fault."

She felt him standing behind her, then his hands cupped her shoulders.

"Kat, honey." Slowly, he turned her to face him, his arms sliding around her, drawing her close, his hand caressing her hair.

Fighting tears, she sank against him, wrapped her arms

around his waist, taking the comfort he offered, her cheek against his bare chest, the feel of his heartbeat and the shower-fresh scent of his skin both soothing and arousing. She allowed herself to savor being close to him, amazed by how right it felt, unable to keep from remembering what it had been like to kiss him, to have his hot mouth on her breasts, to have his weight pressing down on her. And for a long moment, neither of them moved.

Then Kat slowly, reluctantly pulled away. "I . . . I should go."

He crossed his arms over his chest. "Don't you want breakfast? Rumor has it that even reporters need to eat."

She couldn't help but smile. "Thanks, but I want to get a good look at the land around the butte before I head into Denver."

He frowned. "What?"

She walked over to the table and tucked the police report back in the correct file folder. "Looting leaves certain signs. You can see it all over the rez—little holes dug here and there. If there's looting going on at Mesa Butte, I'll be able to tell."

He took a step toward her. "And if you catch someone pinching pots, what then?"

"If I catch anyone in the act, I'll call nine-one-one." Kat took her coat from the back of her chair and slipped it on, her back to him.

"You'd damned well better hope the cops arrive in time." He sounded angry. "If Red Crow's death is somehow related to looting, then what's to keep whoever killed him from killing you?"

"What do you want me to do? Should I just stand by while people say things about Grandpa Red Crow that I know aren't true?"

"And what if you find out that they *are* true?" His words hung in the air.

Kat's fingers fumbled with the zipper of her coat as she forced herself to consider the unthinkable. And some part of her wondered whether she'd be making things worse if through her hard work she managed only to prove that Grandpa Red Crow had been a pot-pinching alcoholic who'd simply staggered off a cliff.

She looked up at Gabe, found him watching her intently, his jaw set. "I'm a journalist. Either way, I have to find out the truth."

"All right. Fine." He set his mug down. "But you're not going there without me. I get off at four. I'll meet you there."

THE DAY TURNED out to be one of the most difficult in Kat's life.

It started out well enough. She called the Denver police immediately after the I-Team meeting to report the death threats and spent nearly an hour answering the detective's questions, while Sophie sat at her desk, pretending not to eavesdrop, a slow smile spreading over her face when Kat told the detective where she'd spent the night.

"We'll need your permission to access your cell phone records," the detective told her. "If we can find the pay phones this person used, there might be surveillance video that can shed light on his identity. In the meantime, we'll increase patrols on your street. If you don't already own a gun, now might be a good time to buy one."

No sooner had the detective walked away when Sophie strolled over to Kat's desk. "I'm sorry you're going through this, Kat. Those calls sound really terrifying. If you don't mind, I'm going to tell Marc about this."

Kat had known Sophie was going to say that. "I'm not sure there's much he can do, but thanks, Sophie."

Then Sophie lowered her voice and smiled. "Is this, um . . . the same ranger who rescued you last summer, the one who intervened when the sweat lodge was raided, the ranger Marc met?"

"Yes, but it's not what you think. He and I . . . we're just friends."

"Ah." The smile on Sophie's face as she walked back to her desk told Kat that Sophie didn't believe her.

And then came the moment Kat had been dreading. She forced herself to read through Grandpa Red Crow's autopsy report, trying to steel herself against her own emotions and failing. Seeing him reduced to a collection of body parts—a brain that had been weighed, genitals that had been examined, subcutaneous body fat that had been measured—seemed to dehumanize him. But worse than that were the toxicology tests that showed him to have alcohol in his stomach—and a blood-alcohol level just below the legal limit for drunk driving.

She didn't want to believe it, couldn't believe it. She'd never once smelled alcohol on his breath, and she'd certainly never seen him under the influence. Yet the proof was right there in black and white. The disappointment she'd felt had been so overwhelming she'd spent a half hour in the women's room crying and the rest of the afternoon trying to figure out how she was going to do her job as a journalist without betraying the memory of someone she loved.

SHE WAS STILL struggling to pull herself together when it was time to make the trip to Boulder and Mesa Butte. She arrived to find Gabe waiting for her at the top of the access road. Still in uniform, he met her at the tailgate, his gun holstered against his hip, the wind ruffling his hair.

He frowned at her from behind his sunglasses. "You okay?"

She shook her head, feeling tears prick her eyes, but willing herself not to cry. "I read the autopsy report, but I . . . I really don't want to talk about it."

"I'm sorry." He reached out, took her hand, held it in the warmth of his own. "Did you contact the police about those calls?"

"Yes."

For a moment, he said nothing, as if expecting her to tell him more. "So what exactly are we looking for?"

Kat tucked her keys and digital camera in her pocket. "Looters leave little holes and trenches. You can see them all over the rez—small pits dug with trowels or shovels. Looters usually don't waste time trying to cover up what they've done. They just grab whatever they find and take off."

"Rape and run."

Kat drew her hair back and tucked it into her coat to keep

the wind from blowing it in her face, then looked about, trying to put aside her unsettled emotions and get her bearings. The sun hung over the mountains, a thin layer of cirrus cloud stretched in ripples across the sky. A handful of crows played in the gale, one moment struggling forward against the current, then tumbling backward, beak over tail feathers like airborne acrobats. To the west, the distant peaks gleamed white in the autumn sunshine.

Thankfully, there seemed to be no one else at the butte, her truck and Gabe's SUV the only vehicles in sight. Even so, a sense of uneasiness had come over her. Maybe it was the sight of the sweat lodge standing cold and empty. Or maybe it was the fact that Grandpa Red Crow had died here.

She shivered, drew her jacket tighter around her shoulders, her gaze coming to rest on the place where Grandpa Red Crow's pickup had last stood, an ache swelling inside her chest. She turned away, swallowing the lump in her throat. "I . . . I've never seen any signs of looting when I've been here, but then it's always been dark."

She felt Gabe's hand on her shoulder, as if he knew what she was feeling. "Well, looting wouldn't happen up here would it?"

Kat looked over at him. "What do you mean?"

"If ceremonies were traditionally held up here, Native people wouldn't have lived here because it's sacred. That means they wouldn't have made pots or hunted or had their trash dumps up here, either, so the artifacts wouldn't be here."

"Oh. You're right." Kat couldn't help wondering why she hadn't thought of that. She was the Indian, after all.

A grin tugged at Gabe's lips. "Hey, I paid attention during my cultural-resource training. The actual butte is on the far west end of the Mesa Butte property. Any encampments would've been east of here—on the plains."

GABE LED KAT around to the east side of the butte. In contrast to the west side, which was a sheer cliff, the east side sloped steeply downward until it leveled out into xeric tallgrass prairie. He was glad to see most of the snow had melted.

Even so, the hillside was steep enough that he was afraid Kat might slip and reinjure her leg. Wearing a long denim skirt and cowboy boots, she wasn't exactly dressed for this kind of terrain. "Watch your step. The grass is slick. I don't want you to fall and hurt—"

She gasped, her feet sliding out from beneath her.

"I've got you." He caught her before she could fall, helping her regain her balance. Then he turned her so that her left side faced downhill. "Walk sideways like this. Let your left leg do all the work."

He sidestepped down the steepest part of the hillside, keeping one hand on her waist just in case, his gaze on their surroundings. If there was any chance that looters were operating here, he didn't want to be taken by surprise. But there was no one else as far as the eye could see. Then out of the corner of his eye, he saw movement—a lone coyote loping its way south at the base of the hill below them.

Beside him, Kat froze, her body suddenly rigid, her gaze fixed on the coyote, an unmistakable look of fear on her face.

"It won't bother us. Coyotes are pretty shy around people."

But she didn't seem to hear him. Her hand found his, held it tight. Then she whispered something, words he didn't understand, her gaze still fixed on the coyote.

"Easy, Kat. I won't let it hurt you."

"I left my corn pollen in my truck," she said at last. "If we cross its path without making an offering, it could bring bad luck."

"Bad luck?" They hadn't covered Native myths or superstitions in their training. "I've got a loaded Glock forty-five semiauto that's guaranteed to reverse most bad luck with a pull of the trigger. But if you want to turn back—"

Her chin came up, her gaze meeting his. "No."

GABE WATCHED AS Kat knelt down beside the plundered earth, rage on slow boil in his gut. She traced her fingers over the deep tread of frozen tire tracks, a stricken look on her sweet face. The tracks came from the east and ended at this spot, where a trench perhaps two feet deep and ten feet long had been gouged in the soil, earth heaped up carelessly on both sides. And it wasn't the only trench. Several more had been dug nearby, some deeper and longer than this one.

"How could anyone do this?" Kat's voice quavered. She reached out, picked up a small potsherd that Gabe hadn't noticed, turned it over in her palm. "They're so desperate to get to the artifacts that they're destroying things."

He squatted down beside her, looked down at other tracks frozen in the mud, their treads farther apart. "Whoever they are, they're using machinery, probably a compact excavator like a Bobcat. This sure as hell wasn't dug with a shovel."

Farther into the trench, they found several more potsherds, as well as a clump of fibers woven together in what looked like a flattened bit of basket, part of a beaded cradleboard, and a small broken shaft of wood that Gabe couldn't identify, but which clearly meant something to Kat.

She held it reverently, turned it over, tears spilling onto her cheeks. "*Chanúpasinté*. A pipestem."

He watched as she set the broken artifact carefully back where she'd found it, then moved to the next trench and the next, where the situation was much the same—the ground strewn with potsherds and pieces of things too old and broken to identify, each of them made by a human hand long ago.

"Son of a bitch! Dammit!" Gabe had known that Mesa Butte was rich in artifacts, but he'd had no idea how rich. There was a fortune buried here—enough to make someone very wealthy.

Was it enough to make someone kill?

"This isn't just looting. It's industrial-scale larceny." He squatted down and picked up a tattered bit of buckskin decorated with what looked like very old and worn porcupine quills—a remnant of someone's clothing. He put it back, stood, and glanced around them, feeling more than a little uneasy. "Time to go. I need to get you the hell away from here and report this."

"I need to get pictures first." She sniffed, wiped the tears from her face, then drew a small silver point-and-shoot camera out of her pocket. "I have to be able to prove this is happening."

And then it hit him. "You're planning to write an article about this."

"Yes." She held up the camera.

"I can't let you do that." He reached out, took the camera from her, and stepped back out of her reach.

"What are you—?"

"I know you're just doing your job, but if you tell the public what's here, this place will be swarming with assholes carrying shovels and buckets. If you care about this place, you're going to have to keep what you've seen here to yourself, at least for now."

"This isn't just about my job. It's about Grandpa Red Crow." She reached for the camera. "If he—"

Gabe heard the rifle's report and had no time to do anything but react. He threw Kat to the ground beneath him as two more shots rang out, hitting the frozen earth beside them and sending up a spray of dirt and bullet fragments.

An AR-15 with .223 rounds, maybe three hundred yards away.

Shit!

Silence.

Kat stared up at him through wide, terrified eyes, obviously in pain and struggling to breathe.

Dread caught in his chest. *Oh, Christ!* "Are you hit?"

She shook her head. "You . . . knocked . . . the breath . . ."

Relief, sweet and pure, rushed through him. But it wasn't over yet.

"Hang on." Knowing he might have only seconds before the shooter took a new position and sighted on them again, Gabe slipped his arm beneath Kat and, holding her tight against him, dragged her deeper into the trench.

"Stay down!" He rolled off her, drew his gun and his cell phone, tossing the phone to her, then racking the slide on the Glock. "Press nine and hold it for dispatch."

Leaving it to her to call for backup, he dragged himself on his elbows to the edge of the trench and looked back toward the butte where the shots had originated, but saw no one. The shooter was probably firing from the cover of the trees high on the butte itself, which meant that he stood between them and their vehicles. He had greater range and God only knew how much ammo, while Gabe had only what was already in his pistol and one spare service magazine—twenty-six rounds. Worse, with the shooter holding the high ground, there was no place for them to run.

The moment they left the cover of the trench, they'd be dead.

CHAPTER 12

SOMEONE HAD FIRED at them. Someone was trying to kill them.

Kat held the phone to her ear with hands that refused to stop shaking. Then, over the thrum of her own heartbeat, she heard a woman's voice. She cut in. "Hello, dispatch? There's shooting at Mesa Butte! There's shooting at—"

She gasped as three more shots tore through the air, the woman on the phone firing questions at her that she didn't hear.

Beside her, Gabe ducked back inside the trench, gun in hand, his dark brows drawn together in a look of focused determination. "Tell dispatch it's one shooter with a high-powered rifle positioned somewhere near the top of the access road. Tell them we're about three hundred yards east of the butte. Tell them you're calling on behalf of sixty-forty-five, off duty."

Kat repeated his words into the phone, doing her best to answer the dispatcher's questions and fighting not to scream as two more shots whined overhead. "No, no one's hurt, but he keeps shooting at us!"

She thought she heard dispatch say help was on the way, then Gabe swore.

"Goddamn it! Tell dispatch I'm returning fire!"

"He's returning—"

Bam! Bam! Bam!

Kat instinctively squeezed her eyes shut and covered her ears against the deafening sound as Gabe shot back, the cell phone falling into the dirt. When she opened her eyes again, she found herself lying on her side, looking at Gabe's profile. Beads of sweat trickled down his temple, and he seemed to be listening, his breathing deep and even, a look of focused concentration on his face.

How could he be so steady when she was shaking like a leaf? He seemed more angry than afraid. And then she saw.

Blood.

It had soaked through the right side of Gabe's coat near his collar, a large hole torn in the black fabric, white fiber batting stained dark red.

"You've been shot!" She crawled over to him, only one thought on her mind—to help him.

He shook his head. "Get down, dammit! Leave it! It's nothing—just a graze. Now listen to me! Whoever this bastard is, he's probably realized he can't hit us as long as we're down here. The only chance he has of getting us before the good guys get him is to come down here. If he tries, I'll do my best take him out. But if anything happens to me, take the Glock and—"

The distant wail of sirens.

"Hear that? The bastard who's shooting at us hears it, too, and is probably high-tailing it away from here. It's going to be okay." Gabe took her hand with his, gave it a reassuring squeeze. "Stay down until I say it's clear. Understand?"

Kat nodded.

"Good." He pressed a quick kiss to her lips, then turned away from her onto his side and peeked carefully around the pile of earth that shielded them.

The next two minutes passed like an eternity. Even as the sirens drew nearer, Kat couldn't shake the feeling someone was watching them, perhaps getting closer to them, waiting for his chance. She closed her eyes, kept her head down, and prayed.

Wailing sirens. Barking dogs. Men's shouts as Mesa Butte and the surrounding land were cordoned off and searched. And finally the sight of two men in Mountain Parks uniforms, guns drawn.

"Hey, Chief, Hatfield. I can't tell you how glad I am to see your ugly faces." Gabe stood, gun in hand.

The ranger Kat recognized as Hatfield looked around at the battered landscape, a look of shock on his face. "Holy fuck!"

Chief Ranger Webb turned in a slow circle, his gaze on the trenches, his face red with rage. "Son of a bitch! What the fuck is going on out here, Rossiter?"

"Isn't that obvious? Someone has turned Mesa Butte into his own private archaeological dig." Gabe took Kat's hands, helped her to her feet, then drew her into his arms, holding her tight. "Are you okay, honey?"

She held on to him, still shaky. "Y-yes, I think so."

He kissed her hair. "Let's get you out of here."

As he helped her climb out of the trench, Kat looked beyond him and saw the butte swarming with law enforcement—park rangers, police, sheriff's deputies. There, not twenty feet away, stood Officer Daniels talking with another cop.

And he was watching her.

"WHAT WERE YOU doing there?"

Gabe looked from Police Chief Barker to Chief Ranger Webb and back again. "I already explained all of this—twice. Wait a minute . . . Am I a suspect or something?"

He'd been at police headquarters for three hours now, filling out paperwork, answering question after question, wanting nothing more than to find Kat and get the hell out of this place. She'd been badly shaken up by the shooting, and he didn't want to leave her alone any longer than necessary. She didn't know it yet, but either she was going to stay at his house again tonight or he would stay at hers. No way was he going to leave her unprotected, not after what had happened today.

"This is just a standard debriefing, Rossiter." Webb gave him a bored look. "Someone shot at you, and you fired back. Just answer the damned questions so we can all go home."

Gabe could tell Webb's patience was worn as thin as his own. "As I told you, she wanted to check Mesa Butte for signs of looting, and I asked her to wait until I got off work at four because I didn't want her going there by herself. If looters were to blame for the old man's death—"

Barker frowned. "Red Crow's death was ruled an accident. You know that."

"Yes, but she doesn't believe it, and after what happened this afternoon, neither do I." How could anyone? It seemed obvious now that Red Crow's death had something to do with looting. "Someone is stripping the place of artifacts and was willing to blow our heads off to conceal that fact. You all saw what's going on there. The investigation into Red Crow's death needs to be reopened."

"We'll make that decision." Barker spoke the words casually, but there was an edge to his voice that said he didn't like taking suggestions from a park ranger.

"Did you see anyone?" Webb tossed a few Tums in his mouth and chewed.

Gabe shook his head. "No. My decision to fire was strategic. I wanted the attacker to know I was armed so that he would think twice before moving in on us. I hoped to buy us a little time so backup could arrive. And it worked. Once I fired, he quit shooting."

Webb nodded. "There's no doubt that you made the right decision."

Barker looked up from his notes. "How many rounds did you fire?"

"Three." They'd already taken Gabe's service weapon and his spare magazine and probably knew the answer to this themselves.

Barker glanced back down at his notes, his brows drawn together in a frown. "What I don't understand is how Ms. James knew to look for looting in the first place. Can you shed any light on that?"

And Gabe realized he was fucked. If he told the truth, he'd lose his job. He took a breath, steeled himself, wondering if the rock gym would hire him. "She—"

Webb cut him off. "She was at the crime scene, remember? She saw the potsherds next to Red Crow's body. That's what she claims at any rate."

For a moment Gabe thought he'd gotten lucky. And then it hit him. "You're questioning her?"

"Of course we're questioning her." Barker glared at Gabe, his voice filling the small room. "Every time we've been called to Mesa Butte, she's been there. Is it too hard to imagine that she's mixed up in this somehow? Maybe the whole lot of them are doing it together—stealing artifacts and selling them, using their ceremonies as a pretext for looting the place and then pretending the shit belonged to their great-grandfathers or some damned thing."

Gabe couldn't believe what he was hearing. "Who's with her? Is it Daniels?"

Barker stood, leaned forward, his face inches from Gabe's. "Daniels is a good cop, a good man, a family man. If you've got a problem—"

"Your *good* cop dragged an innocent woman by her hair and lied—"

"Shut the fuck up!" Webb's voice roared. "Both of you—shut up!"

Barker's face was red. "Get your boy under control, Webb. He's in my shop now, and I've had about enough of his attitude."

Then Barker stood, threw the door opened, and stomped out of the room.

Gabe would have gone after Kat, but Webb shut the door again, a look of unmistakable anger on his face. "What the hell is going on, Gabe?"

"What do you mean?"

"I see how it could happen. You rescue a pretty, young woman. She's grateful. You're horny. The next thing you know she's got your dick wrapped around her little finger, and you're dragged into her problems. Maybe she and her friends are behind this looting. Maybe they've been using their ceremonies as cover like Barker suggested."

Gabe bit back a stream of four-letter words. "Kat hasn't so much as laid a finger on my dick, and she's incapable of stealing."

"You're sure of that, are you?"

"Yes, I'm sure of it. She was totally broken up when she saw what was happening there."

"Maybe she's a good actress."

Then Gabe spoke the words he knew would end his career. "You want the truth? I'll give it you. She only went to the butte to look for looting because I told her about the potsherds. She wanted to know what was in the lines the cops had redacted, so I told her—off the record, of course."

Webb stared at him, his ruddy complexion slowly turning redder. "So she lied to us in order to cover for you."

"She wasn't lying. She was protecting her source." There was a difference—to a journalist anyway.

"Her source? I let you off last time. I sat there in my office and lied to Feinman to save your ass." Webb jabbed him in the chest. "But not this time. You're a damned good ranger, Rossiter. Hell, you're the best. But I won't put my job on the line to save yours, not when you refuse to follow the goddamned rules. You are terminated."

Webb ripped the badge from Gabe's coat and held out one hand.

Some part of him unable to believe this was really happening, Gabe fished the keys to his service truck out of his pocket, lifted the chain that held his key card from around his neck, removed the Glock, and dropped them into Webb's outstretched palm.

Then Webb opened the door and strode down the hallway, leaving Gabe alone.

KAT SAT IN the passenger seat of Marc's SUV, the lights of Boulder passing outside the window. Body armor that was much too big for her pressed into her thighs and bumped against her chin. Beside her, Marc argued on his cell phone with Julian, who was ahead of them driving her truck.

"What do you mean you don't know how to get to US-36 from Twenty-eighth Street? Twenty-eighth Street *is* US-36, dumbass. Yeah, I'm sure. Go straight."

Oddly reassured by their familiar bickering, Kat drew a

deep breath and tried to release the tension that coiled inside her like a spring. For more than two hours, detectives had grilled her, their line of questioning leaving no doubt that they suspected she knew more about the looting than she was telling them. She'd expected compassion from them, given that someone had tried to shoot her. Instead, she'd been interrogated.

More than a little overwhelmed, she'd done her best to answer their questions. No, she'd had no idea there were artifacts at Mesa Butte. No, she'd never heard Grandpa Red Crow or anyone else in Denver's Native community talk about artifacts or looting at the butte. Yes, she knew Native people sometimes dug up artifacts and sold them on the black market, but that typically happened on the reservation where few had good jobs and many went to bed cold and hungry. No, she would never cover for looters, even if they were Indian, because stealing artifacts was wrong.

When they'd demanded to know why she'd wanted to check for looting, she hadn't been able to tell them the truth because that would have exposed Gabe. So she'd told them she'd seen the potsherds beside Grandpa Red Crow's body. Then they'd wanted to know why she hadn't mentioned the shards in her statement to police.

"I was very upset that night. I forgot about it."

"You forgot about it," the older of the two detectives had replied, his tone of voice implying that he didn't believe her.

She wasn't a very good liar.

Some part of her realized they were doing their job, but knowing that hadn't made their suspicion any easier to bear. She'd left the interrogation room feeling weary, shaken, violated—only to find Marc and Julian waiting for her in the lobby. The sight of them very nearly unleashed the tears she'd been holding back.

"How did you know I was here?" she'd asked them.

"You called Tom, remember?" Marc had explained, giving her a hug.

She hadn't remembered.

"You're in shock," Julian had suggested. As tall as Marc with dark hair he kept back in a ponytail, he had the kind of presence that intimidated even hardened criminals. "Flying bullets have a way of shaking people up. Let's get you home."

But she hadn't wanted to leave—not yet. She'd wanted to find Gabe, to thank him, to make sure he wasn't badly hurt, but the person at the front desk told her he thought Gabe had already gone. So Marc and Julian had sandwiched her between them and escorted her out to Marc's waiting vehicle, Julian helping her inside and shutting the door behind her before jogging over to her truck, her keys in his hand. They were taking her to Marc and Sophie's house, where they wanted her to stay till this was over.

Someone had tried to kill her today. Someone had tried to kill her and would probably have succeeded if not for Gabe. He'd recognized the sound of the rifle firing when she hadn't. He'd knocked her to the ground, covering her body with his to protect her. Then he'd scooped her into one arm and used his strength to drag both of them deep into the trench where the bullets couldn't harm them.

If she hadn't waited for him, if she she'd gone to Mesa Butte alone . . .

She shuddered, an image of herself lying dead in the darkness, her blood frozen in pools on the dirt, flashing through her mind. Gabe had saved her life. He'd been wounded trying to protect her, and she hadn't even had a chance to thank him.

"Turn around!" The words were out before she realized she'd spoken.

"Turn around? Did you forget something at the cop shop?"

"No, I . . . I want to see Gabe. I need to see Gabe." How could she explain this when she didn't entirely understand it herself? "I . . . He was hurt, grazed by a bullet, and I want to see him. I want to stay with him tonight."

And if he didn't want her there?

Though she couldn't see Marc's face in the dark, she knew he was watching her. "I'm not so sure this is a good idea. Do you think he can handle keeping you safe?"

"He handled it this afternoon, didn't he?"

"I guess you have a point there. If you're sure this is what you want . . ."

"I'm sure." She'd never been more certain of anything. "I need to know he's okay. I need to see for myself."

Marc reached out to the cell phone on his dash, punched a speed-dial number, then spoke into his Bluetooth headset. "Hey, Dorkangelo, change of plans. Take the next right."

CHAPTER 13

GABE SAT IN the dark on his couch still wearing his coat and boots, a tumbler of whisky in one hand, the bottle on the floor at his feet. Echoes drifted though his mind—rifle fire, the thud of bullets striking dirt, Kat's terrified screams. He raised the glass to his lips, took another sip, but it did nothing to drown out the noise in his head.

Hello, dispatch? There's shooting at Mesa Butte! There's shooting at—

Goddamn it! Tell dispatch I'm returning fire!

You've been shot!

Leave it! It's nothing—just a graze.

Something twisted in Gabe's chest at the image of Kat crawling to him, eyes wide with fear, dirt on her cheek and in her hair. She'd been so afraid, but she'd set aside her panic and risked her own safety—to help him. Most women probably would have let fear paralyze them. But Kat wasn't like most women.

At the time, Gabe had been too pissed off to be afraid. Not that he was used to getting shot at. He'd only faced live fire once in his career, only drawn his weapon against another human being a handful of times, only squeezed the trigger to put down sick or injured wildlife. Still, the moment he'd heard that first shot, his training had kicked in, and he hadn't hesitated. At least he could feel good about that.

Not that he'd earn a promotion or even a high-five for his actions. In a rather fucked-up twist of fate, one of his most valiant days on the job had turned out to be his last day on the job.

You're a damned good ranger, Rossiter. Hell, you're the best. But I won't put my job on the line to save yours, not when you refuse to follow the goddamned rules. You are terminated.

Gabe supposed he ought to feel angry or upset. He'd just lost the only real job he'd ever had, the only job he'd ever wanted. But strangely, he couldn't seem to give a damn. He'd done what he'd believed was right. He wasn't about to let Kat take suspicion onto herself in an effort to protect him. If this was the price he had to pay, then he was willing to accept that.

Way to stick to your convictions, Rossiter.

He raised his glass in a mock toast and took another sip, feeling whisky burn its way to his empty stomach, where it smoldered.

So, if he didn't regret what he'd done to get himself fired, then why, exactly, was he sitting in the dark drinking alone?

Maybe it was the fact that he *was* alone.

Webb's words ringing in his ears, he'd left the briefing room and gone in search of Kat, only to learn that she'd already left with Hunter and another cop. For some reason that had felt like more of a blow than getting shit-canned. As much as he'd been relieved to know Kat was with friends and safe, he'd wanted talk to her, had needed to hold her and reassure her and see for himself that she was okay.

Apparently, she'd just wanted to get home.

Had she thought about him at all?

He took another drink, some part of him aware that his night was turning into a pity party. Well, it wouldn't be the first time, would it? Not by a long shot.

This is getting to be a habit, buddy.

Yeah, he supposed it was.

He took a deep breath, looked at the drink in his hand, then stood, picked up the bottle and carried it and the whisky glass to his entertainment center. He set them down and walked away. Drinking wasn't going to solve anything, and the last thing he needed was another damned hangover.

He kicked off his boots, slipped off his parka—he'd have to patch it or pitch it—then walked into the bathroom and got undressed. He glanced in the mirror and saw an angry groove carved in the skin beneath his right clavicle, flecks of dried blood around it. It looked deeper than he had imagined it would. Though he hadn't felt the impact, he knew from the height and angle exactly when it had hit him.

Somewhere in the millisecond between when he'd shoved Kat to the ground and when he'd followed after her, that first shot had whizzed between them, catching Gabe as he'd gone down. The bullet hadn't so much struck him as he'd struck it. That fact, together with the height of the wound, told him that the round hadn't been meant for him. Some son of a bitch had sighted on Kat and pulled the trigger. If Gabe hadn't heard the rifle fire, the shot would have blown her head off.

When he thought about how close it had been . . .

Christ!

In a rush of delayed panic, Gabe's hands started to shake, his heart thudding hard in his chest, his stomach threatening to revolt. He closed his eyes, leaned against the sink, forced himself to take slow, steady breaths until the nausea subsided. When he opened his eyes again, he found himself staring at his own reflection.

You saved her life, man.

The thought struck him right between the eyes, seeped through him, leaving him with a bone-deep sense of . . . satisfaction. He was used to saving lives, but not like this. To know that Kat was alive tonight because of something he'd done . . .

Maybe you don't suck after all, Rossiter.

He turned the water in the shower and stepped under the warm spray, washing dirt, sweat, and blood from his skin, letting the water loosen his tense muscles. Then he got out, dried off, and dressed his wound, the sting of Betadine making him cuss a blue streak. He'd just covered it with a large bandage when his doorbell rang.

He skipped the underwear and slipped into a pair of jeans. Taking no chances, he picked up his HK .40-cal semiauto— he'd seen the last of the Glock, which belonged to Mountain Parks—and walked quietly to the door. He looked through the peephole—and felt his heart knock against his breastbone.

Kat.

She stood on his doorstep flanked by Hunter and someone else—a man in a black leather jacket whose face he couldn't see. He tucked the firearm into the waistband of his jeans, unlocked the door and opened it. And for a moment all he could do was stand there, staring into her eyes. She looked exhausted, overwhelmed, beautiful.

Had she been crying?

"Good to see you in one piece, rock jock. I see you took a hit."

Gabe tore his gaze from hers, gave Hunter a nod, rubbed his fingers over the bandage. "It's just a graze. Hey, Darcangelo, how's it going? You hang with this guy? That's ironic."

Julian Darcangelo, the best damn detective Gabe had ever met, shrugged, then reached out and shook Gabe's hand, a grin spreading over his face. "What can I say? Every superhero needs a sidekick. Plus, it's a good way to keep an eye on him, keep him out of trouble."

Hunter glared at Darcangelo, muttering something that sounded suspiciously like "fuck you." Then he frowned, pointing back and forth between the two of them. "So, you two know each other?"

"Of course we know each other. We met chasing your sorry ass through the snow. Rossiter here is pure hell on a pair of skis." Darcangelo shifted his gaze back to Gabe. "Is Kat going to be safe here with you tonight?"

Gabe met Kat's gaze again. "Yeah, she will. Do you boys want to come in?"

Hunter's gaze dropped to Kat, as if trying to gauge his response from her. "I think we'll head home and let you two get some rest." Then his gaze shifted to Gabe. He drew out a business card and held it out "Give me a call. Let us know what we can do."

"Will do." Gabe pocketed the card, watching as Kat thanked her friends and said her good-byes. Then he took her hand and drew her inside, the two men's voices drifting back as they headed down his front walk.

"You didn't tell me Kat's rock jock was Gabe Rossiter. He's not a rock jock, Hunter, he's a rock god."

"How the hell was I supposed to know you knew him?"

Gabe closed the door and locked out the night, while Kat hung her coat on the coat rack and slipped off her boots. They turned and faced one another, and for a moment neither of them moved or spoke, Gabe drinking in the sight of her, from the dirt smudge on her cheek to the shadows in her eyes. Then he did the only thing he could do. He drew her into his arms, and held her, just held her, his face pressed against her silky hair, the honey scent and soft feel of her a balm for all the rough edges inside him.

"I'm scared, Gabe." She pressed her cheek against his bare chest.

"I know." He held her tighter. "You're safe here."

"I had to see you. I had to know you were okay."

"I'm glad you came." He drew back, tucked a finger beneath her chin, tilted her face upward—and then he kissed her.

AT THE FIRST soft brush of Gabe's lips against hers, Kat felt tears prick her eyes, the heat and gentleness of his kiss cutting through her numbness, through her shock and fear, opening some vulnerable place inside her that needed him. And she did need him. She needed his touch, needed his strength, needed him to make the day's horror go away. She didn't want to think about the differences between them or the promises she'd once made herself or what tomorrow might bring.

She just wanted him.

She stood on her tiptoes, slid her fingers into his wet hair, and drew his head closer, parting her lips for him, meeting the thrust of his tongue with her own. He tasted faintly of whisky and smelled like pine-scented soap and shampoo. He groaned and kissed her harder, plundering her mouth, stealing the breath from her lungs and giving it back again. She heard herself whimper, felt her knees go weak. Then he broke the kiss, ducked down, and scooped her into his arms.

She gasped, wrapped her arms around his neck, clinging to him, her gaze colliding with his. "Wh-what . . . ?"

"I won't drop you." He nuzzled her temple, carrying her in long strides to the dark of his bedroom.

She'd never been carried like this before. It left her feeling intensely feminine, like something priceless and precious and worth protecting, some part of her delighting in his raw strength, his male power. And for a moment she forgot to feel nervous about where he was carrying her—and what might happen when they got there. She found herself kissing him, nipping his earlobe, trailing her fingers down his spine, his muscles tensing beneath her hands as he walked.

He laid her back on his sheets and stretched out beside her, his face inches from hers, his fingers slowly unbuttoning her blouse. "I want you, Kat. But I won't do anything you don't want me to do. Tell me to stop, and I will."

A bolt of heat shot through her, making her shiver. "Gabe, I . . ."

Whatever she'd meant to say vanished from her mind as he drew off her blouse, his lips brushing over hers, his knuckles sliding in slow circles over her bare belly. And then, abruptly, he withdrew from her, his weight shifting. She heard a soft click—and found herself looking up at him in the light of his bedside lamp, the yellow glow casting the ridges and valleys of his muscles into high relief.

His gaze met hers, his blue eyes dark. "I need to see you—all of you."

She shivered again, the idea of him seeing her body in the light both startling and erotic, nervousness twining with anticipation in her belly. Barely able to breathe, she watched as he finished undressing her, removing first her bra, then her skirt, tights, and panties, leaving her completely naked. Without meaning to, she found herself pressing her thighs together and fighting the urge to reach down and cover herself.

No man had ever seen her like this.

He let out a gust of breath, his brows drawing together, his gaze moving over her from her breasts to the most private part of her like a caress, scorching her skin and making her nipples draw tight. "You are so beautiful. *Jesus.*"

With a moan, he lowered his mouth to her belly and scattered hot kisses over her skin, his lips and tongue seeming to leave a trail of fire as he slowly worked his way upward.

Her breasts grew heavy, memories of how it had felt to have his mouth on her making her impatient. But when at last he reached her breasts, he didn't kiss her nipples as she'd thought he would. Instead he pressed first his lips and then his cheek against her heartbeat, as if the feel of it mattered to him, as if the fact that her heart was beating meant something to him, as if . . .

As if her being alive meant the world to him.

Kat's throat grew tight, a feeling that could only be love—yes, love—swelling inside her, tears trickling down her temples. She was alive. Thanks to this strong, brave, beautiful man, they were both alive tonight. She swallowed the lump in her throat, kissed his damp hair, desire for him driving through her veins like a pulse.

He raised his head, his gaze meeting hers, the intensity in his eyes making her breath catch and her belly fill with heat. "Kat."

His lips came down on hers in a deep, slow kiss that made her feel like she was melting from the inside out, his tongue claiming her mouth with skilled strokes. One of his hands slid up her rib cage, his knuckles teasing the underside of one breast, before he took the weight of it in his hand, cupping and plumping it, his thumb making lazy circles over her puckered areola. Then with a hungry groan, he dragged his mouth from hers, lowered it to her nipple, and sucked.

She gasped, her fingers digging into his shoulders, pleasure surging through her in a liquid rush, making her inner muscles clench. "Gabe!"

He moved from one breast to the other and back again, teasing her nipples, tugging on them with his lips, flicking his tongue over their sensitive tips, until she was out of breath, her body arching toward him, the ache inside her excruciating. Then he did something she never would have imagined.

He took her right hand, drew it downward, and pressed it against her *there*, his hand holding hers in place. "Help me, Kat. Show me what you like."

Gabe was so turned on that it took him a moment to realize that Kat's expression had changed from arousal to shock, a blush creeping slowly from her breasts to her cheeks. She tried to pull her hand away from him, as if he'd just touched it to a hot stove and not her own sweet muff. "I . . . I . . ."

He gaped down at her and released her hand, so stunned that for a moment he couldn't speak. "Don't tell me you've never given yourself an orgasm."

"Well, I . . ." Her blush deepened, a look of genuine shame on her face. "I grew up in a hogaan, and my grandmother is very traditional."

He thought about that for a second, imagined sleeping in a single room with ten other people—one of them being a very strict grandma—and thought he could see why that might have been a problem. "What about during college?"

She shook her head. "I had two roommates, and . . ."

Gabe'd had one roommate, but by then he'd been getting enough tail that on the rare occasion when he needed to take matters into his own hands, he'd just marched his dick to the shower. "After college?"

She looked away. "Well, I . . . I tried a few times, but . . . I guess I didn't really have the patience or know . . . what I was doing."

Gabe felt an unexpected rush of tenderness at her embarrassment. "Well, honey, we'll just have to figure you out together, won't we?"

Letting his fingers brush lightly through the dark curls of her muff, he ducked down and drew one ripe nipple into his mouth, wanting to carry her past her inhibitions to a place where arousal took over. It didn't take long—a few flicks of his tongue, a nip of his teeth, a slow tug with his lips. He felt her fingers clench in his hair, her hips shifting as she instinctively tried to find relief, her innate responsiveness turning him on in a way that other women's theatrical moaning never had.

"God, Kat, I could kiss your breasts all night long. *Mmm.*"

He wasn't exaggerating. The taste of her skin, the beaded velvet of her nipples, the way her belly quivered when he sucked—she was driving him insane. His cock felt like it might bust through his jeans, lust throbbing in his groin, his blood burning. Needing more of her, he slid his hand between her thighs and cupped her, pressing the heel of his hand against her in slow, deep circles.

She gasped, her hips giving an involuntary jerk, her thighs still doing the virgin clutch. Her hands left his hair, one gliding over his back, the nails of the other digging into his forearm. For a moment, he thought she would pull his hand away. Instead, she dug in—and held on.

"Does that feel good?"

Eyes closed, she answered on a breathy exhale. "Oh, yes!"

"Good."

He lost track of time after that, one minute stretching seamlessly into the next, nothing in his world but Kat. Her pleasure became his pleasure, every whimper, every shiver guiding him as he sought new ways to please her, his brain buzzing, strung out on her musky scent, the honey taste of her skin, the sight of her sweet body.

And she opened for him like a flower. Her hips answered the motion of his hand with circles of their own, her thighs parting to give him better access. Attuned to her cues, he nudged one finger between her lips to tease her entrance, unable to stifle a groan when he discovered that she was slick, drenched, ready.

She gave a little squeak, and her eyes flew open, her grip on his arm growing tighter. "Gabe, I don't—"

"Let me make you come. Then I'll stop. I promise."

For a moment she watched him, her pupils dilated, her breathing unsteady. "What if . . . What if I can't?"

"Are you kidding? As sensual and responsive as you are?" He gave her clit a little flick just to make the point and was immediately rewarded with a gasp and a jerk of her hips. "Just relax, honey."

He ducked down and nibbled her throat, then rubbed her own wetness over her clit, felt her body tense. "Do you like that?"

Kat answered with a little whimper, her eyes squeezed shut.

Gabe found a rhythm, felt her swollen little nub grow harder, fuller. Soon her breath was coming in ragged pants.

He could tell she was close, her face flushed, her breasts swollen, every muscle in her body taut. The tension inside her built until he thought she would break like glass. But something seemed to be holding her back, and he was pretty sure he knew what it was.

"There's no one here but me, Kat. No one can hear you or see you but me." He ducked down again, brushed his lips over a wet and puckered nipple—and slowly slipped his finger into her slippery heat, careful not to break the fragile barrier of her virginity.

"Oh, Gabe!" She called out his name, her nails digging sharply into his skin.

She was tight, impossibly tight, her vagina so snug against his finger that he almost came in his jeans imaging how she would feel clenched around his cock. Slowly, carefully, he began to stroke her inside and out, her breathing frantic now, her body clearly on the naked edge.

"It's okay to let yourself go, honey." He whispered reassurances to her, nibbled the skin of her throat, his heartbeat in sync with the wild pulse he felt beneath his lips, his hips moving of their own accord, rubbing his erection against her hip. "Let go, Kat!"

Then her breath broke, and she came with a shuddering sigh, arching off his bed, her inner muscles contracting tightly against his finger, a look of bliss on her beautiful face. He rode through it with her, kept the pressure and rhythm steady, trying to prolong her pleasure in every way he could, his mouth on her breasts, her throat, her lips, as the quaking inside her slowly subsided.

How long they lay there in the quiet Gabe couldn't say. He held her, unable to take his gaze from her, as her breathing slowly returned to normal, her body now limp, a sheen of sweat on her flushed skin. Then she opened her eyes and shyly met his gaze, the emotion he saw there causing a warm tug in his chest.

"Gabe." She ran her fingers over his lower lip, cupped his cheek, then drew him down, her lips meeting his in a soft kiss. "I . . . I don't know what I'm supposed to say."

He ran his thumb over her cheek, the warmth in his chest

growing until there was almost room for nothing else. "You don't have to say anything."

"Is . . . Is that what it's always like?"

He grinned, still stroking her cheek. "Yeah—except when it's even better."

She looked at him for a moment as if she didn't believe him, and he felt a fleeting surge of masculine pride. Then she smiled, a soft, sated smile, her eyes slowly closing. In a matter of moments, she was sound asleep.

IT WAS ONLY after Gabe had turned out the light, cocooned Kat in his arms, and drawn the covers over both of them that he realized he hadn't come. For the first time in three long years, he was sleeping with a woman, truly sleeping with a woman, and he hadn't even gotten inside her. But as he drifted off, it wasn't sexual frustration he was feeling, but contentment.

"WHERE THE FUCK have you been? I've been calling all night!"

"I've been busy."

"I thought we agreed there would be no more violence!"

"I thought we agreed that you'd get that bitch Katherine James off my ass! She was there sniffing around the trenches with Rossiter! What the fuck did you expect me to do?"

"I don't know! I don't know! But trying to kill a reporter and an armed ranger wouldn't have been at the top of my list!"

"I thought I could take them out and then bury the bodies on site."

"Well, you missed! It's over now, you know. You can't go back there. You're done. It's time to cover our tracks and wait for this whole thing to blow over."

"Do you really think it will blow over? When they discover what's buried there, certain plans of yours will go up in smoke. It will only be a matter of time before they put all the pieces together."

"I've covered my trail. There won't be any pieces for them to put together."

"What if you're wrong about that?"

"Then you'd best improve your aim—or choose a different weapon."

CHAPTER 14

KAT ROLLED OVER and snuggled deeper into the warm, soft bed, still floating on the edge of sleep. It was a scent that woke her, catching her attention, slowly rousing her. His scent. Salt, spice, man.

Gabe.

Her pulse skipped. She opened her eyes to find the big bed empty, a hollow in the pillow where his head had rested. She reached over, ran her hand over the pillowcase, and found it cold, his body heat long since having dissipated. The distant thrum of bass told her he was somewhere in the house, probably getting ready for work. But Kat wasn't ready to face real life—not yet.

She had slept with a man.

No, she hadn't had sex with him, but she had slept with him. It was so new to her, so different, that even in her sleep, she'd been aware of him beside her, his arms around her naked body, his long legs tangled with hers. At one point during the night when a bad dream had awoken her—she couldn't remember what it had been about, but it had terrified her—he'd been there, drawing her closer, holding her tight, whispering to her in a deep, sleepy voice.

Shhh, honey. It's okay. You're safe. I've got you.

And her fear had left her. She'd slept dreamlessly after that, feeling more secure than she'd perhaps ever felt.

She stretched beneath the warm blankets, feeling deliciously languid, the sheets soft against her bare skin. She let her thoughts drift, aware of her body, aware of every nerve, in a way she'd never been before, as if her memories from last night were imprinted not only in her mind but also on her skin, heart, and womb. She could recall every touch, every kiss, every stroke of his tongue and fingers, her body seeming to echo with sensation as she remembered.

The tug of his lips on her nipples.

Her breasts tingled, and her nipples tightened.

The shock of feeling his finger inside her.

Her inner muscles clenched.

The shattering bliss of orgasm.

Her belly fluttered.

She'd understood the mechanics of sex since she was a teenager—Tab A into Slot B, and nine months later out comes a baby. She'd learned the rudiments of reproduction in high school and had read sex books in college, trying to fill in the gaps and assuage her curiosity. She'd heard Holly and her other I-Team friends talk about their sex lives. She'd even looked at photos of naked men and women in various Tantric poses.

What she hadn't known—what no book and none of her friends had been able to tell her—was what an orgasm would do to her, how it would feel, how she would feel afterward.

Don't tell me you've never given yourself an orgasm.

Yes, she'd touched herself—more than a few times. But she hadn't been able to make herself climax, partly because she'd never taken more than a few minutes to experiment and partly because she hadn't been able to get away from the feeling that what she was doing was wrong. Her grandmother had been very traditional about such things, and although Kat tried to live as a modern woman, there were some parts of a person's upbringing that were harder to move beyond than others.

Of course, she'd had a difficult time trying to explain that to Gabe. She'd been afraid that a man of his experience would find it laughable. But he hadn't.

We'll just figure you out together.

The memory of his words brought another flutter to her belly. Nothing in her life could compare to what she'd experienced with Gabe last night. Even as new to physical intimacy as she was, Kat knew he'd gone out of his way to make sure he pleased her. His awareness had seemed focused completely on her, as if nothing had existed for him beyond her, as if his sole purpose in that moment had been bringing her pleasure.

Let me make you come. Then I'll stop. I promise.

What if I can't?

Are you kidding? As sensual and responsive as you are? Just relax, honey.

He'd made her feel like she was burning up, his touch both the cause of her torment and her only hope for relief. She'd fought to stay in control, some part of her genuinely afraid of what might happen if she didn't. But Gabe had taken control away from her, never giving her a moment to catch her breath.

Let go, Kat!

His words had set her free—and the fire inside her had exploded. Waves of shimmering ecstasy had washed through her until it seemed that her body was made of light—weightless, radiant.

He'd done all of that for her without taking anything for himself.

She had opened her eyes to find that she was still flesh and blood after all, Gabe looking down at her, an emotion in his eyes that she'd never seen before. If she hadn't already realized she was in love with him, that right there would have done it.

She was in love with Gabe. She loved Gabe Rossiter.

The thought left her feeling both euphoric and terrified. Falling in love with him was the last thing she'd expected. The two of them came from different worlds, different cultures, vastly different attitudes about love and sex.

Still, she knew he at least cared about her. The mark of a bullet on his chest was proof of that—as was her presence in his bed. She hadn't had sex with him, yet he'd slept beside her all night. That had to mean something, didn't it?

Kat wanted to believe it did, but she wasn't naive enough to think that her feelings for him could change his feelings for her.

Is that the mistake her mother had made? Had her mother felt so worn down by her loveless marriage that she'd fallen for some charming *Bilagáanaa* stranger—and then let herself believe that her love for him would make him love her? How sad.

The world Kat had been trying so hard to ignore came into sharp focus around her. She sat up, reached for the alarm clock on Gabe's nightstand, and turned it so that she could see the time. It was 7:15—later than she'd thought. She needed to take a shower, get dressed, and get to Denver by nine, or she'd miss the I-Team meeting.

Conscious of the fact that she was still naked, she got out of bed and gathered her clothes, which lay on the floor where Gabe had tossed them. She slipped on her panties, then grabbed the T-shirt of his that she'd worn last night, pleased to find that it still smelled like him. She closed her eyes, inhaled his scent and let herself imagine for a moment that he was still in bed with her, still holding her.

SUSPENDED FROM HIS hangboard by the tips of his chalked fingers, Gabe gutted it out, keeping his breathing slow and steady as he counted off the repetitions to the grinding beat of Metallica's "The Unforgiven II." He needed to drown out the sound of his own thoughts, to burn off his excess sexual energy. He had a date with his right hand later in the shower, but that wasn't going to be enough to get Kat out of his system.

Ninety-seven. Ninety-eight. Ninety-nine.

One-twenty-seven was his own personal best for fingertip pull-ups, and he wanted to break it today, if for no other reason than to drive her out of his mind. He didn't love her. Wouldn't love her. Couldn't love her.

One hundred six. One hundred seven. One hundred eight.

His forearms, shoulders, and lats burned, his muscles completely pumped, sweat dripping down his temples and chest. He ignored the pain, kept his gaze focused on the A-Basin poster on his wall. Steep slopes. Deep powder. Glades.

One hundred ten. One hundred eleven. One hundred twelve.

He'd warned himself not to get tangled up in her, but when

he'd woken up this morning he was about as tangled up as a man could get, his arms around her, her face nestled against his chest, her scent all over him. His cock had been rock hard and ready, apparently oblivious to the fact that it was still imprisoned in his jeans, which he'd had the good sense not to remove last night.

He'd watched her sleep, savoring the feel of her in his arms, relieved to see that her nightmares had gone, protectiveness mingling with some other emotion inside him. It was only after he'd realized what that emotion was that he'd begun to panic.

One hundred fifteen. One hundred sixteen. One hundred seventeen.

He hadn't held a woman like that for three years, hadn't slept with a woman or woken up with a woman since that last night with Jill. And the last time he'd made a woman come without getting off himself . . .

Well, that had never happened.

Until Kat.

One hundred twenty-four. One hundred twenty . . . five.

His entire body shaking with the effort, his breath coming in grunts, he forced out the last three pull-ups, then let go, stumbling when his feet hit the crash pad. Winded, he turned to reach for his water bottle—and felt like he'd been kicked in the gut.

Kat stood at the bottom of the stairs watching him, dressed in one of his old T-shirts, her long hair gloriously tangled. The shirt was much too big for her, but damned if she didn't look hot. The frayed bottom hung to a few inches below her scrumptious ass, leaving her legs beautifully bare, the worn cotton clinging softly to the swells of her breasts, revealing the points of her nipples.

Gabe needed that shower—now. If he didn't beat one out soon, he was going to embarrass himself. Somehow he managed to speak. "Morning."

"Morning." She smiled shyly, then looked away, her cheeks flushing pink.

Damned if that wasn't the most adorable thing he'd ever seen—a genuine case of post-orgasmic shyness.

Dude, look at you! You are so fucked!

Ignoring that observation, Gabe walked over to her, brushed a strand of hair from her cheek, unable to keep his hands off her. "Did you sleep well?"

She nodded. "Thanks. How about you?"

Her gaze dropped to his chest. She reached out and ran her fingertips through the sweat-damp hair on his chest, the contact making the muscles of his abdomen jerk.

His mouth went dry. "Yeah. Fine. Hungry?"

One touch, and you're reduced to monosyllables. Yeah, you're screwed.

She nodded, withdrew her hand, and met his gaze again, her cheeks burning even pinker. "I can just have toast or—"

"Just give me a few minutes to shower"—*and take care of business*—"and then I'll whip us up some omelets."

"I don't want to make you late for work."

"No worries." Gabe took a drink. "Last night, Webb wanted to know why you'd suddenly taken an interest in possible looting. When I told him the truth, he fired me."

"What?" The color drained from her face, her eyes wide with shock. "Oh, Gabe, no! I'm so sorry!"

"Don't be. I know you tried to protect me, but I couldn't let you lie for me, Kat."

"But what will you do for—"

He pressed a finger to her lips. "Don't worry about it. I've got lots of money in savings, and the house is paid off. You know what this means, don't you?"

She shook her head, her face still pale.

He grinned. "Since I don't have a job and don't really need one, you've got yourself a full-time bodyguard."

"THEY MUST BE CONNECTED." Kat flipped on her turn signal and turned off Speer onto Colfax on her way to the paper. "Can it just be coincidence that looting is going on at the butte at the same time the *inipi* is shut down and Grandpa Red Crow is killed?"

She and Gabe had already been to her place. Marc and Julian had met them there. The men had checked the condo inside and out before they'd let her enter, then they'd evaluated the condo for security weaknesses and had agreed that Gabe's home was by far the safer of the two. So she'd changed into fresh clothes—a dark blue broomstick skirt and ivory sweater—and packed a small suitcase. Then she and Gabe were off again, this time for the newspaper.

"It could be a coincidence, but I'd say that's pretty damned unlikely. I can't help but think Daniels is part of this somehow. He's the one who called the raid on the sweat lodge ceremony. He was the first cop to respond when Red Crow's body was found, and he was quick to reach the scene yesterday."

"You noticed that, too."

"Of course I did. I also noticed the bastard couldn't keep his eyes off you."

Kat glanced over at Gabe, touched by the aggressive edge in his voice—another sign that he cared about her. He sat in the passenger seat beside her, dressed in business casual—gray tweed sports jacket over a black turtleneck, jeans, and black leather shoes. His jaw was clean-shaven, his eyes concealed behind black sunglasses. But there was nothing casual about the gun he carried in a shoulder holster beneath his jacket.

A full-time bodyguard.

He hadn't been joking.

"When we get to the paper, you'll have to go through security. I'm not sure they'll let you bring your gun into the building." For some reason, the idea of bringing Gabe into the newsroom made her nervous.

"They'll probably make me check it. As long as they give it back again when we leave, I've got no objections."

"We usually have an I-Team meeting at nine. My boss, Tom Trent, can be a difficult man. He's a great journalist, but he's got a terrible temper and tends to intimidate people."

Gabe grinned. "Well, honey, he won't intimidate me."

"I'm afraid you're going to get really bored and—"

"Would you relax?" Gabe looked over at her, gave her thigh a squeeze. "I'm here to watch over you, not have you watch over me. I'll be okay."

Kat turned into the paper's main parking lot, parked the

truck, and waited while Gabe got out and walked around to the driver's side as they'd discussed. She waited for Gabe to open her door, then climbed out of the truck. Shielding her with his body, he looped an arm around her waist and hustled her to the paper's employee entrance, then opened the door for her and followed her inside.

She reached for her press card, which always hung around her neck when she was working, and held it up for Gil Cormac, the regular morning security guard. A former corrections officer, Gil had gotten a job at the paper thanks to Sophie, who'd felt sorry for him after his role in abetting Marc's escape from prison had gotten him fired. With a big beer belly and deep smile lines etched in his cheeks, he always brightened Kat's day.

"Good morning, Gil. This is Gabe Rossiter. He's—"

"I'm Ms. James's bodyguard." Gabe took out his driver's license and a small piece of paper, then opened his jacket to reveal his holstered gun. "I've got a permit for concealed carry."

Gil stood, a frown on his face, his gaze shifting from Gabe's driver's license and what must have been the concealed-carry permit to the weapon that lay against Gabe's side. "You'll have to check the firearm, sir."

Gabe drew the gun out of its holster and handed it, barrel pointed down, to Gil, who gave Gabe back his license and permit, took the gun, and bent down to lock it in some kind of safe behind the desk. "What's happened that you need a bodyguard, Ms. James?"

Kat was grateful when Gabe answered for her.

"She's gotten death threats related to one of her investigations. Yesterday afternoon someone fired several rounds at her with a high-powered rifle."

Gil stood upright with a jerk, his eyes wide, his gaze shifting to Kat. Then a look of gritty determination came over his face. "You're safe here, Ms. James. No one's going to get past me. Glad to have you watching over her, Mr. Rossiter."

"Thank you, Gil." Kat turned and took a few steps toward the elevator, but Gabe wasn't finished yet.

"Would you mind if I came back a bit later this morning to ask you some questions about the building security?"

"Not at all. I'd be happy to help, sir."

"Nice guy," Gabe said in a low voice as they walked away. "But I doubt he's fit enough to run a fifty-yard dash much less fight off an armed assailant."

Kat glanced back over her shoulder to see Gil still watching them, a worried look on his dear face.

CHAPTER 15

GABE HAD NEVER been in a newsroom before and had no idea what to expect. Taking up one entire floor of the six-story *Denver Independent* building, it looked like a maze, desks in clusters from wall to wall divided by shelves, filing cabinets, and periodic banks of televisions. He'd hate to be the techie whose job it was to keep these hundreds of computers plugged in, networked, and online.

"That's features over there—news features, entertainment, fashion, food," Kat said, pointing to divisions in the room that he couldn't discern. "Sports is in that corner. General assignment reporting is toward the middle near the copy desk. Opinion, obits, calendars are all toward the far wall, and the I-Team is up ahead."

"The I-Team are the rock stars of the paper, right?" Gabe had seen the advertisements and billboards.

Bringing you news that matters. The I-Team.

Her lips curved in a smile. "Don't let the opinion columnists hear you say that."

Still, it was clear to Gabe that the I-Team were the elite of the reporting staff. Their part of the newsroom was less crowded, with fewer desks and ample room for bookshelves and filing cabinets. Posters with quotes by Thomas Jefferson, Maya Angelou, and Martin Luther King Jr. hung in frames on one wall, while framed awards covered almost every square foot of another. He didn't have to look to know he'd find Kat's name on some of those.

He spotted her desk right away. A small dream catcher

adorned with four small turkey feathers hung in the window beside it. Aging bouquets of white flowers stood in vases toward the back. Manila folders sat in organized stacks off to one side, a framed photograph of an old Navajo woman standing in front of a hogaan on the other. The old woman's face was a mass of deep wrinkles, reminding Gabe of an old apple. She wore a blue headscarf, a green long-sleeved shirt and long black skirt, a traditional squash blossom necklace of silver and turquoise hanging around her neck.

Kat set her purse and briefcase down on the desk and turned on her computer. "That's my grandmother. She—"

"Kat! God, I'm glad you're safe!" Another I-Team member—a pretty woman with strawberry-blond hair—stood, hurried over to her, and gave Kat a fierce hug.

Kat hugged her back. "Thanks, Sophie."

"I heard about what happened. I'm so sorry!" Sophie looked up at Gabe, held out her hand, and gave him a warm smile. "You must be Gabe Rossiter, the rock jock. I'm Marc's wife, Sophie Alton-Hunter. Marc tells me you saved Kat's life. I'm so happy to meet you and to have the chance to thank you in person. I hear you were hit."

So this was the woman Marc Hunter had taken hostage at gunpoint—and then married. Gabe shook Sophie's hand. "It was just a graze, so—"

"Oh, Kat!" A woman with long dark hair and the features of a porcelain doll came up behind them, still wearing her coat, briefcase in hand, and gave Kat a quick kiss on the cheek. "I just about had heart failure when Tom told us someone had tried to shoot you. Bless your heart! Are you okay?"

The woman spoke with a southern accent of some kind. New Orleans?

Kat took the woman's hand, gave it a squeeze, the look in her eyes telling Gabe that she was deeply touched. "Thanks, Natalie. Yes, I'm fine—thanks to Gabe."

Natalie held out her hand. "Oh, the park ranger. Hi, Gabe. I'm Natalie Benoit. I work the cops and courts beat."

"There she is! *Mi chula!*" A young Latino with a camera

bag over his shoulder hurried down the hallway toward them. He dropped his bag on the desk and drew Kat into his arms in a way that instantly raised Gabe's hackles. Then the kid drew back, one hand lingering on Kat's shoulder. "Did they catch the bastards yet?"

"No." She put her hand on Gabe's arm. "Joaquin, this is Gabe Rossiter. I wouldn't be here this morning if not for him."

Joaquin stepped away from Kat and held out his hand to Gabe. "Thanks for watching her back. She means a lot to us."

Gabe found himself wondering exactly how much she meant to Joaquin. *Mi chula*, huh? He had an absurd impulse to put his arm around Kat's shoulders to mark his territory and warn the kid away.

You're a Neanderthal, Rossiter. You've got no claim on her.

Instead, Gabe shook the young man's hand. "I'm glad I was able to help."

He watched while Kat gave her friends the *Reader's Digest* version of what had happened yesterday at the butte, answering a dozen questions and reassuring her friends she was fine before everyone went back to their desks.

"You can sit here if you want." Kat motioned to a vacant workstation beside hers. "This is usually the intern's desk, but we don't have an intern at the moment. The computer is connected to the Internet if you need to check e-mail. Can I get you a cup of coffee or some water?"

"I'm fine for now. If there's a cafeteria here, I might head down while you're in your meeting and get some—"

"Hey, Harker, what's up, man?" Joaquin called. "You look like hell!"

Gabe followed Kat's gaze and saw a young man with reddish hair walking slowly down the hallway. Unshaven and sporting a serious case of bedhead, he looked like someone had just run over his dog.

Kat took a few steps in his direction. "Matt, what's wrong?"

The man—Matt—stopped and looked up at Sophie. "The city's finance director . . ."

"The man who embezzled city pension funds?" Kat prompted.

Matt nodded slowly, anguish on his face. "He committed suicide last night. In front of his wife and teenage kids. Blew his own head off."

There was a collective gasp.

"Oh, Matt!"

"Jesus!"

"Harker, you're late." A big bear of a man strode into the newsroom, a newspaper and notepad under his arm, a cup of coffee in his other hand. "Snap out of it. If a corrupt public official decides to be a coward and kills himself to avoid lawful prosecution, that's not your fault."

So this is Tom Trent.

He was almost Gabe's height but probably outweighed Gabe by a good sixty pounds. He exuded an air of a man who was used to being in charge and didn't put up with bullshit. He turned to Gabe. "Who the hell are you, and what are you doing in my newsroom?"

Kat stepped forward. "Tom, this is—"

"I'm Gabe Rossiter, the park ranger who saved Kat's life yesterday." Gabe didn't need her help dealing with this prick. He held out his hand. "I'm acting as her bodyguard until this is over."

Tom took his hand and shook it, measuring him through cool blue eyes. "Good to meet you. You can stay. The rest of you get to the conference room. We've got a newspaper to make. Not you, Harker. You go home, take a shower, and get yourself together. I want you in my office in an hour."

The I-Team members sent Matt looks of sympathy—and glared at Tom's back as he walked off down a side hallway.

Kat walked over to her desk and picked up a notepad and pencil. "Are you going to be okay here? This usually takes about an hour."

"I'll be fine." With Joaquin still in the room to see, Gabe gave in to his inner caveman, ducked down, and planted a light kiss on Kat's lips.

Her eyes went wide for a moment, pink spots blooming in her cheeks.

He watched her walk away, then sat and booted up the computer. He had a few things he wanted to research.

"WELL, THIS IS quite the conundrum." Tom tapped his pencil against his notepad, his gaze fixed on Kat's. "We're damned if we do and damned if we don't. If we report that there's looting of artifacts at Mesa Butte, we'll be letting every pot pincher in North America know that Mesa Butte is worth a visit. On the other hand, our readers have a right to know what is happening out there, including the truth—whatever it turns out to be—concerning Red Crow's death."

With those words, Tom summed up the dilemma that had been gnawing at the back of Kat's mind since breakfast. As a Native woman, she wanted to do all she could both to clear Grandpa Red Crow's name and to protect the artifacts at Mesa Butte. But now those two goals seemed to contradict one another. Should she protect Grandpa Red Crow's name and preserve all that he meant to Denver's Native people, or protect Mesa Butte and its heritage? What was more important—her duty to Grandpa Red Crow and the present or her duty to the land and the past? And what about her duty as an investigative journalist—a duty to tell the truth?

"Does it make any difference that they've closed the butte?" Natalie held up a press release. "The city of Boulder just announced that the place is now closed to the public and under round-the-clock surveillance."

Kat considered that for a moment. "What happens when this blows over and they quit watching the site? Anyone interested in looting Mesa Butte simply has to wait till the coast is clear."

"Maybe these bastards have stolen everything worth stealing," Joaquin offered.

Sophie shook her head. "I don't think they'd have tried to shoot Kat and Gabe if that were true. People don't kill to keep secrets that aren't worth keeping."

"That's right." Tom leaned back in his chair. "Clearly, someone didn't want James and the park ranger to see what they saw. But I'm not certain that our priority as the press is to conceal the existence of these artifacts so much as to expose the looting and the public officials who allowed it to happen."

For a moment, the conference room was silent.

It was Tom who spoke next. "James, what do you think we should do?"

Kat hesitated, choosing her words carefully. "I think our priority should be to find out exactly what's going on at Mesa Butte and to report it in a way that's culturally sensitive. That might mean being vague about what kind of artifacts are there, or it might mean reporting on the issue of looting in such a way that the public comes to see how damaging it is from the Native perspective."

Tom tapped his pencil a few more times, his brow drawn into a thoughtful frown, then pointed the eraser tip at Natalie. "Benoit, you cover the shooting. The *News* had a paragraph on it this morning, but nothing worth reading. Interview James and the park ranger and see what you can put together."

Syd, who'd sat silently this entire time, turned to Tom. "Will ten inches do?"

Tom nodded. "James, you stay on the main story. Get us something for the front page. I don't care what. Just keep the Mesa Butte story moving. We'll leave the cultural sensitivity to you. Let's get to work."

And the meeting was over.

Kat walked back to the newsroom with Natalie, the two of them working out a time for their interview and strategizing about how Kat could get the documents she'd requested from the city last week without waiting till after Thanksgiving.

"I read about a reporter who bought a portable copy machine, carried it with him to some government office, and started going through files and photocopying everything," Natalie told her. "As long as the documents are public, they can't stop you from walking in there and looking through them."

But Kat barely heard her. Ahead of them in the newsroom

she spotted Gabe standing by the intern desk, a cup of coffee in his hand, a smile on his face. He was deep in conversation with Holly, who leaned in, touched her hand against his arm, and said something that made him laugh.

Kat's step faltered, a strange, jagged emotion catching in her chest.

Beautiful Holly, with her blond hair, big brown eyes, and perfect body. Horny Holly, who went through men . . . the way Gabe went through women.

They were as alike as two kernels of corn from the same cob. And they were obviously enjoying one another's company.

"Don't let it get to you, Kat," Sophie whispered from behind her. "Holly knows better. Besides, the way that Gabe was watching you this morning, I'd say she wouldn't stand a chance anyway."

Kat felt strangely reassured by Sophie's words, as if what she were feeling were . . . jealousy?

At that moment, Gabe turned and caught sight of her, and his smile broadened.

"See?" Sophie whispered. "He's not interested in Holly."

But Kat wasn't so sure.

"I DON'T UNDERSTAND. If Grandpa Red Crow had been drinking in secret all these years, why was his liver not damaged?"

"Maybe he didn't drink that often." Gabe looked over at Kat and saw that her knuckles were white, her hands wrapped tightly around the steering wheel. "Are you sure you don't want me to drive?"

They'd done their interviews with Natalie and were on their way back into Boulder, where Kat hoped to use the new portable copier she had just talked her boss into buying to photocopy all documents in the city's Mesa Butte files. Gabe thought it was a bad plan, one that was more likely to get her arrested than get her the documents she wanted, but she was determined.

She tossed him an angry look. "I'm fine."

He didn't know whether he should call her on her lie or not. She hadn't been fine all morning. Ever since she'd come out of the I-Team meeting she'd seemed upset. He couldn't shake the feeling that she was irritated with him, though he couldn't figure out why. For once, he couldn't think of anything he might have done to piss her off—unless she'd checked the intern computer and had seen what he'd been up to this morning.

While she'd been in the meeting, he'd called Hunter and arranged to meet with him and Darcangelo for lunch. Then he'd gone back down to speak with Cormac, the security guard, and had worked with him to arrange special parking for Kat in the secured underground parking garage so that he wouldn't have to worry about some asshole firing at her while she walked from her truck to the building. When that was done, he'd come back upstairs and had spent the next thirty minutes reading about Navajo traditions—Navajo sexual traditions, specifically.

What he'd read online had proved to him that Kat was very much a modern Navajo, caught between her people's mores and the very different beliefs of the world around her. It had also made him realize how he must look through her eyes.

Can you say "man slut," Rossiter? Sure you can.

Traditional Navajo culture held that sex was for making babies and that masturbation was evil, beliefs reinforced by Navajo creation stories. From what Gabe had read, solo sex was a forbidden topic, something people simply didn't discuss, lumped in with sodomy, homosexuality, pedophilia, and rape. Exposing one's genitals, even to one's husband or wife, was still considered shameful by some, sex something to be done at night in the dark in silence. And until recently, oral sex had been illegal on the rez. Taken together, he could see why Kat was still a virgin—and why she'd looked so shocked when he'd asked her to show him how she brought herself to orgasm.

It's a wonder she didn't smack your face, buddy.

But she looked like she wanted to hit something now, a

kind of angry expression on her face he'd never seen before. This was about Grandpa Red Crow's autopsy report. It had to be. He'd seen her looking through the report again this morning while Natalie was interviewing him and had later glanced at it himself. The old man's blood-alcohol content had come back just under the limit for drunk driving.

"I just think that the coroner would have found something—some sign that he was an alcoholic." She was obviously still in denial.

"I know how upset you must be." He knew better than most what it was like to feel betrayed. "It isn't easy being let down by someone you loved and trusted."

She stiffened. "So he fell off the wagon and then somehow managed to fall off the cliff, is that it?"

"I don't know. I think it's very possible that foul play—"

"It's possible?" She shot him a scathing glance.

And once again Gabe got the distinct impression she was pissed at him. He drew a deep breath and took the plunge. "Are you upset with me about something?"

"Upset with you? Why would I be upset with you?" she asked in that female tone of voice that said, "Of course, I'm upset with you, and if you don't know why, then you're just a stupid man!"

So that's a universal female thing.

Gabe found it strangely reassuring to know that Navajo men had to put up with it, too. He waited a moment, not sure whether to press the issue or just let it drop.

"I saw you talking to Holly earlier," Kat said after a moment. "It looked like you two get along well."

Holly was the sexy blonde who'd walked up to him, looked him up and down, and then started flirting with him. And then Gabe understood. As hard as it was for him to comprehend, he knew it was true. "You're jealous."

He'd expected Kat to deny it or grow enraged with him. Instead, she seemed to crumple, her shoulders slumping, the anger on her face dissolving into a look of misery. "I'm sorry. I'm acting like a mole. I have no claim on you, no right to feel upset if—"

"Acting like a . . . a what?" He wasn't keeping up here.

"A . . . a mole—being cross to you, being angry." She drew a breath and went on. "Holly's a beautiful woman. All men want her. I know that. I have no right—"

"You mean a shrew." Gabe bit his lip to keep from laughing. He forgot sometimes that English wasn't Kat's first language.

She looked over at him, clearly confused. "Shrew? Are you sure?"

He nodded, fighting to keep a straight face. "Yeah."

"Well, either way, I'm sorry. I saw you taking with Holly, and I just . . . I care about you more than you want me to care, Gabe Rossiter."

The sincerity of her words struck him in the chest, the truth they'd both been avoiding laid bare before them. But, surprisingly, it wasn't a cynical rebuke that came to Gabe's mind. Instead, he found himself feeling like an ass. Here she was, miserable and vulnerable, telling him how she felt with no pretence, making no demands and no excuses, and until this moment, he'd been amused by the whole thing.

"Pull over." Gabe pointed to the shoulder of the highway.

She glanced at him in surprise. "What? But—"

"Pull over." He couldn't let her go on feeling like this. "Just do it."

She flipped on her turn signal. "Okay, but you can't walk here. The highway is closed to pedestrians, and it's—"

"I'm not getting out."

She drew over to the shoulder, braked, and put the truck in park. Then she turned toward him. "What—"

Gabe slipped his hand behind her head, leaned over and took her mouth with his in a deep kiss, his tongue dominating hers, caressing, coaxing, until his lips ached, until he'd tasted her mouth in every way he could, until they were both breathless. Then, pulse roaring in his ears, he drew back, tucked a finger beneath her chin, and forced her to meet his gaze, her pupils dilated, her lips swollen and wet.

"You're right, Kat—you've got no claim on me. I've made

no promises, and we both know I never will. But you've got no reason to feel jealous of Holly. I'm sure there are lots of men who'd do or say anything to get inside her, but I'm not one of them. I don't want her. I want you."

Then, unable to help himself, he kissed her again.

CHAPTER 16

ACTING WITH A calm she did not feel, Kat stuck another document in the little copier and pressed the button. A flash of light, a whirring sound—and another copy emerged. Gabe took it, tucked both it and the original into their respective folders, while Kat stuck another page in the machine and pressed the button again.

It was an efficient system, but Kat wished they could go faster. In the office next door, Mr. Feinman was having a heated discussion via cell phone with his boss, Paul Martin, the city manager. Though she couldn't hear what he was saying, she knew that if he had his way, he'd shut down their little operation, confiscate the copies they'd made, and have them escorted from the building by security. It had made him angry enough when he'd seen Kat with the Mesa Butte files in her hands. But when he'd seen Gabe and the copy machine, he'd come unglued.

"You!" he'd shouted, pointing a finger at Gabe. "You shouldn't be here! Your employment with the city has been terminated! I might not be able to throw her out of the building, but I can have you arrested!"

Kat had been about to explain that Gabe has as much right as any other citizen to look at public records, but Gabe had cut her off.

"Relax, lawyer man," he'd said, the gleam in his eyes telling Kat that he was enjoying himself. "I'm here on behalf of the newspaper, too. As you may have heard, someone tried to kill Ms. James yesterday. Since I no longer work for the city, I accepted a position as her bodyguard."

He'd appointed himself her "bodyguard," of course, but Kat had let that little misstatement slide.

A troubled expression had passed over Feinman's face, his gaze dropping to the floor. "I did hear about that. Regrettable." Then he'd looked at Gabe, obviously still angry. "As for your being her bodyguard, you've been helping her all along, haven't you? Mr. Martin will not tolerate this."

Then Mr. Feinman had stormed into the office and slammed the door behind him.

Kat hadn't bothered to tell him that the receptionist had already called Mr. Martin, and Mr. Martin, having a cooler head than his staff, had told the receptionist to help Kat and Gabe in any way she could. Of course, there was always a chance that Mr. Feinman would change Mr. Martin's mind.

Feeling a keen sense of urgency, Kat took out the next document and discovered that it was a folded map and much too big for the copier.

"Do it in sections." Gabe took the map to show her what he meant.

Kat pressed the copy button, then leaned forward and lowered her voice to a whisper. "If he comes out and tells us we have to stop, take the documents we've copied and go back to my truck."

"You're not walking out of this building alone." He leveled her a look that brooked no argument.

"Just put the documents in my truck, and then you can come back for me." She flipped the map over, pushed the button.

"If you promise me to stay inside and away from the front door."

"I promise."

The door opened and Feinman emerged, his face mottled but his expression calm. "Mr. Martin tells me he has no objection to this, so you're free to continue."

"I think we already know that," Gabe said with a grin, taking another copy from the machine. Then he repeated almost word for word what Kat had told the receptionist. "Whether he objects or not, Mr. Feinman, what we're doing is permitted under the Colorado Open Records Act. Check the statute yourself if you have any doubts."

"I am familiar with the statute," Feinman ground out from behind a tight smile.

"Good. Then I guess that means you'll drop the threats and get busy doing whatever it is the city pays lawyers to do."

Both shocked and amused at Gabe's rudeness, Kat looked up—and caught an expression of utter loathing on Feinman's face just before he turned and walked away.

"You didn't have to say that last part, you know," she said later as they headed back to Denver, a fat folder of documents on the seat between them.

Gabe grinned. "I know. I was just having fun."

GABE SAW KAT safely back to the paper, turning his firearm over to Cormac, who clearly viewed his job—and himself— with a renewed sense of importance.

"Nothing out of the ordinary to report, sir," the security guard said gravely.

"Thanks, Cormac. I'm glad you're on our side." Gabe gave Cormac a solemn nod—but didn't miss the tiny smile that played on Kat's lips at this exchange.

When they got to the elevator, Gabe stopped, his mind made up. "Are you going to be here a while?"

Kat nodded. "I've got an article to write by deadline at four, and then I have to organize these files. I won't be going anywhere."

"Do you mind if I borrow your truck? I have some things I need to do."

"Sure." She fished her keys out of her pocket and handed them to him.

He touched a finger to the tip of her nose. "Just promise you won't leave the building for anything. If something comes up, call me."

"I promise."

"Good." He ducked down, pressed a kiss to her forehead. "I'll be back by midafternoon at the latest."

Twenty minutes later, he walked through the front door of the local community clinic and up to the reception desk, where a young woman with short red braids sat chewing gum and typing into a computer. A goldfish bowl filled with condoms in colorful wrappers sat on the counter, while a poster on the wall behind her blared, "Do you know your HIV status?"

Gabe didn't, and that's why he was here.

The woman looked up and smiled. "Can I help you?"

"I'm here for the walk-in testing." For someone who'd fucked as freely as he had for the past three years, Gabe felt strangely embarrassed. He didn't want to do this, but for Kat's sake he would. If there was any chance that he might end up having sex with her, he wanted to know for certain that he wouldn't hurt her.

The young woman handed him a pen and a medical history form. "If you could grab a clipboard, fill out this form, and sign the back, we'll get you signed in. Which test do you want—HIV, hepatitis, syphilis, HPV, chlamydia or—"

"All of them."

"MAYBE IF I had gone to him privately and shown him the evidence I had and given him the chance to come clean . . ." Matt didn't finish the sentence, but left the thought hanging, his lunch of Chinese takeout seemingly forgotten.

"It's not your fault, Matt." Kat sprinkled a packet of soy sauce over her rice. "Tom could have been more tactful—"

"When is that not the case?" Tessa interjected.

"—but what he said is the truth. This man stole from his coworkers, and when he got caught, he stole from his wife and children by ending his own life and depriving them of a husband and father."

It was a rare occasion when the I-Team, past and present, came together. Usually, it meant that something terrible had happened. The last time they'd all been together in the same room, Sophie had been taken hostage by a convicted murderer—Marc—and was missing in the mountains. This time, Kat had narrowly escaped being shot, and the man Matt had exposed for embezzlement had killed himself. Knowing Kat couldn't go out to lunch, Kara and Tessa had brought lunch to the office, each carrying a box loaded with takeout containers into the conference room. Now a buffet of egg rolls, sesame chicken, kung pao beef, moo shoo pork, fried rice, and steamed vegetables, together with soy sauce, rice, and fortune cookies, was spread out across the large conference table, the mingled scents making Kat's mouth water.

Across the table, Kara dipped an egg roll in mustard sauce. "Kat's right. You've got to quit blaming yourself, Matt."

Matt slid his fingers through his hair, his face screwing up in a look of anguish. "I wanted to grab a headline, to break big news, and I ruined his life—and the lives of his wife and kids."

"No!" A chorus of denials filled the room.

"You didn't ruin his life." Kat picked up her fork. "He did that himself."

Natalie reached over and laid a hand on Matt's arm. "He made his own choices, Matt. He chose to steal and to keep stealing. Then he chose to shoot himself—in front of his family, no less. You didn't choose any of that for him."

Sophie nodded, dabbing her lips with a paper napkin. "You did exactly what you're supposed to do—your job."

"I once panned a local songwriter's album." Holly poked at her steamed veggies, not a single grain of rice on her plate. "It was his second album, and it wasn't nearly as good as the first. He died of a drug overdose the night after my article ran. I always felt bad about that. But I didn't sell him drugs. I didn't stick the needle in his vein. Sometimes what we do hurts people's feelings or gets them into trouble, but that's not our fault. They're to blame for how they react, not us."

It was the most profound thing Kat had ever heard Holly say.

Matt drew a deep breath and seemed to consider this. "Thanks, everyone. What would I do without you?"

"You'd drink a lot more," Tessa quipped, making everyone laugh.

Then Kara looked over at Kat. "So, Kat, I want to hear everything about—"

"Oh, God, he's so hot!" Holly interrupted, a bright smile on her face.

Kara glared at her and went on. "—the shooting at Mesa Butte and this story you're working on. And if you want to toss in any details about this super-sexy ranger who saved your life, I won't stop you."

Kat couldn't help but smile.

ON HIS WAY back from the clinic, Gabe grabbed a quick burger with Hunter and Darcangelo, the three of them trying to come up with a game plan to find the bastard who'd threatened Kat and tried to kill her. They agreed to focus on two objectives: tracking down the source of the death threats and learning everything they could about the illegal trade in Native artifacts. Gabe and Hunter would focus on the former, while Darcangelo, with his federal contacts, would tackle the latter.

With that sorted out, Gabe drove back to the paper and made his way toward the newsroom, stopping in the men's restroom to take a leak and remove the little bandage the lab tech had taped over his vein when he'd finished drawing Gabe's blood. He didn't want Kat to see it. He planned on having the STD conversation with her before they had sex—if they had sex—but he didn't want to have that conversation here.

He'd gone in confident that he was fine. After all, he didn't have any symptoms. Then the public-health nurse had come in to discuss his sexual history and his risk factors, and his confidence had begun to fray.

"The most common symptom for someone infected with an STD is no symptoms at all," she'd said. "But you say you've always used condoms, so that's good."

He'd been deeply relieved when the results had come back negative. He'd saved the paperwork so he could prove to Kat that he was safe. He didn't want her to have to take his word for it.

He found her at her desk, typing furiously on her article, a frown of intense concentration on her face. She glanced up at him, started to rise from her chair.

"Just keep doing what you're doing. Never mind me." He sat at the intern desk and logged into his e-mail to see whether Hunter had sent him the information he needed yet. Finding nothing but Viagra spam—the last thing he needed was another damned erection—he began to surf his favorite climbing websites. But he couldn't seem to concentrate, his gaze drawn back to Kat again and again until he finally gave up and let his eyes do what they wanted to do.

She typed without looking at her fingers, glancing down at her notes from time to time, typing, deleting, then typing again. If he told her that watching her work turned him on, she'd probably just think he was coming on to her. But watching her work *did* turn him on—the way she nibbled lightly on her lower lip, the way she tilted her head slightly to the side, exposing her throat, the way she absentmindedly tucked her hair behind her ear, only to have it slide free again and brush against her cheek. He found himself watching the clock, impatient to get her home so that he could take up where he'd left off in the truck on the side of the road this morning.

"Oh, this is so frustrating!" She leaned back in her chair and stretched, then looked over at him and stood. "I think I need to clear my head a bit and get a cup of coffee. Do you want to come with me?"

"Sure." He stood. "I could use a cup of coffee, too."

Like hell you could, Rossiter. What you need is a cold shower.

KAT WALKED TOWARD the elevator, trying to shake loose her tangled thoughts, only too aware of Gabe beside her. Last night, he'd undressed her, held her, touched her in ways and in places that no man ever had, made her feel things—

Don't think about that now, Kat.

No, she couldn't think about that now, or she'd never get this story written. "I feel bad knowing you're spending the whole day here for my sake when you probably have important things to do. Are you bored out of your mind yet?"

"Stop worrying about me." His lips curved in a smile that

made her pulse trip. "Tell me what's got you tied up. Maybe it will help if you think out loud."

She reached out to push the Down button for the elevator, but his arm was much longer, and he beat her to it. "I just don't know how to handle the looting aspect of the story. If I say too much, it would be disrespectful to the Old Ones who lived at Mesa Butte. If I say too little, I won't be doing my job as a journalist."

"I can definitely see the conflict there."

And Kat knew he understood. "I thought I could write a nut graph—"

"A 'nut graph'?" He sounded amused by the term.

"That's kind of a summary paragraph at the beginning of an article," she explained. "I can state that Mesa Butte is the site of a continuing land dispute between the city of Boulder and local Native people, who consider it sacred and use it for ceremonies. Then I can give the history of that dispute—the *inipi* raid, Grandpa Red Crow's death, the protest—and end the paragraph with something about discovering evidence that someone has been digging in search of artifacts."

"You'll want to say that it's under surveillance."

Kat nodded. "I'll also want to try to make people understand why looting is wrong. But if I don't confirm that artifacts have been found and stolen, maybe people will think someone is just digging around, hoping to find something."

The elevator doors opened with a ding.

Kat stepped inside, Gabe behind her, his hand on the small of her back, sending currents of awareness skittering along her spine. She pressed G for "ground floor" then turned toward Gabe as the doors slid shut. "I don't know what Tom—"

"Oh, to hell with Tom!" With a groan, Gabe pinned her up against the elevator wall with his body and kissed her hard and deep, one hand clenched in her hair, tilting her head upward, the other grasping her hip.

In a blink, Kat forgot that she was at work. On deadline. In an elevator. She forgot about the shooting. She forgot everything but him and what he was doing to her, his tongue seeking and subduing hers, his lips so hot and smooth against hers, his body pressed hard against hers.

He broke the kiss, traced the line of her jaw with his lips from her mouth to her ear, nudged her with his hips, giving away his erection. "See what you do to me, Kat?"

Before she could take in this rush of sensation, he drew up her skirt, forced her knees apart with one of his, and reached between her thighs to cup her through her tights and panties, pressing against her in slow circles. Her knees went weak. She knew where that touch could lead, what would happen if he kept touching her just . . . like . . . that.

"Oh!" She pushed against the pressure, liquid heat spreading through her belly. And when he flicked the aching nub of her clitoris, she moaned, the sound reverberating in the tiny space.

She heard a ding, felt the world move beneath her feet. It took her mind a moment to register that the ding was the elevator arriving on the ground floor and that the motion was the car coming to a halt.

Gabe drew back with a frustrated growl, his gaze burning into hers for the briefest moment, before he turned his back to her, shielding her as the doors slid open. Out of breath, her pulse still pounding, Kat struggled to compose herself, making sure her skirt was in place before following Gabe into the lobby and toward the cafeteria.

CHAPTER 17

GABE WOULD HAVE liked another quick and dirty make-out session in the elevator on the ride back upstairs, but he and Kat weren't alone this time. Some guy in a suit—probably a member of the ad sales team—stepped on just before the doors closed, briefcase in one hand, cell phone pressed against his ear with the other.

"I tried to close him on a fifty-two-week contract with four-color, but he wants thirteen weeks at the same discounted rate." He kept talking even after the doors had closed, sparing neither of them a glance.

That was fine with Gabe.

Holding his coffee in his right hand, he moved closer to Kat, close enough to feel the warmth of her body against his. Then he slipped his left hand behind her back and ran his fingers slowly up and down her spine. She tensed beneath his touch, gave a gratifying little gasp, a blush rising to her cheeks.

"What time do you usually head home?" He kept his voice casual.

She struggled to do the same. "I . . . I usually leave close to five. I thought you said you weren't bored."

"Oh, honey, I'm not bored." Frustrated. Blue-balled. But not bored. He leaned down and lowered his voice to a whisper. "I'm just looking forward to getting you someplace more . . . private."

He heard her breath catch and knew his words had hit their mark.

The elevator stopped. The doors slid open. And they were back in the newsroom.

Kat returned to her writing, while Gabe went back to surfing climbing websites. He was skimming an interview with Dean Potter and Steph Davis when his cell phone rang. He saw Hunter's number on his caller ID. "Rossiter here."

"Hey, it's Marc. I thought I'd let you know that we've hit a dead end on the pay phone angle. None of the calls were made from a phone that was near city surveillance cameras."

"Damn." Gabe had hoped they'd be able to catch the caller in action by matching the date and times on city surveillance tapes with the times of the calls. "Do you still have the addresses?"

"Yeah. I'll e-mail them to you. Darcangelo is meeting with his FBI buddy tonight, so we'll see what he turns up on the looting end." Hunter paused for a moment. "How's she holding up?"

Gabe glanced over at Kat, who seemed entirely focused on writing her article. "All things considered, she's doing amazingly well. I got her a permit for the secured underground parking garage, so we don't have to worry about anyone sighting on her while she's entering or leaving the building."

"Good idea." Hunter sounded surprised that Gabe had thought of it. "Have you ever considered ditching bunnies and deer and becoming a real cop?"

"Hunter, fuck you."

Hunter chuckled. "Sorry, Rossiter, I don't swing that way."

KAT READ THROUGH the completed draft of her article and was surprised that any of it made sense. She'd had a hard enough time staying focused as it was with Gabe in the newsroom. But after what he'd done in the elevator, pinning her against the wall, kissing her until she'd felt like she was going to melt, touching her so intimately, she'd found it all but impossible to keep her mind on her work.

Oh, the man knew how to kiss! Her body still felt aroused, her lips tingling, an ache between her thighs where he'd touched her. No matter how she sat or how hard she tried not to think about it, she couldn't escape the feeling.

You're drifting again, Kat.

She forced her mind back on the article, rereading the paragraph that had taken her so long to craft.

In the latest development, the Denver Independent *found evidence that someone has been illegally digging for artifacts on Mesa Butte, including trenches that appeared to have been dug with heavy machinery. This raises troubling questions about recent events at Mesa Butte, including the recent death of George Red Crow, a Hunkpapa Lakota elder and spiritual leader.*

Whoever was behind the looting—and yesterday's shooting—would read between the lines and know that Kat suspected him of killing Grandpa Red Crow. It was a small step toward justice, but it gave Kat a sense of satisfaction all the same.

She had just sent her story off to the copy editors, when Sophie appeared carrying the day's mail. "I grabbed yours, too, because your box was overflowing."

"Thanks." Kat took a stack of envelopes from Sophie and set them down on her desk, glancing over at Gabe. Despite his denials, she knew he must be bored. He was used to spending the day in the mountains, after all, not sitting in front of a computer. Still, he seemed to be occupied, studying what appeared to be a Boulder street map.

I'm just looking forward to getting you someplace more . . . private.

Kat felt that familiar fluttering sensation in her belly. Would he want to have sex with her tonight? Would she stop him if he did?

She didn't know.

She forced her mind back to her stack of mail and began opening envelopes. Most were press releases from Denver-area environmental businesses trying to get her attention—green builders, a community-supported organic farm, a biodiesel collective. But there were other things, as well. A state health department notice of violation against a pharmaceutical plant. New recycling guidelines for the city's single-stream recycling program. A letter from a citizens group concerned about the impact of Denver's brown cloud on air quality in the mountains.

Then she came across a small padded envelope with no return address. She could feel something round and hard inside, and, assuming it was just another product sample or some kind of promotional swag, she opened it. A light brown something fell into her palm. She held it up, turned it over. It wasn't much bigger around than a pencil and was wider on both ends than it was in the middle, giving it a bonelike shape . . .

The breath left her lungs in a rush, her blood turning to ice, her pulse thrumming in her ears. It was a bone. A human bone?

Yee nadlooshii.

The horrifying words—words that no traditional Diné would willingly speak—forced their way into her mind, leaving her dizzy, sick, shaking.

Skinwalker.

Even as she told herself that skinwalkers didn't exist, that they were nothing more than a superstition, that a bit of old bone couldn't hurt her, she felt a chill of foreboding settle in her stomach.

GABE HAD JUST written down the cross streets near the second of five pay phones in downtown Boulder when he heard Kat gasp. It took only a glimpse of her bloodless face and wide, terrified eyes to get him on his feet. "Kat? What is it?"

She held out a hand as if to keep him from coming any closer, even as her legs gave and she sank to her knees, her gaze still fixed on whatever it was that lay on her open palm, her breathing erratic.

"Kat, talk to me. What's wrong?" He knelt beside her, wrapped an arm around her waist to steady her, and leaned forward, trying to get a better look at whatever she was holding. It looked like a . . . bone.

A human bone. The distal phalanx of a human finger, to be specific.

He drew her tighter against him and reached for a piece of paper, which he folded like a taco shell in his hand. "Drop it in here, Kat. Drop it in here. It's evidence."

Slowly, Kat tilted her hand, the small bone rolling off her palm and onto the paper. "D-don't . . . Don't touch it!"

"I won't. I don't want to get my prints on it." He set the piece of paper with its grisly burden on her desk.

The rest of the I-Team had noticed something was wrong and gathered on the other side of Kat's desk, whispering in hushed tones.

Matt leaned in for a better look. "What is it?"

"It looks like some kind of bone," Natalie answered.

Gabe kept his voice calm, only too aware of Kat's trembling and her fast, irregular breathing. "Sophie, call your husband or Darcangelo. Ask them to send over a couple of detectives. Is there a break room or a staff lounge anywhere?"

Tom's voice came from behind. "Bring her to the executive conference room. It's got a sofa she can lie down on. Alton, get Chief Irving on the line while you're at it. This bullshit has gone far enough. I don't want another member of my staff getting hurt."

Rage building in his chest, Gabe drew Kat to her feet. Limp as a rag doll, she leaned against him, her face still deathly pale. "Let's get you to the conference room so you can rest for a minute."

Kat walked, took a few steps, letting him guide her, then she froze and looked down at her hand. "I need to wash my hands. I need to wash—"

"Okay. I'll take you to the women's room first."

Natalie appeared beside them. "I'll come with you."

Kat drew back from them. "You shouldn't touch me. Neither of you should touch me."

"Don't be ridiculous!" The words came out harsher than Gabe had intended. He tried again. "I'm not letting go of you. I don't want you to faint and hurt yourself."

Natalie linked her arm through Kat's. "In case you've forgotten, I'm from New Orleans, voodoo capital of the United States. It's going to take something more macabre than one little old bone to scare me."

Gabe met Natalie's gaze, grateful for her help. He wondered what it was about the bone that terrified Kat so much. He knew lots of cultures had taboos about death and dead bodies. Was it something like that, or did these things hold some darker meaning for her? And not for the first time, he found himself wanting desperately to comfort her and not knowing what to say or do.

"THE BONE LOOKS human to me and very old, but I'm no expert. We'll get these to the lab and see what the forensics team has to say."

Feeling tainted and unclean despite five minutes of hand washing in hot water, Kat watched as Julian, still wearing gloves, held up the plastic evidence bag in which he'd placed the bone, examined it under the fluorescent lights, then passed the bag to Police Chief Irving, an older man with a bristly white crew cut and big belly. She wished neither of them had touched it, though she supposed their gloves and plastic bag gave them a measure of protection.

It can't hurt them. It can't hurt anyone. You have a college degree, Kat! Stop being superstitious, for goodness sake!

That was easier said than done. Until she'd realized what she was holding, Kat hadn't known exactly how much of a grip the old stories had on her. If someone had asked her yesterday whether she believed in skinwalkers, she probably would have laughed. But one piece of bone was all it had taken to prove that she didn't know herself as well as she'd thought she did.

No sooner had Natalie and Gabe gotten her to the women's room than her stomach had revolted. She'd spent the next ten minutes in a bathroom stall throwing up while Natalie offered her reassurance from the other side of the door. When her stomach was finally empty, she'd felt weak and shaky, but the worst edge of her fear was gone. She'd scrubbed her hands until they were red, unable to wash away the unclean feeling.

When at last she'd left the women's room, she'd found Gabe standing just outside the door, a worried look on his face. He'd held out a disposable coffee cup. "Chamomile tea. It will help calm your stomach."

And it had.

But now, seeing the bone again—incontrovertible proof that someone wanted her to die—she found herself once more growing queasy, her hand seeming to burn where she'd held it.

Frowning with concentration, Chief Irving looked at the bone, then set it down on the polished conference room table. He met Kat's gaze, his eyes filled with the weariness and compassion of a man who'd seen too much. "I can see how getting a bone in the mail could be frightening, but I think this means something different to you that it does to us. Can you help us understand?"

Feeling both embarrassed and afraid, Kat glanced around the table from Chief Irving to Julian, who sat across from her, to Tom, who sat at the head of the table, to Gabe, who sat beside her. "It's . . . It's not something we talk about." Her body gave an involuntary shiver. She folded her hands tightly together in her lap, trying to keep them from shaking.

"Take your time," Gabe said, resting a hand reassuringly over hers.

"No Navajo person would willingly touch anything dead. It's one of our strongest taboos. Bones, bodies, even the bodies of animals—they're unclean." She searched for the right English words. "Traditional Navajo believe that there are . . . that there are those who walk among us . . . witches disguised in the skins of humans or animals. They might take strands of your hair while you sleep and work evil on them. Or they might take an arrow, a bead, or a piece of . . . of bone . . . and shoot it into you. We call them . . . skinwalkers."

She could barely say the last word, her heart thudding. "You grow sick or go mad and then die. The only way to cure the sickness is to . . . find and kill the witch."

Find and kill the witch.

That sounded good to Gabe. If he ever got his hands on the son of bitch behind all of this, he'd be only too happy to pull the trigger. He'd seen Kat gravely injured and in pain. He'd seen her devastated by grief. He'd seen her afraid for her life. But he'd never seen her like this—shaken to her very core.

Irving picked up the plastic bag and examined the contents

again. "By sending this to you, they're trying to cast some kind of spell on you?"

"Or trying to tell me that I'm cursed, that I'm already as good as . . . dead." Her voice dropped to a near whisper. "It's hard to explain."

Tom, who'd been silent and busy taking notes, looked over at Kat. "Are skinwalkers common to all American Indian cultures?"

Kat shook her head, her gaze fixed on her hands. "Only Diné. Only Navajo."

"So whoever sent this knows you're Navajo and knows it would upset you." Irving shifted his gaze from Kat to Tom and then to Darcangelo. "It seems to me we ought to consider the possibility that the person behind these death threats and yesterday's shooting is American Indian—someone who knows Ms. James and is familiar with Navajo beliefs."

Gabe could see from the troubled expression on Kat's face that the idea was upsetting to her. "Not necessarily. With the Internet, anyone could find out about skinwalkers."

Or Navajo sexual mores, right, Rossiter?

"Good point." Irving nodded. "Still, it's something we ought to consider. Ms. James, is there anyone who comes to mind who might have done this, anyone in the American Indian community?"

"No, not in the Indian community." She shook her head. "I don't know any Navajo in Denver, and everyone I do know loved Grandpa Red Crow, too. They've been praying for me, hoping I'll get to the bottom of this."

"What about non-Indians?"

Kat's gaze met Gabe's as if seeking his guidance. "I . . . I don't have any proof, but Officer Daniels, the officer who pulled my hair, made the decision to raid the *inipi*. He was the first officer to respond when we found Grandpa Red Crow, and he was one of the first officers to respond to the shooting yesterday. Every time I looked his way, he was . . . watching me."

"I can corroborate that." Gabe then filled Irving in on everything he knew about Daniels, including the complaints he and Kat had filed against him for excessive use of force and Feinman's apparent attempt to get Gabe to withdraw his complaint. "It was clear to me they were trying to cover for him."

Irving seemed to consider this, then he turned back to Darcangelo. "What have you and Hunter learned from the Boulder boys?"

Darcangelo shrugged. "The Boulder PD is being territorial. We had one hell of a time getting the locations of the city's surveillance cameras, and we still don't have the report from yesterday's shooting. So far, we've been polite, but . . ."

"Really? You? Polite? That's a first." Irving raised an eyebrow. But Gabe wasn't fooled. He could feel the affection between the two men. "You have my permission to be yourself. This has spilled over into our jurisdiction now, and that means I want everything they've got going all the way back to the raid on the sweat lodge."

Darcangelo grinned. "Yes, sir."

"In the meantime, we need to keep you safe, Ms. James. Where are you currently staying?"

"I'm staying at Gabe's house in Boulder, and he's acting as my . . . bodyguard."

"Are you satisfied with that arrangement?"

Kat nodded. "Yes."

"Mr. Rossiter, do you think you're up to it?"

"Yes, sir." Gabe filled the chief in on his experience and tactical training, feeling oddly like he was in a job interview.

He was grateful when Darcangelo vouched for him. "I worked with him when we were chasing Hunter. Rossiter here is rock solid."

They spent the next several minutes debating whether Kat was safe enough at his place or whether she ought to be set up in a police safe house under twenty-four-hour DPD surveillance or secreted in a hotel. In the end, they agreed that she was probably safe at Gabe's—with a little additional plainclothes police surveillance that Chief Irving promised to provide as soon as possible, jurisdiction be damned. Gabe found himself both liking and respecting the old man.

"One last thing: secrecy." Irving looked over at Tom, who'd sat silent through most of the meeting. "Ms. James will need to keep her location secret, and that means not sharing it with anyone outside this room. It also means limiting her time in public or in the office. We don't want to give the perpetrator an opportunity to follow her home."

Tom turned to Kat. "James, take what you need to work from home."

"Okay." Kat still looked deeply shaken, and it took everything Gabe had not to put his arm around her. "And thanks, everyone. I'm grateful for your help."

With that, the meeting was over.

Tom left the room with Irving. Darcangelo picked up the two evidence bags—one holding the bone, the other the envelope in which the bone had been mailed—and dropped them into a much larger envelope. "Hunter was sorry he couldn't make it. He and the rest of the SWAT team are doing some kind of training exercise today. You know how those SWAT boys just love to play with their toys."

That made Kat smile. "Thank him for me. And thank you for coming. I know this isn't the sort of case you usually handle."

"Hey, it's no problem. You're family to us, Kat." Darcangelo walked around the table and ducked down to kiss Kat on the cheek. "Call if you need anything, got it?"

She nodded. "Thanks."

Darcangelo met Gabe's gaze. "I'll be in touch."

Gabe waited till he and Kat were alone, then he gathered her into his arms. She leaned into him, as if he was the only thing keeping her on her feet, and he knew she was near the edge. "Let's get your things together and get you home."

CHAPTER 18

"ARE YOU OKAY?"

Kat buckled her seat belt. "Yeah."

She stuck the key in the ignition, turned on her headlights, then slowly backed out of the parking space, aware Gabe was watching her.

"Why don't you let me drive?"

She shook her head. She needed to drive. It would distract her, give her something to do, help her feel in control again. "I'll be fine."

But the moment she said it she knew it was a lie. She could barely think in a straight line, let alone drive. She felt sick, shaken, confused. And suddenly Gabe's house in Boulder seemed a million miles away. She slipped her truck into park and squeezed her eyes shut, fighting back her tears. She heard the passenger door open and close, and then Gabe was there opening her door, unbuckling her seat belt, smoothing her hair from her face. "It's going to be okay."

Feeling ashamed, she slid over to the passenger seat and buckled up again, staring out the window as Gabe drove her truck out of the underground garage, an enormous steel mesh gate lifting to let them out. Julian was there, waiting for them in his unmarked police car—a dark Chevy Impala. Gabe drove through the parking lot, turning west onto 13th Street and heading toward Speer, while Julian followed a couple of car lengths behind to make sure no one tailed them.

For a time, they drove in silence, Kat's sense of shame growing. She deserved to feel ashamed, reacting as she had.

There was no such thing as skinwalkers. She knew that. Skinwalkers were no more real than witches or fairies or goblins or any other creature dreamed up to explain the unexplainable. And yet, when she'd realized it was a human bone . . .

She shivered, chills skittering down her spine.

Without a word, Gabe reached over and turned on the heater.

Kat supposed she should call Uncle Allen and tell him what had happened. He'd hold a special *inipi* for her so she could sweat out the evil. But Allen had enough on his mind without having to worry about her. Besides, the evil, if there was any, was inside the heart of the person who'd mailed that package, not inside her. No skinwalker had sealed that envelope, addressed it, stuck a stamp on it, and dropped it in the mail. A human being had done that. That's what she had to remember.

Whoever had sent it was trying to use her culture against her, trying to make her believe her life was almost over, trying to frighten her.

And he succeeded, didn't he?

Beneath the dregs of her fear she felt it—anger. Anger at herself, at the person who'd done this, at Officer Daniels and those who protected him. White-hot, it built slowly, moving upward from her stomach, chasing away her chills, dispelling her lingering sense of dread. She wasn't some helpless victim. She had her mind, her courage, her spirit. She wasn't a sheep to be spooked and herded. She wouldn't let anyone, *Bilagáanaa* or Indian, manipulate her.

She looked over at Gabe, hesitant to say anything, but feeling the need to redeem herself in some way. "You must think I'm silly."

"Silly?" He frowned. "Why would I think that?"

For a moment she thought he must be teasing, but when he glanced over, his expression was serious. "How I reacted . . . It was . . . ridiculous."

"No, it wasn't." He reached over, took her hand, gave it a squeeze. "You're being way too hard on yourself."

"But skinwalkers . . ." She wanted to explain, but it was still hard to say the word out loud. "They don't exist."

"I know there's no such thing as ghosts, but if someone rigged my house so that I started hearing clanking chains at night and seeing strange transparent shapes drifting past my bed, I'd get pretty creeped out." He glanced over, gave her a lopsided grin. "I'd run the other way faster than Shaggy and Scooby."

"Are they friends of yours?"

He laughed. "You've never heard of Scooby-Doo?"

"Scooby who?"

But this only made him laugh harder. "Never mind. The point is that every culture has its mythical monsters, and just because we know in our rational minds that they don't really exist doesn't mean people can't play on those fears."

He looked over at her, all trace of humor gone from his face. "I'm not going to let him hurt you, Kat. Whoever he is, I'm not going to let him hurt you."

GABE PARKED KAT'S truck in his garage beside his SUV so that no one would see it and know she was there. He disarmed the alarm system and carried her suitcases inside to his bedroom. "Make yourself at home. Let me know if you need anything."

He left her to settle in and went to double-check the doors and arm the alarm system. Once he was certain the place was secure, he went downstairs and grabbed his hunting rifle and extra ammo for both the rifle and his HK semiauto, which he still wore in his shoulder harness. He loaded the rifle and carried both it and the extra ammo upstairs, leaning the rifle against the wall beside the entertainment center and stashing the ammo on the floor beside it. He'd never taken anyone's head off before, but he was ready to do just that.

Get past this, motherfucker, whoever you are.

He'd just started digging around in the refrigerator, trying to figure out what to make for supper when he smelled it— smoke. He walked toward his bedroom and saw Kat holding what looked like a bald eagle feather over a curling tendril of smoke rising from a bundle of white sage that sat in a large abalone shell on top of his chest of drawers. Eyes closed, she spoke soft words he couldn't understand, wafting the smoke over her head with the feather.

She was smudging—praying and purifying herself to wash away the feeling of taint that receiving and holding the bone had left on her.

Feeling like an intruder, he started to turn away, but just then she opened her eyes and saw him. She picked up the abalone shell and took a hesitant step toward him, feather still in hand, uncertainty in her eyes.

Gabe nodded.

She walked over to him, then used the feather to waft sage smoke against his body, whispering foreign words. He caught the smoke in his hands, drew it over his head, the pungent, earthy scent somehow revitalizing, the moment strangely intimate.

By the time she stepped away, the sage bundle had stopped smoldering. She set the abalone shell down on his dresser and placed the eagle feather in a long, slender box that looked like it had been carved by hand. Then she looked up at him and gave him a tremulous smile. "Thank you."

"Are you hungry?" He wasn't sure her stomach was up to eating just yet.

"A little." She seemed to hesitate. "I really just want to take a bath."

At the word "bath," an image of her naked and sitting in his tub blindsided him, sending his thoughts in a distinctly nonspiritual direction. "You go ahead. I'll make supper. Let me know if you need anything."

Like my help undressing or washing your luscious body or . . .

Yeah, he was despicable.

He willed himself to walk away, heading back to the kitchen where he rummaged mindlessly in the fridge and the cupboards, unable to concentrate on dinner, testosterone shorting out his brain, making it terribly hard to think about anything but what was happening in that tub.

He grabbed stuff to throw in a salad and set it on the

counter, then opened the freezer. He had chicken, of course, but he also had elk fillets, buffalo rib eyes and trout. But could her stomach handle any of that? Maybe he should just make omelets.

He decided to ask. He walked to the bathroom, leaned toward the door, and opened his mouth to speak, but nothing came out. Kat had left the door open just a crack, and there, in the bathroom mirror, he could see her reflection.

His mouth went dry.

She sat with her back against the foot of the tub, shaving her legs, her dark hair tied in a hasty knot at the back of her neck, tendrils spilling around her face. Her breasts swayed gently with her movements, her dusky nipples tight, her caramel skin rosy from the heat of the water, the scents of white sage and honey rising with the steam. Then she raised one slender leg out of the water and slid her razor over glistening skin.

Sweet Jesus, Mary, and Joseph!

He was in so much trouble.

KAT RINSED THE shaving cream from her leg, set her razor down on the side of the tub, then reached for her soap, which had slipped into the water and bobbed near her toes amid floating leaves of white sage.

"It's the soap, isn't it?"

She gasped and looked up to find Gabe watching her. He was leaning against the bathroom sink, black turtleneck stretched across his chest, his pistol resting against his left side in its shoulder holster. He looked more than a little dangerous—in an oddly appealing, very male way. His gaze slid over her, his eyes dark.

She fought the urge to cover herself. He'd already seen her completely naked, had already touched her everywhere. "The . . . the soap?"

"Your skin always smells like honey." His voice was deep and warm and seemed to fill the small room. "It's the soap."

The soap.

She stared at it for a moment, the way he was looking at her making it hard for her to think. "It's honey soap. A friend of mine . . . She, um, makes it in her kitchen using honey." *Of course she makes it from honey, Kat!* "Honey from her own hives."

For a span of heartbeats, he just stood there, watching her, his gaze all over her, a look of restrained male desire on his face. Heat flooded Kat's cheeks, her body seeming to come alive with memories of last night as the silence stretched between them.

Then, at last, he spoke. "Do you want me to go?"

And she realized she didn't. "No."

He crossed the small room in a single step and slowly knelt beside the tub, his gaze never leaving hers. Then he pushed up his sleeves, took the soap from her, held it to his nose, and inhaled, his eyes drifting shut. "Mmm."

The masculine rumble of his moan sent a rush of heat to her belly, anticipation coiling inside her.

He opened his eyes, rubbing the soap between his hands to work up a lather, his lips curving into a smile that made her pulse skip. "Just lie back and close your eyes. You're in good hands."

Good hands.

Oh, yes, he did have good hands, and the thought of them touching her almost made her squirm. She leaned back against the tub and closed her eyes, only to have them pop open again when she heard the clink of the soap dropping into the soap dish.

He chuckled. "I said close your eyes."

Barely able to breath, she did as he asked, her nipples drawing tight, her entire body tense, as she waited, impatient, wondering what exactly he would do. But what she felt first wasn't his hands on her breasts, but his lips as they brushed warm and whisper-soft over hers once, twice, three times.

"Kat." He kissed her upper lip, then her lower lip, flicking it with his tongue, catching it between his lips, nipping it.

Then his hands slid over her breasts, soap slick and hot,

cupping and shaping them. His fingers caught her nipples, teased them to aching points, giving them little tugs she felt all the way to her womb. She gasped and arched her back, offering herself to him, awed by the delicious feeling of skin sliding over soapy skin. The sensation unleashed a torrent inside her, left her feeling hot, wet, empty.

Oh, she wanted him! She couldn't deny it, couldn't ignore it, couldn't lie to herself about it. She wanted Gabe.

"You're driving me out of my mind." Gabe drank in the sight of her, inhaling deeply, her musky scent mingling with the scents of honey and white sage. His groin throbbed, his cock almost painfully hard, but there was nothing he could do about it at the moment. He'd thought about unzipping his jeans, just to relieve some of the pressure, but he didn't want to do something that would make her pull away. Besides, he couldn't seem to take his hands off her.

She lay against the back of the tub, her eyes squeezed shut, her lips parted, her breathing rapid. She held tightly to the sides of the tub, as if she thought she might drown. Her wet skin was flushed from the heat of the water and the heat of her own blood, her cheeks rosy. Her dark hair had come loose from its knot, the ends floating in the water around her. And her breasts . . .

They filled his hands, her wine-dark areolas like puckered velvet, their tips hard little nubs that pressed against his palms. He caught one between his thumb and forefinger and rolled it lightly before doing the same with the other, gratified by her little whimper and the way she arched upward, pressing her thighs tighter together to ease the ache he'd built there.

He couldn't let her get away with that.

He scooped up water with his hands and let it trickle over her breasts to rinse the soap away, knowing the heat would intensify her pleasure. "Do you like that?"

She answered with a gasp. "Gabe!"

The way she said his name was like a plea—a cry for release that he was more than willing to answer. He slid one arm behind her neck to cradle her head, lowered his mouth to hers and kissed her deep and hard, needing to bury himself inside her any way he could. Then he reached down with his free hand, skimming circles over the smooth skin of her belly, over her hips, over her thighs.

Her wet fingers clenched in his hair, and she drew him closer, whimpering into his mouth, her tongue warring with his, her hips lifting almost out of the water, letting him know without words where she needed his touch most.

He dragged his mouth from hers, slid his hand between her thighs, forcing them down and apart. But the tub was narrow, too narrow to give him the access he wanted. He lifted her right leg so that her calf rested on the side of the tub, opening her fully. And, hell, yeah, he looked—stared—her erotic beauty hitting like a punch to the gut. "Do you have any idea how beautiful you are?"

"I . . . I don't . . ." She watched him through wide eyes, her breasts rising and falling with each shallow breath, and he could almost feel her uncertainty. Well, that uncertainty would end right here and right now.

"You are beautiful. I'll show you." He slid his arm out from beneath her neck, stood and grabbed his shaving mirror off the shower wall, its little suction cups making popping sounds as they pulled free from the tile.

"Wh-what are you . . . ?" She started to sit up.

But Gabe was already kneeling beside her again. He caught her right leg with the back of his right arm, pinned it where it was, then held the mirror between her legs, angling it so that she could see. "You are beautiful. See?"

At first she kept her gaze on his, then slowly, she looked into the mirror.

He shifted the mirror into one of her hands, then parted her labia, teasing her inner lips with a fingertip. "Like rose petals. And your clit—perfect, erotic, so sexy."

He flicked it—and felt her tense in response. "I want to taste it, to suck on it just like I suck on your nipples. I want to feel it swell in my mouth."

She exhaled a long shuddering breath, and he knew his words aroused her, every bit as much his hands did.

Then he parted her farther, running slick circles over her clit, teasing her entrance. "I want to taste you. I want to slide my tongue inside you here and feel you come against my mouth. I want . . ."

But then he found himself looking at something he'd never seen before—an intact hymen. Proof that she was more innocent than any woman he'd ever touched.

What the hell are you doing, Rossiter?

The pang of conscience struck unexpectedly, stopping him midsentence. Was he taking advantage of her, using his sexual experience to manipulate her into having sex with him? What the hell kind of bastard was he?

He didn't get time to answer his own questions, because just then she dropped the mirror, took his hand, and pressed it against her, her eyes drifting shut, a look of aroused anguish on her face. "Please!"

Gabe quit listening to his conscience, quit thinking of anything but how much he wanted to see her come again. He pressed deep circles against her just where she seemed to like it most, taking care to catch her clit with each pass, his other hand busy with her breasts. He tried to reassure her, words pouring out of him in urgent whispers. "Yeah, honey. Take it! Take what you need from me!"

She held his hand in place, her grip tight. Her breathing was ragged, her head turning from side to side against the tub, her hair floating in the water around her. Then she stiffened and arched, her head going back as she came with a long, shuddering sigh.

Gabe kept up the rhythm, wanting to prolong her climax, to give her every bit of pleasure he could, the sight of her almost enough to make him come in his jeans. Slowly, the tension drained from her body, leaving her limp. She lay still, her back against the tub, her eyes closed, her hand resting lightly on top of his. He laced his fingers through hers, raised her hand to his lips, and kissed it, the musky scent of her orgasm filling his head, sharpening his own sexual hunger.

She opened her eyes, gave him a shy smile. Then without

taking her gaze from him, she slowly sat up, sloshing water onto his jeans, her smile turning decidedly sultry. "When are you going to let me do that for you?"

It wasn't the most blatant offer Gabe had ever received from a woman—but it was the first ever to leave him speechless.

CHAPTER 19

KAT SAW GABE'S pupils dilate, heard his breath catch, and felt the thrill of knowing she could affect him. Still drenched in pleasure, her mind filled with erotic images of her own body, of watching his hands touch her in the most intimate way, she didn't feel like holding back. "You should enjoy this, too, and . . . And I want to touch you."

He exhaled in a rush, brushed a strand of wet hair from her cheek. "Are you sure? I don't want to push you. I don't want you to do anything you don't—"

She wrapped her arms behind his neck and kissed him hard, answering his question the best way she knew how, excitement shooting through her when he moaned and crushed her against him, his tongue welcoming hers inside his mouth, his fingers fisting in her hair. He felt so hard against her, the heat of his body burning through his clothes to her wet skin, his pistol pressing into her ribs.

He lifted her out of the tub and into his arms, not bothering with a towel, his lips still hot on hers. A handful of long strides later, she found herself lying on his bed in the semidarkness, light spilling in through the open door. She watched as he unclipped the holster and hung it, with the gun, around his bedpost. Then he drew his shirt over his head and let it fall to the floor.

"Turn on the light." Kat repeated what he'd said to her just last night. "I . . . I need to see you. All of you."

He reached over—*click*—and she couldn't help but stare. At the strength of his arms and shoulders. At the heavy planes of his chest with its dark curls and flat nipples. At the ridges of his abdomen. At the line of dark hair that trailed down his belly, disappearing behind his zipper. At the unmistakable bulge in his jeans.

Kat's pulse picked up, warmth building in her belly. She wouldn't have imagined that she could feel sexually aroused again so soon after such an earth-shattering climax, but she did. She sat up, tucking her legs beneath her, her shyness gone.

Without taking his gaze off her, he unbuttoned the single button at the top of his fly, unzipped his jeans, then pushed them down his narrow hips, letting them fall to the floor. And for a moment, he stood there, wearing only gray boxer briefs, his thick erection jutting upward, stretching the fabric. "Like what you see so far?"

It was on the tip of Kat's tongue to remind him that she'd seen him undressed once before, but nothing about watching him take off his clothes when he was stumbling around drunk could compare to now. "Yeah."

He hooked his thumbs beneath the waistband of his briefs and drew them down, freeing his erection and standing completely naked before her.

Kat's mouth went dry, her pulse spiking.

There was no mistaking his virility. His penis stood against his abdomen, rising from a nest of dark curls, its thick head fully exposed this time, the gleaming skin stretched tight and almost purple. His testicles rested at the juncture of powerful thighs, full and heavy, one slightly lower than the other. He stood still but not passive, sexual tension humming just beneath his skin as he let her look her fill, clearly at ease with his naked body.

Nizhoni. Beautiful man.

The word came to her mind and refused to leave.

"I'm all yours." A grin on his lips, he took a step toward the bed, then stretched out beside her, offering himself to her. "Look and touch all you want."

GABE WATCHED KAT'S gaze travel over him, resting for one long moment on his cock, and he wondered for a fleeting second whether this was the first time she'd seen a man with a hard-on. It seemed impossible in the age of Internet porn that anyone could reach adulthood without getting an eyeful of stiff dick and spread-eagle—

She ducked down and kissed him, and every thought in his head vanished. His arms went around her—an instinctual response—and he drew her down against his chest, her breasts soft against his ribs, her skin unbelievably smooth, her hair spilling around him. He let her control the kiss, his tongue giving way to her exploration, while his hands moved down the curve of her spine to cup the mounds of her bare ass, his blood so hot he felt like he might spontaneously combust.

Then she dragged her lips from his, laid a hand against his chest, and raised herself up, her fingers fanning through his chest hair, her lips tracing a path from his mouth, down his throat, to his left nipple. She licked it once, twice, three times, sending bolts of pleasure to his groin, the muscles of his abdomen jerking each time. "Jesus."

He wanted to be inside her. Christ, he wanted to be inside her! He wanted to turn her onto her back, wrap her legs over his hips, and slide into her. It would be good. It would be so good—for both of them.

Not possible, Rossiter. You know that.

His mind knew it, but his body didn't give a damn. This was torture, pure and simple—feeling her body against his, her hot little mouth leaving a burning trail on his skin. He groaned out his frustration, slid the fingers of one hand into her hair, the honey-clean scent of her skin mingling with the musky scent of her climax, filling his head, settling on his tongue.

Taste her.

Hell, yeah, he wanted to taste her. He wanted to flip her onto her back and bury his face between her thighs. He would suck her clit, slide his tongue inside her, make her come again and again until the taste of her clung to the back of his throat.

And risk having her think you're a perv? Not a good plan—at least not till you know how she feels about that.

"Your body . . . It's so beautiful. So hard." She made a little mewling noise, then kissed and licked his right nipple, her hands exploring his pecs, his shoulders, his biceps, her body moving against his in a rhythm that told him she was turned on, too.

He damned well hoped so, because what she was doing to him was threatening to send him over the edge, his skin hypersensitive, his balls drawing dangerously tight. She found his navel, kissed it, teased it with her tongue, and his cock jerked. He sucked in a breath, willed himself to relax. He'd never jizzed prematurely, and he wasn't about to start now.

She sat up on her knees and met his gaze, her lips swollen and wet from kissing him, her nipples puckered, her breasts rising and falling with each shallow breath. She took his hand and drew it downward. "Show me."

He curled his fingers around his cock. "Do you want me to show you how I get myself off—or do you want to help?"

"Both." She gave a shy little smile made all the sexier by her breathless voice, by the heat in her eyes.

And he damned near came.

Almost unable to breathe, Kat watched as Gabe gripped himself and began to move his hand slowly up and down the length of his erection, his fingers sliding up the underside all way to the tip, before moving down to the base again. She knew he was watching her, but she couldn't take her gaze off what his hand was doing. Everything about him fascinated her—the soft skin that covered hard muscle, the dark hair on his chest, the veins that threaded over his biceps and lower belly.

And his penis . . .

A bead of moisture emerged from the slit on the tip, the head rising from a thick ridge of flesh, the shaft straining upward.

Wanting desperately to touch him, wanting to make him feel the way he'd made her feel, she reached out and cupped his testicles, kneading them gently. The feel of them was unlike anything she'd touched before—heavy, firm, and yet somehow . . . fragile.

Still watching her, he groaned deep in his chest, his hand moving faster—up-down, up-down, up-down. His motions were nothing like the delicate touches that had brought her to orgasm. They were much more forceful, more potent, and she

realized this was how he would move if he were inside her—
hard, strong, and fast.

And her inner muscles clenched.

The next time his hand moved upward, she closed hers
around the base of his penis. His hips jerked, and he all but
growled. Then his hand fell aside, his fingers closing in a fist.

Slowly she moved her hand upward, surprised at how hard
he felt. Not just firm, but hard. She touched the sensitive
tip, letting her fingers explore him, excited by his gasp, then
slid her hand to the base again. She was about to ask him
to help her, when his hand closed over hers and he began to
guide her.

He tightened her grip, his fingers gentle, and then he began
to move her hand, gradually increasing the pace, whispering to her almost frantically. "Spread your legs, Kat! Let me
touch you!"

She moved her knees farther apart, and his other hand slid
insistently between her thighs, his fingers gathering her slippery wetness and rubbing it over her clitoris, stroking her with
such skill that she almost forgot to focus on him. "Gabe!"

Somehow, touching her seemed to arouse him even more.
His eyes drifted shut, his head turned to the side, and his grip
on her hand tightened. His hips thrust upward, the rhythm
almost violent as he drove himself into her fist like a piston.
His body was drawn so tight she thought it might snap, the
cords of his neck standing out, his chest slick with sweat, his
hand still busy between her legs.

She knew he was on the edge, but so was she. Oh, the
man knew how to touch a woman—and where. He teased
her, probed her, then slowly slid a finger inside her, his wrist
flexing so that the heel of his hand pushed against her right
where it felt best. She moved against his hand, her motions
making his finger slide in and out of her, bringing her to the
very brink.

"That's it, honey. Ride my hand!" Gabe opened his eyes,
looked at where his body joined hers. "God, you're so wet!
Oh, Christ!"

With a deep groan, Gabe arched, his hips giving three
more hard thrusts, his penis convulsing in her hand, shooting

ribbons of thick, white semen over their fingers and onto his belly. The sight was more erotic and stirring than she could have imagined, and the raw sexuality of it sent her over the edge with him.

FEELING STRANGELY CONTENTED, Gabe cradled Kat's head against his shoulder, watching through half-closed eyes as she trailed a fingertip through the pool of ejaculation on his belly. She dabbed at it, made little circles in it, rubbed it into his skin like lotion, her actions somehow both innocent and amusing.

"So this makes a baby." There was a note of awe in her voice.

"Not like this." He reached for the box of tissues on his nightstand. "Mostly, it just makes a mess."

FIVE MINUTES LATER, Gabe sat at the table in his boxer briefs, watching as Kat, wearing that same old T-shirt of his she'd worn this morning, made them a dinner of buffalo steaks, roasted potatoes, and salad. Where she came by this sudden burst of energy when he could barely think and would rather be dozing in his bed with her still in his arms was beyond him. He supposed it was one of the great mysteries of life—how having a good orgasm knocked a man out, but reenergized a woman and left her ravenous.

Maybe it was an evolutionary thing that had enabled women to fatten up for pregnancy and produce healthier offspring back in the day when life was hard and food scarce. He could kind of see that. A cave woman has sex with a cave man, and while he's lying on the mammoth skin in a postcoital stupor, she raids his cave for leftovers. Still, Gabe supposed human males had it easy. If he were a male black widow or praying mantis, Kat would be munching on him right now, not carrot sticks.

Not that he and Kat had mated. Not that they'd actually had sex. They'd done nothing more than get each other off like a couple of high school kids. And yet it had satisfied him in a way that three years of hard-core fucking hadn't. Later, when his brain was working again, this would probably scare the shit out of him, but for now he wanted to savor the moment.

He watched Kat sprinkle salt and pepper on the rib eyes. Then she bent down to slide them in the oven to broil, and his gaze shifted to the curve of her ass and her cute lavender panties. And some of his drowsiness lifted.

She shut the oven, then stood and turned to him, half-eaten carrot stick in hand. "Do you like onions in your salad?"

Despite what had happened today, she seemed relaxed, almost happy, the ordeal she'd been through temporarily forgotten. Some macho part of him found this more than a little gratifying. Distracted by the sweetness of her face, he barely heard himself answer. "Uh-huh."

It was a good thing she hadn't just asked him if he liked rat turds in his salad.

You're in over your head, buddy!

Yeah, he was. But at the moment that didn't seem so bad.

KAT DABBED HER lips with the napkin, then leaned back in her chair, her belly full, her body replete. "That was delicious. Thank you."

Gabe gave her a lazy grin. "You're the cook. Thank yourself."

Something in the way he looked at her made it hard for her to think. Or maybe it was the fact that he was still half naked. Or the sight of his hand—the same hand that had made her come twice this evening—resting against the table.

That's it, honey. Ride my hand!

Heat flooded her cheeks, and she found herself struggling to remember the thread of their conversation. "It . . . It was your food we ate, so . . ."

His eyes narrowed. "You're blushing."

She sat up straight, pressed her hands to her cheeks and looked away. "No, I'm not. It's just warm. I . . . I should start the dishes."

Feeling embarrassed that he had noticed, she stood,

grabbed their plates, and carried them to the sink. She had just turned on the water to rinse them when she felt Gabe come up behind her. His hands settled against the countertop on either side of her, his lips nuzzling the sensitive skin beneath her ear, his breath hot on her skin.

"You were blushing." His voice was deep and dark as midnight. "It couldn't have been the topic of conversation, so it must have been something you were thinking. What were you thinking, my sweet little Kat? Hmm? Tell me."

"I . . ." Kat sank back against him, tilting her head to make more room for his kisses as he traced the curve of her neck down to her shoulder. "I . . . wasn't blushing."

He chuckled. "You're such a bad liar. I think you were thinking about—"

In the other room, his cell phone rang, the jarring sound giving Kat a mini adrenaline surge, her pulse pounding.

"Damn." He pressed a kiss against her hair, then strode off to answer it.

And with her next breath, everything she'd been trying so hard to forget came crashing in on her. The bone fragment. Bullets flying. Looting at Mesa Butte. Grandpa Red Crow's death.

One little Indian . . . dead.

"Rossiter."

Not wanting to eavesdrop but unable to shake the feeling that this call in some way had to do with Mesa Butte, she turned off the water, reached for a towel, and walked slowly toward the living room.

"Go ahead," she heard Gabe say, the gentleness that had been in his voice moments ago now gone.

She stepped into the hallway, her heart beating faster.

"Were they able to ID it?" he asked.

And she knew he was talking about the bone.

Her stomach fell.

She took another step.

"Was he able to say where it came from? Where would anyone get a hold of something like that?" A pause. "Really? Son of a bitch!"

She reached the end of the hallway and found Gabe standing with his back to the fireplace, cell phone to his ear, his face grave.

"She's handling it pretty well. Yeah. Thanks, man. I'll be in touch." He hung up, then turned and saw her. His gaze met hers, his eyes troubled. "That was Julian. There were no fingerprints on the bone besides yours. Forensics identified it. Like I thought, it's human—and at least three hundred years old. The soil traces he recovered from it are a dead match for the soil in the trenches at Mesa Butte."

THE COYOTE CAME from behind her. Yipping and howling, it ran circles around her in the darkness. She shouted at it, told it to leave her alone, but her voice disappeared in the wind. She tried to kick it, tried to run, but her legs wouldn't move.

Then the coyote froze beside her, bared its teeth, growled, the fur on its neck and back raised. But it wasn't growling at her. It was growling at something else—something that moved in the shadows, something that stood just beyond the circle of firelight, something that was coming nearer.

A skinwalker.

She screamed.

"Kat, honey, wake up! It's okay. I've got you."

She heard Gabe's voice and found herself in his arms, in tears, shaking, drenched in cold sweat. She buried her face against his chest, his embrace a refuge. He whispered reassurances, stroked her hair, held her. But it was a long time before she was able to fall asleep again.

CHAPTER 20

IT WAS THE second morning in a row that Gabe had awoken in his own bed to find himself holding a woman in his arms. The same woman.

Kat slept deeply, her head resting on his chest, her breasts pressing softly against his ribs, one of her legs tucked intimately between his, her peacefulness at odds with the salty tearstains on her cheeks and the dark circles beneath her eyes. She'd had a rough night, whatever she'd dreamed so terrifying that she'd actually screamed, waking Gabe from a dead sleep. He'd sat bolt upright and reached for his HK before he'd realized she was just having a nightmare. It had taken most of an hour for her trembling to subside.

He needed to take a leak, but he didn't want to wake her. And so he watched her sleep, something he hadn't done since . . .

What kind of game are you playing with her, Rossiter?

Hell if he knew.

He didn't want to hurt her, did *not* want to hurt her, but that's exactly what he'd do in the end. She had feelings for him. He'd seen it last night—that soft glow a woman got in her eyes when she thought she was in love. But he knew what she wanted from a man—a loving husband, a lifelong partner, a devoted father for her kids—and no matter what she believed, he was none of those things.

He'd given everything he had to Jill. He had nothing left to give.

And then he understood, as if somehow he'd worked it out in his sleep. The reason he hadn't yet pushed Kat away like all the other women he'd fucked is that he hadn't actually fucked her yet. Like any horn dog, he was busy chasing what he hadn't caught, all the kissing and even last night's mind-blowing hand job nothing more than foreplay. If he ever were to get inside her, the protectiveness he felt for her, this strange tenderness, would vanish. He'd come—and it would go. Then he'd have to watch that glow in her eyes turn to hurt and maybe even to hate.

That's why you need to keep your cock to yourself.

Yeah, right.

Who was he fooling? The only reason he hadn't fucked her yet is that she hadn't let him. If and when she did, he couldn't imagine himself being noble enough to refuse. Wasn't he already taking advantage of her vulnerability and using his sexual skill to move her slowly in that direction?

No.

Something in him rejected that idea. He was an asshole when it came to women, but he wasn't that much of an asshole. There had to be more to his need for her than scratching his insatiable sexual itch.

Like what, dickhead?

When no answer came to him—at least not one he was willing to consider—he knew he couldn't trust himself where she was concerned. It was time he put some distance between them. No matter how badly he wanted her, he needed to go back to keeping his hands to himself and sleeping on the couch.

He could forgive himself for a lot of things, but hurting Kat wasn't one of them.

WILLING HERSELF TO concentrate, Kat tried once again to read through a memo from the city's real estate department to Paul Martin, the city manager, discussing the proposed purchase price for Mesa Butte. The owners—a company called Mesa Butte Corporation—wanted three million dollars, but the city Realtor felt the land was worth at most half that amount and . . .

The back door opened, and Gabe stepped in, his arms full

of firewood, fresh, cold air rushing in behind him, a dusting of snowflakes on his shoulders and in his hair. He dropped the wood next to the fireplace, then walked back outside without sparing Kat a glance. It was as if he'd forgotten she was there.

You're being ridiculous, Kat.

He was probably just giving her space to work. Hadn't he told her that he didn't want to distract her? She ought to be grateful that he respected her enough to let her do her job. Except that . . . It felt more like he was trying to avoid her.

She couldn't put a finger on it. He hadn't done or said anything rude. All morning he'd been polite, making sure she was comfortable and had what she needed—coffee, a pen, enough light. But she might have been a stranger for all the warmth he'd shown her. Half the day was now gone, and they'd barely spoken. He hadn't once held her, hadn't kissed her, hadn't so much as touched her. It was as if the past two nights had never happened, as if she were a guest in his house—and nothing more.

She'd been telling herself all day that it didn't mean anything. He cared for her. She knew he did. He'd been there for her these past two weeks without fail. He'd watched over her, protected her, saved her life more than once and been injured in the process. He'd lost his job helping her do hers. He'd respected her sexual boundaries. And now, after years of working in the mountains, he'd chosen to stay cooped up indoors with her in order to keep her safe, when he could easily have washed his hands of the situation and let Chief Irving put her in a police safe house.

A man did not do those things for a woman if he didn't care about her, and what a man did mattered more than what he said—or didn't say.

Or so Kat told herself.

But the truth was that she'd fallen in love with a man who'd loved another woman and had lost her—a man who wasn't ready to love again. If only Kat knew what had happened, if only she knew how Jill had died, then she might understand what was going on inside him. She'd already guessed that Jill's death had something to do with rock climbing. Maybe Jill had fallen and Gabe blamed himself. Or maybe . . .

Kat, listen to yourself!

What was she doing? Was she hoping for something that would never happen? Was she hoping for a kind of love from Gabe that he couldn't give?

You're right, Kat—you've got no claim on me. I've made no promises, and we both know I never will.

She blinked back a surprise rush of tears, trying to ignore the growing ache in her chest. She needed to pull herself together. It was almost two in the afternoon, and she'd barely made headway through the stack of documents she and Gabe had copied at Martin's office yesterday. She had a job to do. People were depending on her. She couldn't let her emotions get in the way of her responsibilities.

The door opened, and Gabe stepped inside again. He dropped another armload of firewood. "Chief Irving's men are here. They're sitting across the street in a black Impala. I thought you'd want to know."

Before Kat could respond, he was gone again.

GABE STARED AT the map of Boulder and the five dots he'd drawn in red marker until his head ached. Someone had called Kat from pay phones at these seemingly random locations and threatened her life. But because none of the phones happened to be near any of the city's surveillance cameras, Gabe didn't know whose ass to kick.

He'd hoped that by looking at the locations on a map and noting the time of each call, he'd discover a pattern or find a common center point. No such luck. The phones were spread across town from Table Mesa to a North Boulder grocery store. The first two calls were made twenty minutes apart, but the others had been made at completely arbitrary intervals, forty-five minutes being the shortest and two hours being the longest. Gabe had lived his entire life in Boulder and knew the intervals had nothing to do with the distance between the pay phones.

He was looking for a pattern, but there was no pattern.

Goddamn it!

He threw his pencil down on the table, feeling ready to explode.

Any more bright ideas, Rossiter?

No. Not a single one.

He leaned back in his chair, closed his eyes, and drew a deep breath. He needed to work out or have a beer or do something to take the edge off. He felt frustrated, tense, angry. It was as if his skin were on too tight, and the damned death threats were only part of his problem. The other part had soft skin and big eyes and long dark hair and was sitting upstairs on his living room floor.

What an idiot he'd been to think he could just ignore her! All day long, X-rated images from last night had filled his mind, making it damned hard to concentrate. Kat naked in the bathtub. Kat exploring his body, wrapping her fingers around his cock. Kat riding his hand, a look of bliss on her sweet face as they both climaxed.

Hell, yeah, he wanted to get inside her, but the truth was that somehow she'd gotten inside him. He didn't just want to fuck her. He wanted to talk to her, to sit and watch her work. He wanted to banish her fear, to make her feel safe. He wanted to hear her laugh, to see her smile again. And it pissed him off. He felt torn between going upstairs just to be with her—and running as far and as fast as he could.

Call Darcangelo. Ask him to move her to a safe house.

Even as the thought occurred to him, he knew he wouldn't do it. He wouldn't be able to stand being away from her. So if he couldn't take not being around her and he couldn't face her without risking his sanity, what exactly was he supposed to do? Hide in the basement all day?

Coward.

He glanced at the clock and saw that it was almost five—time to think about making supper. And that meant facing Kat.

Maybe he could order pizza and distract himself with a few climbing videos. If they watched TV while they ate, they couldn't talk. In his experience, nothing made the average woman's eyes glaze over faster than watching scruffy men inch their way up some big wall in Canada or a mountain in Nepal. Yeah, tonight might be the perfect night to catch up on *Masters of Stone*. How many of those damned DVDs did they plan on making, anyway? The series had more sequels than *Rocky*.

With that plan in mind, he stood, glanced down at the red dots on the map. "Well, you son of a bitch," he said to the dots, "you sure were lucky."

Somehow, the bastard had managed to pick pay phones that were nowhere near city surveillance and was probably going to get away . . .

And then Gabe knew.

That was the pattern.

The son of a bitch who'd made those calls hadn't been lucky. He'd chosen those phones precisely because they weren't under city surveillance. Gabe might not be able to prove it, but he knew in his gut he was right.

He headed for the stairs, took them two at a time. He'd call Hunter or Darcangelo—whoever answered first—and get them on it. They could find out who had access to information about the city's surveillance system, and that would give them a list of potential suspects. They'd finally have something to go on.

KAT RUBBED THE back of her neck, tried to ease the stiffness. She'd read halfway through the file of documents, but she hadn't found a single thing that might explain what was happening at Mesa Butte. There was nothing to indicate the city knew Indian people used the land. There was no mention of looting or Indian artifacts. There were no complaints about the *inipi* ceremonies either from city land-use officials or nearby residents. The documents she'd read so far indicated that Mesa Butte was just a boring plot of land on the outskirts of town. But she knew that wasn't true.

She leafed through the remaining documents and saw only more of the same—property-line surveys, various plant and wildlife studies, GPS surveys, soil studies, groundwater surveys. Was something missing?

She pressed her fingers to her temple to soothe away a nagging headache, feeling sleepy despite three cups of coffee, her mind sluggish. Maybe she needed a fourth cup of coffee or more water—or a break. Realizing it had been at least two hours since she'd budged from this spot, she set the documents aside.

She got to her feet, started to stretch, but she must have stood too quickly. Blood rushed from her head, leaving her dizzy. She stumbled forward a step, catching the arm of the sofa, the toes of her left foot hitting something hard, sending whatever it was skidding across the floor. Only when the wave of dizziness and the pain in her toes passed did she see what it was.

A photo album.

It must have been just hidden beneath the sofa. Now, it sat near her foot, its cover kicked open to reveal the first page. Without meaning to, without even thinking, she reached for it, picked it up, her gaze fixed on an image of Gabe and Jill.

They sat next to each other near a campfire, leaning toward one another, but not touching, smiles on their faces. Gabe had the same long hair he'd had in their engagement photo, but no goatee. He was wearing a flannel shirt over climbing pants, while Jill, her hair pulled back in a messy ponytail, was wearing a hoodie and blue jeans.

"The day we met," read the caption, the words printed on a little strip of paper. "Camp 4, Yosemite, September 15, 2004."

Slowly she turned one page and then the next, lost in the photographs, years of Gabe's life laid out before her. Gabe walking along a rope strung high in the air between two pine trees while his friends watched from below. Gabe and Jill skiing, ice climbing, camping in the snow, always with the same group of friends. Gabe and Jill sitting in front of a Christmas tree, looking sleepy and very much in love. Jill catching snowflakes on her tongue. Gabe and Jill naked in a hot springs together, Gabe's hands cupping Jill's breasts to hide them from the camera. Gabe and Jill drinking beer with a group of friends beside a row of overturned kayaks as the seasons came around to spring.

Kat knew the man in these photos, and yet she didn't know him at all. She'd only ever glimpsed this happier, lighter side of him. And she wondered again what had happened to change him from a man who had loved so deeply to a man who no longer believed in love.

GABE STARED. KAT sat on his sofa, leafing through Jill's photo album. He forgot what he was doing, forgot what he'd been about to tell her, anger rising hot and thick from his gut. "What the hell are you doing?"

She gasped, looked up, clearly startled. She'd been so busy snooping into his past that she hadn't even known he was there.

"Where did you find that?" No one had seen these photos except for him and Jill. No one knew what they meant to him, how much he hated them, how much he hated himself for holding on to them.

"It was under the sofa. I . . . I tripped on it, and it came open, and I—"

He crossed the room in two strides, jerked the photo album from her hands, and slammed it shut. "Just because we've fooled around a little doesn't mean you can pry into my life!"

Kat's head snapped back as if he'd slapped her. "I . . . I'm sorry! I didn't mean to pry. I stubbed my toes on it—"

Some part of him saw her distress, but he was too damned angry to care. "You didn't mean to pry? Why the hell were you looking though it then?"

Kat stood up straighter, glaring defiantly up at him. "Maybe I was trying to understand why a man with so much heart acts like he no longer has one."

"What the hell does that mean?"

"You know exactly what it means!" And then she blind-sided him. "How did Jill die?"

The question was like a body blow. His heart slammed against his breastbone, and it took him a moment to find his voice. When he did, his words came out low and gruff. "That's none of your fucking business."

But Kat only pushed him harder, her soft voice cutting

deeper. "You say you don't believe in ghosts, but she haunts you."

He took a step back. "You don't know a damn thing about it."

She reached out, put a hand on his chest—as if she cared, as if she had some idea what she was doing to him. "I know you loved her. I know you wanted to marry her. I know you were happy with her and that her death hurt you horribly."

She doesn't know anything, Rossiter. She doesn't understand.

Gabe squeezed his eyes shut, his hands clenching into fists at his sides, rage and grief and regret churning in his stomach. He could not go there. Could not go there. He drew a deep breath, willed his hands to unclench. "Look, Kat. I know you've convinced yourself that you're in love with me or some damned thing, but you're not. You only think so because I saved your life, and because I'm the first guy to make you come. Fooling yourself into believing you love me makes it easier for you to do what your hormones want you to do—which is to get good and fucked."

"If that's what you truly believe, then you know nothing about me." Her voice quavered as she spoke, her face flushed with rage.

"In the morning, I'll call Chief Irving and ask him to move you to a police safe house. I think it would be best."

Tears shimmered in her eyes. "Okay. If that's what you want."

Then, she turned and, cloaked in that damnable dignity of hers, walked to his bedroom, and locked the door behind her. As he stomped out the back door, desperate to get some air, his heart still pounding, he heard her break into sobs.

CHAPTER 21

KAT AWOKE, HER head throbbing. She hadn't meant to fall asleep. She sat up, gasping in shock at the pain in her head, dizziness washing over her, forcing her back onto the pillow. What was wrong with her? Was she sick?

The answer came with a wave of body aches and nausea.

Maybe she'd caught the flu—except that she'd gotten a flu shot. Or maybe she'd picked up something like food poisoning. Or perhaps it was a migraine. She'd never had one before, but she'd heard they made some people nauseated.

Outside the window, the sun had already set. She lay on her back in the darkness, fighting overwhelming drowsiness. She needed to get up and get some aspirin and water. Somehow, she needed to make it out of bed and out of the bedroom if . . .

And then she remembered why she was in the bedroom. Gabe had come upstairs. He'd seen her looking at the photo album. He'd yelled at her—hurtful words, horrible words, words that had made her think of Samantha crying on his doorstep.

Just because we've fooled around a little doesn't mean you can pry into my life!

Is that how he saw it? They'd fooled around?

For her it had been so much more than that. And now it was over. In the morning, he'd call Chief Irving and have them move her to a safe house, and she probably wouldn't see him again. But if he'd truly meant what he'd said about "fooling around," he was probably doing her a favor, as painful as it might . . .

She drifted again, only to be awakened by the throbbing in her head. Knowing she had no choice but to get up and get aspirin if she wanted to feel better, she pushed herself into a sitting position. Overwhelmed by dizziness and pain, her heart racing, she fought to stay upright. She couldn't think of the last time she'd felt so sick. Maybe when she'd had pneumonia as a kid. But even then, her heart hadn't raced like this.

She held a hand to her forehead and was surprised to find that she wasn't burning up. She thought of calling for Gabe, but she didn't want his help. She didn't want anything from him. Not anymore.

That thought got her on her feet. Out of breath, she steadied herself, her palms splayed on the bed. Then slowly she turned and step by step made her way toward the bedroom door, her heart slamming in her chest as if she were running up stairs. She grabbed the doorknob, turned it, stepped into the hallway—and felt her knees give.

Unable to stop herself, she sank to the floor. "Gabe!"

She managed just his name—and then the world went black.

IT WAS THE sound of his name that woke him.

"Kat?" Gabe lifted his head and glanced around, surprised to find that he'd fallen asleep. On the television, Steph Davis was making her way up El Cap. Certain he'd heard someone call for him, he sat up.

It was only then he realized how dizzy he was and how much his head hurt. Hell, his entire body hurt. He sat back, drew several deep breaths, his heart thrumming erratically in his chest.

What the fuck?

He never got sick. Ever. Well, not unless he'd gotten drunk—but he hadn't touched a drop today, not even when the sound of Kat's tears had left him hating himself and wanting to drink away the echo of his own words.

Well, you sure as hell are sick now, buddy.

Trying to ignore the pain in his skull, he fought to sit up, but found he could barely move, as if some unseen force were holding him down on the couch. "Shit!"

Again he sank back, his breathing as ragged as if he'd just climbed El Cap himself, and some part of him wondered if he should call an ambulance. But even as he decided that he was being a big wimp, he fell over onto his side, his head landing against the armrest. And that's when he saw her.

Kat lay unconscious in the hallway, her arm outstretched as if she were reaching for him, her dark hair a tangled mass on the polished wood.

"Kat?" He called out her name, but she didn't move.

Adrenaline punched through him, got him on his feet. Spots swam before his eyes, as he took one step toward her and then another, his legs threatening to buckle. And then his paramedic training kicked in.

Dizziness. Rapid heartbeat. Confusion. Drowsiness. Headache.

Carbon monoxide poisoning.

They were dying of carbon monoxide poisoning.

There was no time to dial 911. If they didn't get fresh air, they'd be dead before the ambulance arrived. But there was another possibility . . .

Gabe turned on unsteady feet toward the living room window, drew his HK, flicked off the safety, then fired, aiming for a spread, hoping to God the rounds didn't make it past his security fence and kill somebody.

Bam! Bam! Bam!

The window cracked, three clean holes appearing in the pane—but the glass held.

Dammit!

The handgun's recoil sent him staggering. He dropped the weapon, caught the edge of the entertainment center, barely managing to stay on his feet.

Kat!

She lay still, so still he thought she must have stopped breathing.

Oh, God, Kat!

He had to get her outside, had to get her outside right fucking now.

He drove himself forward, fell to his knees beside her, his heart hammering. Her cheeks and lips were flushed cherry red—a sign that she was dying or already dead. Bolstered by another shot of adrenaline, he lifted her into his arms. "Stay alive, honey. Stay alive."

There was no time to see whether she was breathing, no time for CPR. If he collapsed, if he passed out, they would both die.

Somehow, he made it back to his feet, his legs threatening to give, his heart beating so hard it hurt, his head throbbing. One step, two—and he sank against the wall, Kat's weight drawing him off balance. He fought to steady himself, fought to catch his breath, knowing that the harder he breathed, the more carbon monoxide he was pulling into his lungs, his heart, his brain.

Another step. Another. And another.

He pushed himself forward, the front door only a handful of steps away. His vision grew spotty again, black dots dancing before his eyes. He forced himself to focus on the doorknob, willed his feet to keep moving.

Another step. Another.

He reached for the deadbolt, turned the lock, then grabbed for the doorknob and jerked the door open. Cold night air hit him full in the face. He staggered forward trying to reach Irving's men, who were already running toward him. But then his legs gave way, the cold concrete of his front porch rushing up at him, his vision going black. With his last shred of consciousness, he wrapped his arms around Kat, trying to shield her from the fall. And then there was nothing.

"I THINK HE'S coming around."

"His SAT rate says ninety-six."

"It's bullshit. Ignore it. Carbon monoxide poisoning gives false high readings, so keep the oh-two running at one hundred percent."

Gabe had no idea whose voices he was hearing or where he was. His head throbbed, his heart pounding hard. Faces swam in and out of his vision. Flashing lights. The crunch of boots on ice. And, slowly, the picture came together.

He was lying on a stretcher next to an ambulance. An oxygen mask covered his mouth and nose. There was an IV in his right arm and electrodes on his bare chest, a pulse ox monitor clipped to his forefinger.

What the fuck had happened? Had he fallen?

"Hey, big guy. Welcome back." A man in a blue Boulder Ambulance cap smiled down at him. "Can you tell me your name?"

"Gabriel . . . Rossiter," he answered, his voice muffled by the oxygen mask.

"We're going to take good care of you, Mr. Rossiter." The paramedic covered Gabe with a warmed blanket, and then they were moving.

As the stretcher turned, Gabe saw two ambulances and four or five police cars. They were sitting in front of his house, takedown lights and floodlights turned toward his front yard. And then he remembered.

Waking up. Terrible dizziness. Kat unconscious in the hall. His head and heart pounding as he carried her toward the door.

Carbon monoxide poisoning.

"Kat!" He tried to sit, couldn't. "Where is she? Is she . . . ?"

Then he saw her—or, rather, he saw where she was.

Ahead of him, four paramedics worked around another stretcher, two guiding it into the other ambulance, one walking alongside, pumping oxygen into her lungs with a hand-held ventilator, another straddling her, doing chest compressions. He knew what that meant—imminent cardiac arrest, agonal respiration. Her heart was beating too slowly, and she was struggling to breathe on her own.

Oh, Christ!

She couldn't die. Not Kat. He couldn't lose her, too.

"Kat!" Gabe jerked himself upright, tearing at tubes and wires, trying to get off the stretcher to reach her, dread twisting cold and sharp in his chest. "Get this shit off me! Kat!"

"Easy now!" Strong arms forced him onto his back and held him there.

Too weak and too out of breath to fight back, Gabe struggled but couldn't break free. "Goddamn it! Kat!"

She can't die! Not Kat! Please, God, not Kat!

"Hey, big guy! Take it easy! They're doing all they can for her. You need to let us take care of you, okay? Hey, Eric, I think we're going to have to sedate him."

"IV Ativan?"

"Yeah."

"Kat!" Gabe didn't hear them, his gaze fixed on her stretcher as she was lifted into the other ambulance and the doors were closed behind her. Nor did he see the paramedic who approached him with a syringe or notice when they injected the sedative into his IV line.

Flashing lights. The shrill wail of a siren. And the ambulance holding Kat disappeared down the street.

"Kat!" *Christ!* If she died . . .

But the thought unraveled before he could finish it, and he was drifting.

GABE STROKED HIS thumb across Kat's cheek, his gaze drifting back to the monitor beside her hospital bed, the normal rhythm of her heartbeat holding him together. He'd come so close to losing her, so unbelievably close.

She was breathing on her own now, but they still had her on oxygen. None of her organs had failed, and though they couldn't say for certain that she hadn't suffered any permanent injury, she wasn't showing the typical signs of brain damage. Still, she hadn't once moved during the hours he'd sat here beside her, hadn't opened her eyes, hadn't shown any sign that she knew he was there.

He'd awoken in the emergency room, disoriented and drowsy, as much from whatever they'd given him to knock him out as from the carbon monoxide. Fighting to control his temper so they wouldn't sedate him again, he'd refused to answer a single question, even from police, until someone had told him how Kat was doing.

"She's still critical," a sympathetic nurse had finally told him. "They've got her in a hyperbaric oxygen chamber."

The nurse had then gone on to explain what that meant, but he already knew—doctors were using pressure to force oxygen into her cells in an effort to keep her alive. And Gabe, who had never given any credence to the idea of deities and who had certainly never prayed, had begun to pray in earnest.

The next few hours had been a blur—doctors, blood tests, questions from detectives. Gabe had found it painfully hard to stay awake and had been forced to admit that he was in worse shape than he'd realized. He'd been unconscious when they'd finally moved Kat into intensive care.

He'd come to in his own hospital room after sleeping through most of the night. When he'd remembered why he was there and what had happened, he'd gotten out of bed, slipped into his jeans, and, battling dizziness, had dragged his IV pole to the nurse's station, where he'd demanded to know where Kat was. He must have looked half out of his mind to them—hospital gown, IV, jeans, bare feet—and maybe he had been. Perhaps that's why, rather than forcing him back into bed, a nurse had escorted him to intensive care, where he'd sat at Kat's bedside for the past three hours, holding her hand.

He leaned in close. "Kat, honey, can you hear me?"

Why was she so much worse off than he was? Even as he asked himself the question, Gabe knew the answer. He'd gone outside several times during the day to get firewood, while she'd stayed inside, breathing poison.

What had happened? He'd put a new filter on the furnace in September, something he did every fall. Had he done it wrong? Had something gone wrong with the machine itself? And the irony of it struck him. He'd brought Kat to his house to keep her safe, and doing so had almost killed her. If she'd suffered brain damage . . .

Her lashes lay dark against pale skin, her eyelids still swollen from crying, the tear stains on her cheeks proof he'd hurt her deeply.

*Just because we've fooled around a little doesn't mean
you can pry into my life!*

God, he was a bastard! What had he been thinking?

He hadn't been thinking. He'd seen her looking through
that damned photo album, and the past and present had col-
lided. All the rage he felt about Jill's betrayal, his grief about
her death, his confusing feelings for Kat had come together—
and exploded. His temper had gotten the best of him, making
him say things he wouldn't otherwise . . .

No, that was lie, a lame-ass excuse. He'd said what he'd
said, knowing his words would hurt her, some sick part of
him hoping to drive a wedge between them so that he could
go back to being in control of his emotions again, back to the
guarded emptiness that had been his life before he'd met her.
And despite the pain he'd caused her, she'd still cared enough
about him to show him compassion.

*You say you don't believe in ghosts, but she haunts
you.*

How could she see through him so clearly? He'd never even
spoken to her about Jill. As far as he knew, Kat knew nothing about Jill's death, apart from what she'd heard Samantha
say. Yet, Kat had cut right to the heart of it. And it had shaken
Gabe to his core—so he'd thrown her compassion in her face
and pushed her away.

*In the morning, I'll call Chief Irving and ask him to move
you to a police safe house. I think it would be best.*

Okay. If that's what you want.

No matter how he tried, he couldn't erase from his mind
the image of her as she'd turned and walked away from him,
tears in her eyes. But that wasn't what he regretted most.
What ate at him, what gnawed at him, was the fact that she'd
almost died believing he didn't care about her, that he'd used
her, that he no longer wanted to be near her.

It wasn't true. None of it was true. If only she could know
how he'd felt when he'd come to and seen paramedics fighting
to revive her . . .

Jesus!

Had he ever felt that afraid, that helpless?

"I'm sorry, Kat. I'm so sorry." He kissed her cheek, watched her sleep.

"You're not very good at following doctor's orders, are you?" A deep voice came from behind him.

Gabe jerked awake, unaware he'd drifted off again. "Hunter."

"How is she?"

"She hasn't regained consciousness. We won't know if there's brain damage until . . ." Gabe's throat grew strangely constricted, making it hard to talk.

Hunter laid a hand on his shoulder, and for a moment neither of them spoke.

"I'm sorry," Hunter said at last. "Everyone's shaken up by this."

Gabe nodded.

"I came by to check on you both—and to let you know this wasn't an accident. There's nothing wrong with your furnace. Someone packed your flue with wet leaves, forcing your furnace to vent carbon monoxide into the house."

The words took a moment to sink in, but when they did, a fire began to build in Gabe's gut, anger every bit as potent as adrenaline. He fought to keep his voice steady. "How do you know it was deliberate?"

"There were blades of grass and traces of muddy snow mixed with the leaves," Hunter told him. "Those leaves were raked up. They didn't drift in off a tree branch. Besides, you don't have a cottonwood in your yard, and neither do your neighbors. Whoever did it obviously wanted it to look like an accident but got sloppy."

It was a sick, insidious way to kill someone—turn a home into a gas chamber.

"I promised her I'd keep her safe. I did a great job of that, didn't I?"

"Knock that shit off." Hunter glared down at him. "Whoever did this is playing dirty. I don't know how you realized what was going on or found the strength to carry her outside. That was quick thinking to fire those three rounds, by the way. It didn't shatter the glass, but the guys outside heard. If you hadn't gotten to them, they'd have gotten to you. You're a damned hero, Rossiter. Get used to it."

But as Gabe watched Kat sleep, he didn't feel like a hero.

"WHY ARE YOU here, Kimímila?"

"I don't know." Kat looked up to see Grandpa Red Crow, joy spreading through her like sunlight, the burdens of her life—whatever they had been—slipping away, leaving her with a sense of peace she'd never felt before, as if all were well and had always been well. "I'm happy to see you."

From the distance came the steady beating of a drum and a bright light like the glow of a thousand fires. Her people were waiting for her there. She wasn't sure how she knew that, but she knew it just the same. Perhaps Grandpa Red Crow had come to take her to them.

"My sweet, brave Kimímila." Grandpa Red Crow smiled. "For most of your life, you've felt alone, but you aren't alone now. He is a good man."

"He doesn't want me." A shard of half-forgotten pain pricked her happiness.

But Grandpa Red Crow's smile didn't falter. "He is far from himself and no longer knows what he wants. You must help him."

"I'm not going with you?"

"No." Grandpa Red Crow's brown eyes twinkled, as if the thought of sending her away didn't bother him. "You must do what I asked you to do. It will be the fight of your life. Be strong, Kimímila."

Kat opened her eyes, the grief she felt as Grandpa Red Crow vanished from her dream bringing her awake. Or was she still dreaming? She didn't recognize this place.

Murmuring voices. Something that beeped. A quiet hissing sound.

It was the IV bag hanging above her bed that told her she was in a hospital.

Why was she in a hospital? She tried to remember, tried to remember—and then it came to her. She'd gotten very sick.

She'd woken up in Gabe's room, and she'd been very sick. She'd gotten out of bed to get some aspirin and . . .

He must have brought her here.

The moments passed slowly, and gradually things around her began to make sense. There was an oxygen mask covering her nose and mouth. That's what made the hissing sound. The murmur of voices was nurses talking at a nearby workstation. The beeping came from a monitor that was connected by wires to electrodes on her chest.

She felt something move near her hip and looked down to find Gabe, asleep, his head resting beside her on the bed. He looked exhausted, dark circles beneath his eyes, his hair rumpled, his jaw unshaven. She reached toward him.

Just because we've fooled around a little doesn't mean you can pry into my life!

She hesitated, drew her hand back, the argument they'd had after he'd found her with the photo album coming back to her with painful clarity, stopping her short. He didn't want her. He wanted Chief Irving to put her in a safe house so he wouldn't have to deal with her any longer.

He is far from himself and no longer knows what he wants.

Grandpa Red Crow's voice echoed in her mind—a voice from a dream. And she decided that Grandpa was right. If Gabe didn't want to be near her, why had he fallen asleep watching over her?

She reached out again, ran her fingers softly over his hair. He gave a jerk. Then his head snapped up. He met her gaze, and for a moment he looked confused.

"Kat?" He sat upright, took her hand in his, a look of naked relief spreading over his face. "You're awake. Oh, thank God! How do you feel, honey?"

She had to think about that for a moment. "Tired. Sore."

"I bet." He kissed her fingers. "Do you remember my name?"

"Gabe Rossiter." Why had he asked her that? She pushed the oxygen mask aside, not liking the way it muffled her words. "You silly goat. How could being sick make me forget your name?"

He settled the oxygen mask in place again. "You weren't

sick, honey—at least not with a disease. You had carbon monoxide poisoning. Someone almost killed you. Someone almost killed both of us."

That's when she noticed the IV in the back of his right hand and the hospital bracelet around his wrist.

"Wh-what happened?"

CHAPTER 22

"HE CARRIED YOU out. Did he tell you that?" Sophie sat in the chair next to Kat's hospital bed, Tessa standing beside her, Holly sitting near Kat's feet. Matt stood alone in the corner, looking distracted, his wrinkled blue shirt hanging out of his pants in back.

"Gabe said he got me out of the house, but he didn't say how. I guess he would've had to carry me if I was unconscious." Kat hadn't thought of that.

Then again, this whole thing was surreal. She still had a hard time believing that she'd almost died, that she had, in fact, quit breathing, that her heart had almost stopped beating. But the truth of it was written on her body. Her breastbone was so sore where they'd done chest compressions that it hurt to breathe. Her muscles felt as if she'd been to a gym, and she still had a dull headache—both left over from the carbon monoxide.

Holding her hand, Gabe had told her how he'd woken up feeling sick, had seen her lying on the floor and had realized they were both dying of carbon monoxide poisoning just in time to get the two of them out of the house. "When I came to, I saw them trying to revive you, and I thought . . . I should have kept you safe. I'm sorry."

The remorse on his face had told Kat how sorry he was. She'd given his hand a squeeze. "It's not your fault. How could you have known? Please don't blame yourself. Besides, we're both still alive, aren't we?"

His words and his tenderness in that first hour after she'd

regained consciousness had touched her so deeply that she'd
forgotten about their argument and the things he'd said. Then
a doctor had come in to examine her and had ordered Gabe
back to his own room. She'd seen Gabe once since then.
Shortly after she'd been transferred out of ICU, he'd come
to her hospital room wearing his own clothes to tell her he'd
been discharged.

"I'm going to meet with Chief Irving to work out where
we can put you to keep you safe." His face had been expressionless, the concern and tenderness he'd shown earlier gone.
"I'll be back this afternoon."

Then he'd turned and walked away. He hadn't even
kissed her.

That's when she'd remembered.

*In the morning, I'll call Chief Irving and ask him to move
you to a police safe house. I think it would be best.*

And she'd felt so confused. How could he care enough
about her to hold her hand, to kiss her cheek, to sit by her
hospital bed for hours when he ought to have been in bed
himself and yet still want to be apart from her? Not that she
could stay at his house, not when the person who wanted her
dead knew she was there. But that didn't mean they had to be
apart. Then again, it was perhaps safer for him to be nowhere
near her.

This was the second time he'd almost been killed while
trying to protect her.

She'd found it hard to sleep after that, her thoughts on the
man who cared about her but couldn't seem to love her.

Natalie had arrived just after noon. She was covering the
story and had needed to interview Kat. Tessa and Sophie had
come together as soon as Sophie had gotten off work, while
Holly and Matt had each driven separately. Kara's kids were
sick with strep throat, so she'd sent a card and flowers but
hadn't been able to come in person. Their kindness and concern lifted Kat's spirits more than they could know.

Sophie stood and arched her lower back, rubbing it, as if
it ached. "Mike and Troy—the two cops who were watching Gabe's place—told Marc they heard the shots, called for

backup, and were running toward the house with their guns drawn, when Gabe stumbled out of the front door and collapsed on his front porch with you in his arms. They thought you'd both been shot. Troy said Gabe tried to fight off the paramedics to get to you. They had to sedate him."

Kat hadn't heard any of this.

"God, that's so romantic!" Holly gave a dreamy sigh. "I want some hot guy to carry me in his arms and rescue me!"

"Do you?" Tessa asked sweetly. "You should ask Kat whether she found it romantic, because before the rescuing bit came the part where someone nearly killed her—or did you miss that?"

"Sometimes you say the stupidest things, Holly." Matt shook his head, then crossed the room and gave Kat a kiss on the cheek. "I'm really glad you're okay. I think I'm going to head home."

Everyone stared at Matt in surprise, Holly's cheeks flushing pink. It wasn't like him to say anything sharp. Kat suspected he hadn't stopped blaming himself for the city finance director's suicide.

She took his hand, gave it a squeeze. "Take care of yourself, okay?"

"Yeah," he said. Then he walked out the door.

An awkward silence filled the room.

Seeing the hurt Holly was attempting to hide, Kat tried to reassure her. "I wasn't upset by what you said, Holly. I know what you meant. Matt has his own troubles right now. I don't think he would have said that to you otherwise."

Holly gave a shrug. "I suppose what I said was pretty stupid. You did just almost die. It's just that . . . All of you have met men who really love you, who would do anything for you, even risk their lives. The men I meet only want one thing. They wouldn't risk anything for me."

It was without a doubt the most honest thing Kat had ever heard Holly say, and for a moment Holly looked like she might cry.

Tessa walked over to Holly, put her arm around her shoulders. "You'll find him one of these days, girl. You just need to stop trying so hard."

"And let's hope that when you do find him, you're not in need of rescuing." Sophie glanced at Kat and smiled. "There are other ways to test a man's love."

"Gabe doesn't love me." The words were out before Kat knew she'd spoken. She hesitated, not used to talking about her personal life with others. "He . . . He cares about me. I know that. But he doesn't love me."

Her three friends looked at her as if she'd just spoken in Diné, perplexed expressions their faces.

Sophie frowned. "Why do you say that? From what Marc and I have seen, Gabe is head over heels for you."

Kat was about to speak when Holly cut in. "I thought you two were lovers. Are you still a virgin?"

Tessa shot Holly an irritated glance and went on as if Holly had never spoken. "For goodness sake, the man has almost gotten himself killed twice trying to keep you safe. Do you think a man would do that for just any woman?"

Kat understood the point they were trying to make. It was the same thing she'd told herself so often these past few days. "I know he cares about me. When I woke up, he was sitting beside me, asleep. He seemed so worried. But then, after he was discharged, he was like a different man. He seemed so . . . distant."

Sophie gave a dismissive wave of her hand. "That's just him being a man. Trust me. He's crazy about you, even if he doesn't know it yet."

"I wish I could believe that." Tears pricked Kat's eyes, catching her by surprise. "Before I got sick yesterday, I upset him, and h-he said some things . . . He made it clear that he didn't want to be around me any longer. I was—"

Holly gave a little gasp, her eyes going wide.

And there just inside the doorway stood Gabe.

Kat saw the unreadable expression on his face, and knew he'd overheard her talking about him.

He met her gaze. "I didn't realize you had visitors. I'll wait out in the hall."

"No need. We were just about to leave." Sophie picked up her purse, leaned over, and gave Kat a hug. "Feel better, okay? And stay safe. Call me on my cell phone any time. If there's any way Marc and I can help, you know we will."

"Okay. *Ahéhee'*. Thank you, and thanks to Marc, too."

Then Sophie stood on her tiptoes and kissed Gabe on the cheek. "I'm so grateful you and Kat are both okay, Gabe. And thank you."

Gabe looked startled. "You're welcome."

Tessa and Holly followed, each giving Kat a hug and thanking Gabe for all he'd done. And then Kat was alone with him.

He stood at the window still wearing his parka, his back to her, his hands thrust in the pockets of his jeans. Even without seeing his face, she could tell he was angry. Something about his posture radiated tension.

"I . . . I'm sorry, Gabe." She sought for the right words, certain she'd widened the rift between them. "I shouldn't have been talking about you like that. I don't usually . . . I'm not sure why I—"

"DON'T WORRY ABOUT IT." Gabe heard the fear in Kat's voice, the sound of it adding regret to the emotions that already churned in his gut. "After all you've been through, you needed to talk to someone."

Besides, after what he'd said to her, he deserved it. He'd hoped she had no memory of yesterday afternoon, that she'd forgotten it. Clearly, she hadn't. And that meant he needed to apologize. More than that, he needed to keep his promise to himself.

He needed to tell her.

He turned, saw the uncertainty in her eyes. She looked fragile, vulnerable, an IV in the back of her left hand, her face pale, her hair tangled around her shoulders. He crossed the room, shrugged off his coat, and sat down beside the bed, fighting the urge to hold her hand. "How are you feeling?"

You're a fucking coward, Rossiter.

Yeah, he was.

He'd sworn to himself that if she lived, he would tell her how Jill had died. She had asked, and she deserved to know. Not that it would change anything between them, but at least then she'd understand that the problem wasn't her. It was him.

Something inside him was broken, and he didn't know how to fix it.

The truth was that he *did* care about Kat. The past twenty-four hours had made him face that fact. He cared about her, wanted her, needed her more than he'd needed anyone in three long years. And he didn't know what the hell to do about it.

"I'm better. Thank you. How about you?" She unconsciously rubbed her breastbone, and he knew the paramedics had left her bruised and sore.

"I'm fine."

Her gaze searched his. "And you're sure you're not angry?"

Oh, he was angry all right—but not with her. He was angry with the goddamned son of a bitch who'd packed his flue with leaves and almost killed her, angry enough to want to hunt the fucker down and blow his head off. And he was angry with himself for having hurt her. "Yeah, I'm sure."

Tell her!

She seemed to relax, her guileless eyes still wide and searching. Then she reached up to run a hand over his jaw, her fingers sliding through the hair at his temple. "You shaved. And your hair is damp."

He nodded. "I went home and took a shower. They gave me a police escort. It's strange taking a shower when your house is full of cops."

Why not talk about the weather while you're at it, dumbshit?

She looked away from him, a troubled expression on her face. "Gabe, I . . . I'm sorry I looked through your photo album. I didn't mean—"

He pressed his fingers against her lips. "Shhh. Don't. I'm the one who needs to apologize, not you."

She met his gaze, confusion in her eyes.

"I said things I shouldn't have said, things I didn't mean, and I'm sorry. I was way out of line. I left the damned photo album under the couch. I know you weren't snooping. If I tripped over a photo album with pictures of your life growing up on the rez, I'd probably look through it, too."

Find your balls and tell her, Rossiter.

"I'm sorry you lost her."

It was now or never. "You asked about Jill. You asked how she died."

Kat shook her head, her fingers closing around his. "You don't need to—"

"Yes. I do." He drew his hand away, stood, and turned back toward the window, unable to take the sympathy in Kat's eyes, hating how exposed it made him feel. "We met on a climbing trip to Yosemite. She'd driven from Moab with a couple of girlfriends. I'd come with my best friend from high school. His name was . . . Wade."

How long had it been since he'd spoken that name aloud?

"Jill was funny and sexy and one hell of a climber. Wade and I ended up hanging at Camp Four with them and a bunch of other Yosemite regulars that first night. He hooked up with one of her friends and went off to fuck in the forest, and I headed back to our camp alone. I was almost asleep when Jill crawled into my tent and, well . . ."

Jill had blown his mind, shimmying out of her jeans and hoodie, unzipping his sleeping bag and going down on him without a word. She'd climbed on top of him as soon as he was hard, getting them both off in under two minutes. It had been animal sex at its best. But Kat didn't need the details.

"She moved to Boulder a month later, and soon we were living together."

That had been a wild time, every day an adventure. Everything had seemed perfect. He'd had a job he loved, a woman he loved, a group of close friends—and all of the action he could handle, both outdoors and in the sack. But it had all been a lie.

"You must have loved her very much."

Gabe nodded. "Every guy who climbs fantasizes about meeting a woman who loves the sport as much as he does. Rock climbing, alpine climbing, ice climbing, rafting, mountain biking, skiing—Jill loved it all, and she was good at it."

Somehow he'd reached the window again. He stared out at the darkness, willing himself to stay numb. He hadn't talked to anyone about Jill since her funeral, and he wasn't sure he could handle losing it again like he'd done in the sweat lodge.

"We'd been living together for a couple years when I asked her to marry me. I took her to her favorite rooftop restaurant, surprised her with a one-carat diamond ring, got down on one knee—the whole thing. She said yes. I was on top of the world."

He could still remember how the setting sun had turned the sky over the Foothills pink, how Jill's eyes had misted up, how everyone in the restaurant had applauded when she'd said yes. It had been another perfect moment in his perfect life.

"She wanted a fall wedding in the mountains when the aspens were gold. I liked that idea. She wanted a honeymoon in the Himalayas the following spring. That was cool with me, too. She wanted me to get a vasectomy so that she could go off the pill. I wasn't too excited about that. Putting my nuts to the knife had never been part of my plan, but when you love someone . . . She didn't want kids because pregnancy would interfere with climbing."

"About six weeks before the wedding . . ." Suddenly he found it all but impossible to speak, his control cracking, the abyss inside him yawning wide, three years of pain, of grief, of rage roiling inside his chest, threatening to tear a hole right through him. He'd known where telling this story would lead him, but still the raw hurt astonished him. He forced breath into constricted lungs, willed himself to go on. "About six weeks . . ."

Kat heard Gabe's voice break, saw his hands clench into fists, and her throat grew tight. Ignoring her dizziness and the soreness in her chest, she slid out of bed and wrapped the extra blanket the nurse had given her around her shoulders for modesty's sake, then crossed the cold tile floor one unsteady step at a time, pulling her IV pole along with her. She stopped behind him, hesitated for a moment, then rested her palm against the middle of his back, offering what little support she could.

He stiffened, but he didn't draw away. Then he turned his

head and looked back at her, his brows drawn together in a frown. "You shouldn't be out of bed."

"Don't worry about me."

"You almost died, Kat. Don't be ridiculous." He sounded irritated, but his actions were gentle as he wrapped his arm around her shoulders and guided her back to bed, holding her IV line clear while she settled beneath the sheets. "There you go."

He sat down in the chair beside her, his gaze fixed far-away. And for a long moment, there was silence. When he spoke again, his voice was stripped of emotion, flat. "About six weeks before the wedding, she said she needed . . . to get away. A camping trip with her bridesmaids. I was working."

A muscle clenched in his jaw, some kind of battle raging beneath his skin, and Kat wished she knew what to say or do to make this easier for him.

"She was late getting home. I'd made dinner. The doorbell rang. It was a state patrolman. He said . . ." Gabe's voice broke again. "He said . . . Jill was dead. Car accident in Boulder Canyon. A drunk driver had crossed the yellow line. Her car had rolled into the canyon. The coroner needed me to ID the body."

Kat tried to imagine what it would be like to be asked to identify the dead body of someone she loved—and remembered how hard it had been to see Grandpa Red Crow lying broken on the ground. But what Gabe had gone through had been much worse. Jill had been his fiancée, the woman he loved. "Oh, Gabe! I'm so sorry."

But he didn't seem to hear her. "The officer drove me down. I thought there must be some kind of mistake. It couldn't be her. It couldn't be. But it was. Her face . . . Her face was bruised, bloodied. I touched her cheek, kissed her. She was so cold. I stood there, looking down at her. I didn't . . . I didn't want to leave her there . . . *alone*."

His voice dropped to a whisper on that last word, his eyes squeezed shut, the sight of his anguish making it impossible for Kat to hold back her own tears. She reached out, took his hand.

"I asked about her friends, the other women who'd been with her, but . . ." He drew a deep breath, as if trying to steady himself. "The coroner told me there hadn't been other women in the car. The passenger . . . had been a man."

CHAPTER 23

THE PASSENGER HAD been a man.

It took Kat a moment to understand what this meant, the truth dawning slowly. If Jill hadn't been with her bridesmaids, then . . .

She'd lied to Gabe. She'd been unfaithful. She'd betrayed him.

"That's when I noticed the other gurney, the other body. Wade was draped with a sheet, but part of his arm was exposed. I recognized his tats. My fiancée and my best friend. Killed in a car accident together."

To lose the woman he loved and his best friend on the same day would have been bad enough. But to lose them like this . . .

Tears gliding down her cheeks, Kat held tighter to Gabe's hand. "I-I'm so sorry!"

"At first, I thought there must have been some explanation. Maybe her girlfriends had driven separately. Maybe she'd run into Wade and given him a ride back into town." Gabe shook his head, gave a little laugh, his gaze hard. "God, I was an idiot."

"No! Don't say that!" Kat sat upright, her words coming out with a ferocity that surprised her. "You weren't an idiot. You were grieving and in shock. You loved them, trusted them, and wanted to believe the best of them."

It isn't easy being let down by someone you loved and trusted.

Words he'd spoken just the other day came back to her, and she understood he'd been speaking from painful experience.

No wonder it had been easy for him to believe that Grandpa Red Crow had been hiding a drinking problem or looting artifacts. After a betrayal like that, Gabe would find it terribly hard to trust anyone again.

Especially women.

"I spent the next couple of days half crazed, trying to uncover the truth. I went through her e-mail, her cell phone messages, her credit card receipts, and found shit I wish to God I hadn't. I confronted her girlfriends. They'd known she was going away with him and had been ready to cover for her. Then one of my climbing buddies came by. He told me Jill had been fucking Wade off and on ever since she'd moved to Colorado. Their trip together was supposed to be one last pre-wedding fling before she settled down."

"He knew? Your friend knew—and he didn't tell you?"

"He said it wasn't his business. He said Jill loved me but couldn't give up the single lifestyle. He called her a sex addict, and I wondered how many of my other friends she'd fucked." Gabe spoke through clenched teeth, his voice shaking with barely suppressed rage. "I told him to get the fuck out. I work with him, but we're no longer friends. As for the rest of them—I haven't spoken to any of them since."

"I don't blame you." What kind of friends would let a buddy marry a woman they knew had already been unfaithful? No friend worth keeping, that much was certain.

"I didn't go to Wade's funeral, but I went to Jill's. I left the engagement ring I'd bought her on her finger to remind her of the promise she'd broken and watched as they lowered her casket into the ground, not knowing whether to hate her or . . ."

Kat swallowed a sob, finished for him. "Or whether to grieve for her."

He nodded. "My life with her was a lie. The woman I loved, my circle of close friends. None of it was real. I believed in something that never really existed."

And Kat understood. He hadn't just lost Jill and Wade. He'd lost all of it—the people he loved and the life he'd lived.

"The autopsy came out the day after her funeral. She'd

died almost instantly of a broken neck and massive internal injuries. The coroner found semen inside her—live sperm, still moving. She and Wade were both dead, but his sperm were still alive inside her. Kind of funny when you think about it."

"I don't think it's funny at all." Kat could only imagine how hurtful it had been for him to read through the report, proof of Jill's infidelity and Wade's betrayal spilled across the pages of a public document, a document anyone could read.

"We were going to get married, but she fucked my best friend." Gabe met Kat's gaze, anger sharp in his eyes. But behind the rage, she saw hurt, torment, desolation. "She said she loved me, but she fucked my best friend."

Unable to speak, Kat drew him into her arms.

Gabe allowed himself to sink into Kat's arms, the comfort she offered a refuge from the turmoil inside him, her embrace holding the pieces of him together. He felt shattered, empty, a gaping hole in his chest where his heart should have been, the edges torn and still bleeding. He wrapped his arms around her and held on, hating himself for needing her, but needing her just the same.

It was only then he realized she was crying, her slender body shaking with the effort to contain her tears, her breath coming in shudders. Something twisted in his chest to know she cared. But he hadn't put himself through this to provoke her sympathy, no matter how deeply it touched him. He'd done it so she'd understand.

He drew back, looked down at her face, her cheeks wet with tears, her eyes glistening. "I'm telling you all of this so you'll understand that it's not you, it's me. I can't be the man you want me to be. I'm broken. Inside, I'm broken. Don't waste your time hoping for things that can't happen."

She looked up at him through her tears, her gaze soft with compassion. "You're not broken, Gabe Rossiter. You're just afraid to let yourself feel because feeling hurts so much. But feeling is part of living. You can't escape it. If you try, you'll hurt yourself worse than Jill ever could."

Gabe opened his mouth to object, but nothing came out,

her words knocking the breath out of him. Then she leaned forward—and kissed him.

Her lips brushed over his, petal-soft touches that shocked his system, made his mind go blank. Surprised, he watched, eyes open, as she leaned into him, deepening the kiss, her arms sliding behind his neck. Then her tongue flicked his, and he couldn't help but respond, her touch calling him back from the edge of the abyss, the storm inside him igniting into something even more elemental.

He took control of the kiss, his tongue subduing hers, his body shaking with the sudden force of his craving for her. She felt warm and alive in his arms, her heart beating hard against his. He rained kisses over her face, her tears salty on his tongue, the scent of her skin making him want to devour her. "God, Kat, what have you done to me?"

It wasn't a rhetorical question. Somehow, she knocked him off balance, getting past his guard, breaking through the wall he'd built around the pieces of his heart. He'd let her stay at his house. He'd slept beside her. He'd told her things he'd never told anyone. And now, after he'd spent the past hour explaining to her why she shouldn't waste any more time or emotion on him, he couldn't keep his hands off her.

He didn't wait for her to answer, kissing her again, drawing her closer. She whimpered into his mouth, melting against him in a way that sent heat shooting straight to his groin, her fingers curling in his hair. It was only when his hand bumped against her IV line that he remembered she was supposed to be resting in bed.

He dragged his lips from hers, looked into her eyes and saw a need that matched his own, both of them breathless. "It's a good thing you're off the heart monitor, or we'd have set off the alarm. Nurse Ratched would have come and kicked my ass."

He'd wanted to make her laugh, but she didn't even smile. Tears filled her eyes again, and she reached up to rest her hand against his cheek. "Don't push me away, Gabe. I know you're hurting, but please don't push me away. Don't ask Chief Irving to put me someplace where I can't be with you."

He lifted her back onto the bed, then drew the covers up around her and sat beside her. "I'm not a saint, Kat. Far from it. If we spend much more time together, we're going to end up having sex. Are you sure it's worth the risk?"

She nodded. "Yeah."

And some part of Gabe was relieved.

GABE ARRIVED LATE the next afternoon to find Kat sitting on her bed, dressed and talking on the phone. Given what she was talking about, he guessed she was speaking with her editor. He sat in the chair and glanced at his watch. They had a schedule to keep and needed to be on the road in fifteen minutes.

"He said that artifacts from this area have been showing up on the black market as far away as Beijing and Riyadh, everything from pots to moccasins to human remains. He couldn't say whether they'd come from Mesa Butte specifically, but the designs on the pottery indicate that they were painted by Cheyenne during the century prior to the arrival of settlers."

So she'd spoken with Darcangelo. His FBI contacts had put him in touch with an Interpol agent who'd noticed a sharp uptick in artifacts from this region. Apparently, he'd arranged for Kat to interview the agent. Strange that Darcangelo hadn't mentioned it—or maybe not so strange, given how busy they'd been.

Gabe had spent yesterday afternoon and all day today with Darcangelo and Hunter, getting things ready. They'd used the time to talk over her case but hadn't gotten any closer to piecing things together than they'd been yesterday. The *inipi* raid. Red Crow's death. Threatening phone calls. Looting. Attempts on Kat's life. Lots of puzzle pieces, but no clue as to how they went together. Then Gabe had remembered the hunch he'd gotten just before he'd gone upstairs and seen Kat with the photo album.

"The person who'd made those death threats knew that the phones he was calling from were beyond the city's surveillance cameras," he'd told them.

"What makes you say that?" Hunter had asked.

"Just a hunch."

Darcangelo and Hunter had stared at him, then looked at each other. Darcangelo had called Irving, who'd agreed to ask the city of Boulder for a list of everyone who had access to information about the city's surveillance system. Gabe was pretty damn certain he'd see Daniels's name on that list. It wouldn't prove anything, of course, but it would be a step in the right direction.

He glanced at his watch again, then back at the woman he couldn't seem to get out of his mind. All night long what she'd said had run through his head, permeating his dreams, waking him again and again until he'd given up sleeping.

You're not broken, Gabe Rossiter. You're just afraid to let yourself feel because feeling hurts so much. But feeling is part of living. You can't escape it. If you try, you'll hurt yourself worse than Jill ever could.

Well, Kat was right that he couldn't escape feeling. And his feelings for her were confusing the shit out of him. One moment he was certain the best thing he could do for her—for both of them—was to get the hell out of her life. The next he wanted her so badly that he could barely stand being away from her. It was a wonder he hadn't given himself whiplash.

He let his gaze travel over her, unable to help himself, her femininity enticing him even from across the room. She had tucked her long hair behind her ear, her cheeks a healthy rose color once more. She was wearing the same sweater she'd worn at the restaurant with a pair of sleek jeans, her legs tucked beneath her, her toes peeking out from beneath her, her feet covered with adorable fuzzy pink girl socks.

Adorable fuzzy pink girl socks? Damn, Rossiter, listen to yourself!

So many things had changed since she'd come into his life. He had changed. It scared the hell out of him, and yet, he couldn't deny that when'd woken up this morning he'd felt . . . lighter. Faced with the undeniable fact that Kat meant something to him—and that he was going to be holed up with her for the foreseeable future—he'd decided he had no choice but to take it day by day and see what happened.

You know what's going to happen, dumbass. You're going to fuck her brains out, and then walk away and leave her broken, too.

No, he'd keep his prick in his pants—or at least out of her.

He caught Kat's gaze and pointed at his watch. "We need to go."

She nodded. "Yes, but I'm only about halfway through the documents. That's as far as I made it before . . . Yes, I'll try to have a story ready for you by deadline on Monday. But I have to go now. I've been discharged, so they're moving me."

Gabe scowled at her and shook his head, wishing she hadn't said that.

Kat rolled her eyes at him.

They'd planned to move her in secret, without anyone knowing when she was leaving the hospital besides the three of them, Chief Irving, and the hospital's security staff. Though Gabe was certain no one at the paper would deliberately endanger Kat, the fewer people who knew, the better. The hospital wouldn't acknowledge that she'd been discharged until later this afternoon in order to keep whoever was after her in the dark for as long as possible. Hopefully, by the time the bastard found out she was gone, she'd be far beyond his reach.

"Thanks, Tom. Tell everyone I miss them. Bye." She ended the call and slid off the bed, just as a gray-haired nurse entered pushing a wheelchair. Kat stared at it, then shook her head. "Thanks, but I'm fine. I can walk."

The nurse shrugged. "Hospital policy."

Gabe couldn't help but smile at the dismay on Kat's face. "Just sit back and enjoy the ride, honey."

THEY TOOK KAT out through a basement exit that led to the employee's underground parking garage, where Marc and Julian were waiting. First they had her put on a Kevlar vest. Then she and Gabe, who was also wearing Kevlar, got into Marc's SUV, Kat sitting in the backseat and Gabe riding up front, while Julian followed in an unmarked police car.

"Where are we going?" she asked Marc.

He slid his Bluetooth headset into place, meeting her gaze

in the rearview mirror. "That's for us to know, and no one to find out."

They left the parking garage and emerged onto the street, Julian lagging a few car lengths behind them as they drove south on Broadway. Fifteen minutes later, they'd left Boulder behind. Forty-five minutes later, they were on I-70 and heading into the snowy mountains.

Kat watched the foothills give way to deep canyons and rising peaks, her thoughts drifting once again to what Gabe had told her yesterday. Now she understood why he didn't believe in love, why he thought sex was only about pheromones. How could he believe anything else when the woman he'd loved— the woman who'd said she loved him and who'd agreed to marry him—had hurt and misled him so completely? If what Gabe's so-called friend had told him was true, Jill had been unfaithful from the very beginning. She'd taken Gabe's love under false pretenses—and she'd squandered it.

Kat might have despised her for what she'd done, but Jill was dead. It wasn't right to think bad thoughts of the dead.

And though Kat hadn't considered it until last night, she also understood why he lived his life so completely alone, no longer surrounded by the big group of friends she'd seen in the photographs. He'd lost Jill, discovered the truth about her and Wade, and then learned that his friends had known but hadn't been brave or loyal enough to tell him. His hopes, his dreams, and his faith in other people had been smashed with a single devastating blow. In his grief and rage, he'd cut himself off from everyone.

I can't be the man you want me to be. I'm broken. Inside, I'm broken.

Kat didn't believe that. He wasn't broken. A broken man wouldn't have risked his life to save hers. But she knew he hadn't healed, either. And as she considered it, she thought perhaps she understood why.

Gabe had never let himself grieve for Jill because he was hurt and angry that she'd betrayed him, but he'd hadn't been able to express his hurt or rage, either, because he'd still loved her and had been overwhelmed with grief. One emotion blocked the next, bottled them up inside him. The grief, the hurt, and the rage were still there. She'd seen them all yesterday. Like a man who didn't know which way to turn, he was lost, trapped between irreconcilable emotions.

Don't waste your time hoping for things that can't happen.

Was that what she was doing? Was she hoping for something impossible, something that could never be? No. She refused to consider that.

Kat might not uphold all the traditions of her people. She might not believe everything her grandmother had taught her—the Navajo creation stories, the tales of mythological creatures, the prophesies about the Time of the End. But she was Diné. And she knew that nothing in life was random. Things happened for a reason.

It hadn't been coincidence when the rocks had fallen from beneath her feet, bringing to her side the one man who was both willing and able to watch over her, protect her, and save her life, a man who cared about Native people and respected the land. It wasn't an accident when she'd tried to push him away and events had conspired again and again to bring them together until she'd fallen in love with him. So it couldn't be a mistake that he'd bared his soul to her, revealing to her the shattered part of himself that he'd shared with no one else.

Somehow, Kat was supposed to help him heal.

She knew it in her heart, knew it in her soul, knew it just as she knew the sun would rise in the morning. What she didn't know was how to do it.

He is far from himself and no longer knows what he wants. You must help him.

Grandpa Red Crow's words came back to her.

But how? What should I do?

She closed her eyes and prayed.

She didn't realize she'd fallen asleep until Gabe woke her with a kiss. "Wake up, Sleeping Beauty."

"Where are we?" She sat up, zipped her coat, and looked around to find herself in another parking garage, this one full of people carrying snowboards and skis.

"Nowhere yet."

He and Marc hustled her through the parking garage, Marc walking in front of her, Gabe walking behind her, both of them alert. People seemed naturally to make way for them, taking one look at Marc and Gabe and finding some better place to be. And for the first time all day, Kat felt nervous.

Someone was trying very hard to kill her.

Then abruptly Marc glanced over his shoulder, one hand on his Bluetooth headset. "Copy that. You need backup?"

Kat felt her pulse skip. She looked over her shoulder and caught just a glimpse of flashing police lights before Gabe's arm went around her shoulders, compelling her to move faster. "Now isn't the time to be curious, honey. Keep moving."

Marc had picked up the pace, as well. "We're almost out. Don't worry about us. Take care of yourself."

"Was it Daniels?" Gabe asked.

"Yep."

"Son of a bitch!"

"Frank Daniels?" Kat stopped in her tracks—only to be dragged forward again. "What happened to Julian?"

"Nothing." Marc opened the door to a stairway that led up. "Someone tailed us up the canyon. Darcangelo pulled the car over and found Frank Daniels behind the wheel. I imagine the two of them are having a nice little chat."

Kat didn't know whether to feel relieved by this news—or afraid for Julian.

"I'd like to have a chat with him," Gabe muttered under his breath. "Darcangelo gets to have all the fun."

Marc grinned. "Not today he doesn't."

CHAPTER 24

KAT UNDERSTOOD WHAT Marc meant when she saw the snowmobiles. They sat on a trailer hitched to Gabe's SUV, which was parked in a nearby parking lot. Immediately she realized two things. The first was that they'd put a lot of preparation and effort into this secret plan of theirs. The second was that wherever they were going, they'd be riding these. A swarm of butterflies took flight in her stomach. She'd never even touched a snowmobile, much less driven one.

"Don't worry." Gabe rested his hand reassuringly on her back. "You'll be riding with me, safe and snug."

"Thank goodness!" she muttered.

He chuckled.

The three of them climbed into the vehicle, Gabe in the driver's seat, and left the expensive condos and inns of what turned out to be Vail behind, taking a snow-packed mountain road that wound its way behind the ski area, heading into what looked like backcountry wilderness.

Kat had never seen this part of Colorado. And never had she seen so much snow, the evergreen forest blanketed in deep white as far as the eye could see. The bright sun made the landscape sparkle, snow gleaming so bright and white that it almost hurt Kat's eyes, the sight so breathtaking that she momentarily forgot why they were here. As she took in the beauty that surrounded her, she half listened to Marc and Gabe talk about skiing, the two of them speaking a language she didn't understand.

"We hit the coulie in early March, and it was nothing but

champagne powder and face shots all the way to the bottom," Gabe said.

"Sounds epic. Until yesterday, I hadn't skied anything but snow farms since getting out of prison," Marc replied. "Sophie skis only blues and greens, and when she's pregnant I don't want her on the slopes at all."

"I don't blame you. Ever tried snowboarding?" Gabe asked.

"Yeah, but I prefer skis."

"You're good, too. That was some sick terrain yesterday." There was a note of admiration in Gabe's voice. "At first, I was pretty sure I was going to have to come back for you with a toboggan and a warm blankie."

Marc chuckled. "So I surprised you?"

"Hell, yeah, you did. You jumped out of the chopper, and it was on."

That got Kat's attention. She gaped at the two men from the backseat. They had jumped out of a helicopter? On skis?

"I did all right, but you were amazing. Darcangelo's right. You're absolute hell on a pair of skis." Marc shook his head. "I don't think I've ever seen anyone take deep powder the way you do. Gee-zus! I didn't know whether to follow you down the slope or get on my knees and kiss your ass."

The two men laughed, and Kat saw on Gabe's face something of the man he'd once been, smile lines crinkling around his eyes, a broad grin on his tanned face. It made her happy to see friendship growing between him and Julian and Marc. They were men Gabe could trust, men who knew what it was to suffer betrayal and loss—and to find happiness again. And Kat hoped with all her heart that Gabe would find happiness again, too, whether with her or without her.

They took a right turn—then the truck stopped. Ahead of them stood a closed steel gate, the road beyond buried beneath a good five feet of snow. And Kat understood why they needed the snowmobiles.

"Here we are." Gabe looked back at her and grinned.

Yes, here they most certainly were. But where was here?

"So . . . are you ever going to tell me where we're going?"

GABE ACCELERATED, POURING on the gas to get the snowmobile up the steep hillside. Ahead of him, Hunter, a high-powered rifle on his back, cleared the hill's crest and caught air, snow spraying up behind him as he flew over the top and disappeared on the other side. Gabe would have liked to do the same, but he couldn't—not with Kat riding behind him and towing a sled. It would likely scare the hell out of her, and it was just too risky while weighted down with supplies. Besides, Marc had the better machine, one built for high performance on mountain steeps, while Gabe had the snowmobile equivalent of the family station wagon.

Not that he really minded. Having Kat behind him, her thighs pressing against his, her arms wrapped around his waist, offered its own rush. It felt good just to be near her. She seemed more relaxed than she'd been when they first started out. In his mirror, he could see that she was smiling, her long hair blowing around her face, her cheeks flushed from excitement.

Eyes front, Rossiter.

Cold wind whipping against his face, Gabe felt himself begin to relax, too, sunlight, fresh air, and the beauty of the mountains taking the edge off his temper, almost making him forget about that son of a bitch Daniels. He knew Darcangelo could handle anything Daniels could throw at him, but that wasn't what bothered Gabe. No. What bothered him was the fact that he'd missed a chance to kick Daniels's ass. He'd told Hunter as much when Kat had been in his vehicle putting on ski pants.

"Believe me, I sympathize." Hunter had clapped him on the shoulder. "But it's probably better that you aren't there right now. You won't be able to help Kat if you're in the county lockup for assaulting a police officer. And—you'll have to take my word for this—life behind bars is seriously overrated."

Okay, so Hunter had a point.

Gabe accelerated a bit more, reaching the crest of the hill with enough speed to catch just a bit of air before starting down the other side. Behind him, Kat gave a squeal, but it wasn't a squeal of fear. She was enjoying herself.

So you like that, do you, honey?

Below them, Hunter was carving deep turns in the powder, clearly having too much fun for a lawman on the job. Gabe revved the engine and headed straight down the fall line, taking a couple of bumps, and then carving a few easy turns, the sled sending up a spray of powder. Behind him, Kat laughed, the sound uninhibited and sweet. He grinned back at her and shot after Hunter, who was already climbing the next slope.

They ought to reach the cabin within the hour. He and Marc had chartered a chopper yesterday and dropped most of the supplies. Then they'd heli-skied in and gotten the place ready for Kat. And as soon as his skis had hit the snow and he'd seen how deep it was, Gabe had known he'd made the right decision. He'd had some doubts at first, certain he wouldn't be able to keep his hands off Kat if they were alone together in close quarters. But then he'd compared the cabin to the places Chief Irving had had in mind, and he'd known it was the safest place for her.

Few people even knew the cabin existed, much less knew its GPS coordinates. And no one would be able to get to it without cross-country skiing all day, heli-skiing, or riding in on a snowmobile. As of this afternoon, Kat would seem to vanish, and no one but Gabe, Hunter, Darcangelo, and Chief Irving would know where she was.

As long as Gabe kept his dick in his pants, it would be perfect.

KAT STARED AT the little cabin, amazed to find it here in the middle of the wilderness. It looked like an image from a Christmas card. Built of gray stone with a steep, sloping roof, it sat at the top of a hill, overlooking a vast evergreen forest, high peaks rising up behind it, nothing man-made as far as the eye could see. It was all but buried, snow covering its roof and rising to the middle of its shutters. Beside it stood a log outbuilding, where they'd stowed the snowmobiles and the supply sled.

"Is this yours?"

"Only in my dreams." Gabe chuckled, digging a key from his jacket and sliding it into the lock. "It's a U.S. Forest Service guard station. Rangers stay here from snowmelt to snowfall to watch for poachers, illegal logging, and forest fires."

Marc came up beside them, helmet tucked under his arm, a broad grin on his face, rifle still on his back. "But now the Forest Service is renting it to the Denver Police Department for winter tactical training."

That answered Kat's next question.

Gabe pushed the door open. "It's not fancy, but it's warm and dry and, most of all, very few people know it exists. You'll be safe here."

Kat followed him inside and immediately felt at home. A large woodstove meant for both heating and cooking sat against one wall, firewood stacked high beside it on one side, a sink, small refrigerator, and countertop on the other. A small wooden table and four chairs stood in front of the stove. A double bed sat against the back wall in the center of the room, covered with a comforter she recognized as Gabe's. Beside the bed sat a nightstand with a kerosene lamp. There were two doors in the far wall, one that led to a little walk-in pantry and the other that opened to reveal a small bathroom.

It wasn't octagonal like her grandmother's hogaan, but, as with all hogaans, its door faced east—a good sign.

"We've got solar electricity, so we'll have lights and hot water during the day, so you can keep your cell phone and laptop charged. At night, of course, we'll have kerosene lamps. The rangers who stay up here communicate via radio, so there's no landline, but we got a wireless card for your laptop so you could connect with the paper. Because this place is meant for summer use, the only heat is the woodstove, but there's plenty of wood in back." Gabe turned to face her. "It's not much, I know, but hopefully you'll be able to work in peace."

Kat loved it. Her throat grew tight, warmth swelling inside her at the sight of what her friends had done for her. She stood on her tiptoes, kissed Gabe on the lips and then Marc on the cheek. "It's perfect. *Ahéhee'!* Thank you both so much!"

Both men looked extraordinarily pleased with themselves.

"CAN YOU REPEAT that?" Gabe paced impatiently around the cabin in the moonlight, trying to find a place where the signal was clear and wishing he'd taken time to get a satellite phone, Julian's voice breaking up on the other end.

"We found a Colt AR-15 in his trunk . . . two-two-three rounds and a folder of . . . written by Kat . . . muddy gloves."

That was the same type of round the shooter had fired when he'd tried to kill Kat at the butte. By itself it might have meant nothing, as that model of rifle and that type of ammunition were so common among both law enforcement and civilians. But together with Kat's articles and muddy gloves, presumably used to scoop up wet leaves, it passed Gabe's test for clear and convincing evidence.

"Did you arrest him?"

"Yes . . . hearing tomorrow. He says he was assigned . . . assure Kat's safety, and . . . Barker backed him up at first . . . but the evidence we found . . ."

Dammit!

Gabe hated cell phones. "How'd he know when we were leaving?"

"He . . . told by a friend of his. . . . hospital security staff . . ."

So much for all of their careful planning. "Does he know where we are?"

". . . don't think so . . . can't be sure . . . Daniels . . . to cooperate fully. Old Man Irving and Barker . . . major dick fight . . . angry that his boy is a suspect . . . have to see what we find . . . still too many missing pieces for . . ."

A burst of static.

Well, this conversation was going nowhere.

Gabe had one last question. "Has Hunter checked in yet?"

Hunter had eaten a quick lunch, then hopped on a snow-mobile and headed back the way they'd come, hoping to make it back to Gabe's vehicle before dark. Gabe had no doubt the man could handle himself if he got benighted, but spending a night in the freezing cold with no shelter wasn't fun, as Gabe knew from experience.

"He . . . from the road about fifteen minutes ago . . ."

Kat would be relieved. "Tell him thank you for me."

"How's . . . she okay?"

"She's fine. She seems to feel at home here." That was an understatement. The moment Hunter had taken off, she'd gone to work unpacking her things and putting away the food and dishes as if she'd lived here all her life. From the scent wafting out of the cabin, she was busy making dinner.

"That's good to . . . been through a lot . . . Of all the women on the I-Team, she's . . . vulnerable somehow. . . . special . . . we all care . . ."

Then the line went quiet, the call dropped.

Next time, buy the damned satellite phone, dumbass!

Gabe would have to call Darcangelo back later and get the details he'd missed. He pocketed his cell phone, trudged back around to the front door, and took off his snowshoes. His mind on Daniels, he stepped inside the lamp-lit cabin's toasty warmth—and stopped in his tracks.

The scene before him so natural, so intimate, so domestic that it made his mind go blank, appealing to some long-forgotten part of him, his chest constricting at the sight, the sensation bittersweet. Kat stood at the table mixing something in a wooden bowl. Her hair hung down her back, held in place by a silver and turquoise barrette, lamplight making the dark strands gleam. She'd tied a towel around her waist to serve as an apron, its red-and-white checks streaked with flour. Beside her, a cast-iron pot sat on top the woodstove, giving off a scent that made his mouth water.

Inside his skull, alarm bells went off, warning him that he didn't want this. He didn't want a woman in his life. He didn't want these feelings inside him. He didn't want Kat—not beyond the bedroom at least.

Oh, but he did. Yes, he did.

He shucked his parka and untied his boots, trying to reconnect his brain with his mouth. "Um . . . Hunter made it back.

Darcangelo said he checked in from the road a little while ago."

"That's good." She looked up at him, a relieved smile on her face, flour smudged on her cheek.

Then he remembered. "They arrested Daniels. He had a Colt AR-15 in his trunk along with boxes of two-twenty-three ammo, muddy gloves, and a folder of articles you've written."

She stopped kneading and sank into a chair, her face going pale. "So it was him."

"Seems so." Gabe let the anger come, his fury with Daniels so much easier to deal with than the other emotions he was feeling.

"But why? Why does he hate me so much?" Her eyes revealed a storm of emotion—confusion, fear, anger.

Gabe had no answers for her. "I don't know. But it looks like this might be over. If detectives can tie him to the looting, they'll have a strong case against him both for what he's done to you and possibly for the murder of Red Crow."

She stood, began kneading the dough, clearly still upset. "Does this mean we'll be going back tomorrow?"

He might have pushed her to tell him what she was feeling if his own emotions hadn't already been in chaos. "No. First we need to know for sure that Daniels really is our man and that we've got him and anyone who worked with him in custody."

"That makes sense. Are you hungry?"

"I am now." He dropped the subject, followed his nose to a bubbling pot of chili con carne, then looked in the bowl. "Biscuits?"

She scooped out the dough, plopped it onto a floured cutting board, and began to pummel the hell out it, hiding her feelings behind a smile. "Frybread."

He crossed his arms over his chest. "I didn't realize you knew how to cook on a woodburning stove. I guess you've done this before."

She looked at him as if he'd lost his mind. "I grew up in a hogaan with no electricity or running water, remember? How do you think we cooked?"

He'd known she'd grown up on the reservation, but he'd thought she was exaggerating when she'd mentioned the hogaan without electricity. "Tell me about it."

Kat put the last bite of her frybread on the Spirit Plate. She'd spent most of the meal answering Gabe's questions about her life on the reservation—herding sheep, driving a big pickup to fetch water from the nearest pump, gathering wood and chunks of coal for cooking and heating. He seemed interested in a way most people weren't, listening to every word, asking more questions.

It touched Kat more than she could say.

"There were pictographs carved on the rocks not far from our homesite—creatures with square heads, strange bodies, and zigzag necks. Sometimes my grandmother would take me there and tell me stories about the time before we came to this world, when those creatures were alive."

"It sounds like you and your grandmother are very close."

Kat nodded, unable to keep from smiling at the memory of her grandmother teaching her how to plant corn. "Every spring she catches and kills a crow. Then she stretches its wings out and ties it to the fence she puts around her cornfield as a warning to all the other crows not to eat her corn."

Gabe chuckled, watching her from across the table, his gaze soft, the smile on his face making her pulse trip. "Does it work?"

"No." Kat laughed with him. Oh, how she loved to see him smile! "But when I was little, I thought crows flew away from us because they were afraid they'd be next."

His smile grew. "What else did she teach you?"

"She taught me everything—how to grow food, how to use corn pollen, how to be a good Diné girl, how to . . ."

Surprised to find a lump in her throat, Kat swallowed, her words lapsing into silence. She felt Gabe's big hand close over hers.

"You miss her."

Kat nodded, blinking back tears, the news about Daniels having already left her at an emotional edge. Had he been following them in hopes of getting another chance to shoot her? "My grandmother doesn't know . . . She doesn't know about any of this. It would terrify her. The bone . . . She'd think I've . . . been witched."

Gabe's thumb stroked the back of her hand, the touch comforting. "Denver is a long way from the reservation. Why did you leave?"

Kat hadn't planned on talking about this, didn't want to talk about this, but given how hard she'd pushed him to tell her about Jill, it was only fair that she answer his question. "I'm the youngest of eleven children—my mother's youngest child. I have seven half brothers and three half sisters. My mother was married to a much older man. They grew apart, and my mother met a *Bilagáanaa* man."

That was it in a nutshell, and Kat hoped Gabe would understand without her needing to say more. But he didn't.

"So your mother's husband . . . wasn't your father?"

"No, he wasn't." Kat looked away, unable to meet his gaze.

"Your father was a white man."

She nodded. "I . . . I never met him. I don't even know his name. My mother never told me. Sometimes I doubt she knows. He stayed on the reservation only long enough to find out my mother was pregnant. Her husband divorced her after I was born. She blamed me, so my grandmother raised me."

Gabe took in what Kat had told him, trying to piece it together. So her mother had fucked some white guy, had gotten pregnant by him, and then had blamed Kat. Well, it certainly explained the color of Kat's eyes—not to mention her mistrust of men. And then he remembered what she'd told him in the restaurant.

I decided a long time ago that I would never be any man's conquest, so I don't date. I've never been with a man, and I won't be until I find the one who wants to be a part of my life and isn't just looking for a one-night stand.

Clearly, she didn't want to make the same mistake her mother had made and saw every man as just another guy looking for a quick lay, no strings attached.

You've certainly gone out of your way to prove her wrong

about that, haven't you, dumbshit? No wonder she sized you up so quickly. You're a lot like her father.

As true as that might be, there was one major difference— Gabe would never have left a woman he'd gotten pregnant to face that situation alone. And he would never have abandoned his own child. Whoever Kat's father was, the man was garbage.

He squeezed her hand. "I'm sorry. It couldn't have been easy growing up without a father or to have your mother leave you like that."

"She didn't leave me, at least not the way you think." Kat drew her hand away, stood, and carried their plates to the sink, clearly upset to be talking about this. "She still lives in my grandmother's hogaan. She and my brothers and sisters have never wanted me there. Only my grandmother . . ."

Kat's voice trailed off, but Gabe understood.

Only her grandmother had loved her and wanted her around.

He could see how that might make a person want to leave home. "So you packed your things and moved to Denver."

Kat shook her head, her back to him as she filled the sink with water. "Not right away. I went to college and studied journalism, wanting to help my people, hoping to make a difference. I got a job in Window Rock and worked at the paper there for a while, sharing the money I earned with my family. But it didn't matter. Nothing I did changed anything. My mother says I remind her of my father. My brothers and sisters call me Half-ajo and tease me about my eyes."

Gabe heard her voice quaver and knew she was close to tears. He stood, walked over to her, and turned her to face him. "You have beautiful eyes."

She gave a shy smile, then looked up at him, her smile fading. "I'm not my mother, Gabe. And I'm not Jill. I would never promise to love a man forever and then betray him with someone else."

It was only then that it hit him.

Both of them had suffered because of another person's infidelity. She'd been blamed for the accident of her own birth, while he'd lost everything that had ever mattered to him except for his life.

And now. He hadn't lost now.

"Sweet Kat." He slid his hands into her hair, ducked down, and brushed her lips with his. "Did your grandmother tell you to avoid *Bilagáanaa* men?"

"No." Kat met his gaze straight on, a kind of boldness in her eyes he'd never seen before. "But she did teach me never to look a man in the eyes because when a Diné girl looks a man in the eyes, it means . . . It means she wants to have sex with him."

CHAPTER 25

KAT WILLED HERSELF not to break eye contact with Gabe, her heart pounding. He stared down at her, his pupils dilated, the astonishment on his face turning to something darker, his brows bent in a frown.

He ran the pad of his thumb over her lower lip. "Are you sure?"

She couldn't say when she'd reached this decision. Maybe it had been this morning when she'd prayed for him, looking for some way to help him regain the part of himself Jill had stolen. Maybe it had been that terrible afternoon when he'd saved her from being shot, proving his courage. Or perhaps it had been the moment she'd realized that the wind knew him, that he belonged to this land as much as she did. Regardless, her heart had decided.

She had finally found a man who was worth it, a man she loved so much that going on without him felt unthinkable.

"Yes, I'm sure." She caught his hand where it cupped her chin and kissed his palm. "I love y—"

"Shhh!" He pressed his fingers to her lips. "Don't say it. 'Yes' is enough."

He ducked down as if to kiss her, then abruptly stopped, glancing around them. "No. Not like this."

"Gabe?"

He stepped back. "Why don't you go soak in a hot bath and pamper yourself a bit? The sun only set about an hour ago, so the water ought to still be fairly warm. There's a camping lantern on the counter."

Take a bath? Did she smell bad?

Something of her feelings must have shown on her face, because he leaned down to rest his forehead against hers. "Hey, trust me, okay? If I can't be man enough to keep my hands off you like I should, then at least let me be man enough to do this right. I'll tell you when you can come out."

Confused, Kat walked into the bathroom, turned on the camping lantern, and shut the door behind her. She found herself staring at her own bemused reflection in the lantern's half-light. This certainly wasn't the response she'd expected from him.

If I can't be man enough to keep my hands off you like I should, then at least let me be man enough to do this right.

What did he mean by that?

And then her pulse began to race again as she realized what was about to happen.

Gabe was going to make love to her. Tonight.

Suddenly, she was grateful for the extra time. What she'd said a few moments ago had been entirely spontaneous. She hadn't stopped to think that it had been a couple of days since she'd shaved her legs or that she needed to brush her teeth or that she might want to take a bath first.

Quickly, she set her razor and a washcloth near the tub, then turned on the water, relieved to feel it was still quite warm. While the tub filled, she flossed and brushed her teeth and tied her hair up in a knot. Then she undressed and stepped into the soothing heat, noises coming from the other side of the door—the clanging of dishes, the opening and closing of cupboard doors, the creaking of floorboards, the front door opening and closing again and again.

She might have tried to figure out what he was doing if she weren't so nervous. Instead, it was all she could do to focus on shaving her legs, questions chasing one after another through her mind. How much would it hurt? Would she be able to have an orgasm with him inside her? Would he compare her to Jill and be disappointed? Would he push her away afterward as he had so many women?

Stop doubting, girl. Trust yourself. Trust Gabe. Trust that you've come to this place and time for a reason.

Her belly full of butterflies, she reached for her soap,

inhaled its sweet honey scent and remembered how much he seemed to like it. Then she lathered her skin, trying not to worry about things she couldn't control. She'd just pulled the plug from the bathtub drain and begun to dry herself when he knocked on the door.

"Kat? Whenever you're ready . . ."

Her heart gave a hard knock. Was she ready? After all these years was she ready for what was about to happen? She wrapped herself in a soft towel and drew a deep, calming breath. Then, without glancing at the mirror, she opened the bathroom door—and stared in amazement. "Oh, Gabe!"

The cabin had been transformed. The dirty dishes had been cleared from the table, and the kerosene lamps had all been stored away. Dozens of small emergency candles sat here and there on saucers and in bowls, the room warm with their radiance. Pine boughs had been wrapped around the bed's four posters and its headboard, their scent fresh and enticing. The air was warm, a strong fire burning in the woodstove.

His gaze fixed on her, Gabe stood in the middle of the room, wearing only his jeans, the candlelight giving his skin a tawny glow, seeming to accentuate the ridges and valleys of his muscles. And Kat felt that familiar flutter in her belly.

Oh, yes, she was ready—for him.

He crossed the space between them in two lazy strides, slid his fingers into her hair, and undid the knot, spilling it down her back and around her shoulders. Then he brushed his knuckles over her cheek. "I can't make any promises about tomorrow, Kat, but for tonight at least, I'll do my damned best to be worth it."

Then he reached down, tugged off her towel, and let it fall to the floor.

Kat willed herself to stand strong while his gaze traveled over her body, desire naked on his face, the breath leaving his lungs in a gust.

"God, honey, you're beautiful."

But he was the beautiful one.

Hasteen nizhoni. Her beautiful man.

Barely able to breathe, she laid her hand over one of his pecs, the hard slab of muscle more than filling her palm, his nipple flat and dark. She flicked it with her thumb, watched it tighten. And then she couldn't stop herself, her hands finding their way over his chest with its mat of dark curls, over his abdomen with its ridges of hard muscle, her heart beating faster when her touch made his belly jerk. She took hold of the button that fastened his jeans, but her hands were so unsteady that it wasn't until he reached down to help her that she was able to undo it.

"Easy, honey." His voice was a deep purr.

They drew down his zipper together. He wasn't wearing underwear, his erection springing free, his hands guiding hers beneath the skin-warmed denim, over his narrow hips, and over the muscled roundness of his buttocks, as he shucked his jeans and tossed them aside. And then they were both naked, male and female, the perfection of the moment striking Kat deep in her soul.

Gabe let his gaze rake over her again, hungry for the sight of her. The scent of warm honey rose from her damp skin, one taut nipple peeking out from between strands of dark hair, her breasts rising with each rapid breath. He hadn't thought it was possible to want a woman this badly, to truly want *her*, to want to please her. Somehow it heightened his need for her, but it also left him feeling something he hadn't felt for a long time—bona fide nerves.

Got a case of performance anxiety, buddy?

Hell, yeah, he did. He'd never had sex with a virgin, and he didn't want to disappoint her or, worse, hurt her. And yet he was pretty sure she would feel at least some pain. If he hadn't been fairly certain it was sacrilegious, he'd have asked the Patron Saint of Men Who Fuck Virgins to help him do this right.

Shit!

"Come here." Heart hammering in his chest, he caught a finger beneath her chin, ducked down, brushed his lips over hers, gratified by the little shivers that passed through her. He would take this slowly, giving her body and her mind all the time she needed to adjust and truly enjoy it. And then . . .

He fought back the desire to kiss her, instead letting her anticipation build as his mouth wandered. He tasted the honey-sweet skin of her throat, sucked her earlobe, teased the whorl of her ear with his tongue. Only when she was shaking in his arms did he bring his lips back to hers, kissing the corners of her mouth, nipping her lower lip, tracing the outline of her lips with his tongue. Then, at last, he kissed her, inhaling her whimper, his mouth filling with the taste of mint as their tongues met.

She seemed to melt in his arms, every soft, sweet inch of her pressed against him, the feminine feel of her making his body tense, a bolt of heat shearing through his gut. But if he'd thought he was in control of this kiss he was wrong. She kissed him back with all the fire in her soul, matching him stroke for stroke, her erotic exploration of his mouth blowing whatever was left of his mind. He was lost in her, lost in the scent and feel of her, need for her thrumming in his veins.

He dragged his mouth from hers and scooped her into his arms, carrying her the few short steps to the bed and stretching out beside her, his mouth retaking hers the moment her head touched the pillow. Tongues invaded, sparred, ravished, hers as much as his, teeth scraping skin, biting, nipping. But he wanted more.

He lifted his head, pinned her arms above her head with one hand, then reached down with the other to cup her breasts, teasing her petal-soft nipples into tight buds, tugging them with his fingers, flicking them with his thumb.

She gasped, then moaned, a sound of unmistakable female arousal.

"God, I love your breasts." Natural and soft, they yielded to his hand as he cupped and plumped them, their tips so sensitive that the merest flick of his thumb made her shiver. When he couldn't wait another second, he ducked down, greeted each puckered peak with an eager flick of his tongue, then closed his mouth over her right nipple and sucked.

She cried out, whimpered, arching her back, offering herself to him, her arms still pinned above her head. "Oh, Gabe, *ayor anosh'ni!*"

He didn't speak Navajo, but the urgency in her voice got at least some of her message across. Driven by her pleas and his own desperate hunger, he tugged on her nipple with his lips, flicked it with his tongue, suckled it, cupping her other breast with his free hand, his thumb tracing circles on the sensitive underside.

God, she was responsive! Her breathing came in shudders, her body trembling, her eyes squeezed shut, a look of torment on her sweet face. Brain buzzing with lust, he shifted his mouth to her other nipple, grazing her with the edge of his teeth, then sucking hard. He wanted to please her, wanted so goddamned bad to please her, wanted to make her burn for him the way he burned for her.

"Gabe, please!" She squirmed against him, her hips lifting off the bed, seeking relief.

He raised his head, released her wrists, and felt her fingers clench in his hair. He flicked a nipple with his tongue, teasing her. "Please what? Please stop?"

She gave a frustrated moan. "Please *don't* stop!"

Only too happy to oblige her, he lowered his mouth to a wet nipple, sucking and nipping her as he nudged his hand between her thighs, lifted her right leg and draped it over his hip, spreading her wide. His hand sought the sensitive skin of her inner thighs, teasing her, working his way slowly upward.

Christ, he could feel her heat. It radiated from within her, her sultry, musky scent igniting every drop of testosterone in his blood. She whimpered his name, her nails digging into his scalp, her hips rising each time his hand drew near, then twisting in sexual frustration when he drew his hand away again. When he was certain he had her on the edge, he cupped her damp curls—and eased a finger inside her.

She gave a breathy moan, her hot, slick vagina gripping his finger tight.

He heard himself growl like some kind of damned animal,

his hips flexing as if his cock were buried inside her instead of thrusting against her thigh.

Slow down, Rossiter.

He forced breath into his lungs, doing his best to relax. He stroked her, sliding a second finger inside her, stretching her. "In a few minutes, my cock is going to be inside you, stroking you just like this."

She shivered, tensed, and he knew she found the idea both arousing and a little frightening. And that was okay, because so did he. He did not want to hurt her, but damned if he could hold back much longer.

He gathered her body's own moisture, then withdrew his fingers and rubbed the silky wetness over her clit, the little pink bud swelling at his touch. Then he penetrated her again, sliding his fingers in and out, taking care to catch her clit with each deep stroke.

Her breath came in ragged pants as he kept up the rhythm, her faced turned against his chest, her eyes squeezed shut, her body wracked with tension that seemed to arc through her and into him, shooting straight to his groin.

"I want you, Kat." His words came out in urgent whispers as he flicked her nipples with his tongue, unable to keep his mouth off her, his cock so hard it ached. "I want to fuck you so bad it hurts."

Then she gasped, seeming to hold her breath as the tension inside her peaked—and shattered. She came with a shaky sigh, her inner muscles clenching around his fingers, a look of excruciating pleasure on her beautiful face. He rode through it with her, keeping his rhythm steady, trying to make her pleasure last, raining kisses on her breasts, her throat, her lips, as the quaking inside her slowly faded.

When her climax had passed, he held her, a bittersweet ache in his chest at the sight of her lying in his arms. Her eyes were closed, her lips slightly parted, her breathing soft and easy. Her hair lay in a tangle around her face, her lashes dark against her cheeks, her lips curved in the faintest of smiles.

And Gabe made up his mind. If she'd had enough, if she fell asleep, he wouldn't push her. They'd forget the whole "take my virginity" thing, and he'd just go wank in the bathroom like he'd been doing these past few days.

Noble of you, Rossiter. Stupid, but noble.

But she didn't fall asleep. Almost as soon as he'd finished arguing with himself, she opened her eyes, gave him a shy smile, then turned on her side to face him, her lips closing over his. His arms went around her, the two of them twisting and rolling on the bed in a tangle of limbs, hands exploring soft skin, seeking out new ways to give pleasure. And then she was beneath him, both of them breathless.

On fire for her, Gabe reached beneath a pillow and drew out the condom he'd stashed there, ripping off the wrapper with his teeth, his mouth filling with the taste of latex and spermicidal lubricant. He was about to slide it down the length of his erection, when her hands caught his, stopping him.

"No. No condom. Please! This first time, let it be what it's meant to be. Let me give all of myself to you. Let me have all of you." She looked at him through those big eyes of hers, and he knew she was serious.

His heart seemed to stop. "I've been tested, so I know I can't make you sick. But I never got the vasectomy, Kat. I *can* make you pregnant. Do you know what you're risking, what you're asking me to risk?"

"Yeah, I do." She nodded. "Just this once. Please."

"No condom" had always meant "no sex" as far as Gabe was concerned. He hadn't had sex without a condom since . . . Well, he couldn't remember when. But the thought of being inside Kat, of truly feeling her, with no barriers between them . . .

He groaned, let the condom fall to the sheets, then stretched himself out above her, wrapping her left leg around his waist. "I don't want to hurt you."

She slid her hands up his chest, looked into his eyes. "I know."

His gaze locked with hers, he slowly nudged the tip of his cock into her slippery heat, her body resisting his intrusion, his access impeded by that thin ring of flesh. Then, with the slightest thrust of his hips, he broke through.

Her eyes flew wide, and she gasped, then squeezed her

eyes shut, biting her bottom lip. And it struck him as unfair somehow that what felt so indescribably good to him caused her pain.

"Easy, honey." He held himself still inside her—no easy task. She was slick and impossibly tight, the head of his cock teased by sensations he would never have felt if he'd been wearing a condom—subtle textures, wetness, heat. Every instinct he had urged him to drive deeper, to bury himself in her snug warmth, the first stirrings of orgasm tugging at his belly. But this was about her, about pleasing her, about giving her everything he could give her, because what she'd given him—*Jesus!*—what she'd just given him was priceless, far beyond anything he deserved.

Kat tried to relax, the pain gradually subsiding, her nervousness giving way to a sense of exhilaration at the thought that Gabe was inside her.

"I'm sorry." He stroked her hair, raining kisses on her cheeks, her eyelids, her lips, her forehead, as if trying to kiss away her discomfort, the tenderness on his face almost breaking her heart.

"It's not bad, really." And it wasn't—not anymore.

Watching her face, he repeatedly withdrew, then nudged himself inside her again, going deeper each time, gradually stretching her past the pain until he filled her completely, the sensation both strange and pleasurable.

He moaned, whispered her name, his body shaking. "Oh, honey, you feel so . . . *Jesus Christ.*"

And then he began to move in deep, slow thrusts, stroking the hidden places inside her, the slippery friction making her ache. Oh, the sweetness of it! She was so glad she'd waited for this moment, for this man, for Gabe. No matter what happened tomorrow or next week or next month, this was beyond her dreams.

Unable to get enough of him, she slid her hands up the sweat-slick planes of his chest, over the hard curves of his shoulders, and down the tense muscles of his back. *"Ayor anosh'ni! Ayor anosh'ni!"* I love you! I love you!

The words spilled out of her in a breathless rush, carrying

the spirit of her love to him, returning at least some of the love Jill had stolen, even if he couldn't understand what she was saying. And then Kat couldn't think, let alone speak, the ache inside her drawing together in a tight, shimmering knot, as he moved over her, against her, inside her, his breath hot on her face, his skin slick with sweat.

"Oh, Kat, honey—Christ!—I can't . . . hold off . . . much longer!"

An image of his penis thrusting in her closed fist flashed through her mind, and she realized that's exactly how he was moving inside her now, his hips thrusting hard, strong, fast. And in a moment, hot semen would shoot from him into her, just as it had shot over her fingers that night. The thought was so erotic, so deeply arousing, that Kat found herself on the brink of another climax.

But this was like nothing she'd felt before, the feel of him inside her carrying her higher than she'd ever been. Orgasm overtook her with the force of a flash flood, drowning her in pleasure, a riptide of bliss that threatened to carry her away. She heard a woman cry out, and realized it was she, her nails instinctively digging into his back as she fought to hold on, her teeth finding his shoulder, her inner muscles clenching around him.

He groaned, his pace quickening, as he answered her cries with whispers of encouragement. "That's right, honey! Come for me!"

She heard his breath catch, felt his control shatter, his body shuddering as he came apart in her arms, losing himself inside her with a deep groan.

GABE LOOKED DOWN at the woman who slept so deeply in his arms, her head resting on his chest, her sweet face completely relaxed, one silky leg tucked between his. He ought to hate himself. Instead he felt overwhelmed by a sense of . . . peace.

The candles had long since burned themselves out, the fire burned to embers in the woodstove. Though he knew he should get up and add more wood, he didn't want to move. He didn't want to let go of her.

For so long, sex had been about nothing but physical release. He'd hook up with an attractive woman and fuck her, craving those few seconds of forgetfulness that came when he did. Then he'd pack up his prick and leave, feeling empty and wanting to be alone. In the end, he'd felt the same disgust for each and every one of those women that he'd felt for himself.

He'd been afraid the same thing would happen tonight. But it hadn't. Instead of wanting to scrape Kat off his skin and leave her, he'd wanted to hold her, to kiss her until she fell asleep, to feel the warmth of her skin against his. Somehow she filled the emptiness inside him, made him feel whole again.

You love her, buddy.

He wanted to deny it, but he couldn't. The truth of it lodged in his chest, swelling behind his breastbone until it almost hurt.

He loved Katherine James.

That fact ought to scare the hell out of him, but it didn't. Instead, it left him grinning like an idiot.

Silly goat.

Still grinning, he drew the covers up to her chin—and fell into a deep sleep.

"VAIL?"

"They're probably holed up at a condo with twenty-four-hour security."

"Maybe. Maybe not."

"You have some idea where they went?"

"Let's just say I've got a hunch."

"You might as well give up. You're not going to get to them. Besides, there's too much attention on them as it is. If you somehow did manage to kill them—you've bungled it so far—every reporter in the state would jump on the story."

"Hey, they got lucky last time. The trick is to get to him first. Once he's out of the way, killing her will be easy."

"Do you really think you can do it? Do you really think you can kill a woman?"

"Are you kidding me? If it's a choice between her dying and me going to prison, then she's already dead."

CHAPTER 26

KAT AWOKE THE next morning, her body floating, her nose cold.

"Morning, beautiful." Gabe leaned over her and kissed her, brushing a strand of hair off her cheek. "I was wondering if you were going to sleep all day."

"Mmm." She stretched, feeling as lazy as a cat, her heart warm with memories from last night. "Maybe I should."

He chuckled. "Well, at least stay in bed until I get the fire going. It's cold outside these covers."

Used to getting up in the cold, she was about to offer to help when he slipped out of bed and, still completely naked, strode over to the woodpile, the mounds of his buttocks shifting as he walked, his body available for her casual perusal. And she decided she was fine with letting him do it himself.

Even without an erection he seemed big. Had that part of him really been inside her? She squeezed her thighs together, felt both moisture and a twinge of soreness, and almost smiled. Yes, he most certainly had. And it had been more wonderful than she could possibly have imagined.

I can't make any promises about tomorrow, Kat, but for tonight at least, I'll do my damned best to be worth it.

His words came back to her, warmth blossoming behind her breastbone when she thought of all he'd done to please her. The candles and pine boughs. The way he'd gone out of his way to make sure she enjoyed it, taking his time, holding back for her sake. The tenderness and concern on his face when he'd finally pushed inside her. He'd made her feel beautiful. He'd made her feel wanted. He'd made her feel loved.

He'd even been willing to give her a first time that was pure, with no barriers between them. He wasn't Native, so she hadn't expected him to understand how important it was for the male and female waters to mingle. But even if he hadn't understood what it meant to her, he'd done as she asked.

She might not know much about sex, but she'd learned enough from listening to her I-Team friends talk about it to know that last night had been more than special. It had been perfect.

She watched Gabe as he bent down, opened the stove, and put wood on what remained of the embers one piece at a time. His body was different from hers in so many wonderful ways—the muscles of his back that narrowed to a V just above his butt, his flat, smooth nipples, the muscle just above each hip that curved down toward—

"Enjoying the view?" He grinned.

Kat felt herself blush, but met his gaze, determined to put shyness behind her. She'd made love with this man. She'd trusted him with everything she was. She had no reason to feel embarrassed or shy, no reason to hold back. "Yes, I am."

AMUSED, GABE CLOSED the woodstove, the fire now rekindled, and took a step toward the bed. "Want a closer look?"

Kat laughed, sat up, then winced, her laugh becoming a gasp.

Gabe had a pretty good idea what was wrong. He'd seen flecks of dried blood on the sheets and on himself. He'd figured she'd be sore.

It's called "hymeneal laceration," Rossiter. And you caused it.

Yeah, thanks. He already knew that.

There'd been no way around it, but it still bothered him that he'd hurt her. He walked over to the sink. "Lie back and rest for a minute."

"What—"

"You'll see." The sun had been up for a while, so the water was nice and hot. He filled a bowl and tested the temp with his fingers. Grabbing a clean dishcloth, he walked back to the bed, setting the bowl down on the nightstand. He took the cloth, dipped it in the water, then squeezed it out and slid into bed beside her. "Bend your knees."

When she'd done what he'd asked, he slipped his hand beneath the covers and between her thighs, pressing the hot cloth against her.

Her eyes drifted shut, and she gave a little sigh.

"Does that help?" Unable to help himself, he ducked down and kissed her temple.

"It helps a lot. Thanks."

"You should probably soak in the tub a couple of times today. It will ease the soreness and help you heal." He turned back toward the nightstand, dipped the cloth in the bowl again, and squeezed it out, then held it against her once more.

Again, she sighed. "Mmm."

He studied her face, grateful to see no sign that she regretted last night. Then again, he'd never met a woman who knew her own mind quite the way Kat did. Despite the hardships of her life, she seemed to know exactly who she was. That was more than he could say for most women—or for himself.

She opened her eyes and caught him watching her. She reached up and touched her hand to his cheek, running her thumb over the stubble on his jaw. "In case you're wondering, Gabe Rossiter, last night was the most wonderful night of my life. You were—and you are—more than worth it."

Something swelled in Gabe's chest. There was so much he wanted to say to her, so much to explain. But this was all so new to him, and the words got stuck somewhere in his throat. "I'm glad."

Why don't you tell her it was special for you, too, Rossiter? Why don't you tell her that it blows your mind to think she spent her virginity on you? Why don't you tell her you love her?

He would—later.

He turned back toward the nightstand, wet cloth in hand, but stopped when she caught his arm. He looked down to find her staring at his shoulder, eyes wide with shock. He turned his chin, glanced down—and saw a bruise surrounded by teeth marks.

She looked up at him, shame on her face. "I did that, didn't I?"

Gabe couldn't help but grin. "Yeah, you did, and at the time, honey, it felt good. Don't worry about it. Given what women go through, a man ought to be tough enough to take a little pain for the sake of his woman's pleasure."

GABE TOOK ADVANTAGE of Kat's soak in the tub to call Darcangelo and repeat the conversation they'd tried to have last night. Perhaps it was pointless, but he wanted to shelter her from as much of this as he could. She didn't seem to remember it, but twice last night she'd had nightmares, once muttering something about a coyote. It had made him want to beat the shit out of someone—specifically Frank Daniels.

"Daniels claims he has no idea how the clippings of Kat's articles got into his trunk." Julian's voice came through crystal clear this time. "In fact, he's all but accused me and Hunter of planting them there."

"No one's going to believe that bullshit. So what's his excuse for following us?"

"He says he wanted to make sure the two of you got safely out of Dodge. He says he and Chief Barker were sick of the Boulder PD getting slammed in the papers. Barker backed Daniels up, admitting they'd had that conversation about it and saying that Daniels volunteered to make sure we got safely outside Boulder PD jurisdiction."

Gabe gave a snort. "We were outside their jurisdiction once we left the city limits. How does he explain following us across three counties and over the divide to Vail? Did he suddenly get the urge to go skiing?"

"He says he knows Kat thinks he's behind it and he wanted to make damned sure nothing happened to her."

"This from the man who yanked her by her hair." Gabe wasn't buying it.

"The AR-15 and the ammo belong to him. His prints are on both. But there are no prints on the folder with Kat's articles, and there are no prints on the articles themselves.

Same with the muddy gloves. There are no fingerprints inside or out."

"He's a cop. He knows how not to leave prints."

"True, but he also knows his rights better than most people. Why let me search his car if he knows there's shit in the back that could incriminate him? Why keep a rifle on hand that could easily be pin tested and matched with the evidence found on Mesa Butte? He's stupid—I'll give you that—but he's not that stupid."

"You sure about that?"

"Pretty sure. And here's another thing. My FBI contacts looked into him and found no way to connect him to looting. They tracked his credit card use for the past year, and found no strange pattern of travel, no heavy equipment rental, no purchases of Indian artifacts, no history of collecting antiques. Nada."

"So you're saying you think he's being set up?" This was not what Gabe wanted to hear. It meant that the person behind all of this was still out of their sights.

"That's what Hunter thinks, and he's got more experience being set up than anyone I know." Darcangelo laughed at what was obviously a private joke. "But if the pin tests show it wasn't Daniels's rifle, I'm going to say Hunter's right."

"When will you get the test results back?"

"Hard to say with this being a short week because of Thanksgiving. I'm pushing to get them by Wednesday."

Gabe had forgotten about Thanksgiving. "Does Daniels have any idea who might be behind this?"

"He wants to peg it on someone in the Native community, but I'm not leaning in that direction. We've questioned a few of Kat's friends, and my gut tells me they're clean. They're simple folks—hardworking, honest, and scared to death for her."

"Dammit! I wish there was something I could do, some angle I could follow from here while you work your side of it there."

"You're doing the most important thing—keeping our girl safe. Oh, speaking of angles . . . Daniels did turn up on the list of city staff who have access to info about the city's

surveillance system—but so did a thousand other people. So
that tells us nothing."

Well, that figured, didn't it? "Thanks for checking. Keep
me posted."

"Will do." There was a moment of silence. "We're going to
catch whoever's behind this, Rossiter. I promise you that."

"Damn straight we will."

"There's a winter storm warning in effect for later in the
week. You need anything up there?"

"No. I think we're set. I'll check in every day at oh-eight-
hundred and sixteen-hundred hours."

"Good enough. Oh, one last thing. Tessa sends her
regards—" There was a moment of muffled discussion on the
other end, a woman's voice in the background. "Tessa says
I'm supposed to use her exact words. She says to please give
Kat her love and tell her that Sophie had an ultrasound and
it's a girl and to act surprised when Sophie calls because even
though Sophie didn't tell Tessa not to tell Kat, Tessa thinks
Sophie will probably want to tell Kat herself. Got that?"

Gabe chuckled. "Yeah, I think so."

"Women!" But as exasperated as he sounded, Darcangelo
wasn't fooling anyone. Gabe could tell the man loved his wife
to the point of distraction.

He hung up the phone just as Kat walked out of the bathroom, wrapped in a peach-colored towel, her hair hanging
dark and wet down her back.

"Who was that?" She kept her voice casual, but he could
sense her anxiety. She must have been able to hear more than
he'd thought she would.

"Oh, that was just Julian. He said to let you know Sophie's
having a girl."

Kat smiled. "I know. Kara and Holly sent me text messages, but I'm supposed to act surprised when Sophie calls
because they think she wants to tell me herself."

Gabe shook his head. *Women.*

"I'M GOING TOO fast!" Breathless, Kat looked to Gabe,
who skied down the hill backward in front of her, coaching

her. How he managed to do that when she couldn't even ski forward without falling she couldn't say.

"You're fine! Go into the snow plough if you need to slow down, or turn your skis away from the fall line. There you go. You've got it. Now point and turn left."

And just like that, her feet seemed to take off without her, landing her on her butt in fluffy powder. It didn't hurt, of course. But the snow was cold, and getting up with big, slippery planks strapped to her feet wasn't easy.

She didn't know what had gotten into him that he'd suddenly decided to teach her to ski. She'd spent what was left of the morning going over her notes from her interview with Julian's Interpol contact and reviewing the documents she'd read in the Mesa Butte file. She'd promised Tom an article tomorrow by deadline, and with everything that had happened, she felt completely out of touch with the investigation.

But Gabe had made it impossible for her to concentrate just by being in the room with her. He'd taken the documents away from her, kissed her silly, then made long slow love to her, every bit as caring and tender as he'd been last night, making her climax three times with him inside her before he'd finally let himself go. And though he'd worried about hurting her again, it wasn't nearly as painful is it had been last night.

"A woman ought to be tough enough to take a little pain for the sake of her man's pleasure," she'd said, echoing his words.

"For her man's pleasure?" he'd teased, arching a brow. "Who came three times? And have you seen the scratches on my back?"

Then he'd declared it time for the two of them to get a bit of fresh air. "Leave the work for tomorrow. You deserve a damn break."

And because she really just wanted to spend time with him, she'd let him talk her out of the cabin and into a pair of boots and skis.

It was a beautiful day. The sky overhead was big and clear and blue, the sunlight striking diamonds off the snow, the air fresh as only mountain air could be. And more than once she'd caught sight of bald eagles soaring above a nearby cliff, their wings broad and dark, their heads snowy white.

If only she could stay upright on skis . . .

A broad grin on his face, Gabe turned sideways and side-stepped up the hill toward her, his boots creaking, his skis crunching in the snow. He reached down and helped her to stand. "Up you go. Dust yourself off."

"Every time I fall and have to get up . . . I get so out of breath!"

"That's just the altitude. We're above nine thousand feet here. You'll get used to it." He brushed snow off her jeans as if she were a child. "You almost had it there. Don't let speed psyche you out. This hill isn't very steep so you can't get up that much speed anyway. And you can slow down anytime you want by turning and cutting across the fall line or going into your snow plough."

Kat looked down the tree-strewn hillside. "It looks steep to me. I'm from the Arizona desert, remember?"

"No excuses, rez girl. You can do it."

A part of her wanted to say she'd had enough and hike back up the hill to the cabin. But she refused to give up so easily. She knew how much Gabe loved the outdoors. That's one of the things that had drawn him to Jill—she'd loved outdoor sports as much as he did.

Every guy who climbs fantasizes about meeting a woman who loves the sport as much as he does. Rock climbing, alpine climbing, ice climbing, rafting, mountain biking, skiing—Jill loved it all, and she was good at it.

There was no way that Kat would ever be able to equal Jill in that respect. But she could at least learn to ski. Or at least she hoped she could.

She drew a deep breath. "When we're done with today's lesson, can you give me a demonstration? I'd like to see you ski."

His grin widened. "Okay, honey, you've got yourself a deal."

AN HOUR LATER, Kat sat outside the cabin, bundled in a blanket and dressed in a warm, dry skirt, feeling exhilarated

by her success on the slope. She'd made it to the bottom of
the hill three times without falling. Somewhere along the way
she'd decided Gabe was right—skiing was fun. The smile
he'd given her when she'd told him this had made her heart
ache. It was the same bright smile he'd worn in those photos.

Now he was keeping his end of the bargain. She watched
through binoculars as he trekked, skis on his shoulder, up the
side of the nearest mountain in search of what he called "sick
terrain." He disappeared behind a large outcropping of rock
and emerged a short time later some distance above it near
the timberline. How he managed to move so quickly on such
steep terrain and at this altitude with the weight of the skis on
his back she couldn't say. Maybe it had something to do with
all that muscle.

Soon he stood at the base of the cliff where she'd seen
the eagles soaring. She watched through the binoculars as
he stepped into his skis, tied the snowshoes onto his backpack, and drew a pair of goggles over his eyes. With a glance
in her direction and a smile on his face, he turned his skis
downhill—and was off.

At first she thought he was falling, snow spraying in all
directions around him, obscuring her view, moving down the
steep slope like a mini-avalanche. Then he turned, and she
saw that he hadn't fallen at all. He was in complete control, a
man at the center of a whirling cloud of powder.

It was like watching poetry. His body seemed almost still,
and yet it wasn't, his legs shifting subtly, his weight leaning
slightly from side to side as he made small turns, adapting to
the terrain, his poles and the top of his head the most visible
parts of him. Then he reached timberline, shooting through
glades of pine and bare aspen with such speed that it left her
breathless.

And then Kat saw.

He must have forgotten about the rocks. He must have
forgotten about the rock outcropping, because he was headed
straight toward it. He didn't seem to realize it was there,
didn't seem to know that if he kept skiing in that direction,
he'd have a drop of at least fifty feet to the snow below.

"Gabe!" Kat ran forward, screamed to warn him, but he couldn't hear her.

He skied right over the top of the rocks—and shot into the air.

Her legs gave out, and she sank to her knees in the snow, binoculars landing in her lap. Unable to breathe, her pulse tripping, she grabbed them and watched as he landed in a spray of powder and shot down the mountainside, a wide grin on his face.

Only then did she realize he'd done that deliberately.

FEELING MORE ALIVE than he had in years, Gabe skied up to the cabin and knew he was in deep shit the moment he saw Kat's face. She glared at him, a wool blanket wrapped around her shoulders, binoculars dangling from one hand.

"You should have warned me about those rocks." She didn't yell, but her voice shook with anger, her accent stronger than usual. "What would have happened if you'd broken your leg or died? How could I have helped you out here?"

"You were afraid for me?" He jammed his poles into the snow and stepped out of his skis, setting them upright against the cabin wall.

"*Yáadilá!*" She muttered something beneath her breath, glowering at him, and he wondered if he'd just heard her swear for the first time. "Of course I was afraid! I saw you heading for the rocks, and I thought you were going to break your neck!"

"Believe me, I've skied much hairier things than that." He reached for her, ducked down, and kissed her on the mouth—only to have her plant her hands in the middle of his chest and give him a shove.

Surprised, he laughed, rocking back on his heels. "Come on, Kat! I didn't mean to scare you. I know what I can handle."

She stood there glaring at him for a moment—then she jumped into his arms and kissed him hard on the mouth.

He caught her, the two of them falling backward into the

snow. She didn't seem to care that they were outside, that she was lying on top of him on the ground, her tongue teasing his, her hands searching for a way beneath his parka.

So watching him ski had scared her—and turned her on.

Adrenaline from his run down the slope mixed with testosterone in his blood, the volatile combo blanking out his brain. He undid his parka, ripped his shirt out of his ski pants, and pushed his shoulder holster to the side, giving her easier access to his chest. And then his hands were beneath the blanket, lifting her skirt in fistfuls, cupping the sweet curves of her ass, slipping beneath her panties to caress her clit. She was slick, hot, ready for him.

She moaned, her thighs parting to make room for him, her hands sliding all over him. "Now!"

He drew out his cock, and, forgetting she was sore, pushed the crotch of her panties aside and thrust upward, impaling her. "Oh, gee-zus!"

She gasped, then moaned, biting her lip, her head falling back.

He grasped her hips to guide her, but she'd already begun to find a rhythm, her slick inner muscles stroking him as she rode him to within an inch of his life, the two of them coming hard and fast, his groan mingling with her cries.

THEY LAY THERE for a while, both of them regaining their breath, Gabe stroking Kat's hair, her head resting on his chest. "I'm sorry I scared you."

"I've never seen anyone do anything like that. Even if you did scare me, you're amazing, Gabe Rossiter."

He held her, waiting until his cock slid out of her on its own, the contact so precious he didn't want to end it, even if he was freezing his ass off—literally. This was the third time he'd come inside her without wearing a condom and he wasn't sure he could get used to wearing latex ever again. "Let's get indoors. The temp's dropping."

Or maybe that was just all the snow in the back of his pants. He sat up, steadied her while she got to her feet, then rose, adjusting his shoulder holster and grabbing handfuls of packed powder and slush out of his ass crack, icy chunks sliding down his legs inside his pants.

He looked up to see Kat covering her mouth with her hand, clearly on the brink of laughter. She pointed to the snowy ground.

Gabe looked down to see the vague outline of a man with a very clear imprint of an ass. He chuckled. "Well, that's one way to make a snow angel."

CHAPTER 27

KIMÍMILA!

The *Ma'ii* called to her with Grandpa Red Crow's voice again and again, sending shivers up her spine. She walked in her moccasins to the door, opened it, and saw the coyote pacing back and forth in front of the hogaan. Bigger than any coyote she'd ever seen, it saw her, stopped pacing, then threw back its head and howled.

It was trying to warn her.

She took her pouch of corn pollen from her woolen sash belt and held it out with trembling hands, an offering. "What is it? Tell me! Please!"

Gabe appeared at her side. He pushed past her to stand between her and the coyote. Then the ground gave way from beneath him, and he fell out of sight.

Kat screamed . . .

And found herself sitting up in bed in the cabin covered in cold sweat.

Then, Gabe was there, drawing her against his bare chest, holding her tight. "Shh, honey. It's okay. It's all right. It can't hurt you."

And then she heard the howl.

Caught between sleep and wakefulness, it took her a moment to realize that it wasn't a dream. The coyote was there. Outside the cabin door.

"Nidaaga!" No! Feeling almost sick, she stared at the door, part of her wanting to close her eyes and go back to believing it was a nightmare. But it was real, and she couldn't hide beneath the covers. She knew what she needed to do.

She drew away from Gabe, pushed aside the covers, and walked to the cupboard where she'd placed her pouch of corn pollen. Then she walked to the door, her pulse thrumming in her ears.

"What are you doing?" Gabe got out of bed, reached for his handgun. "You're not thinking of opening the door are you?"

The coyote howled again.

"Wh-when the *Ma'ii* comes to your home and calls to you, it's a warning from the spirits. I-I must—"

"Whatever you have to do, can you at least put something on? It's four degrees out there." He tossed her a blanket, and only then did she realize she was naked.

She wrapped herself in the blanket, unlocked the door, and slowly opened it.

The coyote sat not ten feet from the doorway, its thick coat covered with snow, its breath a light mist on the cold night air. The moon gleamed in its dark eyes like starlight on black ice. When it saw her, it tipped back its head and howled again, the sound sending shivers down her spine.

Just like her dream.

Praying in Diné, she stepped outside, snow beneath her bare feet, a bit of corn pollen between her fingers.

"Kat . . . It's a wild animal. Don't get too close." Gabe came to stand beside her, rifle still in his hands.

But Kat barely heard him, the words of her prayer helping to calm her as she moved closer, thanking Brother Coyote for being a messenger tonight.

The coyote shifted its front paws, stood, howled once more, then trotted away.

She watched until it disappeared down the hillside, then hurried forward and sprinkled corn pollen in its footprints, moving clockwise. Next, she put a pinch of corn pollen on her tongue and on her head, speaking the sacred words. Then, she turned to Gabe, who had followed her out of the cabin, and held a pinch of corn pollen to his lips. Though he clearly had no idea what she was doing, he opened his mouth and accepted it, bowing his head so she could sprinkle some on his head, as well.

Then the tension drained from her body all at once, leaving her weak and shaking.

"Let's get you back inside. You're freezing." He wrapped his arm around her shoulder and guided her back inside. "Get back in bed."

Shivering, she did as he asked, watching as he lit one of the lamps, then filled the coffeepot with cold water and set it on the woodstove to boil.

"I wish I could do something so you wouldn't feel afraid," he said at last. "You've been dreaming about coyotes almost every night, did you know that?"

She shook her head. "I'm sorry if I woke you."

"I don't give a damn about that. What does the coyote mean to you? You said something about not crossing its path when we saw that one at Mesa Butte. Does crossing its path bring bad luck?"

"Not exactly. When a coyote crosses your path, you have to show respect. If you don't, your life can be thrown out of balance, and that can bring bad things. But sometimes a coyote can be sent by the spirits to warn you." She shivered, the plaintive howl echoing in her mind.

Gabe slid in bed beside her, drew the covers closer around her, kissed her hair.

She wanted to explain, to make him understand. "I crossed a coyote's path the day I fell. I wasn't able to stop and make an offering. And then the day we found Grandpa Red Crow, just as I was leaving home to meet you, I saw a coyote was standing at the end of my driveway, watching me. I made an offering, said the sacred words but . . . Then at the butte, we both crossed the coyote's path. I didn't have my corn pollen, and we were almost shot. I know it probably sounds silly and superstitious to you, but I can't get past the feeling that something terrible is going to happen."

He stroked her hair. "It doesn't sound silly and superstitious. It sounds like post-traumatic stress. You've been through hell. But just in case, the door is bolted, and I've got a loaded rifle and a forty-five semiauto right here where I can grab them on a moment's notice. Anyone who tries to hurt you is going to have to get through me first."

But that might have been what terrified Kat the most.

* * *

WHILE GABE CHOPPED wood outside, Kat peeled and
sliced potatoes to add to the beef stew she had bubbling on
the stove. She was used to making mutton stew, so she wasn't
sure about the flavoring. She needed to make dough for frybread, too, because no one ate stew without frybread. But
dough could wait a little while.

She sat down at the table and opened the Mesa Butte file,
feeling a sense of urgency that wouldn't leave her alone. The
coyote's visit both in her dream and outside the cabin had left
her feeling shaken. She needed to find the answers so this
ordeal could end, and that meant focusing on her investigation. There had to be something in this file that explained
what was happening at Mesa Butte. Clearly, the raid on the
inipi, Grandpa Red Crow's death, and the looting were all
related, but how?

She'd already met today's news deadline and was hoping
to get a jump on tomorrow's article. The story she'd turned in
today had been more a feature story than hard news, offering the reader an overview of how the international black
market for American Indian artifacts worked and attempting to explain how looting hurt the Native community. She'd
made the most of her interview with the Interpol agent and
had taken time to interview several Indian leaders, including
Uncle Allen.

It had given her an excuse to check in and hear how everyone was doing—Uncle Allen with his new responsibilities
as leader of their *tiyospaye,* or spiritual family, Glenna with
her chemotherapy, Pauline with studying for her GED. They
were all very worried about her, of course. Uncle Allen had
asked if he could come see her. When she'd told him that she
was in protective custody and couldn't even tell him where
she was, much less welcome him for a visit, he'd seemed to
understand.

"We've been holding sweats up in Conifer every weekend,
and we've been praying for you and your ranger, Kimímila. I
hope he's keeping you safe and happy."

"He is, Uncle Allen. He is."

And he was. If it hadn't been for the sense of foreboding she couldn't seem to shake and the circumstances that had brought them here, these past three days would have been the happiest of her life.

Oh, how she loved Gabe! She loved that he was at home in the wild, that he knew how to survive and thrive. She loved that he was strong and courageous, every inch the warrior. She loved that he was passionate in bed and that he brought out the passionate side of her. Now that she knew what she'd been missing where sex was concerned, it was hard to imagine living without it. But it wasn't just sex—it was sex with Gabe.

Yes, she loved him, and she was pretty sure he loved her, too, even if he hadn't told her so. There was simply no way a man could fake the kind of caring he'd shown her each and every day—the way he protected her, the way he'd held her last night when she'd been afraid, the way he made love to her.

And yet he'd made her no promises. He'd been careful to let her know that he couldn't make promises. Even so, she refused to worry about it. She didn't want to undermine the connection they'd made these past few days with negative thoughts. She'd given herself to him knowing that he might pull away. She still believed she'd done the right thing. It had been the only way to reach him, the only way she could think of to help him restore harmony in his heart.

And if you're pregnant?

If she was pregnant, she'd have a baby for Gabe. And she would love that baby forever, whether Gabe was in her life or not.

Clearing her mind, she sorted through the remaining documents, pulled out a surface-water survey, and began to read.

THAT'S HOW GABE found her, highlighter in hand, gaze on some official-looking piece of paper, a thoughtful frown on her face. He'd worried about her all day and had known without asking that she was still thinking about last night's visit from the coyote. To be truthful, he'd found the whole thing to be damned eerie, particularly given what she'd told him. Though he was a man of science and wanted to believe this was all freakish coincidence—coyote crossings, coyote night-mares, late-night coyote visitors—he couldn't help but won-der whether there wasn't something to this coyote business.

He dropped an armful of wood on the dwindling wood-pile. "Find anything?"

Whatever she was cooking, it smelled like heaven.

She looked up, shook her head, dark circles beneath her eyes. "No. And that's what bothers me. There's nothing in this file to explain what's happened at the butte—no history, no mention of artifacts, no indication that the city even knew Indian people used the land."

That *was* strange.

"Those things should definitely be there. The file must be incomplete." He walked back outside for another armload, shutting the door behind him, his gaze shifting to the western horizon.

The temp was dropping fast, and dark storm clouds were moving in from the northwest. Within the hour, they'd be in the midst of a blizzard. That's why Gabe had shifted pri-orities from worrying about Kat—and ogling her discreetly while she'd worked—to chopping firewood. He'd wanted to bring in as much wood as possible before the storm hit. As long as they were warm, he and Kat could ride out whatever the mountains could throw at them. And he had all kinds of ideas about how to pass the time while the storm raged. He filled his arms with firewood, walked around to the front door, and nudged it open with his boot.

She was standing by the stove, stirring what could only be beef stew. "You say those documents should be in the file. Do you know that for sure?"

He dropped the load of wood, glanced into the pot, his mouth watering. "Are you making frybread? 'Cuz you know I love your frybread, honey."

She rolled her eyes, a smile tugging at her lips. "Yes, I am making frybread. Only crazy people eat stew without frybread."

He grinned, ducked down, and kissed her nose. "Got to check in with Darcangelo and get more wood. Snow is about to fly."

By the time he'd made the call and gotten the last load in, the storm had begun and they'd lost electricity for the night. Kat had already lit a few lanterns and was kneading dough, a skillet of oil heating on the stove.

"It's coming down pretty hard already. I'd say we're in for a genuine Rocky Mountain blizzard." He stripped off his gloves, parka, and boots, then walked over to the sink and washed his hands. "I'm betting we'll get at least a foot."

She took her lump of kneaded dough and began to divide it into little balls. "Is that what you would call 'sick powder'?"

He knew she wanted to talk about the Mesa Butte file, but she wasn't pestering him. She'd asked the question, and unlike most women he knew, she trusted him to answer it. That was just another thing he'd discovered that he loved about her. "I see you're getting the lingo down."

She smiled, took up one of the little balls, and began to stretch it into a tortilla shape. "I have no choice but to learn it being around you. Otherwise I might never know what you're talking about."

"I'm glad you've accepted that." He laughed, drew out a chair, and sat, watching the delicate motions of her hands as she worked the dough. He could get used to having her cook for him, to sharing all of his meals with her. He could get used to a lot of things where Kat was concerned—if he let himself.

You haven't told her you love her.

No, he hadn't, but that's only because he was a damned coward. He'd get to it eventually. It's not like either one of them was going anywhere. There'd be plenty of time to talk about all that stuff whenever he found the cojones to do it.

He reached for the Mesa Butte folder, which she'd set aside on a chair, and began to look through it. Groundwater studies. Property-line surveys. Noxious weed surveys. Four prairie-dog population counts. Raptor studies. But nothing having to do with the cultural history of Mesa Butte. When he finished, he dropped it on the table. "This file is definitely incomplete."

The sound of sizzling filled the room as Kat put the first piece of bread on to fry. "How can you be certain?"

"When the city buys a piece of property, one of the first things it does is conduct a survey of cultural resources. A historian researches its recorded history, while an archaeologist does a survey on the land looking for artifacts. Depending on what they find, the city is required to make sure those cultural resources are preserved. In the case of Mesa Butte, that job falls to Mountain Parks."

She turned the sizzling, bubbling bread over, glancing back at him. "So, if there's no archaeological survey or historical study in the file—"

"Then someone in the city government removed them."

"If this is true, then whoever removed them has broken state law. The newspaper will sue. Are you absolutely certain?"

"Absolutely one hundred percent certain."

KAT HAD JUST lost her third straight game of checkers when Gabe leaned back in his chair, crossed his arms over his chest, and looked at her through narrowed eyes. "You're not into this game, are you?"

Outside the wind howled, the sound reminding her of the coyote's call.

"I'm sorry." Kat handed Gabe back the few black pieces she'd managed to steal from him. "I guess I'm a bit preoccupied."

He handed her the red. "This wouldn't have anything to do with Mesa Butte, would it?"

His tone of voice made her laugh. "I know we can't do anything about it tonight, and I know we've already talked it out. I just feel bad that I didn't realize the file was incomplete sooner. I remember wondering about it last Thursday, but I forgot—"

"Is that the same Thursday where your workday was cut

short by near cardiac arrest? Because if it is, I think you're being way too hard on yourself."

It was, of course, that same Thursday. Kat had stopped reading the file because she'd been sick, though she hadn't known it at the time. She hadn't gotten back to it till today. "I see your point. But this isn't just about getting a story, and it isn't just about me or my safety. It's about finding the person who killed Grandpa Red Crow and who plundered Mesa Butte. It's about protecting my people's right to pray in peace. I'm an investigative journalist. If I don't do my job right . . ."

He reached across the table and took her hand, stroking her knuckles with his thumb. "You're doing everything you can. Tomorrow morning, I'll call Mountain Parks and get the name of the archaeologist. Then we'll track him down and see if we can get the information straight from him."

Kat nodded, drew a deep breath, resolving to put it out of her mind for the night. They had a plan, and it was a solid plan. And there wasn't anything more she could do about it until tomorrow.

"What you need to take your mind off this is a new game." Gabe folded the game board, picked up the checkers, and put them back in the battered box. "And I have the perfect game in mind."

"HERE ARE THE rules." Gabe had no idea how she'd react, but it was worth a try. "Take your three little scraps of paper, and write a sexual fantasy you have on each one. It can be something you want me to do to you, or something you want to do me, or even something you want us to do together, like a role-playing game—teacher and schoolgirl or caveman and cavewoman or cowboy"—he winked—"and captive Indian maiden."

Kat gaped at him openmouthed.

"We'll roll the dice to see who draws first. Then we get naked, and whatever gets picked out of the ski hat is what we do."

She closed her mouth, and her eyes narrowed. "And what are the objectives of this little game of yours and how does one determine the winner?"

"Well, that's the cool thing about this game. It's one where no one wins and everyone wins. But the objective of the game is simple." He leaned across the table, looked straight into her eyes and smiled. "Intense. Sexual. Pleasure."

Her pupils dilated. "Wh-what if one of us writes something down that the other one doesn't feel comfortable doing?"

"That's another one of the rules—all players must agree to be open-minded." He could see that she was wondering exactly how open-minded he would expect her to be.

You probably should've left the role-playing thing out, douche bag.

Too late now.

He reached out, took her hand, brought it to his lips. "Trust me, okay?"

"Okay." Looking somewhat apprehensive, she took her three strips of paper and a pen and walked over to the dimly lit corner.

Gabe quickly filled out his slips of paper, folded them, and dropped them in the ski hat. Then he undressed and stretched across the bed and waited—and waited. She was probably trying to come up with three fantasies and then worrying that he'd think she was too kinky. Finally, she turned around and, nibbling on her pen, walked over to the ski hat and dropped her three slips of paper inside.

She looked over at him, her gaze traveling over him. "I thought we're supposed roll the dice before getting naked."

Gabe grinned. "How about we skip the dice, and you draw first?"

Looking more than a little nervous, she turned her back to him, drew her sweater over her head, took off her bra, then shimmied out of her skirt. Then she caught her panties with her thumbs, wiggling her sweet ass as she drew them down, bending almost to the floor, giving him a glimpse of paradise, all the while looking back at him over her shoulder.

His heart gave a thud, his dick rising to attention.

So his rez girl had a playful side. He liked that.

Then she stood upright and walked naked to the table, her long hair hiding her breasts from him. She drew a slip of paper from the hat, unfolded it—and turned beet red, her eyes going wide, her gaze flying to meet his.

"Read it. Out loud." Gabe watched her, pretty certain what the slip of paper said and trying to gauge her reaction. He could tell by the way she hesitated that she was shocked by the idea. But the way her breathing had quickened and her nipples had instantly drawn tight told him she also found it arousing.

"It says . . . 'Kat lets Gabe make love to her . . . with his mouth.'"

Kat looked up from the piece of paper, watched a sexy grin spread slowly across Gabe's face, her pulse skipping. "Y-you really want to do that?"

In one fluid motion, he rose off the bed to his feet. "Remember what I said that afternoon when I was drunk?"

"You said a lot of things." And she remembered them all.

"I said I'd suck your clit till you came. I said I'd make you scream. Well, I've thought about going down on you every day since that day we met at the restaurant. The need to taste you has kept me awake at night, and, honey, tonight I get lucky."

He scooped her into his arms, and laid her out on the table, knocking his ski hat to the floor with an impatient swipe of his arm, folded bits of paper scattering across the polished wood. Without giving her a chance to breathe, he kissed her hard, cupping her breasts with both hands, roughing her nipples with his thumbs. Then his mouth dropped to her breasts, as he sucked, licked and nipped his way down her body, teeth and lips and tongue raising goose bumps on her skin, making her shiver.

Was he really going to do this? The thought that he actually wanted to put his mouth on her shocked her—but not as much as it made her burn. And she was burning, anticipation licking through her like flames, his lips scorching her skin. Then his tongue dipped into her navel, circling her, flicking her, making her think of what it would feel like to have it stroking her in other places. That thought unleashed a flood between her thighs, leaving her wet for him.

"God, Kat, your scent—it's driving me insane!" He sank to his knees between her legs, kissed her low on her belly. Then he lifted her legs and draped them over his shoulders, parting her gently with his fingers, his gaze fixed on the most private part of her, a look of raw male hunger on his face. "I've wanted to taste you for so long."

Barely able to breathe, she watched as he settled his mouth against her and gave her clitoris a teasing flick, the sensation like nothing she'd felt before.

She gasped, curled her fingers reflexively in his hair. "Oh, Gabe, I—"

But whatever she'd been about to say unraveled on a moan as he licked her again—one slow drag of his tongue—then drew her into the heat of his mouth.

Kat was lost in a rush of pleasure, her arousal almost unbearable as Gabe gave her his most intimate kiss, his tongue stroking her, flicking her, nudging her entrance, his lips tugging on her aching clitoris. She arched, thrashed, not in control of her own motions or the sounds that were coming from her throat.

Then a strong arm came down across her hips, pinning her down, holding her in place for his mouth, his rhythm relentless, orgasm already building inside her, a tight, reckless ache. Every nerve ending in her body sizzled, her lungs struggling for breath, her body straining, her fingers fisted in his hair as she fought to hold on. Her breath came in ragged pants, the pleasure so intense it felt like torment. She wanted . . . needed him now . . . inside her . . . the emptiness aching . . . aching so badly . . . yearning to be filled.

"Mmm, God, Kat, you taste good!" As if he knew what she needed, he pushed first one, then two fingers inside her, stroking her deeply—and the tension inside her exploded.

She cried out, her body shattering in a white-hot surge of bliss, pleasure pounding through her in an iridescent rush. He rode through it with her, keeping up the rhythm with his mouth and fingers, drawing out her climax, making it last.

"God, Kat, I want you!" And then he was above her, inside her, the deep, rhythmic slide of his cock driving her from one orgasm to another, his kiss carrying her own erotic taste into her mouth. She wrapped her legs around him, offering him all of herself, as he fell over the edge and, with a deep groan, lost himself inside her.

KAT LAY IN Gabe's arms on the bed, her head on his chest, her body feeling languid, her fingers threading through the sweat-dampened hair on his chest. "I like your game better than checkers."

He chuckled, a deep sound that reverberated in his chest. "Here's the best thing about this game—it lasts as long as we last."

He reached for a folded piece of paper, picked it up off the floor, read it—and grinned. "So you want to tie me to the bed, huh? I'll get a rope."

She gaped at him, laughing. "It does not say that! It says—"

In a blink, she found herself flipped onto her belly, her arms stretched out above her head. Gabe spoke in her ear, his voice a deep rumble. "It says you want me to take you from behind. Do you want it like this? Or"—he drew her up onto all fours—"like this?"

"Yes! Oh, like this!"

He grasped her hips and drove into her—hard.

GODDAMN COLORADO WEATHER!

If it weren't for this fucking storm, he'd be done and on his way home. Instead, he'd had to bivouac and was now stuck in this damned tent, waiting for the storm to blow itself out. And he was so close!

According to the last GPS reading he'd gotten before the goddamned batteries had died, the cabin was a couple miles south of him. He ought to have found it by now. He'd have kept going if darkness and whiteout hadn't made it impossible for him to see whether he was skiing in circles or about to go off a cliff. He wasn't going to risk getting seriously lost or breaking his neck. He was here to kill, not to die.

He drew his sleeping bag up tightly around his chin. If he was going to be stuck out here for God only knew how long, he might as well get some sleep. Then, when the storm broke, he'd ski in, nice and quiet, and get rid of them.

CHAPTER 28

THE STORM RAGED into the next morning, the sky so over-cast that Kat and Gabe were forced to ration electricity. While Kat's laptop charged, Gabe checked in with Darcangelo, then heated water so he and Kat could take a bath together. That brought them as close as they could get at the moment to ful-filling her last fantasy—making love in the shower.

"I still say you cheated," she said, lying back against his chest in the cooling water, her eyes closed, her body limp, a look of female sexual satisfaction on her face.

Gabe kissed her hair, lazily fondling her right breast. "I never said you had to write something different on each slip of paper. I really wanted to go down on you, so I did what I could to improve my odds. You're not complaining, are you? From the way you screamed all three times, I'd say you enjoyed it as much as I did."

"No, I'm not complaining." She smiled, then laughed, her cheeks turning a charming shade of red. "But I'll remember that for next time."

Next time.

There would be a next time. There would be lots of next times.

And something in Gabe's heart constricted to think that this smart, beautiful, loving woman was his. Somehow, she'd gotten past the hurt inside him and had given him back himself. He'd never expected to feel this happy again, had never expected to dream about the future again, had never expected to love again. And now they had their entire lives stretched out before them. There'd be more nights of mind-blowing sex. There'd be a wedding. There would be children.

There would be a "happily ever after" after all.

Bet you're glad you never got your nuts cut, aren't you?

Yes, he was. Not having kids had been Jill's plan, not his.

Tell Kat how you feel about her.

He steeled himself, drew a breath—and chickened out. "You're the most beautiful, most amazing, most wonderful woman I know, Katherine James."

She smiled, her eyes still closed. "And you're the most wonderful man in the whole entire world, Gabe Rossiter. I love you."

"THE ARCHAEOLOGIST'S NAME was Phil Getman. Hatfield says he used to do all the archaeological survey work for the city. Here's his number."

Kat took the slip of paper, amazed that it had been so easy. "Are you sure Ranger Hatfield won't end up in trouble for giving you this?"

"Dave knows better than to tell anyone. He's good at keeping secrets."

The edge to Gabe's voice brought Kat's gaze up.

He reached down and ran his fingers through her damp hair. "He's the one who knew about Jill and Wade but didn't tell me. Sorry. I shouldn't have brought it up."

Kat caught Gabe's hand, gave it a squeeze. "Say what you need to say. I don't feel threatened by your past."

He cupped her chin. "You amaze me, do you know that?"

She stood, wrapped her arms around him, offering him the reassurance he seemed to need. "Thanks for getting the number for me. I know it can't have been easy for you to ask him for help."

He held her for a moment, kissed her on the top of her head. "Hatfield owes me, and he knows it."

"Let's just hope I can reach this Phil Getman—and that he'll talk to me."

* * *

REACHING PHIL GETMAN was easy. Getting him to speak was not.

The first time he answered and Kat told him why she was calling, he'd told her to leave him alone and had hung up on her. When she'd called back, he'd been angry. "Fuck off! I told you I don't want to talk about it!"

"But, Mr. Getman—" Kat put down the phone. "He hung up again."

Gabe poured Kat a cup of coffee, his flannel shirt still unbuttoned, giving her a distracting view of his chest. "He lives in Avon. That's only a couple of hours from here as the snowmobile drives. I suppose if worse comes to worse we could pay him a visit now that the storm has blown itself out. Whoa! Did I just say that? Forget it. Bad idea, Rossiter. You're not leaving this cabin, honey."

"Silly goat!" Smiling at Gabe's monologue, Kat took the cup and sipped, the coffee black and strong. "He's obviously afraid. I can't say I blame him. If he'd only listen, I'd offer him whistle-blower protection."

The next time Kat called, she got Getman's voice mail. She left a long message, telling him about Grandpa Red Crow's death and the looting at Mesa Butte and revealing that someone was trying to kill her for reporting on these things.

"I'm trying very hard to piece together the truth about what's happening at Mesa Butte, but I need your help to do it. A good man, someone I loved, died up there, and I think he was murdered. I need to know what's in the survey you did and why it seems the city is trying to hide it from me. Please call me back, Mr. Getman. I'm prepared to offer you whistle-blower protection and full anonymity if you'll talk to me. I know you're afraid, but so am I."

She left her cell phone number, then hung up. She was about ready to call Tom to check in when the phone rang. She answered.

"Ms. James? This is Phil Getman."

"Yes, Mr. Getman. Thank you so much for calling me back."

"Look, I'm sorry I was an ass, but I've got reasons for wanting to stay out of this. What's whistle-blower protection?"

Kat explained how state shield laws enabled her to keep her sources confidential and how state law protected whistle-blowers from retaliation. She promised not to name him in her story or to describe him in any way that revealed who he was. When this seemed to satisfy him, she told him everything that had happened at Mesa Butte from the raid on the *inipi* and Grandpa Red Crow's death to the looting and the attempts on her life. Then she shared with him what she'd unearthed so far, which was nothing.

"There's supposed to be an archaeological survey in the file, but it's missing."

He gave a laugh, his voice rough, probably from years of smoking. "Of course it's missing. Martin doesn't want anyone to see it."

"Paul Martin, the city manager?" Kat glanced over at Gabe, who sat across the table from her, listening intently.

"Yeah, who else?" Mr. Getman paused. "I'll tell you what I know, but you're going to have to keep your promise to me. I wouldn't have thought Martin capable of murder, but I guess you never can tell. I don't want this bastard coming after me the way he's come after you, but I wouldn't feel like a man if I didn't help you out."

"I appreciate that, Mr. Getman. I appreciate it more than you know." Kat gave Gabe a thumbs-up.

"About five years ago when Paul Martin came to work for the city, he talked the city council into buying the Mesa Butte property. The city contracted with me to come in and do the archaeological survey. I found pots and arrowheads dating back a few centuries. I also found what looked like burial sites."

Kat thought back to the trenches and the kinds of artifacts she'd seen there—the pipe stem, the bit of woven basket, the fragments of clothing, the cradleboard. And now it made perfect sense. They weren't just artifacts that had been left behind. They'd come from people's graves.

The looters were desecrating human graves.

She held a hand to her mouth, afraid for a moment that she might be sick, looking over at Gabe in what was a silent plea for support. He stood, walked around the table, and rested his hands on her shoulders. "Y-yes, I . . . I think I've seen the burial sites. That's the key isn't it? He's hiding the report because he doesn't want anyone to know about the burials."

And for Kat a familiar and sad picture began to come together. Indian burials had federal protection. Land that contained Indian burials was off-limits for development. If anyone discovered the truth about the burials, Martin would be blamed for pushing the city to spend two million dollars on land it couldn't use.

"What does he want to do with the land, Mr. Getman?"

"I don't think he gives a rat's ass what the city does with it. Right now, the city council is looking at plans for a recycling drop-off site. All they'd have to do is pave the place, bring in the recycling bins, and they'd be in business. The burials would be hidden for the next several decades or so. But that's not the point, not really."

"What do you mean?"

Getman seemed to hesitate. He lowered his voice, as if he was afraid someone might overhear him. "Martin's big plan wasn't to develop the land, but to get it off his family's hands. The previous owner was none other than his own sainted brother-in-law, who bought the land himself for less than two hundred grand."

It took a moment for the full impact of what Getman had just told her to sink in. "But the city bought it from Mesa Butte Corporation—"

"Which is just a cover for Martin's sister's husband."

So Martin had manipulated the city into buying Mesa Butte for more than ten times what his brother-in-law had paid for it, getting what was a piece of property he couldn't develop off his family's hands—and breaking more than a few laws in the process. Kat was impressed, if somewhat skeptical, of Getman's research. "How did you learn all this?"

"I've got a P-H-fucking-D, okay?" Getman sounded insulted. "I can do research. The man threatened to ruin me. I did some digging on him."

"This was five years ago. Why haven't you gone to the authorities?"

"Hey, the man said he'd make sure I never got another contract. Just be glad I have a sense of chivalry and don't want to see him hurt a lady."

"I'm not judging you. I'm simply curious. I can understand that this has been difficult and upsetting for you." Kat ignored Gabe's snort of disgust. He was obviously listening and putting the pieces together from her side of the conversation.

"I've been looking for a way to get back at him. You said you'd let me be anonymous. This way I can take that bastard down, and he won't even know it was me."

GABE JAMMED THE shovel deep into the snow and scooped it away from the cabin's front door, the burn in his muscles taking the edge off his fury. The snow had let up a little more than an hour ago, leaving about fifteen new inches of powder—and giving him a way to vent his hostility. Of course, he'd rather hop on the snowmobile, make his way to Avon and kick that bastard Getman's ass. For five years the stupid son of a bitch had known that Martin was a crook, and he'd kept quiet to protect his wallet. Now he was using Kat, who'd put her life on the line, to get his revenge against Martin.

The man was a fucking coward.

Gabe would like to kick Martin's ass, too, but he had a feeling Hunter and Darcangelo were going to beat him to it. While Kat had been on her cell phone filling her editor in on everything she'd learned, Gabe had called Darcangelo on his cell phone and brought him up to speed on Martin.

Darcangelo had given a low whistle. "This doesn't prove that he's the one behind the attacks on Kat, the old man's murder, or the looting, but what you've described is certainly a clear motive for murder. If he knew about the artifacts, it makes sense that he might want to cash in on them. And he is on the list of people who have inside information about the city's surveillance cameras. I'd say he just became a person of significant interest in this case. We'll get on it."

Then there'd been nothing for Gabe to do but stay out of

Kat's way. He couldn't help her by stomping around the cabin. Besides, she seemed to have all the help she needed. From what he could tell, most of the I-Team was working on this story now. Sophie and the others were helping Kat track down the records she'd need to prove Getman's claims, while she worked on a draft of the article, filling in details as they were able to provide them.

He had to hand it to her. She was cool under pressure. He knew that what she'd learned had upset her. Few things were more upsetting to Native people than the desecration of graves. For Kat to know that she herself had stood in a burial area and handled things that had been in human graves, however innocently, must have shaken her deeply. And yet apart from her initial shock, she'd been the consummate professional, setting aside her own personal anguish and focusing on the job at hand.

No wonder the I-Team had a reputation for kicking ass.

At least they were moving closer to the truth. Gabe wanted this ordeal to end for her. He wanted to know she was out of danger. He wanted her to be able to put fear behind her and go on with her life—a life that would now include him.

Breathing hard, he trudged back to the woodpile, set the shovel against the wall—and saw something move out of the corner of his eye back near the trees. His pivoted, drew the HK out of its holster, clicking off the safety. He stood there, watching, half expecting to see their good buddy Brother Coyote loping out from among the trees, But there was nothing. He turned to head back inside.

Pop!

He whirled toward the sound, felt a sharp jab in his side—and looked down to see a tranquilizer dart sticking out of his parka. He jerked it out with his left hand and threw it on the ground, knowing that it was already too late. The drug—whatever it was—had injected on impact, and it was already taking effect.

Son of a bitch!

He wanted to shout out, to fire his gun, to do something to warn Kat to protect herself, but the snow was rushing up at him, his gun too heavy to hold, his eyes refusing to stay open. He did a face-plant in the powder, unable even to catch his own fall. And some part of him wondered whether he'd gotten a human-sized dose—or a dose meant to tranquilize a bear. If it were the latter, he'd be dead within moments.

I'm so sorry, Kat. I promised to keep you safe. I blew it. I didn't even tell you I love you.

As if from far away, he heard the crunch of boots on snow, felt a boot nudge him in the ribs, then felt himself being rolled onto his back. He fought to open his eyes, wanting to look into the face of the man who was in all likelihood about to kill him and the woman he loved. He forced his lids up for just a second, and the face he saw smiling down at him made him think he was dreaming. Summoning every bit of his will, he got out three words. "Don't . . . hurt . . . her!"

Laughter. "I'm not going to hurt her. I'm going to kill her."

Kat!

Gabe's heart gave a hard thud, and then—nothing.

KAT SIPPED HER coffee, reread what she'd written, feeling jumpy both from the caffeine and from the adrenaline of closing in on a big story. Or that's what she told herself. In truth, she couldn't shake the sense of foreboding that lingered from last night's visit from the coyote. Nor could she escape the sick feeling that had taken hold of her the moment she'd realized she'd stood in a desecrated burial ground and had touched things that had been plundered from graves. When this was over, she would ask for leave from the paper, drive back to K'ai'bii'tó, and visit her mother's uncle, Uncle Ray, who was a *hataaþhlii*, a singer or medicine man, and would know what ceremonies to perform for her and Gabe to rid them of any taint that still clung to them.

At least she'd made real progress today. Everything Getman had told her had been true, something she'd been able to prove with the help of the other I-Team members. Natalie had tracked down old records on Mesa Butte Corporation and Paul Martin's brother-in-law through the secretary of state's office and Colorado Vital Records. In less than two hours, she'd been able to verify that Martin's brother-in-law had, indeed, owned the land and had profited by selling it to the city of Boulder.

Kat had called Mr. Getman back and talked him into faxing the newspaper a copy of the original archaeological survey with the information on burials intact. Then Sophie had scanned the survey and e-mailed it to Kat, who'd gained a new appreciation for high-speed Internet during the ten minutes she'd watched it download.

While Gabe had reheated the stew for lunch, Kat had read through the survey carefully and had found exactly what Mr. Getman had said she'd find—a report detailing Native people's use of the land for centuries and pointing out the location of a probable burial ground exactly where the trenches had been dug. Then she'd gone through her notes, written up a list of questions, and called Paul Martin.

In the end, her interview with him had been almost a letdown. The moment he'd realized where her line of questioning was leading, he'd clammed up and refused to say another word. Feinman had done the same thing. Martin's brother-in-law had simply hung up on her. So Kat had called the newsroom and asked Sophie and Natalie to fax proof about Martin's dealings to each and every member of the Boulder city council. And the council members had had lots to say.

Kat searched through her notes and found a good quote from Laura Marsh, the council's most outspoken member, then typed it in. *I want a full investigation of Paul Martin and his actions concerning Mesa Butte. If it turns out these documents are accurate, I'd say there's every chance the city will seek both criminal and civil remedies against him.*

Then Kat looked up the specific wording of the federal statute that protected American Indian burial sites and added that to her story. She read through the article once more, checking for holes and typos, and finally satisfied, she e-mailed it to Tom, who replied almost immediately.

Great work, James. We're running it front page, above the fold. Once again the Denver Indy *and the I-Team are making headlines.*

This was why she'd become a journalist—to do a day's work and know that it made a difference in the world.

Of course, there were still many unanswered questions. Was there any connection between Martin and Daniels? Was Martin tied to the looting in any way? If so, why would he wait to steal the artifacts until after the property had passed out of his family's hands? What did any of this have to do with the raid on the *inipi*? And how did Grandpa Red Crow's death—and the attempts on her life and Gabe's—fit into the picture? She hoped Martin would fill in the missing pieces once he'd spent a little time in a police interrogation room.

Could this nightmare truly be drawing to a close? Oh, she hoped so. She was trying to be strong, trying to be brave, but she'd be lying if she didn't admit she was feeling the strain of it. If it weren't for Gabe . . .

If it weren't for him, she wouldn't be alive to feel the strain.

Wondering what he would like most for dinner—besides frybread—she closed her laptop and walked over to the wood-stove to see how much stew was left from lunch. There wasn't much—certainly not enough for a big man like Gabe. Then it occurred to her that she no longer heard him shoveling. He must have finished and have gone back to the woodpile for more wood. She wasn't surprised to hear the front door open.

"Have you worked up an appetite?" She turned to face him. "We've . . ."

Whatever she'd been about to say died on her tongue.

In the doorway stood Chief Ranger Webb. It took a moment for her to recognize him with ski goggles over his eyes, a thick growth of stubble on his jaw, and a hat on this head. Beyond him lay Gabe facedown, unconscious or dead, in the snow.

He grinned. "You're surprised to see me, aren't you, sweetheart? As for Gabe, I don't think he's hungry at all."

CHAPTER 29

KAT'S HEART BURST inside her chest, knocked the air from her lungs, her knees almost buckling. "Gabe!"

Webb looked over his shoulder, then back at Kat. "He's not dead—not yet, anyway. It's a damned shame to have to kill him, but he got himself into this."

Webb's words penetrated Kat's shock and confusion, relief that Gabe was alive shining like a light through a dark fog of terror. "H-he's not dead?"

Webb smiled as if he were proud of himself. "I shot him with a tranquilizer dart. I had to neutralize him to get to you, but I couldn't just pop him, could I? This has to look like an accident."

Just like Grandpa Red Crow's death.

Panic turning her blood to ice, Kat took a step backward, then realized she had no place to run. "B-but why? Why are you doing this?"

"We can talk about it on the way there." Webb tossed something at her feet. A climbing harness? "Get dressed for the outdoors and put that on. We're going for a little winter adventure."

A winter adventure? Where was he taking them?

On the table beside her, her cell phone rang.

Her pulse spiked. If she could reach it, if she could just open it . . .

Webb reached inside his coat, probably grabbing for his gun. "Let it ring."

But Kat wasn't going to die without a fight, no matter how

terrified she felt. The worst thing he could do was kill her, and he was going to do that anyway.

She lunged for her cell phone, grabbed it—then felt her body explode with pain. She couldn't help but scream, every nerve ending on fire. Her legs fell out from under her, her body dropping to the floor as if boneless, the cell phone slipping from her hand and sliding beneath the table.

And then the pain stopped.

Panting, her body shaking, she lay against the cabin floor, struggling to understand what had just happened.

"Want some more?"

She screamed as pain ripped through her again—and then stopped, leaving her feeling as if the room were spinning.

He'd shot her with a Taser. That had to be it.

Two booted feet walked toward her and kicked the climbing harness toward her face. "Do exactly what I tell you to do. It won't save your life, of course—I'm going to kill you either way—but you'll suffer a hell of a lot less if you do."

She felt him tug at her blouse and realized he was removing the gun's probes. She wanted to throw herself against his legs and knock him to the floor, but she still hadn't regained control of her body yet, her muscles caught in painful spasms.

"I'll tell you one more time—put some real clothes on and get into the harness. If you don't cooperate, I'll fry you again."

Slowly, Kat got to her hands and knees, then to her feet, Webb watching her every move. Hands shaking, her muscles strangely weak, she walked on unsteady legs to her suitcase, and took out a pair of jeans, her mind racing for a way out of this.

She couldn't call for help. Her laptop was closed and in sleep mode, her cell phone under the table. Whoever had called would call back and wonder why she didn't answer. But they wouldn't know something terrible had happened, so they wouldn't send help—at least not in time to help her.

And slowly the full horror of her situation became clear.

Unless and until Gabe woke up, she was on her own with a killer, and if she couldn't find a way to stop him, both she and Gabe would die.

She had to find the strength to fight Webb, no matter how much it hurt to get stunned. She had to slow him down somehow. She had to give Gabe time to recover. Webb might have the upper hand now, but he wouldn't have such an easy time of it once Gabe was on his feet again and he had to contend with both of them.

Sending a silent prayer skyward and fighting to subdue her fear, she stepped into her jeans, drew them up beneath her skirt, turning her back to Webb for modesty's sake—but also so that she could look around the room without him seeing.

What she needed was a weapon, something that would take Webb by surprise, something she could hide. Gabe's rifle stood next to the bed, but there was no chance she could get her hands on it. Her gaze moved over the room. Lantern. Comb. Gabe's ski hat. A half dozen little strips of paper.

Her throat constricted, those fantasies they'd lived together now swallowed in this nightmare. *Oh, Gabe!*

Cell phone charger. Coffee beans. Dirty coffee mugs and . . .

A paring knife.

It sat on the counter by the sink on what was the far side of the cutting board from Webb's point of view. Could he see it?

Deciding she had nothing to lose if Webb caught her—and her life and Gabe's to gain if he didn't—she slipped off her skirt and put on a pair of warm woolen socks. Then, heart thudding, she walked toward the sink. "I-I need a drink of water."

Stun gun still in hand, Webb frowned. "Hurry up. We're not on Indian time."

Kat rinsed one of the coffee mugs, filled it, then began to drink, letting her left hand come to rest on top of the knife, steeling herself against the searing pain that would likely follow. But nothing happened.

And then her moment came.

Webb glanced over his shoulder toward Gabe.

Kat quickly closed her fingers around the handle and snuck the knife into her front left jeans pocket. Then she set the mug down on the counter again, her pulse skipping with the thrill of having accomplished this small act of defiance. She hid it under a mask of fear. "C-can I have time to pray? Please?"

He sneered. "You'll be talking to your Great Spirit face to face soon enough. Say whatever you have to say then. Get that damned harness on."

CHILLED TO THE bone, Kat lay facedown in the snow, her lungs aching for breath, her left wrist broken, the pain almost unbearably sharp.

Gabe, please wake up!

"Get up! Get on your feet!" Webb shouted at her from the snowmobile, his face red with fury, Gabe lying, still unconscious, on the supply sled behind him.

"Please . . . I just . . . need to catch . . . my breath." Sucking air into her lungs, she struggled against pain, exhaustion, and the awkwardness of snowshoes to stand. "You're going . . . too fast! I'm not used to . . . altitude . . . or snowshoes!"

It was the truth. They were above timberline now, the air thin and bitter cold, the cabin she'd shared with Gabe swallowed by distance and evening shadows. Even if she'd been in a hurry to die, she wouldn't have been able to keep up.

As soon as Webb had gotten her into the harness—she hadn't been able to figure out the confusing arrangement of leg holes and straps on her own—he'd tied a rope through a strange steel device that hung from its waistband and dragged her outside, where he'd insisted she put on snowshoes. Next, he'd put a harness on Gabe with gloved hands and tied him into the rope, as well, the two of them separated by a thirty-foot length of orange-and-yellow rope. Then Webb had tied Gabe onto the supply sled together with his own backpack and skis, climbed onto the back of the snowmobile, and had driven it slowly westward. Kat found herself being hauled forward at a near run.

At first Kat had thought that Webb was using the rope and harnesses to prevent them from escaping, and she hadn't understood why he'd left her hands free. All she had to do was cut through the rope or unclip the harness. Then she'd realized he was trying not to leave any marks on her that would indicate foul play. Rope burns and fibers on her wrists would have done just that. Besides, he didn't need to bind her hands. One pull of the Taser's trigger, and she was rendered helpless.

Now, seeing where he was taking them, she guessed that the rope and the harnesses weren't just meant to restrain her and drag her along. They were also props. He was planning to throw her and Gabe off the cliff and make it seem like some kind of climbing accident.

Kat had seen this cliff from a distance and admired it. Eagles had soared above it. Gabe had skied down to her from the snowy slope hundreds of feet beneath it. And unless she could delay long enough for Gabe to come around, the two of them were going to die where he'd stood that wonderful afternoon, grinning to himself as he planned how he would show off for her.

She whispered another prayer, let the wind take it.

She'd done everything she could think of to slow Webb down except pull the knife—something she wouldn't do until she had a clear opportunity to use it. It was her only true weapon, and she couldn't squander it. So she'd unclipped the rope from her harness and run, only to be stunned and dragged back. She'd pretended to trip and fall more times than she could count. She'd kicked off her snowshoes. She'd even wrapped the rope around her left arm in an effort to pull Gabe off the sled.

That's how she'd broken her wrist. She'd jerked on the rope just as the snowmobile had surged forward, and the bone had snapped. She'd collapsed to the snow, nauseated and shaking from pain.

"I know what you're trying to do. You're stalling, hoping your boyfriend will wake up and rescue you. If I'd known you were going to be this goddamned much trouble, I'd have tranqued you, too!" Webb shouted.

Kat knew Webb couldn't do that now because the drug would still be in her bloodstream when she died—just as it would apparently still be in Gabe's. A major glitch in Webb's plan.

And yet . . .

Just a moment ago, she thought she'd seen Gabe move. She thought she'd seen his fists clench and his head bob, as if he were trying to raise it. And that had given her hope. If only she could hold out, if she could only be strong . . .

It wasn't much farther. They had almost reached the top of the ridge. Then they would veer to the left and head uphill toward the top of the cliff. And one way or another, this nightmare would end.

Gabe, wake up!

Tears of pain and desperation pricking her eyes, she lost her balance and sank to the snow again. "You said you'd tell me. . . . why you're doing this. Can't I know why . . . you want to kill me?"

"You're a smart girl." He turned off the snowmobile, climbed off, and trudged toward her. "How about you tell me?"

So exhausted that she found it hard to think, Kat made a guess. "You and Paul Martin were . . . making money looting the burial site at Mesa Butte . . . and Grandpa Red Crow found you stealing from the land. The two of you killed him. Did you try to make that . . . look like an accident, too?"

"I tried to get all of you Indian people off the butte, but the old man just wouldn't cooperate. He came back to set up another sweat lodge ceremony and discovered what I was doing. He took a pot from me as evidence. I had to get rid of him." Webb grabbed her coat, jerked her to her feet. "I wish I'd remembered he had that damned pot in his pocket. That's what tipped you off, isn't it? That was my one mistake. Still, I have to give myself credit. For something I hadn't planned in advance, I handled it well."

Kat got the sense that he was proud of himself. "You forced him to drink alcohol, didn't you?"

Webb nodded. "I hit him over the head—not enough to kill him, just to knock him out. Then I carried him up the butte, coaxed some rotgut down his throat—and dropped him over the edge. It was easy."

"You tried to kill me, too." Kat felt a surge of loathing for the man who stood in front of her.

No, not a man. A monster in the skin of a man.

A true skinwalker.

She pushed harder, needing answers. "The death threats. The break-in at my house. The human bone that was mailed to my office. The shooting at Mesa Butte. The leaves in Gabe's furnace flue. You were behind all of that, weren't you?"

"I kept trying to scare you off the story, but you just didn't get the point. After you found the trenches, I knew it was only a matter of time before you uncovered the truth, so I had to get serious. But now I have a question for you. What do you know about Paul Martin?"

She cradled her left wrist with her right arm, breathing easier now, her nausea subsiding. "I know his brother-in-law used to own the land. I know he got the city to buy it and hid the fact that there are Indian burials there. Did you learn about the burials from him?"

Webb gave a snort, his breath rising in a mist. "I've known what was out there since before I became a ranger. At first I just picked stuff up off the ground—pots, arrowheads. It was good money. Then I had to dig. Bones, moccasins, beads— that was better money. Martin and his brother-in-law caught me trespassing once when the land was still theirs, but they didn't call the cops because they didn't want anyone to know that shit was there or they'd have never sold the land. Instead, they asked for a cut of whatever I took. When Martin talked the city into buying the land, I made a deal with him. He would let me take what I wanted, and I wouldn't give away what I knew about him."

Webb spoke of desecrating graves as if it were just a business, showing no respect for those whose bones rested in the earth, or his role as a ranger, or for life. He'd been witched—by money. During the workday he hid behind the face of man who cared for the land. When his uniform came off, he plundered it.

"So this is just about money?" She couldn't help the disgust that leaked into her voice. "That's disappointing."

"Taking artifacts was about money. I've got kids in college, and I like to wager. I have to come up with the money somehow. But killing you isn't about money. It's about saving my own ass. I'm not going to prison."

Kat hoped he'd step closer, her fingers itching to draw the knife. She kept her voice steady. "Was Officer Daniels in on that deal?"

"Daniels? Hell, no. Daniels is just so stupid and so hungry to get promoted that he does whatever Martin tells him to do—and thinks it's his own idea. Martin tells him people are complaining about Indians building illegal bonfires on Mesa Butte and hints that someone needs to act, and the next night, Daniels breaks up your little sweat lodge ceremony. Then Martin gives him a pat on the back. Good dog."

And Kat knew. "You put the file with my articles in his trunk, didn't you?"

But Webb ignored her question. He grabbed her left wrist and bent it back.

She screamed, her knees buckling, the pain so terrible she forgot all about the knife, her mind going blank in a rush of agony.

Webb leaned over her, pressed his grizzled face close to hers. "My turn to ask questions. Who else knows about Martin?"

She sobbed out the words, fighting to hold on, tears streaming down her face. "Everyone! Everyone knows! I wrote about it . . . for tomorrow's paper!"

He seemed to study her, his eyes still hidden behind goggles. "You're lying."

"No!" she sobbed. "I'm not!"

He released her. "Fucking bitch! You'll pay for this."

Dizzy and panting, Kat sank to the ground, then choked out a laugh as the absurdity of his implied threat hit her. "What will you do? Kill me?"

He glared at her, then reached down and took her chin between his fingers. "Watch yourself, or I might find more interesting ways for you to die. Then again, you seem to enjoy pain."

Willing herself to stand, Kat watched Webb's back as he trudged back to the snowmobile. "It's falling apart, Ranger Webb. Your whole plan—it's crumbling. You wanted to make this look like an accident, but there's evidence of a struggle all over this mountainside. The drug is still in Gabe's system.

You struck a deal with Mr. Martin, but he's been exposed. I doubt Martin will sacrifice himself to protect you. You'd be better off just leaving us here and making a run for Mexico."

Webb's back stiffened, but he ignored her. He straddled the snowmobile, started it, and Kat felt herself jerked forward once more.

TRAPPED IN HIS own private hell, Gabe drifted in and out, listening but unable to do a thing while Kat fought Webb with every bit of strength and courage she had, her screams tearing a hole in his chest.

I know what you're trying to do. You're stalling, hoping your boyfriend will wake up and rescue you.

He was trying. God knew he was trying.

Webb had hurt her. Gabe had gotten pieces of it—his threats, her agonized cries and whimpers. But he couldn't put the pieces together, too fucked up to focus.

More than a few times he'd thought he'd shot Webb or beat the shit out of him and freed Kat from this nightmare. But then he'd realized he was still dreaming—or hallucinating. And he'd find himself drifting again.

Still, the ketamine-induced haze was lifting. Little by little it was lifting, his mind growing clearer, his thoughts sharper.

He willed his eyes to open, got a view of darkened sky above him. He willed his eyes to open again, looked toward his feet, and saw Kat being pulled along behind them, barely able to stay upright, her face a mask of pain and fatigue.

I'm so sorry, honey. Hang in there. You're not alone.

KAT ALWAYS THOUGHT she'd die at home surrounded by the Four Sacred Mountains, children and grandchildren beside her, her last words carried into the sky by the wind. Now it seemed as if she would die here, on a mountain whose name she didn't know, no *hataathlii* to sing for her, the man she loved dead beside her in the snow.

She trudged along behind the sled, more exhausted than she could ever remember feeling, her thighs aching, her clothes wet from falling in the snow so many times, her body wracked with cold. She'd quit struggling a while back, realizing she'd need whatever strength she had left at the end. No matter how tired she was, no matter what it cost her, she would fight him.

They were near the top of the cliff now, the wind so cold that it stole her breath.

Or maybe that was fear.

And without realizing it, she began to sing, tears trickling down her wind-burned cheeks. It was a corn-grinding song, something her grandmother had taught her when she was a very little girl pretending to grind corn while her grandmother sat stringing her loom or weaving one of her beautiful rugs. Even though Kat could barely hear herself over the drone of the snowmobile, the words came to her easily, the feel of Diné on her tongue soothing her, easing her fears.

Though she was in pain, exhausted, and freezing cold, she felt strangely alive. A frigid wind caught her hair, its icy breath cleansing, the scents of snow and pine fresh and invigorating. The moon rose over the horizon making the snow sparkle, the landscape coldly serene. Overhead, stars glowed like little campfires, and she found herself remembering the dream she'd had about Grandpa Red Crow.

You must do what I asked you to do. This will be the fight of your life. Be strong, Kimímila.

And then it struck her. Maybe it hadn't been a dream after all. Maybe she'd been so close to death that some part of her had actually spoken with him. Maybe he could see her now and knew that she was still fighting.

I haven't given up, Grandpa. I won't give up.

She kept singing, her words growing stronger as they moved toward the highest point above the cliff. Slowly and carefully, she drew the knife from her pocket, holding it tight in her right hand.

CHAPTER 30

GABE FELT THE snowmobile stop, heard Webb cut the engine, the world silent apart from the melancholy sound of Kat's singing and the beating of his own heart. He felt the sled rock as Webb climbed off the snowmobile, heard the crunch of Webb's boots in the snow. He willed himself to stay limp, to wait just a few more seconds.

Then Webb spoke, clearly facing away from the sled. "Here's as good as any place else, I guess. It's three to four hundred feet to the ground here. I don't imagine it'll hurt as much as what you've put yourself through today. Be grateful for that at least. I could've done anything to you I felt like doing."

Yeah, Webb, you asshole—you're the soul of compassion.

Gabe watched from beneath his eyelashes as Kat stood before Webb, not backing away, not running, her chin held high, her dignity intact despite everything Webb had done to her. But Gabe wouldn't let Webb hurt her again. His muscles tensed for action—for real this time, not as part of a hallucination.

"Y-you're going to throw us over the side here?" She asked the question casually, as if she were asking Webb where he'd like to stop for a picnic.

"That's the idea." Webb drew the Taser from his parka, clearly intending to stun Kat again.

"No!" she pleaded. "Not again, please!"

"I can't imagine you're going to go without a fight, so—"

Ignoring his lingering dizziness, Gabe sprang up from the sled, threw the rope over Webb's head, and drew it tight against his throat. "You want to fight, you son of bitch? Try me!"

He met Kat's gaze for a fleeting second, surprise and overwhelming relief in her eyes, her sweet face lined with pain and exhaustion.

But the ketamine must have turned Gabe into an idiot, because he'd forgotten entirely about the Taser. The force of it took him by surprise, dropping him in one second flat, the pain overwhelming. He couldn't help but cry out, the part of him that could still think amazed that Kat had endured it as many times as she had.

Out of the corner of his eye, he saw her move in on Webb, her right arm making a slashing motion, something in her hand.

A knife.

Webb yelped, dropped the stun gun.

Gabe's pain ended abruptly, and he lay, limp, in the snow, muscle control returning too slowly for him to stop Webb from lifting the rope from around his neck and going after Kat. But if she was afraid, she didn't let it show.

"So much for looking like an accident. Your blood is on the snow, on my hands, on the knife. They'll know you did this." She backed away from him on her snowshoes, crouched like a wildcat about to pounce, while Webb had to trudge, buried up to his knees in powder.

But Webb had the size advantage—and a much longer reach than Kat. The bastard backhanded her, knocking her into the snow. "Goddamn you!"

"Leave her the fuck alone!" But no one was listening to Gabe. "Webb, no!"

Kat landed by the sled, one of her snowshoes coming off, the knife flying from her grasp. But she hadn't given up. She grabbed one of Webb's ski poles from the sled and swung it at his head, making him duck, distracting him, slowing him down.

Way to go, Kat.

Gabe lurched unsteadily to his feet, throwing himself toward the knife, his hand closing over its cold handle just as Webb's hand closed around his wrist. But Webb was determined. He fell on Gabe, the two rolling through the snow.

"Gabe! The cliff!"

He heard Kat's cry of warning and realized he and Webb were perilously close to the cliff's edge. He head-butted Webb, pain splitting his skull at the impact of bone on bone. Webb groaned, his grasp weakening. Then he rolled off Gabe, crawled a few feet away, blood pouring from his nose.

Gabe stood, the knife in his hand. "So this the real you, huh, Webb? A grave robber, a man who tortures women, a cold-blooded killer? I trusted you, you asshole. I admired you. I worked my ass off for you."

"Fuck you, Rossiter, you self-righteous prick." Webb staggered to his feet. "You think those artifacts are better off lying in the dirt? I needed the money to clear up some debts. Someone was going to take them eventually. Why not me?"

"The artifacts don't belong to you." Gabe circled, slowly trying to put himself between Webb and Kat. "They belonged to people who were buried with them."

A strange expression flitted across Webb's face, then he smiled. He reached into his coat and drew his Glock. "I forgot I had this. Since my DNA is all over the place, I might as well blow your heads off and finish this."

Gabe was about to make a desperate lunge with the knife, when Webb pitched forward in the snow, writhing at Gabe's feet, howling like a wounded animal.

Behind him stood Kat, pressing the electrodes of the Taser directly against Webb's back, giving Webb a well-deserved taste of his own medicine. "Do you enjoy pain? Do you?"

Gabe heard the quaver in her voice, something twisting in his chest to think how many times that same weapon had been used on her today. He needed to get her off this mountain and to a hospital. She was exhausted, probably hypothermic, and from the way she'd been holding her left wrist, it was almost certainly broken.

He tucked the knife in his pocket, grabbed the Glock, then pointed it at Webb's head. "It's over, Webb. Where's your cell phone?"

Webb raised his head, his gaze flicking toward the sled, where his backpack still sat, the expression on his face like that of a cornered animal, and Gabe knew he was trying to plot a way out of his own mess. "It's here. In my pocket."

"You're lying. Kat, check his backpack."

That's when Gabe felt the snow beneath him shift with a deep, almost imperceptible *whomp*! And he realized that he and Webb weren't just near the edge of the cliff but past it, their combined weight resting on an overhanging cornice of snow. And that cornice was about to give way.

KAT FELT THE mountain move beneath her feet like the subtle shifting of sand. And then Gabe was shouting to her, running toward her, motioning for her to move.

"Get back! Get back as far as you can! Run!"

Not sure what was wrong and yet trusting him completely, Kat turned and ran as fast as she could in snow that rose above her knees, using the ski pole she still held to help her balance, icy air burning her lungs. But she hadn't run far when the rope brought her up short. She looked over her shoulder, saw Gabe on the ground, Webb's hands holding tightly to Gabe's harness.

Then she heard a *whoosh*!

And all at once Kat was yanked off balance onto her side and dragged headfirst across the snow toward the cliff's edge. But what she'd thought was the cliff's edge was gone—and Gabe with it.

Knowing they would both fall if she couldn't somehow stop herself from sliding, she rolled onto her back, sat up, and dug the heels of her boots in deep. But it wasn't enough, her heels channeling through the powder, the darkness that marked the gaping chasm just ahead of her, the edge rushing toward her.

Then she remembered the ski pole. She took it with both hands, thrust it into the snow at an angle, throwing all of her weight onto it, the pain in her broken wrist tearing a scream from her throat, the snow still rushing by beneath her.

Momentum flipped her onto her belly again, her body coming to rest almost directly on top of the ski pole, which suddenly caught—and held.

Kat jerked to a stop. Out of breath, almost sobbing with relief, she held on to the ski pole, pressing it down into the snow with every ounce of her strength. The harness bit into her hips, Gabe's precious weight on the other end. "G-Gabe?"

He didn't seem to hear her.

Her heart still hammering, she glanced back over her shoulder—and almost screamed. Her boots were no more than ten feet from the edge.

Beneath her, the rope jerked, and she felt the ski pole slip several inches, then catch again. Dread curled in her stomach. If the ski pole came free, if it slid much farther . . .

Then she heard Webb's voice. "Did you feel that? She's slipping. I guess we're all going to die together tonight."

Webb was on the rope, too?

"Sorry, Webb, but hanging with you isn't what it used to be."

The rope jerked violently, and there came the dull sound of fists meeting flesh. The ski pole began to bend.

"Gabe!" She whispered his name.

More blows. The rope twisted. The ski pole bent more— and gave a small slip.

"No! No! No!" Webb pleaded, then screamed, the sound dropping away, then ending abruptly.

Kat squeezed her eyes shut, the thought of what had just happened rousing dark memories, putting her stomach into free fall. And she started to sing again.

GABE LOOKED UP, saw that he was about twenty feet below the edge of the cliff. He could hear Kat singing and knew she must be terrified. He couldn't blame her. They'd both come close to dying, and it wasn't over yet. The slippage had slowed, but it hadn't stopped. He could feel it.

Inch by inch, he was pulling Kat over the edge with him.

"Kat, can you hear me?"

"Y-yes!"

"Webb is dead! I'm going to climb up to you. Find a way to dig in! Try not to slide!"

"There's nothing more to dig in with! The ski pole is bending!" For the first time today, he heard true panic in her voice, and he suspected she was remembering the last time the ground had disappeared from beneath her feet.

"Hang on, honey! I'll be quick." *I hope.*

What Gabe wouldn't give for a set of ice tools and some crampons. Or a headlamp. Or a damned helicopter. Darcangelo would know something was wrong because Gabe hadn't checked in, but would he send help?

Willing his mind to focus, Gabe drew off his gloves and dropped them. This wasn't going to be easy. He couldn't see details of the rock face in the dark, so he couldn't see where the holds were. He'd have to feel his way up and hope he didn't climb himself into a dead end. At least he didn't have far to go.

You can do this, Rossiter.

He felt his way over the cold, slick rock and felt his stomach sink. There was very little exposed rock, most of the cliff face covered in verglas—a slick patina of brittle ice that made rock climbing treacherous under the best conditions. He extended his arms out to both sides as far as he could reach and then upward over his head.

There. At one o'clock. A little crack.

Barely wide enough for his fingertips, it felt like a lifeline. Ignoring the cold, he nudged his fingers into the fissure, only to feel more ice. If he'd had an ice screw, he'd have screwed it in, clipped into it, and gotten his weight off the rope. But his fingers weren't steel.

The knife!

He drew it out of his pocket and began to jab at the ice with the blade.

The roped slipped, and Kat screamed.

Gabe felt himself drop, the fissure now beyond his reach. Son of a bitch! "Hang on, Kat! Just a little longer!"

Starting from scratch, he tucked the knife away and quickly found a small nub for his left foot, the fingers of his right hand catching a crimper. He put his weight into the holds—only to feel the toehold crack and give way.

Verglas, not rock.

In the dark, he couldn't tell the difference.

Shit!

He tried again, feeling down around his knees for something his toes might be able to catch. Nothing but slick ice.

Son of a bitch!

He looked up. "I'm going to try climbing the rope. If you can hold on, I'll be up in less than a minute."

He'd hoped to avoid this. His weight would make the rope swing, putting more stress on the ski pole and increasing the risk that it would slip or bend. He'd wanted to find a way to take his weight off the rope. Then Kat would have been able to crawl forward and dig in again, taking up the slack in the rope. They'd have been able to inch their way to safety. But that wasn't going to happen. He needed to act, and he needed to act fast. His fingers were quickly going numb from cold, and Kat, already hypothermic, wouldn't be able to hold on much longer.

"Nice and easy, Rossiter." He reached up, grabbed the rope between both hands and pulled himself upward, keeping his motions smooth to prevent the rope from swinging. He reached up again, drew himself up higher.

Then Kat screamed, and the rope slipped again, fast this time—then caught. Gabe looked up and saw the toes of her boots jutting out over the edge.

And he knew it was no good.

He thought of all the times he'd risked his life since Jill's death, climbing without ropes or a helmet, defying gravity, daring the rock to defeat him. He'd redpointed routes no one else would touch, set speed records, free-soloed his way into climbing history, and none of it had meant anything to him because life had no longer meant anything to him. And now when he had everything to live for—on what was the single most important climb of his life—he couldn't scale a distance of twenty-five feet.

But he wouldn't let Kat die.

He drew the knife out of his pocket, a sense of calm settling over him. At least he'd lived long enough to die for a good reason. "Kat, can you hear me?"

"Y-yes!"

"When this is over, I want you to dig through Webb's pack and look for anything you can use to keep warm and stay awake—food, a space blanket, hand warmers. Then I want you to find his cell phone and call for help. Darcangelo already knows something's wrong because I didn't check in, but if you call, he'll get here sooner. Stay awake no matter what it takes, do you hear me? And stay away from this edge. Find a way to get out of the wind and take shelter till rescuers find you."

"B-but what about—" She gasped, screamed as the rope slipped again.

Gabe cut faster. "This isn't going to work, honey. I'm just pulling you down with me, so you're going to have to go on without me."

"Wh-what? I-I don't understand. W-without you?"

"All you have to do tonight is survive, Kat. Do you hear me? Stay alive! You can do this. You're strong. You're the strongest, bravest woman I've ever known. What you went through tonight—you kept us both alive. Be strong just a little longer!"

Perhaps she could feel the tug of the knife on the rope, or maybe she'd put two and two together.

"No, Gabe! Don't do this! I can hold on! I'll hold on as long as it takes! We'll find a way! Please don't! Don't leave me! I love you!"

But even as she cried out for him the rope slipped again.

There were so many things he wanted to tell her, so many things he hadn't taken the time to say, but it was too late for that. Only one thing mattered now.

He forced the words past the lump in his throat, words he should have already spoken. "I love you, Katherine James. I love you with everything I am. You're the best thing that's ever happened to me. Remember that."

"No, Gabe, please! Don't do this! I need you! Let me save you!"

He looked up, wishing to God he could touch her. "You already have."

Steeling himself—how much could it hurt to die, anyway?—he pushed the knife through the last bundle of fibers and let himself go, Kat's scream following him into oblivion.

* * *

KAT LOOKED OUT over the edge into the abyss, her face wet with tears, the grief inside her so strong it felt like physical pain. She cried his name again, her voice now a hoarse croak. "Gabe!"

No answer.

He was gone. He'd cut the rope. He'd cut it with the knife she'd carried all day, the knife she'd given him. He'd sacrificed his life to save hers. Now, he was gone, his body lying broken down there, somewhere in the cold and dark.

She wished she could go to him. She wished she could at least put a blanket over him. She wished she could sit beside him until help arrived. Her grandmother wouldn't like her being so near a dead body, but at least he wouldn't be alone.

"Gabe!" She sobbed his name through chattering teeth.

She'd realized what he'd meant to do, but she'd been helpless to stop him. One moment he'd been there, talking to her, reassuring her, telling her he loved her, and the next he'd been gone, his weight no longer pulling on the rope. He hadn't cried out, hadn't screamed. He'd fallen silently into the darkness.

No, Gabe! Don't do this! I can hold on! I'll hold on as long as it takes! We'll find a way! Please don't! Don't leave me! I love you!

I love you, Katherine James. I love you with everything I am. You're the best thing that's ever happened to me. Remember that.

No, Gabe, please! Don't do this! I need you! Let me save you!

You already have.

Again and again, she heard her own desperate cries, then his quiet replies, the terrible beauty of what he'd done for her shattering her heart. He'd died a warrior's death, giving his life for hers. And for a time—she couldn't say how long—she lay there, unable to move, unable to cry, almost unable to breathe.

Then gradually, she became aware that she *was* breathing,

her breath rising in a mist before her face, her heart beating, her body shivering from the cold.

She was alive.

Because of Gabe she was alive. And no matter how impossible it seemed, no matter how much it hurt, she had to stand up, turn her back on this place, and go on without him. It was the only way to survive, and survival was the only way she could honor his sacrifice. She had the rest of her life to grieve for him.

She drew in a shaky breath. "*H-hágoónee'*, Gabe. *Ayor anosh'ni*. I love you."

Remembering what Gabe had told her to do, she sat, scooted back from the edge, then stood, shuffling through snow back to the snowmobile, her legs stiff and slow. There in the sled, next to the place where Gabe had lain, sat Webb's backpack. She opened it with her right hand, then searched through it, pulling out whatever she thought she might need—a sleeping bag, a flashlight, granola bars, a Nextel phone, little tins of food, a chocolate bar. Then she kicked his skis and the one remaining ski pole out of the sled, climbed into it, and crawled into the sleeping bag.

It took her three tries to get Sophie's number right, and she realized she was suffering more from the cold than she had imagined. Sophie answered on the second ring, the concern in her voice bringing tears to Kat's eyes, grief, exhaustion, pain, and relief tangled so tightly inside her that she couldn't tell one emotion from the next.

"Kat? Oh, my God, Kat, are you okay? We've been worried sick about—"

"Oh, Sophie, he's dead. Gabe is dead."

CHAPTER
31

"KAT, CAN YOU hear me? Stay awake!" Sophie's voice came from the cell phone. "They're almost there, but you need to stay awake."

"I'm trying, but I'm so sleepy. And my wrist . . ."

"I bet it hurts a lot, doesn't it?"

It did, but not nearly as much as the hole in her heart. "He cut the rope, Sophie. I tried to stop him, but he cut the rope. He fell."

"I know, sweetie. He must have loved you very much."

I love you, Katherine James. I love you with everything I am. You're the best thing that's ever happened to me. Remember that.

Kat felt a surge of grief, but was too exhausted even to cry. It was even getting hard to speak. "He told me he loved me. Just before he fell, he told me he loved me, but I already knew."

"Are you still sitting up?"

"Yes." Then Kat realized she'd just told a lie. She was lying down again. "No."

"Can you sit up? Can you do that for me?" Sophie sounded worried.

Kat had been talking to Sophie for what seemed like a very long time now. She'd told Sophie everything that had happened from the moment she'd seen Webb standing in the cabin door until the moment Gabe had fallen. Sophie had passed what she'd said along to Marc and Julian, who were on the way with a rescue team to get her.

"Can you still hear me, Kat? Try to sit up!"

Forgetting about her broken wrist for a moment, Kat tried to push herself up, then collapsed with a cry, overwhelmed by pain.

"You used your left hand, didn't you? I should have reminded you." Then Sophie's tone of voice changed, her words quavering as if she were afraid and in tears, and Kat knew she was talking to Marc again. "Yes, she's still conscious, but she's fading. Her words are slurring together. Can't the pilot fly faster?"

All you have to do tonight is survive, Kat. Stay alive!

Kat's eyes opened—when had she closed them?—and she found herself staring at a sky filled with stars, the cold beauty of it making her heart swell. Was Gabe up there somewhere in some kind of heaven? Had he joined Grandpa Red Crow at one of those distant campfires? Could he see her?

And where was Sophie? She'd been talking to Sophie hadn't she?

There came a blinding light and a sound like beating wings, the wind blowing snow all around her. And then Julian was there—and other men, too.

Julian stroked her face. "I'm here, Kat. It's going to be okay. We're going to get you warm and take good care of you."

"Julian." She reached her right hand out to him, feeling a rush of relief to see him. "You have to help Gabe."

He took her hand, held it. "Don't worry about Gabe, sweetheart."

Someone piled heated blankets on her, unfamiliar voices around her.

"Let's get her into the chopper. We'll start oxygen and IV fluids there."

"Watch it!" That was Julian. "Her left wrist is fractured."

Gentle hands lifted her onto a stretcher, and then she was moving, bouncing along, Julian walking beside her.

She held fast to his hand. "You can't leave him there. It's so cold. I don't want him to be alone. Please don't leave him down there."

"See that other chopper?" Julian pointed toward a light in the sky. "Hunter is there with another team on his way to the base of the cliff to see if they can find him. They'll bring Gabe home. I promise."

That was all Kat needed to hear.

She closed her eyes, and finally she slept.

THE SOUND OF a chopper roused Gabe to consciousness. He watched it disappear beyond the top of the cliff, a sharp feeling of relief flooding his chest, momentarily dulling his pain. Darcangelo and Hunter had come through.

Thank God!

Kat was safe. She was safe.

He seized that single thought, held on to it with all of his might, the knowledge that she was going to be okay making each unbearable moment a bit more bearable. He'd long since stopped feeling cold—a bad sign. But he was thirsty, so thirsty, pain making him long to pass out again. One of his lungs had collapsed, the pressure in his chest excruciating. Both of his legs were broken, the left one a bad compound tib-fib fracture that had bled heavily before he'd managed to rig a tourniquet out of his boot lace. It had taken all the strength he'd had left to manage that.

Kat is safe. She's safe.

He felt himself relax, darkness swallowing him whole, his pain growing distant, as if it weren't really in his body. He didn't hear the second helicopter land below him on the mountainside, didn't see the men ski toward the cliff, didn't see the tallest one break into an uphill sprint, then drop down beside him on his knees.

It was the sound of Hunter's shout that awoke him.

"What the . . . ? Get medical up here! Hurry! He's alive!"

Gabe opened his eyes, saw Hunter leaning over him. It took everything he had to speak. "Is . . . Kat . . . ?"

"Julian says she's got a serious case of hypothermia, but she's going to be all right—thanks to you. Jesus! I just can't believe you're alive!" Hunter shrugged off his pack, stripped off his parka, and laid it over him. "The gods of powder really do love you the most."

"Wa . . . ter."

Hunter's gaze traveled over him, and Gabe knew from his grim expression that he was worried by what he saw. He drew a bottle of water out of his pack, lifted Gabe's head, and held the bottle to his lips. "Easy does it. Not too much now."

Gabe swallowed, the mouthful Hunter allowed him not nearly enough to slake his thirst, but better than nothing.

Hunter looked to his right. "So that's Webb?"

Gabe nodded.

Webb lay about twenty feet west of Gabe, most definitely dead. He'd had the misfortune of landing on an outcropping of rock about three feet off the ground, while Gabe had landed in deep powder, much of it probably from the cornice. The snow had broken his fall. If his legs hadn't hit a ledge on his way down, he'd probably be fine.

Hunter laid a reassuring hand on Gabe's shoulder. "Kat told Sophie what happened. You've got balls of granite, Rossiter. I respect the absolute hell out of you for what you did. I'm going to get out of the way so these guys can take care of you."

God, Gabe hoped they had morphine—a gallon bucket of the shit.

Hunter gave Gabe's shoulder a squeeze, then stepped aside to make room for the paramedics. "If you need me, I won't be far. I'm going to let Darcangelo know so he can tell Kat. She's pretty torn up."

Gabe had thought she must be. He'd heard her crying out for him, her voice sounding so small and faraway. He'd tried to answer but hadn't had the breath.

Hunter's voice drifted back to Gabe. "Darcangelo, you are not going to fucking believe this. He's alive! He's seriously hurt, but he's alive."

"KAT, SWEETHEART, WAKE up!"

Cocooned in warmth, Kat heard Julian's voice, some part of her resisting. She didn't want to wake up, didn't want to face what awaited her outside the forgetfulness of sleep. But there was something urgent in Julian's voice.

She fought to open her eyes and found herself still in the

helicopter, a paramedic hanging a bag of heated IV fluids above her, an oxygen mask on her face, Julian looking down at her, smiling.

How could he be smiling?

"Hunter has something to tell you." Julian moved the oxygen mask out of the way, then pressed his Nextel phone to her ear.

"Can you hear me, Kat?" Marc's voice came in clear.

Kat swallowed, her throat rough and sore from shouting. "Y-yes."

"Gabe is alive. He's hurt pretty bad, but he's alive and more or less conscious."

And for a moment Kat couldn't speak, her heart kicking hard, her head seeming to spin. "Wh-what?"

"Gabe is alive!"

Kat glanced up at Julian, looking for proof that she wasn't dreaming, the smile on his face broadening to a wide grin. "H-he's really alive? Gabe is alive?"

"He landed in a deep powder cache. He hit the cliff wall on the way down so he's busted up pretty badly. But he's alive and still himself. Do you want to say something to him? He might not be able to say much, but he'll hear you."

"Yes! P-please!"

There was a pause. Then Marc's voice came from a distance. "Go ahead, Kat."

"Gabe? Gabe, are y-you there?"

"How's my . . . rez girl?" It was unmistakably Gabe's voice. He sounded weak. He sounded hurt. But he was alive.

Hot tears sprang to Kat's eyes, the ache in her heart washed away by a surge of joy. "Oh, Gabe! I-I thought . . . But how . . . ? I love you! D-do you hear me?"

"Yeah." There was the barest hint of a smile in his voice. "Love . . . you . . . too."

And then Marc was on the other end again. "Hey, Kat, they need to move him, so that's it for now."

In the background, she heard Gabe cry out, something twisting in her stomach to know he was suffering. How badly was he hurt? "Thank you, Marc. Stay with him, please! I don't want him to be alone."

"I'll stay as close to him as they'll let me. But you rest easy now, okay? Let them take care of you. Julian's staying with you, and Sophie and Tessa are on their way to the hospital."

A warm feeling spread behind her breastbone at this news. Her friends were there for her once again. "Okay. Bye."

Julian tucked his phone away.

One of the paramedics slid the oxygen mask back into place over her nose. "She really needs to keep this on. We have to stabilize her core temp."

"Uh, yeah, sorry about that." Julian winked at her.

Kat squeezed Julian's hand, a silent thank-you, then closed her eyes, tears spilling down her temples. *He's alive. He's alive.*

Before she knew it, she was asleep again.

GABE DRIFTED THROUGH the next several hours in a morphine haze, the shattering pain in his legs dulled if not gone. He knew when they arrived at the hospital, knew when they reinflated his right lung, knew when they'd taken him for the first of three CT scans. Then a doctor said something about needing to stabilize his core temp and give him a few units of blood before they could operate on the fractures in his legs.

Through it all he wanted one thing.

"I want to see her. I need to see Kat." He said it again and again.

"She wants to see you, too, but she's in surgery, buddy." Hunter rested a reassuring hand on Gabe's shoulder. "Nothing serious. They're just setting her wrist. She's going to be fine. You just let them take care of you now."

And then Hunter was gone, and a man in a surgical cap and mask stood above Gabe. He lowered a clear plastic anesthesia mask over Gabe's mouth and nose. "Take a deep breath for me."

The world faded.

WHEN THE NURSE wheeled her back from having her wrist set, Kat found her friends waiting in the lobby down the hall from her room. Uncle Allen and Nathan were there with Glenna and Pauline. The entire I-Team, past and present, was there, together with Julian and Marc, who'd been up all night. Sophie had dark circles beneath her eyes, and Kat knew she'd been up all night, too. Kara and Reece had come, and Tessa, as well. Matt was the only who hadn't been able to make it. Even Tom was there.

"You sure are popular." The nurse pushed Kat's wheelchair into her room, then helped her into bed. "Are you up for visitors?"

"Yeah." Being with friends would make the wait easier. "Please let me know if you hear anything about Gabe. I want to be there when he wakes up. I haven't seen him since last night. I need to be there for him."

The nurse nodded and gave her hand a sympathetic squeeze. "I'll let you know."

Her wrist still blessedly numb from the anesthetic they'd injected, Kat watched while her two groups of friends filled the room and introduced themselves to one another, Sophie giving her chair to Glenna, Uncle Allen and Nathan taking time to shake everyone's hand, Holly discreetly eyeing Nathan's long hair—and his butt. It felt strangely satisfying to see these two parts of her life—the Indian part and the journalist part—coming together. Somehow it made her feel whole.

And then Kat found herself telling them what had happened, Marc and Julian filling in the missing pieces. She had to back up a bit so that Uncle Allen, Glenna, and Pauline could follow along. She'd already had to tell the story three times—to a sheriff's officer from Vail as well as police from Boulder and Denver—so it was easier this time. Or maybe it was the love and support of her friends that made it easier, Glenna sitting beside her, patting her arm in a grandmotherly way, Pauline standing wide-eyed behind Glenna, Sophie on the other side of the bed, holding her right hand.

Still some parts of the story were harder to tell than others. Gabe lying unconscious in the sled. The long, agonizing battle up the side of the mountain as she tried to buy time for Gabe to wake up. Webb's cruelty with the Taser.

His admission that he'd killed Grandpa Red Crow and tried repeatedly to kill her.

"He told me he didn't want to go to prison."

When she reached the part where Gabe cut the rope and let himself fall, she couldn't stop her tears. "I tried to hold on. I tried so hard, but the ski pole kept slipping. I pleaded with him not to do it, but he was afraid he'd pull me off the cliff, too, so he . . . he cut the rope . . . and fell."

Sophie gave Kat's hand a squeeze, tears in her eyes. "You did everything you could. When I think of what you went through . . ."

But Kat wasn't so sure. "If I'd just been a little stronger, held on a little longer, maybe he wouldn't be in surgery now."

"You're being way too hard on yourself," Tessa said. "Bless your heart! You're not Superman, you know."

Pauline dabbed her eyes with a tissue. "I think you're both very brave."

"Gabe knew what he was doing," Kara assured her. "He made a choice."

Holly gave Kat's foot a squeeze. "If it had been me, I'd be dead. I never could've done what you did. I probably would have jumped off the cliff myself just so I didn't have to be afraid of falling."

Holly's admission—and her strange logic—made everyone laugh.

Then Marc spoke. "You fought a man almost twice your size alone for hours. You endured God only knows how many rounds from the Taser, not to mention a broken wrist and serious hypothermia. I don't know how much stronger any woman could be—or any man, for that matter."

Julian nodded. "What Hunter said. You're my hero, Kat James."

Uncle Allen held up his hand, a sign that he wished to speak. "You did what Grandpa Red Crow asked you to do, Kimímila. You uncovered the truth about what was happening at Mesa Butte. But if my cousin had known what it would cost you, he never would have asked it of you. You almost lost your life helping your people, and your ranger took the warrior's path and gave his life for you."

"Aho!" Nathan said softly.

Uncle Allen went on. "As I see it, Creator was moved by these acts of sacrifice and brought you both safely to this moment."

Everyone seemed to agree.

"When I saw he was alive, I couldn't believe it." Marc shook his head. "The first thing he did when he opened his eyes was to ask about you, Kat."

Julian smiled. "And the first thing Kat did when I found her was ask me to go get Gabe's body and bring him home."

Tears spilled down Kat's cheeks, but she smiled along with everyone else. She sniffed, glanced at the clock. Gabe had been in surgery for five hours now.

Such a long time.

"How did you reach us so quickly? It seemed like forever, but Sophie said it was only about forty-five minutes."

"We were already in Vail when you called Sophie," Julian said. "Martin spilled his guts yesterday afternoon, pointing the finger at Webb, blaming him for everything. We were able to corroborate some of what Martin said and went to arrest Webb, but his wife said he'd gone skiing for the weekend. When you and Rossiter failed to check in and we couldn't reach you, we knew something was wrong."

"But how did Webb know where to find us?"

"Since we can't ask him, we can only speculate." Julian wrapped his arm around Tessa's shoulder and drew her back against him. "I'm guessing he knew about the cabin in the same way Rossiter did—through his job. When he heard that Daniels had followed us as far as Vail, he must've guessed where Rossiter might take you."

"So Daniels wasn't a part of this after all." Tom frowned.

Julian shook his head. "Not directly. He was just eager to get promoted and did anything he could to ingratiate himself to Martin. All Martin had to do was suggest that something ought to be done, and Daniels did it, not realizing he was being used. Webb knew that and took advantage of it by trying to cast more suspicion on Daniels. I expect the Boulder PD will be doing an internal investigation on Daniels."

"What about Feinman?" Tom asked.

Marc shrugged. "Whether he's charged depends on how much he knew. That's up to the Boulder police to uncover. I know they've launched a full investigation."

Natalie looked up from her notes. "So what happens with Martin?"

"Off the record—you'll have to talk to the Boulder DA—I'm sure he's facing a host of felonies including conspiracy to commit murder," Julian said. "He might not have killed Red Crow or tried to kill you, Kat, but those crimes were committed as part of their looting scheme and he knew about them, so he's accountable, too."

"What about the things that were stolen?" asked Uncle Allen. "They should be returned to the land and to our ancestors."

"It's very unlikely we'll be able to get any of it back again," Reece said, speaking for the first time. "I've spent a lot of time these past couple of days researching it. Once an artifact is sold into a private collection, we'd have to prove that it was obtained illegally in order to take it back. I'm going to introduce a bill this next session to strengthen state looting laws and give additional protection to American Indian sacred sites in and around urban areas. I'd like to see sacred sites, including Mesa Butte, set aside for use by Native Americans but we'll see how far the bill goes."

Kat hadn't heard anything about this. "Thank you, Reece. That means a lot to me, to all of us."

Tom folded his notebook. "I need to get back to the paper. You did one hell of a job, James. You've got the front page whenever you're ready to write your account of this. It will be good to have you back in the newsroom."

Tom left. Then it was Natalie's turn to go.

"Deadline beckons. I'll see you soon, okay, Kat?" Natalie kissed her on the cheek. "I'll call if I have any questions. I'm going to try to do this story justice."

Kat smiled. "I'm sure you will."

Then Marc stepped forward. "I'm taking my wife home so she can get some sleep and grow our baby."

Sophie wrapped her arms around Kat, hugging her tight. "I'm so glad you're okay, and I know Gabe's going to be okay, too. Call us if you need anything."

Kat hugged her back as fiercely as she could with one hand, her throat tight. "Thank you for being there, Sophie. I don't know what I would have done without you on the other end of the line last night."

Then Kat's gaze traveled around the room. "I don't know how to thank you all for what you did for us—for your support, for your prayers, for being here today."

There were smiles and muttered "your welcomes."

Marc ducked down and kissed her cheek. "What are friends for?"

Friends.

And it struck her that she had finally found her place—here in Denver. Though the ragged buttes, sandy washes, and wide-open spaces of K'ai'bii'tó would always be her homeland, Denver was now her home. The thought put a lump in her throat.

Then the nurse poked her head through the door. "Ms. James? Mr. Rossiter is out of surgery, and the doctor says it's all right with him if you sit with him in recovery. He's not fully conscious yet, but he's been saying your name."

CHAPTER 32

GABE OPENED HIS eyes, and she was there, sitting beside him, wrapped in a hospital blanket, her hair tousled. "Kat."

He didn't think he'd ever seen a more beautiful sight. Her cheek was bruised, her face lined with exhaustion, her wrist in a cast, but she was here, safe and precious beside him. She stroked his cheek, smiled down at him, her smile not quite hiding the worry in her eyes. "How do you feel?"

Even on a morphine pump, he hurt like hell. "Did the doctor tell you?"

She nodded, her eyes filling with tears that she tried valiantly to blink away. "He said that your right leg should heal just fine, but . . . that they'd had to amputate your left leg just below the knee. I'm so sorry, Gabe."

"Don't be, honey." He reached up to cup her cheek. "I expected to wake up dead today. I got my entire life back—except for part of one leg. Seems like a bargain to me."

Not that he hadn't had a dark moment when they'd revived him in the operating room long enough to tell him what they had to do. The loss of a limb was no small thing, but compared to what Gabe had almost lost . . .

He'd almost lost his life. He'd almost lost Kat.

She looked down at him, her gaze steady and strong. "Whatever it takes, whatever you need, I'm going to be there for you, Gabe. You're not alone."

"I'm a lucky man." And a tension he hadn't realized he was carrying left him.

She still loves you, Rossiter, you lucky bastard.

"How's your wrist?"

She looked at the cast as if she hadn't quite realized it was there, then shrugged, the blanket slipping, revealing red marks on her arm that could only be Taser burns. "It hurts a little, but it's fine."

He was willing to bet it hurt more than a little.

She met his gaze for a moment, then slowly her face crumpled, tears spilling onto her cheeks. "Oh, Gabe! I-I thought . . . I thought I'd lost you!"

He slipped his hand behind her nape and drew her against his chest, holding her while she cried it out, her tears seeming somehow to wash away last night's horror for him, too, the feel of her in his arms more soothing than any narcotic. "It's okay, honey. We're both safe. It's over."

She pressed her cheek into his chest, words pouring out of her. "I-I tried to hold on! I tried, but I couldn't keep myself from slipping. And then I felt little tugs on the rope, and I remembered you had the knife. I begged you not to do it, but you didn't listen. And then you were just . . . gone."

He kissed the silk of her hair, breathing in her scent. "It was the only way to get you out of there alive. There was no way in hell I was going to drag you over the edge with me and let you die, too."

"I-I called for you. After you fell, I called for you."

"I heard you, but I didn't have the strength to shout back. I'm sorry."

She lifted her head and met his gaze, her cheeks wet. "For a while, I couldn't move. It felt . . . like a part of me had died with you. I didn't want to turn away from the cliff because it felt like I was abandoning you."

Something twisted in his chest to think of her up there, alone and hypothermic, trying to watch over his dead body. "But you did it. You got up. You called for help. You went on without me. You did the right thing."

"It was the hardest thing I've ever had to do." The despair in her eyes told Gabe she wasn't exaggerating. "B-but I realized the only way to honor what you'd done for me was to survive, to go on and . . . I-I'm sorry. I have so much to be grateful for. I promised myself I'd be strong for you and here I am crying like a child."

"You have no reason to be sorry." He wiped the tears from her cheeks with his thumb. "You've been strong long enough, Kat."

A look of anguish came over her face. "When I think about what you've lost!"

He knew she wasn't just talking about his leg, but also everything she thought he'd lost with it—rock climbing, ice climbing, skiing. "I haven't lost anything. I'll climb again. I'll show off for you on skis. We'll make more snow angels. I promise."

She sniffed, gave him a tremulous smile, laughed.

"You know what the worst part of this was for me? It wasn't falling or thinking I was going to die, and it sure as hell wasn't losing my leg. It was being able to hear you, to hear that Webb was hurting you, and being too drugged to do a damned thing about it. I tried, Kat. God knows I tried to snap out of it. I can't tell you how many times I thought I'd kicked his ass and freed us both only to realize I was hallucinating and he was still dragging you up the mountain like a dog."

For as long as he lived he would never forget the sound of her screams.

"So you could hear what was happening?" Kat hadn't known that.

"Some of it, and it's the closest to hell I ever hope to come." He stroked her hair, his words slightly slurred from the morphine. "I wasn't able to stop him from hurting you while I was drugged, but hanging from the side of the cliff, feeling that rope slip inch by inch, I knew exactly what I had to do."

She couldn't imagine it. "Weren't you afraid?"

He shook his head. "The moment I realized I had to cut the rope, I felt a sense of calm. It dawned on me how often I had risked my life for nothing. Three years wasted on crazy climbing and meaningless sex, trying so hard to forget. Life meant nothing to me beyond the next punch of adrenaline."

"You were hurt. You weren't in harmony with—"

He shook his head. "I was selfish. I let what happened with Jill change me. I became like her—I only thought about myself."

"That's not true! When I fell in the rockslide, you were there for me, and you didn't even know who I was."

"Sweet Kat." He gave her a weak smile. "Do you remember what you said to me after the *inipi*? You told me that a man who only cared about sex wouldn't have stopped. You were right. You saw things in me I couldn't see and forced me to take a good, hard look at myself. You filled places inside me I didn't even know were empty. You really did save me. If I had to die so that you could live, then I was happy to die. At least that way my death would mean something."

"Oh, Gabe!" Kat couldn't stop the tears that filled her eyes.

And for a moment neither of them spoke.

"When they were loading me into the chopper, I promised myself that if I lived through this, I wouldn't waste another day." He drew a deep breath, cupped her cheek and looked into her eyes. "I have my life back, and I want to share it with you. I love you, Katherine James. Marry me."

Kat stared at him, her pulse thrumming.

Had he just said what she thought he'd said?

"We'll have as many babies as you want—ten if that's what it takes. We'll visit your grandmother as often as you like. I'll eat bowl after bowl of her mutton stew, and I won't complain about the heat or the lack of privacy."

Kat's own words came back to her.

I've never been with a man, and I won't be until I find the one who wants to be a part of my life and isn't just looking for a one-night stand. So unless you want lots of children, love mutton stew, and enjoy spending your summer vacations in one-hundred-fourteen-degree heat in a two-room hogaan without electricity or running water, we shouldn't even start down that road.

And she realized that Gabe was answering the challenge she'd given him that day in the restaurant. Tears spilled down her cheeks, only this time they were tears of happiness. "I thought you didn't believe in fairy tales."

His gaze held hers unwavering. "I believe in us."

Kat stroked his cheek. "Yes, I'll marry you. There's nothing in the world I'd rather do than marry you. In my heart, you've been my half-side since the day I realized the wind knows you."

"The wind . . . huh?" He frowned, looking like a confused little boy.

"The wind knows you. You're a man of this land, of the earth."

"And what's a 'half-side'?"

"My mate—my perfect matching male half."

His lips curved in a sleepy but sexy grin. "I do fit inside you rather nicely, don't I? Hey, don't look shocked. They took my leg, not my libido."

Kat couldn't help but laugh, but she knew she'd already kept him awake too long. He might not complain, but she could tell he was tired and in pain. She pushed the button on the morphine pump, and watched the lines on his face ease as another dose slid into his bloodstream.

Then she leaned down and kissed him, her hand taking hold of his. "Shut your eyes, Gabe. Rest. I'll stay right here beside you. Sleep."

And he did.

GABE STEADIED HIMSELF on the crutches, his right leg in a walking cast, the left leg of his black Armani tux pinned out of the way. "Hey, Hunter, can you check my tie?"

Hunter moved to stand in front of him, grabbed the silver-and-black-striped tie, and fiddled with the knot for a moment. "Tie looks great. Flower thingy looks great."

Darcangelo leaned in. "It's called a boutonniere, idiot."

"And the ring?" Gabe couldn't wait to slide it onto her finger.

"That's quite a ring," Darcangelo said. "It must've cost you an arm and a leg."

"You like it, Dickangelo?" Hunter asked. "I didn't think it was your style, but I guess you never know. Just remember I did all the legwork for it."

"You know, when I'm back on my *feet*, I'm going to kick both your asses." Gabe fought back a grin. Hey, he could tell leg jokes, too. He turned to Reece. "The ring?"

"It's safely in the keeping of the ring bearer," Reece answered. "Connor knows his entire future on planet Earth depends on getting the rings up the aisle to you."

"Relax, Rossiter!" Hunter chuckled. "Everything's under control."

"I just want this to be perfect for her."

Gabe glanced around the little hospital chapel, feeling strangely nervous. A week had passed since he'd lost his leg and regained his life—and it was a week he'd tried to live well. It had been a tough week and painful, but he was recovering more quickly than the doctors had anticipated. Rather than dwelling on his injury and the uphill battles that awaited him, he'd focused on putting together a wedding worthy of the woman who'd given him her virginity and her heart.

Her friends—now his friends—had helped, handling most of the arrangements so that he and Kat could heal. Darcangelo had handled the tux rentals. Hunter had gone out with Gabe's credit card—and very specific instructions—to get Kat's ring. Sophie and Holly had taken Kat shopping for her wedding gown, which Gabe hadn't yet seen, while Kara and Tessa had handled the flowers, the cake, and the invitations.

Uncle Allen, who, as a medicine man, was licensed to perform weddings in Colorado, had agreed to perform the ceremony and had met with Kat and Gabe privately to talk about what would happen. He'd also gone with Nathan down to K'ai'bii'tó and brought Alice James, Kat's grandmother, back with them to Denver to be a part of her granddaughter's wedding. Of course, Grandma had been shocked to learn that there was a wedding, but not as shocked as she'd been when she'd heard what had happened in Kat's life over the past three weeks.

She'd brought her brother, Ray, the *hataathlii*, so that he could sing the right songs and hold the right ceremonies before the wedding. And although the fact that it wasn't a traditional Navajo wedding clearly bothered her, she had embraced Gabe as a grandson when she'd heard that he'd saved Kat's life.

"Blue-eyed Navajo" she called him in heavily accented English.

She sat in the front left pew, wearing her best red velvet skirt and shirt, her gray hair in a bun and hidden beneath a red silk scarf, a squash blossom necklace of silver and turquoise around her neck. She glanced over at Gabe and gave him a slight smile. He winked. Her smile broadened, revealing a few missing teeth.

The pews were full. Some of the faces Gabe recognized— Kat's colleagues from the newspaper, Dave Hatfield, Rick Sutherland, hospital personnel. But other faces were new to him—Kat's Native friends from Denver. One of them— Gabe thought her name was Pauline—watched him and his groomsmen discreetly. He caught her gaze and smiled. She turned beet red, covered her face with her hands, and giggled.

Teenage girls.

Ray and Nathan entered, Nathan sitting behind the altar with his drum, Ray standing beside him. And then with the beating of Nathan's drum and Ray singing in his native tongue, it began.

Ten-year-old Connor, Kara and Reece's son, was the first to enter, carrying the rings with such stiff solemnity that he drew quiet laughter from the adults. Behind him came his five-year-old sister Caitlyn, who looked so adorable in her little black dress, and bobbing brown curls, that the audience let out a collective "aw." She looked to Kara for reassurance that she was doing it the right way, then, having had enough, tossed her petals and ran to climb in her mother's lap.

Holly entered next, holding a bouquet of roses and pine sprigs and wearing a sleek strapless black dress that probably didn't belong in a hospital, much less a chapel. She walked down the aisle with a smile on her lips, her gaze on Nathan.

"Uh-oh," Hunter muttered beneath his breath.

Tessa came next and after her Sophie, both wearing black, Sophie definitely looking pregnant now. The women stood across from their husbands, exchanging glances with Darcangelo and Hunter that Gabe interpreted only too easily.

And then Kat stood in the doorway.

Dressed in a simple gown of virginal white, her hair coiled on top her head and spilling in waves down her back, a wreath of roses and pine sprigs sitting on her head like a crown, she quite literally took his breath away.

The wedding guests rose to their feet as one.

"You okay, buddy?" Hunter whispered in his ear.

Gabe drew a breath to steady himself. "Yeah."

KAT WALKED FORWARD to the sound of Uncle Ray's singing, her heart beating faster than Nathan's drum, her gaze fixed on the man she loved. He was the most beautiful man she'd ever seen, his dark hair and tanned skin stunning against his black tux. And he was standing—using crutches, but standing nonetheless.

He met her gaze, smiled at her, his smile making her belly flutter.

Holding on to the love she saw in his eyes, she walked forward, so happy that she felt like she was floating. She reached his side and waited for him to turn himself toward the altar, then slipped her hand inside his and faced Uncle Allen.

An eagle feather in his hair and wearing a suit, Uncle Allen spoke Lakota words of blessing for the crowd that had gathered, then spoke in English.

"We are all friends here. We are all relatives. And that's the meaning behind 'Mitakuye Oyasin.' All my relations. We are all related—men and women, Indian and non-Indian, the two-leggeds and the four-leggeds and the winged ones. And today we've come together to witness the marriage of our brother Gabriel Rossiter and our sister Katherine James."

Then he told Gabe what would be expected of him as a husband, instructing Gabe to love Kat and be faithful to her, to keep her warm and sheltered and fed, and to be a good father to any children she gave him. "I say this, and yet I don't think there is much I can teach you about the ways of a husband. You have already shown that you are willing to give your life for the woman you love."

"Aho!" came the response from the Indian men in the chapel.

Then Uncle Allen turned to Kat and told her to love Gabe and be faithful to him, to take care of him, and to nurture and cherish any children he might give her. His eyes shimmered with tears. "My dear Kimímila, I tell you these things, but what can I teach you about being a wife when you have already shown your love by fighting like a warrior for this man?"

"Aho!"

"I believe the two of you were husband and wife in your hearts before you even met—each of you the true half-side of the other."

At the word "half-side," Gabe met Kat's gaze and smiled that sexy smile of his—and Kat felt herself blush.

Then Uncle Allen urged Connor forward with the rings. Kat took the ring she'd gotten for Gabe—a white gold band with Boulder's mountain skyline inset in yellow gold all the way around it—and slid it on to his finger, promising to be a good wife to him. He looked down at the ring, then up at her, surprise on his face, clearly recognizing the outline of the mountains.

"I love you," she mouthed.

Then Gabe took the ring he'd gotten for her and cradling her cast in his hand, slid it over her finger, promising to be a good husband to her. Kat stared at the most beautiful ring she'd ever seen—diamonds circling an oval-shaped stone of polished turquoise in robin's egg blue, all set in antique white gold.

"I love you," he mouthed.

And she saw in his eyes that he did.

WHAT PEOPLE TALKED about for days after the wedding wasn't the bride's gown or the mix of cultures in the ceremony or the unique circumstances, but the way the groom had kissed the bride, drawing her against him, holding her as if she were the most precious thing in his world, and kissing her slow and deep and long.

It was true love, they said.

It was the stuff of fairy tales and happily-ever-afters.

EPILOGUE

Ten months later
K'ai'bíí'tó, Navajoland, Northern Arizona

"I THINK GRANDMA knows we've been having sex." Kat rested her head on Gabe's right arm and snuggled backward into him, her heart and body replete, the heat of lovemaking cooling into a feeling of deep contentment.

They lay spooned together on a mattress in the bed of her pickup truck looking up at the night sky, a woolen blanket covering them both, as much to lend them a modicum of privacy as to ward off the September chill.

"Mmm, really?" He nuzzled her hair. "Why do you say that?"

Kat smiled. "She called us 'busy bunnies.'"

He laughed, a deep, sensual sound, his left hand sliding over the bare curve of her abdomen. "Do you think your big belly gave us away?"

"No, silly goat!" She laughed. "I think you make too much noise."

"Me?" He chuckled. "I hate to break it to you, rez girl, but you're the noisy one."

Because Kat was afraid Gabe might be right, she didn't challenge him, instead picking up where they'd left off when her description of Navajo constellations had somehow led to sex under the stars. She pointed to the star that never moved and the four little stars around it. "That is what we call *Náhookos Biko'*."

Gabe repeated the Navajo words. "That means . . . northern fire?"

"Very good." Kat was happy that he was learning the Diné language so quickly. "To us, it looks like the fire in the center of the hogaan. *Náhookos Bika'ii*, Northern Male, and *Náhookos Bi'aadii*, Northern Female, circle around it. To us they represent the family in their home. We believe all things revolve around the family and the hogaan."

She felt the baby move, pressing its heel or elbow against the place where Gabe's hand rested. He gently rubbed the spot, his fingers warm on her skin, then chuckled when the baby nudged again. "It's crowded in there now, isn't it, little one?"

He'd been fascinated with her changing body and the growing baby from the day they'd found out she was pregnant last December. Even when he'd been in rehabilitation learning to walk with his prosthetic leg, he'd pampered her, doing everything he could to make her more comfortable during the ten long weeks of morning sickness, his love—and his sense of humor—never flagging.

"Look at us," he'd said one morning after she'd been very sick and pain had kept him awake most of the night. "We're the eighth and ninth dwarves—Gimpy and Barfy."

Some men might have grown bitter or demoralized after losing a limb, but not Gabe. He'd faced all of it—the physical pain, his temporary limitations, learning to walk again—with courage that had left Kat feeling humbled and even more in love with him than she'd been before, if such a thing were possible.

"I suppose if I'd lost my leg in a stupid climbing accident, I might be angry," he'd said one night as the two of them lay together in bed. "But I know *why* it's gone. That night, I'd have given anything to keep you safe. Half a leg is not too high a price to pay for the woman I love."

The loss of his leg—and the circumstances under which he'd fallen—had made him an instant celebrity in the climbing world. People's fascination with him had grown when, six weeks after losing his leg and almost dying, he was climbing again, using only his arms and one leg to scale several tough routes in the rock gym while people watched and cheered.

The sight of him doing what he loved had brought tears to Kat's eyes, and she'd found herself cheering as loudly as everyone else when he triumphantly reached the top, a smile on his handsome face.

And almost overnight he'd found himself in the position of being a role model for others who'd lost limbs. When a company that manufactured cutting-edge prosthetic legs asked him to come to work for them field-testing legs they designed for elite athletes, he had agreed to take the job, provided he could work it around trips with Kat to the reservation and the needs of the new baby.

"My family is my priority," he'd told them.

They'd agreed.

So now he got paid to have fun, rock climbing, alpine climbing, ice climbing, skiing, even rafting to test-drive various prosthetic designs. Together with the volunteer rescue work he did for Boulder Mountain Parks, he led a very full and active life, every bit the athlete—and the man—that he'd always been.

Kat knew he was as excited as she was to meet their baby. Although her due date was still nine days away, the midwife in Tuba City had told them last week that the baby could come at any time. And Kat was ready.

She was ready to experience the mystery of becoming a mother, to know what it felt like to bring life into the world, to meet the little person she and Gabe had made together. She knew giving birth would be different than anything she'd experienced so far. She'd been with Sophie when Sophie had given birth at home to little Addy and had seen the reality of birth—the hard work, the pain, the blood. Still, she was eager for it.

That's why she'd come home—to have a baby. Kat wanted to give birth on the reservation so that she could have both Gabe and her grandmother by her side—and so that there would be no doubt that her child was a member of the Navajo Nation. She and Gabe had left Denver two weeks ago, wanting to make sure she would have time to meet the midwives who would be with her during the birth. So far it had been like a honeymoon—one that included her extended family.

Of course, this wasn't the first time Gabe had been to K'ai'bii'tó. They'd come in March to introduce Gabe to her family, to help with shearing the sheep and so that Uncle Ray could sing a Blessing Way for her and the baby. Then they'd come again in May to help with the planting of the corn. Gabe had gotten to see her grandmother's dead-crow-on-the-fence ritual for himself.

"Remind me not to mess with Grandma's corn," he'd whispered in Kat's ear.

But Kat's grandmother adored Gabe. The two of them had a teasing relationship that relied on a mix of English and Navajo words—Nav-lish Kat called it—for communication.

Kat's nieces and nephews loved him, too. The smaller children were fascinated by his prosthetic leg, while the older ones seemed to be in awe of him because they understood how he'd gotten it. Only Kat's mother and her brothers and sisters had given him the cold shoulder, but he hadn't taken it personally. He'd seemed more upset by the way they'd treated her than how they'd treated him.

"It's not your fault your mom fooled around, for God's sake!" he'd said one morning after Kat's mother had pointed to Kat's belly and told her that her baby wouldn't really be Diné. "You're family, and that ought to be enough for all of them!"

That afternoon, her grandmother had sent Kat and Gabe on an overnight errand to Tuba City and had sat everyone else down inside the hogaan, making them listen while she'd told them in detail what Kat and Gabe had endured to protect Mesa Butte.

"If any one of you still wants to treat Kat and her man as if they are strangers, then I think that person is out of balance and sick in the heart," she'd told the family. "I wouldn't want that sickness here in my home."

Kat had only learned what had happened when she and Gabe returned the next morning to find her mother gone. But after that night, Kat's brothers and sisters had begun to treat both her and Gabe with respect and even kindness. As much as it had hurt to think her mother still didn't care about her, she was enjoying getting to know her brothers and sisters.

She and Gabe would be staying until they could hold a First Laugh ceremony for the baby, so she hoped to build strong friendships with them.

"Over there, you can see the two stars we call *Hastiin Sik'ai'í.*" She pointed to the western horizon. "That means 'Squatting Man.' He represents . . ."

She felt her womb tighten and heard—or felt—something go *pop.* And warm water trickled out from between her legs. "I . . . I think my water just broke."

"Well, the midwife said sex often induces labor. I guess she was right." Gabe kissed her cheek, then sat up and hopped down from the truck, reaching for her and lifting her gently to the ground, his gaze dropping to the small puddle that formed in the sand at her feet. "Honey, I think you're about to have a baby."

GABE WAS IN awe. His rez girl was pulling this off without breaking a sweat. His arm behind her shoulders, he raised her into a squatting position on the birthing bed as the next contraction began. She grabbed on to her woolen sash belt, which hung from the ceiling, and exhaled softly, her breath barely catching as she pushed.

"Strength, strength," Grandma Alice whispered in Diné.

When the contraction was over, Kat let go of the sash belt, and Gabe eased her back into a reclining position again.

"You're doing so well, honey. Not long now." He bent down and kissed her forehead, taking her hand in his, whispering in her ear. *"I love you."*

Whether she heard him, he couldn't say. Her eyes were closed, her face as relaxed as if she were asleep.

"Nature's anesthesia," the midwife whispered.

Kat had dilated to ten in less than seven hours, and although it had been back labor all the way, she'd stayed unbelievably calm, singing softly to herself and talking reassuringly to the baby in Diné, while Gabe held her hand and Grandma made sure she drank plenty of tea. Still, as quiet and peaceful as her labor had been, he'd known she was feeling intense pain from the way she'd almost crushed his fingers with each contraction. And although he knew women had been having babies for as long as there'd been men on the planet, he wished it were easier.

She'd wanted as traditional a birth as possible, and other than Gabe's absolute refusal to let her give birth in her grandmother's hogaan—Tuba City was a long hour's drive over rutted dirt roads—that's what she was getting. They'd had a small ceremony before she'd come into the birthing room, during which her Uncle Ray had sung the "Singing Out Baby" chant. The bed faced east, so the baby would be born facing the right way. Kat wasn't wearing a hospital gown, but an old T-shirt and a blue cotton skirt, which she'd pulled up around her hips. And the Indian Health Service midwife had mostly stayed out of the way, checking Kat's progress only twice and monitoring the baby's heartbeat with a handheld Doppler every so often.

Another contraction came, and another, and another.

And Gabe wished it would be over so that Kat's pain would end. It boggled his mind to think an *entire baby* had to pass through a part of her body that was so tight—and so exquisitely sensitive. He could only imagine how much it hurt.

Then on the next contraction Gabe saw—a tiny glimpse of the baby's head. And for the first time it really hit him that he was about to become a father. His pulse skipped, and he couldn't help but smile. "I can see the baby's head, Kat. It has lots of dark hair."

Kat met his gaze. "D-dark hair?"

He nodded. "Yep."

A few pushes later, and the baby's head began to crown.

Kat moaned, squeezed her eyes shut, her knuckles white as she clung to the sash belt. "Oh, it hurts so much!"

Without even thinking, Gabe wrapped an arm around her shoulders to steady her, then pried one of her hands off the sash belt and pressed it against the baby's head so that she could at least feel what he was seeing—the birth of their first child.

Her eyes flew wide, and she looked down, seeming to forget her pain as the baby's head slowly emerged, its tiny face looking up at them, its eyes still closed.

"Let me just check for a cord." The midwife felt with gloved fingers around the baby's neck. "No cord. Go ahead and catch your baby."

Kat laughed and met Gabe's gaze, tears shimmering in her eyes, a look of wonder on her sweet face. Then they both watched in amazement as their baby slipped in a liquid rush out of her body and into their waiting hands. Going on instinct, Gabe lifted the slippery-wet baby into Kat's arms, then eased her back onto the pillows.

Tears streamed down Kat's cheeks, the baby cradled in her arms. *"Shi-yazhi! Shi-yazhi! Shi-yazhi!"*

My little one! My little one! My little one!

The baby gave a little cough, then a little cry, its skin flushing pink.

Grandma was the first to check, lifting one of the baby's legs, then chuckling.

"It's a girl." Kat smiled at Gabe, her face radiating pure joy.

Speechless, Gabe leaned down and looked into the open eyes of his newborn daughter, his heart swelling until it seemed there was no more room inside his chest.

He had a daughter. He and Kat had a baby girl.

It wasn't until Grandma reached up and wiped his cheek with her thumb that he realized he was crying, too.

THEY MADE THE drive back to K'ai'bii'tó when little Alissa Gabrielle, whom Kat had named after Grandma Alice and Gabe, was three days old. Still more than a little sore, Kat carried the baby, while Gabe walked beside her, carrying the diaper bag and car seat. Grandma Alice met them at the door, welcoming them home with a smile and hurrying to make juniper ash tea for Kat.

While Gabe carried in wood, Kat sat in the rocking chair near the wood stove and nursed, her breasts aching with milk, her gaze fixed on the tiny baby who looked up at her through unfocused eyes. She'd never known that the human heart could love this much or feel so much happiness. It amazed her to think that Alissa, so perfect, so precious, had grown inside her body. From her ten tiny toes to her dark downy hair, she was a gift—a gift she and Gabe had given to each other. Kat could see both of them in Alissa's delicate face, their blood mixed together in their child.

Giving birth had been harder and more painful than Kat had imagined, but she'd never felt more loved, more cherished, than during those long hours with Gabe and her grandmother beside her, supporting her, holding her hand, helping her get from one moment to the next. Gabe must have told her he loved her a thousand times, his strength never flagging, his voice holding her together.

At the height of her labor when the pain had been most intense, Kat had been amazed to think that her grandmother had gone through this twelve times, several times giving birth alone in the shade of a piñon pine. The thought had comforted her, making her feel connected to the female ancestors of her clan in a way she hadn't before, the timelessness of the act of birthing a bond between her and all women who'd come before her. And even though she could still vividly remember the pain—did anyone really believe that women forgot?—she was already excited to know there would be more babies as precious and beautiful as Alissa.

Kat had just finished nursing when Grandma walked up to her holding a carryout box in one hand and a hand trowel in the other. "Come. It's time."

Alissa still in her arms, Kat stood and followed Grandma Alice out the door, calling for Gabe, who was now splitting wood, to follow them. The sun was beginning to set, washing the mesas and scrub forest in tones of gold and orange, the wind just beginning to pick up, the scent of desert autumn in the air.

Grandma led them over to the sheep corral, then handed Gabe the carryout box, gesturing for him to open it. Kat fought not to laugh at the expression on his face as he glanced inside.

He met her gaze, looking perplexed. "It's the . . . after-birth."

Kat nodded, unable hold back a smile. "Were you hoping for Chinese takeout?"

Then Grandma knelt down and began to dig, speaking in Diné, Kat acting as interpreter. "We Diné bury the afterbirth of our children in the land near our homes because we know that the cord which bound us to our mother for nine months will bind us to the land for the rest of our lives. My mother buried my cord here on this homesite, as her mother buried hers and I buried Kat's."

Grandma reached out and took the nearly dried afterbirth into her hands and began to bury it in the red earth, saying Alissa's Diné name—Shandiin Hozhoni, which meant "Beautiful light that breaks through the clouds."

A lump formed in Kat's throat, the ritual meaning more to her than she'd realized it would. But then Grandma spoke again.

Her throat tight, Kat translated. "Grandma says this cord now becomes Alissa's deep root with the land and that no matter where she goes in her life, K'ai'bii'tó will be her home, as it has been the home of the women of this family all the way back to the days when we returned from the Long Walk." Kat paused to listen to Grandma Alice speak, then repeated her words in English once more, tears blurring her vision. "She says that she doesn't know what happened to your cord when you were born, but that there is some of you in Alissa's cord. This means that you have deep roots here now and that K'ai'bii'tó is your home, too. She hopes you will remember this and know that the door to her hogaan will always be open to you."

Grandma patted the red soil into place with gnarled hands, the placenta and umbilical cord now buried. She stood and looked up at Gabe, patting his arm. "You—Blue-Eyed Navajo."

Then she walked away, leaving the three of them—Kat, Gabe, and the baby—alone together.

Gabe wiped the tears from Kat's cheeks with this thumb.

"I think that means she doesn't want me to keep the two of you in Colorado for too long at any one stretch."

Kat laughed. He hadn't understood at all. "What she was trying to say is that she loves you, that you're like a grandson to her."

Gabe glanced over at Grandma Alice, a muscle tightening in his jaw, a telltale sheen in his eyes. Then he met Kat's gaze, the love he felt for her there on his face for her to see. "A year ago, if you'd told me I'd have a wife and a new baby girl, I'd have laughed in your face. But now I can't imagine living a moment of my life without you. You're the best thing that ever happened to me, Katherine James Rossiter, and I will spend every day until I die loving you."

Cradling the baby between them, Kat rested her cheek against his chest, his heartbeat strong, as strong as the sun-scorched earth beneath her feet. "I could say the same about you. If not for you, neither Alissa nor I would be here today. You gave up your life for mine, and there's not a day that goes by that I don't remember that. You're everything to me, Gabe. *Ayor anosh'ni.*"

Then the wind picked up, sand swirling at their feet, the last rays of sunlight stretching rosy fingers across the sky. Somewhere in the distance a lone coyote howled, as if to say that all was right with the world. And Kat knew in her heart that it was.

"Let's get you inside by the fire." Gabe wrapped his arm around Kat's shoulder and together they walked west toward the welcoming warmth of the hogaan—and the rest of their lives.

Keep reading for a special preview of
Pamela Clare's next I-Team novel

BREAKING POINT

Now available from Berkley Sensation!

IT WAS THE sound of her first strangled scream that had woken him. It had been the feral scream of a woman trying to survive. Then a moment later she'd spoken, her voice soft, young, feminine, her accent unmistakably New Orleans.

Natalie Benoit was her name, and she was what the Zetas hated most after honest cops and soldiers—a journalist.

Zach had found himself sitting upright, straining to hear while Zetas whose voices he didn't recognize—newcomers— joked about raping her, clearly enjoying the rush of having her at their mercy, their laughter colored by lust. Rather than crying or begging for her life, she'd tried to bargain her way out of the situation. Either she had a lot of guts, or she hadn't understood a word they'd said. Given how poorly she spoke Spanish, he was willing to bet it was the latter.

Then one of the bastards had struck her—hard from the sound of it—and two of the men had begun to argue.

"¡La putita me rompió la nariz!" The little whore broke my nose!

Zach had found that remarkable. *Good for her.*

"¡Deja tu verga en los pantalones o te corto los cojones! El Jefe la quiere para si mismo—sin violación." Leave your prick in your pants, or I'll cut off your balls! The chief wants her for himself—untouched.

The words had hit Zach square in the chest.

If Cárdenas wanted her as his personal sex slave, she was as good as dead.

A burst of AK fire had ended the fight.

I don't know who you are or what you want, but my

newspaper will pay ransom to get me back alive. Please call them! Mi periódico pagará dinero para mí—mucho dinero.

Her naiveté had been painful to hear. Clearly, it hadn't yet dawned on her that life as she knew it was over. But the men had long since quit listening to her. Instead, they'd talked casually about what they hoped Cárdenas would do to her, bile rising into Zach's throat at each graphic and brutal description.

Cárdenas had a reputation for abusing women. Zach had heard that he sacrificed women to *La Santa Muerte*—that macabre cult saint of *Narcotraficantes*, Holy Death—as a way of giving thanks for his success in the cartel wars. To think that Zach had been *this close* to taking him, to ending his reign of terror . . .

Gisella should be in that cell now, not Natalie, whoever she was.

Please don't put me in there! Please don't!

She'd become almost hysterical the moment they'd brought her in here, her scream when they'd closed the door and walked away laced with primal terror. And for good reason. This filthy, dark place was probably beyond her worst nightmares.

Now she was in the cell next to his, separated from him by a wall of adobe brick. From the sound of it, she was about to hyperventilate, her breathing shallow and rapid, each exhale a whimper. He thought he could just make out the words of a prayer.

Sorry, angel, God seems to have taken the week off.

Then he realized she wasn't praying. She was reciting a nursery rhyme.

"To market, to market, to buy . . . to buy a fat pig." Her voice was unsteady, and she was clearly having trouble remembering the words. "H-home again, home again . . . I want to go home again . . . jiggety-jig."

The sweetness of it hit Zach hard. He hung his head, the hopelessness of her situation tearing at him.

She might not be here if you'd done your job.

Men like him were supposed to stop bastards like Cárdenas and his Zetas from hurting people. But rather than putting Cárdenas away, Zach was going to have a front-row seat while Cárdenas raped and tortured this girl to death.

Son of a bitch! Damn it!

Zach didn't realize he was trying to break free of the manacles again until his hands were wet, water from broken blisters mixing with sticky, warm blood.

Who are you fooling, man? You can't save her. You can't even save yourself.

No, he couldn't. But he *could* reach out to her, let her know she wasn't alone.

He swallowed, then sucked in as deep a breath as he could, wincing at the pain in his ribs. "Natalie? Can you hear me? My name is . . . Zach."

Manhattan
April, present day

THEY WERE USING her as bait.

Dr. Gina Cappozi could feel them following her. All day
she'd had that peculiar sensation of eyes on her back, the spill
of goose bumps on her flesh for no reason, a tingle in the hairs
on her neck . . . obviously the STORM Corps special ops guys
must be doing what they did best—lurking in the shadows,
watching her from doorways and alleys, scanning the busy
Manhattan streets for danger. Always there for her. Always
watching her back. Waiting patiently for their mutual enemy
to appear.

She wished they would just go away and leave her the hell
alone.

Their constant presence was meant to be reassuring. It
should be a comfort knowing they were there watching out
for her. But it wasn't. Because even though STORM Corps once
heroically saved her life, and was now supposedly protecting
her, she also knew those spec ops guys had an agenda—to get
their hands on *him*, their hidden enemy, any way they could.

And she was their Judas goat.

Well, too bad. They'd have to wait their turn at the bastard.
Because *she* wanted him even more than they did.

Her nemesis. *Captain Gregg van Halen.*

Gina glanced around as she quickly took the steps down
into the black maw of the Lexington Avenue subway tunnel. No familiar faces lingered in the crowd as the crush of

mindless, homebound humanity carried her along in its wake. Would she be able to give her babysitters the slip this time?

Or maybe they'd tired of her game of hide-and-seek, and had already gone away and left her on her own. Maybe it was van Halen she could feel stalking her.

Good. Let the bastard come.

Just let him try and hurt her. She was ready. Her body was healed. And her mind . . . well, her mind was as healed as it was going to get. For now.

She was armed, of course. She never left her Upper East Side brownstone without her weapon of choice. Hell, even inside her home, she was never without her knife. Nowhere was safe for her, indoors or out. Not as long as van Halen still drew breath.

She wrapped her fingers firmly around the handle of the razor-sharp KA-BAR knife tucked in her coat pocket. Oh, yes. She'd been practicing, all right. Lunging and plunging it into the heart of a straw target, over and over, until little piles of cut straw lay scattered on the ground all around and its cloth covering was sliced to ribbons. Day after day, week after week. She'd decimated a hundred targets or more, much to the chagrin of her self-defense instructor.

She was confident now, no longer terrified of the mere thought of coming face to face with the man who'd haunted her nightmares for the past six months. The man who had sold her to terrorists and walked away without a backward glance.

Really, what could he do to her that she hadn't already endured? He couldn't hurt her. Not this time. Not her body. Not her heart. He wouldn't take her by surprise again. He wouldn't get the chance.

No one would. Not ever again.

Because Gina Cappozi was taking her life back.

And Gregg van Halen was going to die.

That was for damn sure. The very hand that had lovingly stroked his skin and caressed his body to fevered arousal was going to be the same hand that ended his miserable life for good.

And if she was very, very lucky, it would happen tonight.

* * *

FUCKING HELL, NOT again.

STORM operator Alex Zane struggled to take a breath. Frantically, he fought against the menacing desert mirage as Afghanistan closed in all around him, binding him in a breathless straightjacket of horror. Desperately, he tried to block the piercing screams.

"No!" he cried. "Get the fuck away!"

Too late. No way out of the nightmare now.

He hugged his rifle to his body and burrowed his back into the rocky hillside above the Afghan village where he'd been sitting for hours, waiting for the signal to attack. Screams of pain echoed through the heat-shimmering air like sirens of death.

His comm crackled and his team leader's urgent voice broke over the headset. "Zero Alpha Zulu, this is Zero Alpha Six, do you read me?" Kick Jackson sounded urgent. But competent. In control. *Unlike Alex.*

He grasped at Kick's voice, clinging to it like a shipwrecked sailor. "What's going on out there, Alpha Six?" Alex asked, fighting the panic. *Fucking breathe, soldier!*

Kick's voice barked out, "Do not move in! It's a trap. Repeat, do not— God*damn* it! Drew! Get back here!" Kick swore again, and Alex could hear his sharp breaths, like he'd taken off at a dead run. In the background, the terrible screams grew louder. "Abort and withdraw!" Kick yelled, cursing. Then the comm went dead.

Suddenly, an explosion ricocheted off the mud walls of the village below. Alex flung his rifle onto his back and scrabbled up the rocky hillside to take a look. No way was he retreating, leaving Kick and the others to—

A dozen village men surged over the ridge just above him, pointing their weapons at his head and shouting. His pulse rocketed out of control. *Fucking hell!* He spun in the dirt and launched himself down the slope. He hit the comm. "Zulu under attack!"

His assailants swarmed after him. He had to lead them away from the rest of the team.

No! Don't do it! his mind cried out. *Don't—*

Gunfire erupted all around. More screams.

Fire scorched across his temple and pain burst through his shoulder. He jerked and stumbled. The world tilted, then went black. But miraculously, he was still conscious. Terror crushed his chest. He scrambled up again and ran. Blind. *My God, he was blind!*

He ran straight into a human hornet's nest. Vicious hands grabbed his arms, fingers yanked painfully at his hair, gun butts slammed into the soft organs of his body. He cried out in agony, striking back, kicking with all his blind fury.

His captors just laughed. And beat him until his flesh turned to red oatmeal.

Then they bound a rope around his ankles and threw him to the ground.

A raw sob escaped his throat. Fuck, no! No. No. Fuck no!

"Alex?" Kick's reassuring voice floated in on a cool breeze.

Alex tried to yell an answer. But his throat had strangled closed on a mute cry. He knew all too well what came next. And there was nothing to do but endure it. *Again.*

Or go completely insane.

Which he might do anyway. *Again.*

"Alex?" Kick called from far away. *Too far.* He'd never reach him in time.

The motor of a Jeep roared and gears ground. He thrashed against his bonds. *Fucking damn it to hell!*

The rope around his ankles yanked taut. *Oh, God, this was really happening.* He tensed his body. Prepared himself for the hideous pain.

"Alex!"

The Jeep jerked forward. So did he. A bloody layer of skin stayed behind on the ground.

He screamed.

"Alex! Wake up!" The order was firm and clear, like the voice of God. It would not be disobeyed.

Alex surged out of his nightmare, wrenched upright with a lurch, and hit his head on the solid roof liner of an SUV.

Jesus!

He looked around frantically as he shook off the dregs of an illusion so real it made him doubt his own sanity. Tall buildings crowded around the vehicle. Horns blared on the busy street. Men in suits chatted on their Bluetooths.

He was back in Manhattan.

"Shit!" he cried, gulping down a painful gasp of much-needed air. *"Shit."* He grabbed the steering wheel and gripped it to steady his throbbing, reeling head. Harsh breaths stung his lungs as he forced himself to calm his raging insides.

Just another damn flashback . . .

On his first op for STORM Corps, he'd spent the day sitting in an SUV on a stakeout—not on some godforsaken mountaintop fighting insurgents. *Thank God.*

All too slowly, the debilitating panic and adrenaline subsided. Until, finally, he was able to haltingly unclench his fingers and stomach. *Fuck.* He'd never been claustrophobic before. But then again, he had never been a lot of things before . . . until the events of the past two years had taken their heavy toll. He shouldn't have been particularly surprised when the insidious panic swept over him, stealing the air from his lungs and thrusting him into a living nightmare of hallucination. But he always was.

"You okay?" Kick asked at length.

Alex exhaled heavily. Looked up into the worried face of his best friend, who was white-knuckling the edge of the open SUV window, leaning in. Not touching or reaching for him. Just observing, at the ready. He'd been through this before, the debilitating flashbacks. They both had.

"Fuck," Alex said aloud, shaking like a goddamn leaf. "Fucking hell."

"Yup," Kick said. Perfect understanding weighted his intense gaze. That day in A-stan when Alex was captured, Kick had been half blown up by a land mine and left for dead. It had been a long, long road back for both of them.

And it wasn't over yet. Not by a long shot.

But *hell.* Alex had really thought he was ready to go back to work. After all, the injury-induced blindness was gone, his body weight was back up to where it had been before the tender loving care of his al Sayika terrorist captors had starved it in half, his muscles were again firm and rippling . . . if under a web of angry red scars. He no longer flinched at sudden sounds or movements.

Much.

It was just the fucking claustrophobia that still got to him. Who'd have thought simply sitting in a closed vehicle would trigger it? He sighed. More damn fodder for his damn shrink.

He steadied his fingers and slashed them through his hair. "I don't know how long I've been out. Did I screw up? Is she home? Did I miss her?"

Her being Dr. Gina Cappozi, the object of the surveillance he may just have goatfucked all to hell. Gina Cappozi had also been a captive of al Sayika for three months, but here in the States, and for entirely different reasons than Alex. They'd brazenly captured her, beaten her, and compelled her to produce a horrific biological weapon to use against her own country, hoping to kill millions in an attack on U.S. soil. But she'd outsmarted them and foiled their plans.

After her rescue, the decimated terrorist organization was out for vengeance and had put a price on her head. A big one. Double the price they'd put on his and Kick's after his own rescue. Everyone, including Alex—hell, especially Alex— was expecting some fanatic *jihadi* to show up and collect on it any minute.

Thus Gina's protective detail, of which he and Kick were part. The operation was being run by STORM Corps—Strategic Technical Operations and Rescue Missions Corporation— Alex's and Kick's relatively new employer. STORM had been contracted for the mission by the Department of Homeland Security.

Initially, Alex had been on Gina's tag team, but he'd kept jumping at shadows, absolutely certain she was being followed by someone other than STORM. But no one else on the team had spotted any kind of tail, or danger, or anything suspicious at all. It was just him being paranoid.

Big fucking shock.

So he'd been reassigned to watch her brownstone—a throwaway job no one had thought he could possibly fuck up . . . though no one had actually said it aloud.

How wrong they all had been.

"No worries," Kick told him now. "Dr. Cappozi's fine. She just got on the subway to come home."

It suddenly dawned on Alex that Kick was supposed to be on tag duty today with Kowalski. "Then what are you doing here?" he asked. "Are you sure nothing's happened?"

"Gina's safe," Kick reassured him. "But there's been a development. NSA picked up some interesting chatter overnight."

Alex was instantly alert. "What kind of chatter? About al Sayika?"

Kick nodded.

Alex narrowed his eyes. For many years both he and Kick had worked as operators for an outfit called Zero Unit, which was an ultra-covert black ops unit run from the deepest bowels of the U.S. Central Intelligence Agency. But after the deadly disaster in A-stan, and another near-debacle six months ago in Sudan, Kick was convinced al Sayika must have a mole working for them—either within Zero Unit itself, or for someone higher up, maybe in another government agency with close ties to ZU. How else could the terrorists have obtained such accurate details of both ill-fated operations? Details solid enough to sabotage the missions and leave most of the teams dead. When Gina had been taken right from under their noses at Zero Unit headquarters, there had been an investigation. Everyone had been cleared. But Kick still had his doubts. *Someone* had betrayed them.

Alex agreed. They were dealing with an inside traitor of the worst ilk.

So they'd both quit Zero Unit and joined STORM, a similar but non-governmental spec ops outfit. They were fairly certain that STORM had not been infiltrated by the terrorists. Last year, the organization had staged Dr. Cappozi's rescue in Louisiana, as well as Kick's retrieval of Alex over in Sudan— all without leaks from their side.

Dr. Cappozi's current protection detail was just part of a bigger mission: to find and eliminate the scumfuck traitor working as a mole in the U.S. government for the al Sayika terrorists. Dr. Cappozi was convinced the man they were looking for was her former lover, Captain Gregg van Halen, a Zero Unit operator who'd gone rogue shortly after her capture. The evidence supported her belief.

If she was right, this van Halen person was directly responsible for Alex's imprisonment and torture, Kick's terrible injuries, and the hideous deaths of their teammates.

For Alex and Kick, the mission was one of pure revenge. God help van Halen when the two of them got hold of him.

And they would. That was a fucking promise.

Kick finally opened the SUV's door and got in. "Quinn called a meeting," he said. "He wants us back at HQ, asap."

"What about the Cappozi place?" Alex asked, glancing uneasily at the three-story brownstone before hesitantly reaching for the vehicle's ignition. "What if I'm *not* being paranoid and—"

"Johnson and Kowalski have her six on the subway. And they're bringing in Miles to finish your shift here," Kick told him. "She'll be in good hands until Marc and Tara take over their regular watch at nine tonight."

Alex pushed out a breath. "All right." He checked the dashboard clock. It was just after five. "I guess that works."

Kick raised a brow as he put the SUV in gear. "You good to drive, bro?"

Alex gave a humorless chuckle. "Worried about my mental health?"

"Hell, yeah. I need to stay alive. Newlywed and all, remember?"

"Like I could forget," he muttered with a wry curl of his lip. Kick had been relentlessly happy since tying the knot. Not that Alex begrudged his friend. He was glad *one* of them was happy, at least.

He gunned the engine to life. "And damn, Kick. In case you hadn't noticed, *every*one behind the wheel in this town is a fucking lunatic. Trust me, I'll blend right in."

* * *

GREGG VAN HALEN followed Gina Cappozi onto the subway car at the last possible second, making sure she didn't dart out again just before the doors closed.

She didn't. Didn't even try.

Not that it surprised him. For the past week, since returning home to Manhattan after her lengthy convalescence upstate, his former lover had done nothing to avoid being found. Nothing to escape the menace that lurked in the corners of the darkness, seeking to hunt her down.

Almost like she was taunting him. Or fate. Except for the occasional furtive, hollow-eyed glances she gave her surroundings, you'd never know she was in a constant state of terror.

Avoiding the vigilant observation of the STORM agent tailing her, Gregg casually grabbed the center pole of the subway car along with the horde of commuters anxious to get home for the night. The sliding doors slammed shut and the wheels lurched forward with the distinctive rattle and squeal of the New York subway.

He turned his back on Gina. He didn't need to face her. In fact, he preferred watching her in the flickering reflection of the grimy window. Better to keep the rage from showing in his face and giving him away.

Her dark green eyes went to and fro as she clung to an overhead strap, her gaze alighting for a quick perusal of each passenger before shifting to the next. Always moving. Always searching.

For him.

He allowed himself a grim inward smile. *So nice to be wanted.*

She'd never see him, though. Yeah, she'd see a man, a tall man, his head and shoulders obscured by a baggy hoodie. But not *him*, not Gregg van Halen. Not until he chose to show himself. Which he wouldn't. Not with those STORM clowns following her every move. But he could be patient when he needed to be.

Gregg had been invisible for so much of his life, it took no effort at all to remain so. Even in plain sight, in broad daylight, he was a true shadow-dweller. A ghost.

A spook.

His lips flicked up. An apt double entendre. The description went far deeper than his job. The shadows themselves drew him. Dark obscurity spoke to him. Even now, it whispered in his ear, beckoned to him from the pitch-black void just beyond the strobing flash of subway window where he watched his own reflection, and that of his woman.

Alas, he could not answer the call and slip back into the void. There was something he must do before returning to the sheltering comfort of anonymity. He must deal with the overwhelming fury in his heart. And take care of this woman. His lover, Dr. Gina Cappozi.

In the mirrored film noir frames of the moving window, he searched her face for any sign of recognition. Or of alarm. And found none. Her eyes passed quickly over him.

But within himself, crouching right next to the anger that simmered and roiled in his chest, he felt a bone-deep physical recognition of her. And had a sudden, overwhelming need to put his hands on her. A need so potent and visceral it nearly sucked the breath from him.

He *knew* this woman, intimately. Knew her flesh and her fears. He had plunged deep inside her and felt her quake with the pleasure his presence there had brought her. And felt her tremble with the fear of his absolute power over her.

He wanted to feel her quake and tremble again.

But she would never allow it. Never accept him again as she once had.

Because he had betrayed her.

He had betrayed everything.

He battled back a surge of sick fury. Steeled his insides and beat back the clot of unwanted emotion. Anger would not help. Emotions would not help. Only action would.

As the train screeched around a curve he released the pole, letting his body wedge into the clutch of commuters surrounding her. No need to hold on. His balance was perfect, honed through years of hard physicality on his job as a

mercenary for Uncle. Bit by bit, inch by inch, he eased closer
to her—the backward bump always accidental, the sideways
step seemingly unintentional. Until his back was at her front.
Not quite touching.

But oh so close.

Close enough to catch the familiar, tempting scent of the
woman he'd once tied to his bed and taken in ways that had
both thrilled her . . . and frightened her to the marrow.

He'd always frightened her. From their first wary, agenda-
filled meeting, he'd scared the pants off her. Literally and
figuratively. It was part of his attraction. And hers. She had
once loved the edgy thrill of it. But now . . . she hated him.
Hated him with a passion that nearly matched his own.

While she'd been at the sanatorium up north, from his
hidden vantage points on the grounds he had watched her
body slowly heal from the terrible trauma she'd gone through.
But in her mind the terror still loomed as large as when she'd
been a captive of al Sayika. She'd learned to defend herself,
studying deadly moves, plunging her knife into the center of
a man-shaped target over and over. Imagining it to be his own
black heart, he was sure.

Over the months he'd observed her and covertly listened in
on her debriefs and conversations via the device he'd planted
in her room at Haven Oaks, one thing had become abundantly
clear: Gina Cappozi blamed him for her capture.

She wanted him dead. And *she* wanted to be the one to
kill him.

Too bad he couldn't let that happen.

The train sliced through the black tunnel, lights flashing
to the cacophony of the steel rails. He cocked his head to the
side and inhaled, picking out his lover's unique fragrance
from the potent olfactory brew of refuse, burning brakes, and
the perfumed sweat of a thousand bodies.

She glanced around uneasily. Nervous. Instinctively sens-
ing a predator close by.

Impassively, he read an ad sign hanging on the wall,
keeping his face hidden. She anxiously caught the eye of the
STORM agent across the car from her, who shook his head
reassuringly. She shuddered out a breath and tightened her

grip on the strap above her again as wheels screamed and the train pulled to a herky-jerky stop at the next station.

Passengers all around disgorged, jostling them so her body was wrenched away from his. New people crowded around. He steered closer. The doors slammed shut again.

Heedless to the danger, he turned and deliberately stepped up right behind her, this time his front to her back. She was tall, especially in her work heels, but he was taller. Much taller. Heartbeat accelerating, he spread his feet and grabbed the strap next to hers.

He hovered over her. *Close. So close.* Silky strands of her long black hair tickled his nose . . . smelling of the woman he had stripped naked and taught to pleasure him as no other woman ever had.

His body remembered those nights. Achingly well. He could still hear the echoes of her groaned sighs and throaty moans as he took her. Could still feel the touch of her fingers and the tip of her tongue as she explored his body with mutual, shivering delight.

His cock grew thick and hard, remembering.

Again the brakes squealed, the car slowed; people shifted in readiness to exit.

He nearly vibrated with the urge to touch her. To step into her. To press his body right up against hers and feel her succulent curves fitted against his unyielding muscle. Just for a fleeting moment.

But he didn't dare.

She must have felt the air around them quicken. Must have sensed the taut, electric thrum of lust, which pulsed through his whole body for want of her. Must have inhaled his eager male pheromones as they sought a way to lure her to his bed again. Suddenly, she went rigid. Her knuckles turned white on the strap she clung to. Her head whipped around and she raked his features with a fear-sharpened glare.

But he had already looked away. Averted his hooded face so she couldn't see the hunger prowling in it like a trapped tiger. Or read the intent lying there, in wait. Waiting for the right moment.

To take her.

The train jerked to a halt and she stumbled backward into him. She gasped. He didn't move. But she felt it—the long, thick ridge that the memories had raised between his thighs. Her breath sucked in. Her hand dropped. To touch him?

He knew better. She was reaching for her knife.

But too late.

He was already out the door.

It wasn't time. Not quite yet.

But soon he would have her.

Very soon.

Pamela Clare began her writing career as an investigative reporter and columnist, working her way up the newsroom ladder to become the first woman editor of two different newspapers. Along the way, she and her team won numberous state and national journalism awards, including the 2000 National Journalism Award for Public Service. A single mother with two teenage sons, she lives in Colorado at the foot of the Rocky Mountains. Visit her website at www.pamelaclare.com.